T0355045

# Book Review

A FAST-PACED story that incorporates time travel, set against a backdrop of family love, friendship, conflict, and forgiveness. Woven into the race to rescue a brilliant scientist who has mysteriously disappeared are captivating scene transitions between the ancient biblical world and the world we know best. Travelers along the journey include a Judas-type friend, a loving nephew, and a feisty, courageous girl who refuses to allow her physical challenges to stop her. The adventure leaves no one untouched.

MARLENE DANIELS
Pastor's Wife, Educator, Avid Reader

## OTHER BOOKS BY DEBBY:

*The Onyx Stones: Mystery of the Underground People* (prequel to *The Onyx Stones 2*)

*His Timeless Touch: Twelve Remarkable Short Stories of Lives Changed by the Healer*

*Cherish: A Still, Small Call*

*Cherish: Behold, I Knock*

*Cherish: Create in Me a Clean Heart*

# The Onyx Stones 2:

## How Alexander and Cricket Save Uncle Chad

### Debby L. Johnston

WestBow
PRESS®
A DIVISION OF THOMAS NELSON
& ZONDERVAN

WestBow Press books may be ordered through booksellers or by contacting:

WestBow Press
A Division of Thomas Nelson & Zondervan
1663 Liberty Drive
Bloomington, IN 47403
www.westbowpress.com
844-714-3454

Scripture quotations taken from The Holy Bible, New International Version® NIV® Copyright © 1973 1978 1984 2011 by Biblica, Inc. TM. Used by permission. All rights reserved worldwide.

ISBN: 978-1-6642-4256-2 (sc)
ISBN: 978-1-6642-4258-6 (hc)
ISBN: 978-1-6642-4257-9 (e)

Library of Congress Control Number: 2021916198

Print information available on the last page.

WestBow Press rev. date: 11/02/2021

Dedicated to our Lord Jesus who rescues us from ourselves by his grace.

A special thank you to Jason Rusk for his review of my early draft.

And so, it continues...

# Contents

# Chapter 1

## Alexander and Uncle Chad

"Admiral! Admiral! The Raptorians have locked onto us and are preparing to fire."

"Understood, Mr. Lasson. Return fire immediately, and increase our shield strength."

"Aye, aye, sir!"

Admiral Callahan stands calmly but his eyes convey concern over whether or not *The Argosy*, under his command, can withstand the hits. Across the starship's observation screen, a series of guided streaks close the gap between the battling adversaries.

Tense music drums wildly as *The Argosy* rocks from two glancing blows. The force of the second impact slams First Mate Lasson into the instrument panel. But the Argosy's protective shield holds and deflects the volley.

In contrast, the Raptorian defenses fail. *The Argosy* officers avert their eyes, cover their ears, and brace themselves against the blinding flash, thunderous explosion, and oncoming collision with flying debris that marks their enemy's annihilation.

A deep silence follows. It is obvious that Admiral Callahan takes no pleasure in his victory. He removes his hands from his ears, draws a deep breath, lifts his chin, and calmly commands the crew to reset the ship's course. The noble quest of *The Argosy Explorer* will continue in next week's program.

———◆———

The television screen flickers. *The Argosy* starship streaks through unknown galaxies, the credits roll, the theme song blares—and I groan. What a bunch of garbage! Doesn't the show's producer know that science fiction doesn't mean ignoring science? This program has been touted for weeks as the *best space-adventure series of all time*. What a letdown!

The episode's inaccuracies are so glaring that I doubt if anyone over the age of six will tune in next week. The last (but not least) of the show's blunders was the crew's reaction to the Raptorian ship's explosion. I knew as far back as the third grade that *The Argosy* officers would not have covered their ears to block out noise from the blast. Sounds do not travel in a vacuum—at least not *normal* sounds. While it is true that some sounds travel through outer space, it is only on wavelengths that human ears cannot hear.

According to my esteemed Uncle Chad, author of numerous well-regarded science articles, "it takes special instruments to pick up the superlong gravitational waves that bear the songs of stars, the gorging of black holes, the groaning of planets"—and, I might add, the relatively teensy explosions of starships.

In any event, I'm swearing off *The Argosy Explorer* serial. I'm not a kid anymore. I, Alexander Tennyson, am finally a teenager, and I'll spend my time in more productive activities, like finishing my rocketry program requirements and tuning in to documentaries that stick to facts.

It's a shame that Uncle Chad, my dad's older brother, couldn't have been here to share my low regard for the serial's premiere. We could have laughed together through the whole thing. No doubt, Uncle Chad would have found a dozen more errors than I managed to catch. He's brilliant!

Uncle Chad is science editor for *Armchair Science* magazine. Joseph Chadwick Tennyson (with a string of academic letters after his name) has translated scores of highly technical subjects into the everyday language of *Armchair Science* readers. He's covered topics like exploring the nervous system of the human body, mapping the human genome, reviewing ice-age theories, uncovering the tools and techniques that built the pyramids, analyzing the rings of Saturn, predicting meteor showers, and proving solar and stellar influences on bird and butterfly migration. And I've read every one.

It's no secret that Uncle Chad has always been my hero. It was through his telescope when I was eight that I first saw the dusty rings of Saturn, and it was through the lens of his high-powered microscope when I turned nine that I isolated my own cold virus. (How cool is that?) I've been hooked on space and science ever since.

My mentor has never brushed me off or belittled my questions. He has always said, "Well, what do *you* think, Alexander?" And I've done my best to respond with logic and facts. That's because Uncle Chad has taught me the importance of properly observing and evaluating evidence when forming conclusions. I have seen his principles at work in his workshop, where I've helped him prepare certain experiments and demonstrations.

For example, once when I was ten, Uncle Chad wanted to explain to his readers a theory of how lava and rock from volcanic eruptions on small planets with weak gravitational fields might contribute to space debris. To present the arguments involved, Uncle Chad photographed a well-known grade school vinegar-and-baking-soda *volcano*—that he let me set up. Then he shared a photo from NASA of an astronaut's toothpaste floating in the weightlessness of his space capsule. Finally, he shared about thrust and force in outer space. From these examples, Uncle Chad made it easy to imagine volcanic matter flying away to become space litter.

Needless to say, I loved helping Uncle Chad. And at suppertime, I would tell my parents everything I had learned that day. By age eleven I had helped with many demonstrations and experiments and had made myself more or less indispensable

But then, two years ago in May, shortly after my eleventh birthday, my lab assistant role dissolved. That's because Uncle Chad disappeared. Without a word, and without a trace. He simply vanished.

———◆———

It happened on a Friday.

As always, I arrived on my bike after school to help in the workshop. But curiously, no one answered the door, not even Uncle Chad's new university-student apprentice, Lawrence Traeger. Usually Uncle Chad or Lawrence met me before I could knock. When neither appeared, I pressed my face against the window and knocked again.

Had Uncle Chad and Lawrence gone somewhere for supplies? Why hadn't they let me know?

A quick trip to the side yard confirmed that the garage was empty. I texted, *Where are you? Will you be here soon? Should I wait?* I spelled out the words in full because although Uncle Chad is a scientist and well-acquainted with cell phones and can decipher ancient hieroglyphs, he doesn't hold with my using acronyms and abbreviations in texts. *There's no excuse for you not to communicate clearly and properly,* he would say whenever I lapsed into what he called *this generation's deplorable decline in distinct expression*. But today, even though I used full spellings and complete sentences, there was no response.

The midafternoon sun felt good, and I had to assume that Uncle Chad and Lawrence would be here soon, so I lazily sprawled on the top step of the porch to wait. I hoped that Uncle Chad and Lawrence would feel guilty when they returned and found me lying there.

Twenty minutes passed, however, and they did not show up. I heard the phone ring in the kitchen at the back of the house, and I jumped. Someone else was looking for Uncle Chad. Or (I sat up straight) perhaps it was Uncle Chad expecting me to answer! He knew I could let myself in with the spare key from under the paving stone beside the back porch. Maybe he had assumed I was already inside and would pick up when he started to leave a message.

In case I was right, I hurried to uncover the key and crack open the kitchen door. It felt odd not to announce myself, so I shouted *hello*, but no one answered. I pushed on in. My footsteps echoed on the linoleum, and the walls seemed to listen as I checked for phone messages. There were none, so I crossed loudly to the refrigerator and collected a cold soda. Everything sounded exaggerated in the emptiness. The pop of the aluminum tab filled the room like a metallic explosion, and the bursting of hundreds of carbonated bubbles added a faint percussive background to my noisy swallows.

With growing unease, I pulled out my cell phone and punched in another text. *Where are you? I'm in your kitchen. Will you be long?*

My eyes scanned the counter while I waited for a reply, and I noted how bare the counter top looked. Where were the dirty dishes? There were always dirty breakfast and lunch dishes stacked and waiting when I arrived. Uncle Chad didn't own a dishwasher (he said it was an unnecessary extravagance for someone who lived alone), and he washed dishes only once—after supper. Hadn't Lawrence and Uncle Chad eaten today? Or had they been gone that long? If so, why hadn't they texted or called? I needed answers.

I looked for a clue scratched on a scrap of paper or a scribbled note next to the house phone, but there was nothing. I circulated through the living and dining rooms and came away empty there, as well. A peek into the bedrooms revealed unmade beds but nothing disturbing—until I noticed that Uncle Chad's eyeglasses still sat on his nightstand. In alarm, I questioned why the glasses weren't on his face. Why had Uncle Chad left his glasses behind? He couldn't see without them, and he certainly would need them to drive.

Had Uncle Chad become ill in the night? Had Lawrence driven him to the hospital? Was Uncle Chad there now? Had Lawrence tried to contact us but didn't yet know our phone number? (I didn't know his.) But surely, Lawrence would have found our number by now—a full eight hours since morning light.

On the outside chance that Lawrence might have left me a note in the workshop, I raced to look. But nothing jumped out at me. The only notes on the worktable were yesterday's penciled observations from our current project. And not one pencil or beaker or test tube had been moved since I had left for home on the day before. There should have been lots of things moved. Uncle Chad and Lawrence should have been hard at work before I arrived. How I wished they were!

With fears mounting, I called my dad's office. The minute he answered, I blurted, "There's something wrong at Uncle Chad's house!" Dad instantly demanded to know if I was OK.

"Yes, Dad, I'm fine." (I should have known he would think the worst, since I never called him at work.) "It's about Uncle Chad," I explained. "He's not here, and I can't get him to take my calls or answer my texts."

Dad sounded busy, and he casually tossed out, "He and Lawrence have probably been delayed on some errand and will be there before long."

"But, Dad," I persisted, "Uncle Chad's eyeglasses are still on his nightstand."

Silence. Then, Dad repeated what I had said.

"Yes, Dad," I replied. "Uncle Chad would never go anywhere without his glasses."

I could hear Dad changing gears; whatever he was working on could wait. Now he told me to hang up. "I'll call you back in a minute."

Several minutes passed. Then Dad called and ordered, "Stay where you are, son. I'm coming over."

As I tucked my cell phone into my pocket, I hoped Dad wasn't angry. I hoped I wasn't being foolish. What if Uncle Chad showed up before

Dad arrived? I supposed it could happen, but something told me it wasn't going to.

I put my soda can in the recycling tub under the kitchen sink, and as I closed the cabinet door, the gloom of a growing list of unreasonable fears swept over me. The kitchen's hollowness felt eerie and alien, so I left the house and sought the sun on the front porch to wait for my father.

Dad frowned when, minutes later, I showed him the pair of glasses next to Uncle Chad's bed. And I walked with him quickly as he checked every room for notes or clues, just as I had done. Then Dad telephoned the hospital. When no one matching Uncle Chad's description was registered by Admitting, Dad called the police.

I was near enough to the phone to hear most of what was said, and I was frustrated when the desk sergeant expressed little concern. Since we could produce no evidence of foul play, besides a pair of glasses, the sergeant calmly advised us to wait 48 hours. "Most missing people turn up and aren't missing at all," he explained. "And perhaps your brother has a spare pair of glasses you don't know about." And although Dad argued with him, the man refused to budge. He told us to check back later; there was nothing more to do. Dad caught himself before he uttered a curse, and then he texted his brother for the fourth time. Before we left the house, Dad scribbled a note to stick on the refrigerator: *Chad, call me when you get in. Thanks. Jonathan.*

Forty-eight hours felt like an eternity. Uncle Chad was never absent from my thoughts. His face was the last image I pictured before I fell asleep, and he was the first thing on my mind when I awakened. Dozens of questions clamored for my attention in a never-ending loop, especially the big question: *Where are you, Uncle Chad?*

At last, Monday arrived, and in late afternoon the police met us at Uncle Chad's house. Dad and I repeated our concerns and frightened observations, and we walked Detective Gorman and a uniformed officer through every room. To match what seemed like his all-too-short, cursory examination of the scene, the detective punched into his cell phone only the briefest of notes. And he touched nothing, except in the bedroom. There, he picked up and squinted through Uncle Chad's eyeglasses before returning them to the nightstand. Within minutes, the detective was handing Dad his business card and reciting instructions about calling him if anything new turned up. Before he could finish, however, a car pulled into the drive.

"It's Uncle Chad's car!" I shouted.

I couldn't race fast enough to get out the door and down the steps. But Uncle Chad was not there. Only Lawrence stepped out of the SUV.

"Why isn't Chad with you?" Dad called from the porch.

Lawrence ignored his question and asked, "What's up with the police?"

We watched impatiently as Lawrence rummaged in the backseat of the car for his backpack, an activity he performed awkwardly with one hand because the other was newly bandaged. Although wound thoroughly in sterile, white strips, the injured hand didn't look broken. What had happened? Had Lawrence and Uncle Chad been in an accident? Was Uncle Chad in worse shape and being cared for somewhere?

Detective Gorman had the same questions. He met Lawrence at the top step with, "I understand that you live here as a student apprentice. We're trying to locate Dr. Tennyson; do you have any idea where he might be?"

"No, I don't," replied Lawrence with a shrug and a shake of his head.

"Isn't that the doctor's car?" Gorman asked. "Where have you been?"

"Dr. Tennyson let me use his car to go to the university this weekend," Lawrence told him. "I needed to pick up some things. He knew I'd be back today."

"So, you've had no contact with him while you were gone?" Gorman pressed.

"No. I have no idea where the doctor is," Lawrence insisted. "When I left, he was planning to finish his experiment with Alexander, and I was to help photograph the results once I got back."

"What experiment?" Gorman asked.

Lawrence explained, "Dr. Tennyson writes magazine articles that present complex science in layman's terms. He's been finishing an assignment to explain *clumping*, a theory on planet formation. And the experiment is a kitchen-style demonstration to be photographed and published with the article. Alexander and I can demonstrate the experiment if you'd like."

Gorman declined the demonstration but asked Lawrence to accompany him through the house. I tagged along as Gorman quizzed Lawrence for any possible clues on Uncle Chad's absence.

"I can't believe this," Lawrence kept saying. "The doctor's article is due in a few days. He would never miss a deadline."

Finally, Gorman asked Lawrence about his injured hand.

"I burned it," Lawrence said. "It was one of those stupid things you do without thinking. I picked up a hot skillet and spilled grease on myself. I had it treated at the university hospital ER, and I'm supposed to have it checked here to avoid infection."

"Hot grease? That's a shame," Gorman said. And then Gorman asked Lawrence if he had another place to sleep for a while. "You won't be able to stay in this house until we finish our forensic work," he explained. (I was grateful for the mention of an ongoing investigation. It relieved my worry that, after today, nothing more would be done to find Uncle Chad.)

Lawrence turned to Dad. "He could sleep at our place," Dad offered. "We have a guestroom."

Lawrence said thanks, and then he disappeared down the hall to retrieve some things from his bedroom. When he returned to the front door, he locked up the house and handed the uniformed policeman his key.

We didn't see Detective Gorman again until Wednesday afternoon. When the detective came to our house, he graciously accepted a cup of coffee from Mom and sank into Dad's favorite chair. We assumed that he had news for us, but we had to wait impatiently while the man leisurely sipped his coffee and made small talk.

Finally, Gorman asked a surprising question: "Has anyone from the Middle East visited Dr. Tennyson recently?"

Dad answered no, but then he backtracked to offer that Uncle Chad had visited the Middle East many months before, in connection with an article he submitted on the pyramids. "But he's not left the country since then nor has he had Middle Eastern visitors that we know of."

Then Dad asked, "Do you suspect that someone from the Middle East is involved in Chad's disappearance?"

Gorman shrugged and revealed that the forensics team had found unusual shoeprints on Uncle Chad's bedroom rug. "The footprints contain dust and materials found only in Middle Eastern deserts," he said.

"But," said Gorman, "the real puzzle is the condition of the footprints. They're fresh, as if someone stepped straight out of the desert and into the house. That's impossible of course, because anyone who would have come here from the desert would have lost the dust on the plane, in the airport, and in the car in which they arrived. Only traces would have remained, not full prints of dust."

Then Gorman watched our faces as he asked, "Does Dr. Tennyson go away often without his glasses?"

Dad immediately told Gorman, "Chad needs his glasses. He wouldn't have gone anywhere without them."

Gorman nodded. "I thought as much, based on the lens prescription. But he seems to have left them behind for some reason."

I couldn't think of a reason.

Gorman also reported that no strange cars had been seen at Uncle Chad's house. But then he admitted, "Dr. Tennyson's neighbors aren't particularly nosey; no one saw Lawrence back out of the driveway on Thursday evening either."

Lawrence frowned. "I wish they had seen me. And I wish they were seeing Dr. Tennyson here today."

I wished, too, that someone had observed something. How does a person disappear and no one notices? I wanted Uncle Chad to text or call— or come ambling through the door with a grin and a perfectly reasonable explanation for his absence. But it didn't happen. When Detective Gorman left, I felt empty. We had more questions, now, than we'd had before he had come.

# Chapter 2

## Two Long Years

Two years have dragged by since Uncle Chad's disappearance. And in that time the police have moved on to more active cases, Lawrence Traeger has completed his studies and graduated from the university, and a new science editor has begun writing Uncle Chad's usual feature in *Armchair Science* magazine.

But I haven't forgotten. I ride my bike past Uncle Chad's little ranch house every day after school. And I still devour everything I can that relates to science and new scientific developments. I've even begun conducting my own experiments. The clutter in my bedroom shows it; the room's beginning to look like Uncle Chad's eclectic workshop.

I'm thankful that Dad hasn't given up hope, either. Mom thinks we should sell Uncle Chad's house and *move on*, but Dad keeps dragging his feet. Whenever Mom mentions *moving on*, Dad heaves a sigh and says, "I imagine you're right, Gwen, but I can't bring myself to do it, yet." Then he tells her, "There's no finality, no neat little ending. Chad could come home any day. We just don't know."

And because Dad holds out hope, he keeps Uncle Chad's house sensors programmed to turn on the inside and outdoor lights at dusk, and he pays a maintenance crew to cut the grass in the summer. The workers also shovel Uncle Chad's walk in the winter and power wash his siding each spring.

I dread the day when Dad finally gives up and sells the house. That'll be the day I'll feel like Uncle Chad has died.

———◆———

Today, I pull up my jacket collar and tuck in my chin so I can breathe warmer air. The October sky is cloudless, but it's a cold Saturday and I've forgotten my gloves. The handlebars feel like ice. I keep alternating hands to steer, and I pedal faster so I can complete my task and return home quickly.

It's Uncle Chad's birthday and, as I did last year, I'm intent on slipping a birthday card through the mail slot in his front door. It makes no sense, of course, but I feel compelled to commemorate his special day.

The mail-slot cover creaks when I lift it. I shove in the card and hear its faint *thup* on the floor inside. "Happy Birthday," I whisper, and I turn to leave. But I stumble over a little dog that has suddenly appeared.

"Where did you come from?" I cry as I recover my footing.

Oblivious to the trouble he's caused, the happy-faced little terrier insists that I pet him, and he makes me laugh. His entire body wags as if we're old friends. I scratch behind his ears, and a girl calls from the sidewalk, "Sorry if he scared you. He's a bit overfriendly."

"No problem," I call back. "We're good."

The girl, who appears to be near my age, sits beside my bicycle in a wheelchair.

"His name's Hero," she offers, and I wonder how she arrived here, alone.

Hero follows me off the porch when I go to introduce myself. "I'm Alexander Tennyson," I say, and the girl shares, "And I'm Cricket Dalton. I live just around the corner."

I try not to stare, but for the life of me, I can't figure out how Cricket got here from *around the corner*. Even though her wheelchair is motorized, I see no switches or levers, and the more I observe, the more I doubt that Cricket could operate them if they existed. Her arms and hands, as well as her legs and feet are motionless, twisted, and shrunken with the atrophy of quadriplegia.

While I contemplate the mystery of her transport, Cricket asks where I live, and I tell her, "Four blocks that way." Then I explain, "This is my uncle's house; I came to deliver a birthday card."

"Too bad he's not home," she says. "You could have sung to him."

I laugh. "I'm not much of a singer."

Then Cricket asks, "Is your uncle ever home? I never see anyone at this house except yard workers."

I'm not sure if she just wants me to tell her the sad story or if Cricket really doesn't know about Uncle Chad's disappearance. I thought everyone in town knew. Either way, I try to be polite, and because I'm cold, I give her a short answer designed to bring our conversation to a quick close. I say, "He works for a magazine and travels."

"Oh, how exciting!" she exclaims. "Which magazine?"

I can tell, now, that Cricket doesn't know the story and that she is a talker who will expect more information. I offer, "It's a long story. Could I walk you home while we talk?"

Cricket agrees, and I leave my bike so I can push her wheelchair. Before I reach her, however, Cricket is already moving. "No need to push," she calls over her shoulder. "I can drive myself."

I watch in astonishment as the girl deftly guides herself down the sidewalk by means of a *chin rig*—a device I've never seen before.

"That's amazing!" I call after her, and I hurry to pick up my bike and catch up. "How does that thing work?"

Cricket stops long enough to say, "I love my chair. Without it, I'm stuck." Then she demonstrates her control over the chair's direction and speed with slight movements of her chin. Before she starts back down the walkway, she instructs, "So, tell me about your uncle."

For the next few minutes, we move together. I explain that Uncle Chad is a scientist and writes for *Armchair Science* magazine, and I tell Cricket about my visits to his workshop. "Uncle Chad used to let me work on projects with him," I say. "Someday I'm going to work for NASA and be a scientist, too."

"And I want to be a teacher," Cricket says.

Then she asks, "So, is your uncle away, now, on a trip for his magazine? Where is he?"

I sigh. "We don't know."

Cricket looks puzzled. "What do you mean, you don't know? Doesn't he keep in touch?"

"He used to," I say. "But something has happened. He's disappeared and has been gone for two years."

"Two years! That's a long time!" Cricket exclaims.

"I know. And we have no idea where he is."

Before I can explain further, we arrive at Cricket's house. A woman standing at the open gate calls out, "There you are, Cricket! I was coming to check on you. It's too cold for you to be out this long!"

Cricket motors her way forward and through the gate. "I'm sorry if I worried you," she tells the woman. "I met someone and we've been talking."

Then to me Cricket says, "This is my house, and this is my guardian, Marlene Grace Fox."

Cricket now introduces me, and she adds, "Alexander's uncle lives in that white house back there."

The expression on Marlene Grace's face tells me that she knows about the white house. She nods her acknowledgement and, noticing that my bare hands are turning blue, she offers, "Alexander, do you have time to join us for a cup of hot chocolate?"

I can't say yes fast enough.

———— • ————

The cup bearing the hot chocolate thaws my hands, and its sweet, rich contents warm my insides. And although I'm sure that Marlene Grace suspects that I'm slipping tiny bits of cookie under the table to Hero, she says nothing.

Instead, Marlene Grace deftly serves Cricket every sip of her drink and bite of cookie. The interaction between the two is so intuitive that I almost forget that Cricket is not serving herself. But I am increasingly aware that without her caregiver, Cricket could not manage anything. She could not lift herself from her chair to her bed, attend to her private bodily functions, blow her nose, or swat a mosquito. Her quadriplegia mercifully ends at her neck and at least allows her to speak, nod, and turn her head.

Marlene Grace never pauses in her attentions to Cricket as she tells me, "I recall reading the news stories about your uncle two years ago. And you say that he still hasn't returned?"

"No," I say. "No one has heard from him since he vanished." And I repeat for Marlene Grace and Cricket the story of the day I discovered Uncle Chad missing. It's a story I haven't told in a long time, and it still has the power to stir pain as I relive it. Tightness grips my chest as I tell of finding Uncle Chad's eyeglasses on the nightstand.

I close my account with, "The police found nothing, and we have no idea where else to look. We just hope that Uncle Chad is safe and that someday he'll come back."

"I'm sorry this has happened," Marlene Grace sympathizes. And Cricket agrees.

"I know what it's like to lose people you love," says Cricket. "A couple of years ago, I lost my family in a car accident—the same accident that left me paralyzed."

Her revelation stuns me, and because I don't know what to say, I simply murmur, "I'm sorry." Cricket hurries to reassure me.

"It's OK," she says. "That was a long time ago. Of course, I still miss my family and my old life, but God has been good. I am now blessed to have Marlene Grace and her husband, William, to care for me. And I know that my family is safe in heaven."

Her brave declarations shame me. I can't begin to compare losses. While I still have my parents and my health, Cricket's family and her mobility are gone forever. I miss Uncle Chad, but I still have hope that one day my mourning will turn into joy. I still cling to the possibility that Uncle Chad will return.

———— • ————

After our snack, Cricket invites me to follow her. "I want to show you my collections," she explains.

I trail her and Hero down the hall, and the minute we enter Cricket's oversized bedroom, spring explodes before my eyes in painted walls of glorious blue skies, fields of wild flowers, and a splash of butterflies. And hanging over a small desk is a wide arrangement of framed butterfly and insect specimens. Scrapbooks of pressed wildflowers lie open on a shelf, and trays of carefully labeled rock samples fill another bookcase. All are evidence of Cricket's freedom to explore and capture nature before her accident.

"Wow!" I exclaim. "This is impressive!"

"I'm glad you like it," Cricket says. "I love studying things and adding to my displays—with help from Marlene Grace and William, of course."

"Of course," I say, and Cricket volunteers the biological names and classifications for a large set of beetles she has carefully preserved and pinned to foam-core under glass. As she describes the habits and environment of a particular Goliath beetle, I shake my head in wonder. Until this moment, I had no idea that Cricket and I shared a love of knowledge. While Cricket's passion lies in earth sciences and biology, and mine is in outer space and physics, we nevertheless speak a similar language—the language of science.

I tell Mom and Dad about my visit once I get home, and Mom raises an eyebrow when I say, "Cricket's really cool for a girl. I told her I'd see her tomorrow after school."

———— • ————

Everyone who knows me knows that I haven't had a girl friend before— not a *girlfriend*, but a friend who is a girl. Most girls are too giggly and silly. But Cricket is down-to-earth and only talks when she has something to say. While most guys are pursuing girls for other reasons, I'm not interested in that, just yet. Right now, I appreciate Cricket as a friend with a brain.

I stop by Cricket's house after school, just like I used to stop at Uncle Chad's. She's usually home by the time I get there, even though Cricket attends a special school at a rehab facility where she can use her voice-activated phone pad to interact in class. Marlene Grace greets me at the door and, in the kitchen, Cricket and I enjoy a snack before we disappear down the hall to talk.

Over several days, I tell Cricket about my rocketry program launches and my plans to one day work with NASA on space exploration. Cricket shares with me her dreams about teaching and one day writing a book. When I ask if the book will be about butterflies or semi-precious stones or wildflowers, she hedges, and I'm surprised. Sporting a cryptic smile, she tells me, "I plan to write about things I've done and places I've been. You can read about it, one day, in my book. But for now, I prefer not to share." I get the message and quit pumping her for details.

As days pass, I find that Cricket holds other secrets, too. I never know when her privacy wall will go up, like on a particular afternoon when I ask about an odd specimen in her butterfly collection.

"I've never seen one like this," I say. "What is it?"

She responds, "I don't know."

I sit back in surprise. "Really? I thought you knew all of your insects. Where did you catch this?"

"You'll laugh," she says. "I found it in my bedroom."

"No!" I say. "This butterfly isn't from around here."

Cricket agrees. "You're right," she says. "I said you wouldn't believe me. But it's true; I found him in my room, and the creature died here. I had Marlene Grace help me mount him."

"But..."

"I know," Cricket says. "He's not from here. I can't explain it to you, now. All I know is that he's a male—the little green dot on his hind wings confirms it, just like the black dot on a male monarch's wings verifies his sex."

"And how would you know about his dot if you haven't seen a female of this species?"

Cricket hesitates. "Well, actually I have seen some females."

"All right, let's hear."

But Cricket disappoints me. "It's a long story," she says. "And I hope you don't mind, but I'd rather leave it for another time."

I start to open my mouth to say something, but I close it again. Cricket must have reasons for her secrets. Perhaps she will share when she knows me better.

# Chapter 3

## Discoveries

Not long before breakfast, Dad shouts for Mom and me to come and look. Over his shoulder, we see the smiling face of Lawrence Traeger and a *USA Today* headline: *Man Finds Pirate Treasure in His Back Yard*. Uncle Chad's former workshop assistant waves a small gold cup high overhead, a trophy from a cache of pirate booty he has reportedly unearthed on his newly inherited property in North Carolina. According to the article, the little plot of land that used to belong to his grandfather is located between the tiny towns of Swanquarter and Engelhard on Pamlico Sound, only a ferry ride away from Ocracoke in the Outer Banks.

Dad reads part of the story aloud:

> Ocracoke, with its ideal harbor, was famously a port of Edward Teach's pirate ship, the Adventurer. Teach, better known as the notorious Blackbeard, was overtaken and killed off the Ocracoke shore by British Lieutenant Robert Maynard in 1718. Legend purports that Blackbeard used the area as a hiding place and regularly off loaded his stolen goods at various Outer Banks coves and on the mainland shore opposite the islands. For 300 years, treasure hunters have scoured every inlet to search for his gold, but they have met with little success. Traeger's discovery in Swanquarter will no doubt ignite a new wave of treasure hysteria.

> When interviewed, Traeger said, 'While walking in the far end of my field, I happened to trip over a patch of stones I thought were the remains of an old well. When I investigated, however, I found it to be a stone-lined hollow that contained a rotted leather bag. My eyes nearly popped when I spilled the bag's contents and found gold and jewels!'

> *Traeger's find is historically surprising because most of the items date from ancient times. For example, the gold chalice photographed with Traeger is from the fifteenth century B.C. and is a pristine Egyptian artifact not unlike those pulled from Egyptian tombs and the pyramids. How Blackbeard acquired such items is a mystery. His raids were thought to have been limited to the eastern U.S. coast and the Caribbean. What ship could have brought items like these to the New World?*

When Dad finishes reading, visions of pirate ships and treasure swim through my mind. "How exciting!" I say.

"What a find!" my dad echoes. "That boy is going to be very wealthy."

But Mom notices something else. "He might be rich," she says, "but did you see that Lawrence still can't use his left hand? He must have really hurt it two years ago."

Sure enough, in every photo, Lawrence's gloved hand hangs uselessly at his side. It surprises all of us. How could a grease burn do so much damage? But in any event, maybe his newfound treasure will bring him a medical miracle. I hope so.

Dad wonders where Lawrence will end up: a mansion in the East, a yacht on the gulf, or an island surrounded by white sands and blue waters? I try to imagine him in any of those places, and I wonder if he ever thinks of us. After Lawrence left our house two years ago, he kept up no correspondence. Except for the *USA Today* article, we might never have known what happened to him. Mom simply smiles and says, "And to think that we played a tiny role in that rich young man's life! I wish him well."

I wish him well, too, but I assume that we will never hear from him. Any connection we once had is long gone. The most I can lay claim to is that I once worked with him, and that he stayed in our home for a short while. I'm even surprised when Cricket, who has seen the *USA Today* article, too, remembers Lawrence's name from my account of Uncle Chad's disappearance.

Her text says, *Wow! Your friend Lawrence has struck it rich!*

I text back, *Who knew?*

My bedroom is a little neater today than yesterday. When Mom puts her foot down, I have to pick up things so she can vacuum my floor and dust. But it's hard to put everything away. I wish I had a workshop like Uncle Chad's where I could leave everything sitting out—like my homemade glass samples, formed from sand in a makeshift backyard kiln; or a series of tiny motors I assembled to test water as an alternative fuel; or my biggest mess, according to my mother (my dad laughs), a collection of dust. Each dust-filled bottle states where I found the sample, what the microscope says is in it, and whether or not it contains mites. That collection, along with my motors, is now on its way to the garage.

Thankfully, I have been allowed to keep my rocket-building corner as is. A magnificent solid-fuel rocket model sits on my desk, and I've stored my assembly tools and extra parts in a box underneath. Every time I look at that rocket, I think of Uncle Chad. He's the one who enrolled me in the national youth rocketry program several years ago, and with his help I advanced rapidly through all the program's primary divisions to where I am today.

My first launch was a simple cardboard-paper tube propelled by effervescent tablets. Next came resin-impregnated paper tubes launched with water from a garden hose. After that, I powered several fiber-glass tubes with batteries and electrical igniters. Then, just before Uncle Chad disappeared, I ordered the sophisticated, state-of-the-art, commercial, solid-fuel rocket kit. Uncle Chad and I were to assemble the project together and I would launch it to complete my program's junior division. But it was not to be. The day the kit arrived on my doorstep was the day after Uncle Chad vanished. In my troubled state of mind and with the future uncertain regarding Uncle Chad, I relegated the unopened box to a corner of my bedroom floor, never expecting to put it together until Uncle Chad returned. Without his supervision (as my sponsor) and his official sign off, I can't apply to launch a solid-fuel rocket until I turn eighteen.

For over a year, I let the unassembled kit lie in its corner. And then one day, I pulled it out and started to put it together. I decided I could surprise Uncle Chad when he came back. I allowed myself to think that by the time it was completed Uncle Chad would be home.

Months have passed, however. The finished rocket, now gleaming in the sunlight on my desk, sits unlauded and unlaunched, and Uncle Chad is still missing.

Having completed the rocket's assembly, I would normally now be hard at work preparing the research report that must be approved before the rocket can be scheduled for launch. But I haven't made a move to start my report.

The subject isn't difficult; the report simply covers a history of rocket pioneers and an overview of the natural laws governing space flight. But the paper's format is a stickler. Everything has to be done *by the book*—the official *Youth Rocketry Program Book*, that is. If I don't follow the book's outline carefully, my report could be rejected. And since I don't have the program book in hand, I can't follow it.

I'm not saying that I don't know where the book is, or at least where it should be. It's locked in Uncle Chad's workshop, somewhere among my old rocketry supplies. But I can't make myself go after it. I haven't been in Uncle Chad's house since the day I discovered him missing.

I don't want to enter that empty house. I don't want to see the uncompleted experiments on the work tables and the accumulation of notes on the desk that haven't been touched. I don't want to hear the echoes of my footsteps in his hallway. And I don't want to feel Uncle Chad's ghostly presence over my shoulder as I sort through my supplies to find the book.

Nor do I want to send someone else to rummage through the workshop and disturb things. I don't even want to ask Mom or Dad to go with me. After all, I'm thirteen years old, and I should be able to handle this. But I can't.

Sometimes, like today, I attempt to work myself up to going. My completed rocket, held in a beam of sunlight on the desk, mocks me. And I argue that I should be able to retrieve the program book with only a quick dash in and out. But I can't make myself go. I can't overcome my aversion to visiting the house alone.

It's too bad I don't have a dog like Cricket's to take with me. A dog might be good company for something like this. A dog wouldn't overreact if I happened to shed a tear or two. I toy for a minute with the idea of taking Hero with me. Perhaps Cricket would let me borrow him. I might even tell her why I need him.

Now I chide myself. Why not simply ask Cricket to come? I could show her where my scientific interests were molded. She could see the kind of experiments Uncle Chad and I used to do. And I could let her see my old rockets. Of all people, Cricket would be sensitive to how much the workshop and my time with Uncle Chad had meant to me, and she would understand why I don't want to linger there. She and I could be in and out of there in minutes.

Before I change my mind, I pull out my phone and text her. And I gulp when Cricket immediately replies that she and Hero would be happy to accompany me on my errand. *Just let me know when you want to go,* she texts.

———◆———

On Saturday, I arrive at Uncle Chad's house to find Cricket and Hero waiting for me on the sidewalk. By the time the wheels of my bike come to a full stop, Hero is wiggling his welcome and bouncing up and down for me to bend and pet him. I take a moment to give him a thorough scratch beneath his collar. Then I take a deep breath and ask, "Are we ready?"

Cricket replies with the real question, "Are *you* ready?"

I let out a long breath and nod. Then, because the walk around the house is uneven, I push Cricket's wheelchair to the back yard. I pull her up the one step to the porch and turn the spare key in the lock.

Now, I draw in a long breath and try to make my heart rate settle. Hero squeezes through the door before Cricket and I enter the kitchen.

Thankfully, the room isn't as spooky as I remember. The morning sun streams through the windows and reflects off the counter top. It looks almost inviting.

I breathe again. "The workshop is through here," I direct, and I lead the way. Hero disappears down the hall ahead of us.

Like in the kitchen, the workshop windows face the sun and let in lots of welcome light. My eyes rove over the familiar desk and tables.

Cricket chuckles at the workshop's ordered chaos. "It looks like my school's science lab," she says, and she's right. A periodic table, a diagram of the solar system, and other such posters paper the walls. Test tubes, beakers, burners, and a litter of assorted materials run down the center of the work surface. And variously divided spaces represent different experiments in progress.

I tear my eyes away from the last unfinished experiment and head, instead, for the rocketry corner across the room. There, on tables set against the wall, stand a row of all my old rockets, flanked by their accompanying essays, framed achievement certificates, and a collection of grinning photographs of me with Uncle Chad and my parents on launch days. Uncle Chad would often pass the display with a smile and say, "someday you'll look back on all of this and tell your children that this is where your NASA career started." I would wrinkle my nose. *Children* meant marriage, and I refused to think about that. But I loved it that Uncle Chad kept all my things on display.

Cricket has been checking out my rocket corner, and she asks, "Are any of these rockets reusable?" I explain that after firing and retrieving them, I've always restored each one to its launch-ready state. I don't share with her my fear that my next launch may never happen. Instead, I concentrate on finding my book. I drop to the floor to search through my supplies.

A curious Hero joins me under the table, and when I pull a promising box into the light, Hero's nose and whiskers are already at work checking its contents.

I don't remember stashing away this many tools and spare parts from my last rocket, but the box is heaped full and there's no sign of the rocketry book. Instead of digging for it, I dump the box upside down.

Hero chases clattering parts across the floor, and the book is now on top, along with another book—a thick leather-bound journal I've never seen before.

"That's odd," I murmur.

Cricket asks what's odd, and I answer, "I don't know what this is. It's not mine, and I don't know how it got into my box."

I thumb through the journal's pages and note with surprise the long entries in Uncle Chad's handwriting, along with carefully sketched illustrations. The sketches include details of ancient Egyptian headgear, hieroglyphs, pyramids, and workers in short tunics. And the title page of the journal contains one penned word: *Proof.*

"It looks like research for my uncle's article on the tools and techniques that built the pyramids," I speculate. "But I wonder why Uncle Chad put it into my rocketry box."

Then, before I close the journal's cover, a note scribbled on the last page catches my eye. I read it out loud: "I'm hiding this journal so that Lawrence cannot find it."

"Whoa!" Cricket exclaims. "What does that mean? Is that the Lawrence who just found the pirate treasure? Why would your uncle want to hide this from his student apprentice?"

"I don't know," I answer. And I wonder again why Uncle Chad chose to hide it here. Was it just a good place, out-of-sight, that Lawrence might never think to check? Or was there some significance to hiding it among my things?

"Are you going to read it?" Cricket asks.

"Definitely," I say.

Cricket suggests, "Wouldn't it be something if the journal contains clues about your uncle's disappearance?"

At that, my heart races. What if Cricket is right?

"We definitely need to read this," I say.

"We could go back to my house and go through it," Cricket suggests. "That is, of course, if you want me to hear the story."

"Of course!" I say. "You were here when I found the journal. This is our mystery book. Let's check it out and see if there's anything interesting in it. Maybe there's nothing, but maybe..."

I stuff the journal and my rocketry book into my satchel and head for the door. At Uncle Chad's desk I stop to look at his picture. "I haven't forgotten you, Uncle Chad," I say. "And if you left this journal for me to find, I'll check it out." Then I add, "I miss you."

I decide to take the photo with me, and when I pick it up, Cricket asks, "May I see that?"

"Sure," I say, and I hold the picture down for her to look at. Cricket stares at the photo for so long that I ask, "What's wrong?"

"This is your uncle?" she asks.

"Yes," I say. "What's wrong?"

"I-I'm not sure," Cricket stutters. But she doesn't take her eyes off the picture.

I see nothing unusual about the photo. Uncle Chad looks distinguished and serious, as he often did for cameras. I look back at Cricket and then back at the photo—and suddenly I see it!

I don't know why I haven't noticed it before. But now I can't unsee it.

Around Uncle Chad's neck is a braided rawhide necklace bearing a single shiny black stone—a stone exactly like the one on the ribbon around Cricket's neck.

Cricket sees me staring at her stone. "What is that?" I ask. "Why do you and Uncle Chad have the same stone around your neck?"

Cricket answers evasively, "It is interesting, isn't it? I had no idea that anyone else had such a necklace."

I sense the wall going up—Cricket's secrecy wall that I can't penetrate. It's obvious that Cricket doesn't want to discuss the stones right now. And although I would love to have immediate answers to the mystery, I know that I will have to wait until Cricket is ready to explain yet another of her many secrets.

# Chapter 4

## The Journal

I can hardly wait to explore the contents of the journal. At Cricket's house, I pull out the chair at her desk. Cricket parks herself by the window, and Hero hops onto her bed. I clear my throat and begin to read.

*June 22, 2015*

*I met someone today, or rather he met me. How he got into my bedroom I don't know, but when I awakened, he was sitting there looking at me. When I jerked up, the young man said calmly, "Don't worry; everything's all right." Then he handed me my glasses and sat waiting for me to come to my full senses.*

*"How did you get in?" I demanded, and he shrugged. "Wasn't hard. Your spare key is in the flower pot by the back door."*

*I supposed that a clever person could have found it, but I couldn't imagine why anyone would bother. I'm not known to be a particularly wealthy man, and I have very little that anyone would want to steal.*

*"But why are you here?" I asked. "Who are you? And why couldn't you wait to see me until I was awake—you know, knock on the door like a normal visitor?"*

*The man smiled as if I had said something amusing, and I studied him. Red hair, blue eyes, early twenties, blue jeans, and T-shirt. He didn't look dangerous. But I didn't appreciate the intrusion.*

*"Go ahead and get dressed," he said. "I can wait."*

*Because my bladder couldn't wait, I had little choice but to grab my clothes and head for the bathroom. When I came out, he was still there staring at the ceiling.*

*"I'm ready for some breakfast," he said now, and I laughed. Some nerve! Breaking in and now demanding breakfast.*

*I stalked past him and down the hall to the kitchen. I had no doubt he would follow me. But when I got to the kitchen, my mouth fell open in surprise.*

*The table was already set, the coffee was done, and so was the bacon. A serving plate of steaming pancakes sat waiting to be buttered and drenched in syrup. Who was this guy?*

*The stranger pulled out a chair for me and I sat. Then he took his place across the table and poured me a cup of coffee.*

*"Eat up, before it all gets cold," he urged, and I looked around the room and out the window to make sure I wasn't dreaming.*

*"It's not my birthday, you know," I said, and the fellow laughed. "Does it have to be a birthday to get a special treat?"*

*"No, I guess not," I said, and suddenly I was ravenous. I stabbed two of the pancakes from the serving dish and filled my plate.*

*The stranger and I ate the entire stack of pancakes and every strip of bacon and then sat back, satisfied.*

*I puzzled again over who this fellow could be. When I asked, he answered cryptically, "I heard you needed some help proving something."*

*I had no idea what he was talking about. I wasn't working on any particular project at the moment. I had just finished an article for* Armchair Science *on tools and techniques that built the pyramids, and I hadn't yet started a new article. No one knew what I would tackle next, not even me.*

*"Proof of what?" I asked.*

*"Several things. Among them is proof of the biblical Exodus."*

*"Ha! What's not proven?" I challenged. "Everyone knows that the Israelites lived in Egypt and eventually left."*

*"But does everyone agree on a mass exodus of hundreds of thousands, perhaps two million, people and how and why they left?" he asked.*

*I shrugged. "Not particularly. There are no records in the Egyptian histories to correspond with such an exodus. It's more likely that the Israelites came and left little by little, over many years, just like people from other nations did."*

*"But," the stranger countered, "weren't the Israelites slaves? How could slaves slip away unnoticed?"*

*I could tell that my visitor was trying to back me into a corner; he was trying to make me say that the biblical record was factual. Perhaps he was some religious zealot who had taken offense at something I'd published—perhaps something I'd said in my article about the tools and techniques that built the pyramids. But I don't remember saying much about Moses in that article. By all accounts (biblical or otherwise), the pyramids were constructed in the Old Kingdom period (c. 2700-2200 BC), long before Joseph and the Israelites were said to have come to Egypt and before Moses is supposed to have led them out. I decided to throw my stranger a bone and said, "I suppose a mass migration was possible but it's not likely to have happened the way it's portrayed in Exodus."*

*"Why not, if the other facts line up?"*

*I didn't want to argue with him, but I said, "Well, there's a heap of mythology wrapped around those facts. Like the business of the sea opening up and over a million people walking through. It's probably a poetic way to say that the water level was low in that spot and they were able to cross over. The biblical writer obviously wanted to give credit to some supernatural being, so he exaggerated a little. People did that sort of thing back then."*

*The stranger listened but smiled his annoying smile again.*

*"Low water, huh? Then how do you suppose that the Egyptian army chasing them drowned? Wouldn't the army have been able to cross, too?"*

*"Ah," I said. "There you go again. The only place that such a drowning account occurs is in the biblical story. There is nothing in the Egyptian records about such a drowning of their army."*

*"And don't you find that to be a little convenient on the Egyptian's part?" my visitor asked. "Especially since you'll not find records of any defeats in the Egyptian annals—not a single one. What king or pharaoh would want to leave that kind of record?"*

*I could tell now that this conversation was never going to be truly productive. As a man of science, I had little use for ancient mythologies like those in the Bible, except when the anecdotal insights of the spiritual records helped fill in gaps of history on ancient customs and thought. Weak-minded people clung to the book's tales as true, but not me. I was determined now to cut this visit short.*

*"Well," I said, "I have work to do. So, if you have nothing else you need, I thank you for the breakfast and hope you have a good day."*

*I stood. The stranger took the hint and stood as well.*

*"Until tomorrow, then," the man said, and before I could object to another visit from him, he turned the knob on the kitchen door and walked out.*

"What an odd encounter!" I say. "I don't recall Uncle Chad ever saying anything about a break-in. I wonder if I should tell Detective Gorman. He might be able to find the intruder and question him."

Cricket doesn't share my enthusiasm, however. She says, "Maybe. But this supposedly all happened three years ago."

And before I can comment, Marlene Grace interrupts with a tap on the bedroom door. The door is already ajar, and I hurry to slide the book off the edge of the desk and to the floor where it can't be seen. I'm not sure why, but I'm not ready to share our discovery with Marlene Grace or anyone else, yet.

"Are you two ready for lunch?" Marlene Grace asks.

"Me too?" I ask.

"That was the idea, child," Marlene Grace replies with a grin.

"That would be great!" I say. "Let me text my mom to make sure it's OK."

I leave the book on the floor until after we have our lunch.

# Chapter 5

## The Stranger Returns

When Cricket and I retreat to her room again, I retrieve the journal from the floor. Hero curls up in my lap, and I scratch his ears. If I didn't know better, I'd think the little Jack Russell terrier understands every word I'm reading. He seems to be waiting for me to pick up where I left off.

*June 23, 2015*

*This morning when I awakened, I was pleased to find that I was alone in my bedroom. As a precaution I had brought the flower pot key inside and left it on the kitchen counter. It must have worked.*

*Or so I thought, until I began to smell coffee.*

*Sure enough, a full breakfast awaited me in the kitchen, along with my stranger.*

*"You're spoiling me, you know," I muttered, and the young man poured coffee into my cup.*

*As I buttered my pancakes, I noticed the Bible from my reference shelf lying next to my plate. The stranger saw me glance at it, and he said, "I thought you might want to reacquaint yourself with the Exodus story."*

*"Oh, I think I remember it pretty well," I retorted. Although my memory isn't photographic, it does retain information, especially details I've read several times. The Bible is one of those reference items that have been useful as I've written some of my magazine articles. For example, I spent a lot of time in the Bible's first chapters when I wrote my article on Genesis Versus Evolution.*

*"Suit yourself," the man said. And then the stranger reached over the table and set a small biscuit-like cake on the edge of my plate. "See what you think."*

*He broke off a bite from another cake and put it into his mouth. As he chewed, I shrugged and bit into the little cake he had placed on my plate. It tasted sweet but not too sweet, kind of like bread, but with a different texture.*

*"What is it?" I asked. "A special family recipe?"*

*"No, silly. It's a cake of manna."*

*I looked at him over my glasses. "Where did you get manna?"*

*"From the desert."*

*I rolled my eyes. Of course. Now I knew why the book of Exodus lay open by my plate. But I was ready for him.*

*"I'm pretty sure I read that God stopped supplying manna after the Israelites entered the land of Canaan," I said. "If that's so, God's not in the manna business anymore."*

*"Very good!" my stranger said.*

*We ate our pancakes and bacon in silence now, because I refused to ask him how or why he had brought me manna. But after several minutes of ignoring each other and consuming our syrupy meal, I began to grow aggravated. What did this*

*guy expect to gain by breaking into my house each morning
and fixing me breakfast? It was very uncomfortable.*

*"Aren't you a little curious about my visits?" the stranger
suddenly asked. And I growled, "Yeah, now that you mention
it. I'm curious and a little upset that you keep showing up
uninvited."*

*"I'm only here because somebody sent me."*

*"OK," I said sarcastically, "who are you and who
sent you?"*

*He said, "I can't tell you that yet."*

*"Can't or won't?" I challenged him.*

*"Both, I guess," he replied with a shrug, and he poked a
last bite of pancake into his mouth.*

*"Look," I said crossly, "are you going to tell me what
you're doing here, or not?"*

*The visitor wiped his mouth on his napkin and said,
"Maybe tomorrow."*

*Then he carried his plate to the sink, rinsed it, and
walked out the door.*

———◆———

Cricket purses her lips when I stop reading. I'm astonished at the story
in the journal and start to say so when Cricket murmurs, "I think I know
the stranger."

"Really!" I exclaim. "Is he dangerous? What's he up to?"

Cricket's response is a decided nod toward the journal. "We need to
read more, so I can be sure."

"Sure of what?"

"Sure that I'm not mistaken," she says.

Then, because Cricket insists, I read on.

*June 24, 2015*

*I was almost disappointed to awaken today and find no
breakfast made and no stranger in the kitchen. I thought*

*that perhaps he would come later in the day, but the fellow never showed up. I think his absence worries me more than his visits.*

*June 25, 2015*

*Still no visit from the red-headed stranger.*

*June 26, 2015*

*Today I smelled the coffee the minute I awakened. Throwing off the covers I ran to the kitchen.*
*"Miss me?" the fellow asked.*
*I felt stupid. I just mumbled, "What happened to you?" as he poured my coffee.*
*"Had some other things to do. But I'm here now. And as I promised, I can now tell you my name. It's Josh."*

———————◆◆———————

The minute I read the name *Josh*, Hero wags his tail and Cricket cries out, "I knew it!" With triumph in her voice, she orders me to keep reading. "Don't stop now!" she insists.

Hero punctuates her command with a happy bark, and I press on to learn more.

*June 26, 2015 (continued)*

*"Josh?" I repeated. "Josh what?"*
*"Just Josh. And I'm here to offer you something."*
*Oh, great. Was this a sales pitch? Had this whole intrusion business been a lead up to selling me something? What a way to get your toe in the door! Feed your patsy some pancakes.*
*I crossed my arms. "I don't need anything. Keep your promo to yourself. I'm not spending a dime."*

*At that, Josh smiled that aggravating smile of his. Then he pulled out something from his pocket and laid it on the table.*

*"Really?" I said when I saw the object he'd produced. "You think I want to buy a rawhide necklace? No thanks."*

*The thought of a crazy salesman began to tickle me now. He wasn't even selling something the world needed, like a portable, personal air-conditioner. Who needs a rawhide necklace with a black stone?*

———— • ————

*The necklace!* I stop reading.

"This is where Uncle Chad got his necklace!" I say. "The one that's like yours." And although I've restrained myself regarding Cricket's secrets, I now press her for information.

"What's the significance of the black stone necklaces?" I ask. "How do you know this Josh person? Why did he give you and Uncle Chad these necklaces?"

Cricket ignores my questions and insists that I keep reading. "It's important," she declares.

I dislike her evasiveness, but I read on because it seems that the answers are in the journal.

*June 26, 2015 (continued)*

*"This isn't just any necklace," Josh said, and I thought how that's what all salesmen would say. I supposed that Josh would tell me next that the stone at the end of the rawhide turns into a night light or something.*

*Then before I could protest his action, Josh slipped the lanyard over my head. I felt the stone land in the hollow of my throat. I grabbed at it and protested, "I said I didn't want to buy this thing."*

*"Oh, there's no cost," Josh said. "It's a gift from the one who sent me."*

"Look," I said trying to sound reasonable, "I'm not in the habit of accepting gifts from strangers. I'm sure he means it as a kind gesture, but I'm uncomfortable with this. Please take it back with my thanks-but-no-thanks."

Josh replied, "But you don't know yet what the necklace can do."

I threw up my hands. "Okay. Let's get this over with. Go ahead and give me your sales spiel so you can get your commission and leave me alone."

That seemed to amuse Josh. He declared, "You are by far the most difficult person I've ever had to offer a present to."

I rolled my eyes at the ceiling. What did it take to get rid of this fellow? "Okay," I said, "what does this wonder necklace do?"

"This," he said.

One word. That was all. And as he said it, Josh clicked the stone on his lanyard against the stone on mine. In a dizzying instant my reality changed! I looked down to see that my feet were no longer on the floor. Josh and I were rising toward the ceiling like a couple of balloons. And then somehow, we passed right through the ceiling and into the sky. Higher and higher we climbed. Through the clouds and beyond.

Faster and faster we flew. When we entered the vacuum of space, I was sure we were going to die. But it didn't happen. We raced on. At the edge of the Milky Way, the nearest stars streaked past us like bullets.

———————◆———————

I snort, now, and stop reading. I have to stop. This can't be Uncle Chad's writing. He would never write something so outlandish. This is not science. If I didn't know better, I'd think this had been concocted by the writers of *The Argosy Space Explorer* television serial.

"This is garbage!" I cry. "Uncle Chad did not write this. No way!"

I toss the book down, but Cricket insists that I keep reading. "Don't stop!" she orders forcefully.

Her tone of voice startles me, and she stares me down. Hero's ears have perked, and I shake my head. But I continue to read the words that I don't believe.

*June 26, 2015 (continued)*

> *Now we acquired a target, a planet. A mere pinpoint ahead of us. The orb expanded every fraction of a second as we approached. Finally, it loomed ominously. Terror filled me. At the speed we were hurtling we were certain to crash at any moment. Instinctively I curled up, shielded my eyes, and screamed.*
>
> *But in the last fraction of a second before our imminent demise, our headlong rush stalled into a marshmallow of slow motion. I can't explain it, except to say that it was as if time expanded, and we hung suspended only inches from the surface. Then we were deposited on the ground as gently as snowflakes on a winter day.*
>
> *Before my brain could catch up, Josh reached out and steadied me. I stared past him at palm trees, sand, and a sun setting behind a horizon of pyramids.*
>
> *Were we back on Earth? I didn't think so, but it was so like the Earth I knew.*

---

I stop reading again and wrinkle my nose. The journal falls back and I spout, "If this is Uncle Chad's writing, he must have gotten into some bad drugs. This is ridiculous!"

But Cricket isn't laughing. "Don't stop reading," she orders again. She gives me the same stare as before, until I give in.

*June 26, 2015 (continued)*

> *"Put this on," Josh directed me. He held out a nondescript tunic. The outfit matched one that I noticed he was wearing. And before I could object, Josh took off my glasses and my*

*wrist watch and ordered me to remove my shoes. He replaced the shoes with a pair of simple leather sandals which I put on. He then proceeded to stash my things into a rough leather pack that he slung over his shoulder.*

*I protested that I needed my glasses, but Josh insisted that I didn't need them. And to my surprise I found he was right. Without a hint of myopic fuzziness, I could clearly see a small group of people walking a short way ahead of us on a dirt road. After I dressed, Josh pulled me into a jog so that we could catch up with them.*

*Our companions proved to be a solemn, sweaty group of workers who seemed too tired to talk. As we passed a series of work sites, more workers abandoned their tasks and fell in to walk with us. Behind each group were scores of spear-toting supervisors watching the workers leave to join the caravan. As far as I could see, thousands, perhaps hundreds of thousands, of people left similar work sites and filled other roads that joined ours. Everyone plodded wearily in the same direction.*

*"Who are these people?" I whispered, but Josh ignored me.*

*Now, in the same way that we had acquired companions, we began to lose members of our company. Groups of men peeled off as we passed what I guessed were their homes— desert-brick huts lit by lamplight and surrounded by stone folds of sheep and goats. I could smell baked bread wafting from the hut windows, and my tummy rumbled.*

*When the last of our companions left us, Josh and I walked on to the edge of the settlement. There, several uninhabited huts hugged the desert sands. Josh led the way into the first hut.*

*"We'll sleep here," Josh said, and I asked in surprise, "We're staying the night?"*

*In answer, Josh simply opened his back pack and pulled out two blankets and a small oil lamp.*

*I quizzed him, "Where are we?"*

*Josh gave me a reproving look. "You know," he said.*

*I wanted to object, but my protest would have been hollow. I did have a good idea of where we were, and Josh knew it. He now produced a hunk of bread, some cheese, and an animal skin filled with water. I ate as if I had missed breakfast and lunch today. And soon it was time for bed.*

———————•———————

The journal entry for June 26 ends, and Cricket frowns when I take advantage of the break in the narrative to flop back and object, "This story is too crazy for me. I don't get it. What's going on? Where have Josh and Uncle Chad landed?" Then I insist, "This is a waste of time."

Hero can hear the frustration in my voice, and he pushes his nose under my hand so that I have to pet him. His eyes don't leave my face.

Cricket resists my questions. "You will get it," she says. "And you need to hear it from Uncle Chad."

Her comment is meant to induce me to continue reading. I know that, somehow, she knows the answers to my questions, but she stubbornly refuses to fill me in. I'm forced to look for my answers in the pages of the journal.

*June 27, 2015*

*In the morning, I expected to awaken in my room at home. My strange dream of travel to an ancient desert had been vivid, and I wouldn't soon forget it.*

*But to my consternation when I opened my eyes, I found myself still in the company of the inexplicable Josh in a pitifully small mud hut. Through the doorway I could see the rest of the worker compound awakening. No matter how tightly I squeezed my eyes, I could not dispel the images and the sensations I had felt yesterday and that continued to unfold.*

*Josh produced a breakfast of bread, cheese, and a few dates. "What, no pancakes?" I quipped.*

*We ate in silence and then Josh said, "Off to work."*

*Josh rose to his feet and slung his pack over his shoulder. I had no choice but to follow him to the road. There we met up with the familiar throng of workers we had walked with last night.*

*Fresh from their rest, our travel companions were talkative this morning. And true to the illusion I was already suffering from, I heard them speaking in perfect English!*

*"Any new word from Moses, this morning?" one man asked. "The locusts are finally gone. They've devastated the fields. Pharaoh will surely let us out of Egypt now."*

*"Don't count on it," a younger man said. "Pharaoh needs workers to supply bricks and build his storage cities. He'll never let us go."*

*Others in the group agreed with the young man. "Just because Moses tells us we're going to leave doesn't mean we are going anywhere."*

*A third man, an excitable fellow, spoke up now. "But maybe God is going to rescue us. Moses has accurately predicted eight calamities in the last six weeks. Our God is showing his power, to make Pharaoh listen."*

*The young scoffer interrupted. "If our God is so powerful, then why has he waited 400 years to get us out of this slavery?"*

*The first man admonished the scoffer. "Would you rather believe that the sun or the moon caused the recent disasters? And if so, how did Moses predict them? He doesn't believe in the sun or the moon gods. Moses claims that our God has spoken to him and that our God intends for us to leave Egypt now—and we are to take the bones of our forebear, Joseph, with us when we leave."*

*A majority of the workers agreed with the God-fearing man, and the young scoffer was forced to hold his tongue.*

*One of those who believed said, "It seems that God has heard our cries and knows our plight. If he is going to save us, we need to listen to his spokesman, Moses. Perhaps Pharaoh will give in today and word will come."*

*I was ready to burst with all the unbelievable words I was hearing. Josh turned to me and asked, "Something wrong?"*

*I whirled around and pointed a finger in his face. "You know exactly what's wrong. This whole thing is wrong. This can't be happening."*

*Josh calmly replied, "But it is happening. As I've told you, this is a gift for you."*

*"I don't need this so-called gift," I snorted. "This is all fabricated. You're just trying to brain-wash me with this illusion. I don't know how you're doing it, but it's not going to get me to accept the biblical account of the Hebrew exodus."*

*Josh did not react to my accusation. He just kept walking. Then he said, "What you want to know is why you hear these people speaking in English."*

*With as much sarcasm as I could muster, I huffed, "What makes you think so?"*

*Josh didn't even blink. "It's part of your gift. You've been endowed for the present with the ability to communicate in the original universal language—the language of all the Earth prior to Babel. Whatever these people say will be heard as English by you, and whatever you say will be heard by them as ancient Hebrew." Then Josh added, "And if you choose, you can even speak and understand ancient Egyptian."*

*I wanted to scream. This was definitely a dream, the stuff of fairy-tales! This language business clinched it. Nothing could be more contrived than the biblical myth that in one day everyone's universal communication was confounded by the Hebrew God so that no one could understand each other and so that the attempt to build the Tower of Babel would be thwarted. Everyone knows that language variances came about over long periods of time when people were separated from one another across the globe.*

*I didn't know how Josh was managing this complicated illusion, but I wasn't going to let it work on me. I kept walking and tried to remain sane.*

*Our traveling company dwindled little by little, and Josh and I left the road with the last group of workers. We entered a vast brick-making yard where thousands of squared brick molds spread across the landscape. The mold-drying field was dotted with scores of massive vats for mixing mud and straw. Under the severe gaze of several taskmasters, our company set to work manufacturing bricks.*

*Like Josh, I made myself useful by hauling straw to the vats, straw that was gathered by others from the surrounding area or carted in from elsewhere. Josh and I passed our itchy armfuls to men who chopped and dumped the binding material into the gooey mud and stirred. A queue of workers filled heavy jugs with the resulting straw-laced mud and passed them along the queue to other workers who bent to fill one empty mold after another, for hours on end. When the molded mud had dried sufficiently in the sun, the bricks were knocked out of their squares and set onto the ground to continue drying. The finished bricks were carefully stacked into little mountains all across the plain. And, no matter how many mountains we produced, more bricks were required. We were constantly told by the supervisors to work harder and move faster. Josh calmly picked up his pace, and I did the same until the drudgery of our work settled into our backs and knees.*

*To take their minds off the toil and monotony, workers around us talked. Several of them recounted the events of recent plagues. I decided that the Egyptians must not understand much Hebrew because they showed no reaction to the repeated stories.*

*"Never before has all of the country's water, everywhere, turned into blood—and stayed that way for a week," one man said. "And Egypt has never had such overwhelming plagues of frogs, lice, and flies."*

*A slender young man with a stir stick at the brick molds smiled when he said, "And then all of the cattle died except for ours in Goshen. God protected our cattle, and that made*

*Pharaoh angrier. You would think that Pharaoh would begin to realize that with the Hebrew God he's met his match!"*

*With sweat dripping, a stocky worker who dropped off an armload of straw hissed, "You forgot to mention my favorite plague: boils! Painful boils that broke out on all the Egyptians, even Pharaoh. Serves him right!"*

*The workers wanted to laugh but were afraid of the whips of the taskmasters. Talking was tolerated but laughing was not allowed.*

*I scowled and glared at Josh. This illusion of his was interesting, to be sure. But I still believed I was dreaming. Josh had somehow altered my reality to press his point about the biblical story. None of this was truly happening.*

*A solemn-faced older man did not seem to share the bitter glee of the younger workers about the misfortunes wrought by the plagues on the Egyptians. "It's all terrible," he murmured.*

*"So, Saul," one of the younger men sneered, "you don't think the Egyptians deserve punishment for crushing us as slaves and working us like dogs?"*

*Saul didn't answer at first. But following more taunts, he said sadly, "This pharaoh is foolish. He has recklessly ignored his history. Our people—especially our ancestor Joseph—saved Egypt when God sent a seven-year famine across the world. And Pharaoh honored Joseph and invited his people to live here, in Goshen. And we were guests until that pharaoh died. The Egyptian people were our friends and neighbors. But new generations and new pharaohs have ignored their history and have wrongly feared our numbers— even murdering an entire generation of our male babies and relegating us to this slavery."*

*"And," interrupted a bitter voice, "they have robbed us, so that we cannot buy our freedom. We cannot redeem ourselves and leave this place!"*

*Saul nodded to acknowledge the man's lament. Then he said, "But I believe that God is calling an end to our misfortune. I believe that God is redeeming us by making Pharaoh pay our price with judgments of pain and plagues."*

*Then Saul quoted an old prophecy from Genesis 15, where God told Abram (who became Abraham, the father of the Hebrew race), "Know for certain that your descendants will be strangers in a country not their own, and they will be enslaved and mistreated four hundred years. But I will punish the nation they serve as slaves, and afterward they will come out with great possessions."*

*"Well," snorted a young man, "God's going to have to hurry on the 'great possessions' part of that prophecy! I don't have a single coin to my name, and I don't know that any of you have, either."*

*At that, an older man said quietly, "Not so fast, Jubal. I think that Saul is right. We may not have a lot, yet, but I think God is paving the way for the wealth of that prophecy to come true. At least in my case, I see the possibility. My daughter has sent word that she is coming home. Her mistress is paying her to leave! The woman has given Elizabeth fine clothing and jewelry and even gold because she wants Elizabeth to ask our God to exclude her and her household from the next judgment on Egypt. The woman has said, 'You are under a great blessing by a powerful God. I have failed to see it, until now. So, allow me to make amends and honor you and your great God. Pray for me that I may be spared his judgments. Use my gold and silver as you see fit to worship your God when you leave this country.'"*

*When the man finished speaking, another man shared, "I haven't said anything, until now, but the same thing is happening with my Deborah. Her owners are releasing her, as well, and are sending her away with money and rich things. I hadn't believed Deborah, but now I think it may be true, since you say the same thing is happening with your daughter."*

*Then, throughout the workforce, others quietly affirmed that the same things were happening to members of their families, but they hadn't told anyone or dared to believe it, until now.*

*Even so, the scoffing young man persisted. "You're all dreaming!" he sneered. "It's all a pipe dream. Nobody's offered me money. Every Egyptian I know hates us and agrees with Pharaoh that we should continue to be slaves. I don't believe the tyrant will ever let us go."*

*"But Pharaoh will let us go," declared Saul more boldly, now. "With every plague the time draws closer that we will be given permission to leave. We must not lose hope. I believe it will be soon."*

*"I hope so," the young man growled. "The taskmasters are becoming crueler every day."*

*"That's because the taskmasters are afraid," suggested another worker with an empty mud jug. "If our God leads us out of here, the taskmasters will have to make the bricks themselves."*

*"That'll be the day!" a sneering man said a little too loudly, and several other workers chuckled under their breath. But then the man said, "The taskmasters may be afraid of our God, but they still have the whips that we feel on our backs."*

*A comical fellow jested, "And to think that for the last four weeks I've had my bags packed and ready to leave. I've even composed a sweet bon voyage song to sing to my favorite taskmaster."*

*In spite of themselves, everyone laughed at that. And immediately a contingent of overseers laid lashes from their whips across our backs. I managed to elude the thrashing, but I found that my shoulders and knees ached from bending and lifting.*

*And then it dawned on me. What was I doing? I didn't have to work! Nobody has to work in a dream, even an elaborate one created by Josh. So, I stopped. And when I did, I instantly felt the whips sting my back. Lash after lash. The Egyptian overseer who scourged me shouted, "Get back to work!" Dream or no dream, I was compelled to pick up my jug of mud. This much reality in a dream was too much. I wanted to curse Josh for bringing me here.*

*But before I could give my mysterious companion a piece of my mind, someone turned out the lights—completely.*

*In an instant the morning sun disappeared. Everything grew dark. It was as if light had never existed. Nothing glimmered or twinkled or danced with shadow. Darkness deeper than any cloud cover on any midnight pressed in all around us with a heaviness that could be felt.*

*My first thought was that Josh's dream was finally ending. But I was wrong. I continued to hear and touch and even smell my surroundings. Only my sight was gone.*

*And I wasn't alone in my blindness. I heard workers around me puzzling over what had happened. Most were afraid to move; there were too many obstacles one could trip over and become seriously injured. And yet no one wanted to stay trapped in this place. Even the taskmasters called out in their confusion.*

*As the minutes passed, panic among my companions grew. One worker cried out, "Our God has destroyed the sun! Because Pharaoh wouldn't listen to him, Moses has taken the light. How will anyone live now? Without light everything will die!"*

*I admit that it did feel like the end of the world. But I remembered the story of the plague of darkness, and I expected the sun to return in a few minutes. The writer of Exodus claimed that the darkness lasted for days, but I had always doubted it. Scientifically, it had to be no more than a solar eclipse. Granted, this was the darkest solar eclipse I had ever experienced (usually the sun's corona was visible and gave some light), but I was convinced that there was a rational explanation for what we were experiencing, as there were rational explanations for all of the previous plagues. All of the plagues could be explained as natural (albeit extreme) occurrences in nature. In this case, the light of the sun should be peeking through any minute. No eclipse could last longer than seven minutes and 31 seconds.*

*But ten minutes, twenty minutes, thirty minutes passed and the eclipse did not end. I couldn't understand it, and I was becoming confused in the blackness. What was happening? Something was very wrong.*

———◆———

"Wow!" says Cricket. "What your uncle is describing is exactly what the Bible says happened. The ninth plague was total darkness for three days."

"But Uncle Chad says it was just an eclipse..."

"No, Alexander. Your uncle says that it wasn't an eclipse. It was lasting too long."

Then Cricket says, "It must have been frightening to not be able to see even a glimmer of light—no shadows, no passing clouds, no sun, and no stars."

I try to imagine it, and I offer, "I was in a cave, once, where the guide turned off the lights for a couple of minutes. It was totally dark in there. And it was scary."

Then Cricket grows solemn. "That's what blindness is like. As I've told you, after my accident I was blind for many days. Thankfully, my sight returned, but I didn't know that it would. I thought I was going to be blind forever, and unable to feel. It was the most hopeless feeling I've ever had."

Cricket seems so somber that I wish she didn't have to relive that terrible time.

Finally, I say, "But didn't you say that the darkness in the Bible lasted only three days?"

"Yes." Cricket smiles, and I say, "OK. Let's read some more."

*June 27, 2015 continued*

*Something was very wrong.*
*Then I thought, this was Josh's doing. How far was he going to let this dream go? I wished I could find him. I'd give him a piece of my mind.*

43

*And then I saw a tiny spark that burst into flame. Josh had lit a fire. He had made a makeshift torch out of a wooden staff and a torn strip from his tunic. Hungry for the light, everyone drew near and crowded in. Other garment strips were torn off and more torches were made. The lights were passed around.*

*Now Josh called out, "Hold hands and make a chain. Follow the torches home."*

*The Egyptian supervisors rushed in and tried to commandeer the torches. But every torch they pulled from the hands of a worker went out. Only the torches in Hebrew hands stayed lit, and the line of workers moved with their torches to the road to begin their march home.*

*As the company approached the first living compound, we could see lights in the windows of every house. Oil lamps flickered and looked homey and inviting, as on every other evening.*

*At one house nearest the road, we watched a scuffle. I recognized an Egyptian taskmaster who had followed us and who now tried to steal the oil lamp from the home. With his spear in one hand he kept the house owner and other workers at bay while he lifted the lamp from the table with his other hand. But the moment the lamp left the table, its flame went out. The Egyptian set the useless lamp back on the table and would have tried to slip away, but the minute the lamp left his hand, its flame returned. Again, he picked up the lamp, and again the flame went out. He replaced the lamp on the table, and the flame rose again. It became clear to him that only the Hebrews had the power to keep the flames lit.*

*The workers, also, began to realize their power, and they banished the overseer to the darkness. "Go home!" the workers shouted at him. And the man was forced to stumble back to the road and crawl blindly away.*

*Following this little victory, the workers milled about and cheered. When the celebration settled, someone called* out, "How long will this darkness last? Does anyone know what Moses has said about it?"

Josh answered, "Three days. And Moses told Pharaoh that only the Hebrews would have light."

Again, the crowd cheered. It dawned on them that they didn't have to work, and that they were in a position to help themselves.

"Should we pack our things?" one woman cried. "Should we leave Egypt now?"

In answer, Josh called out, "We must wait. It's too dangerous to travel with only torches in the dark with children and animals. Moses will tell us when it is time to go. Our God will tell him."

"Remember," Josh said, "that Moses not only called down the plagues, but he also turned them back. He will tell us when the darkness will end, just as he predicted when the blood would turn back to water and when the frogs and lice and flies would leave. He also predicted when the boils would heal and when the hail and locusts would cease."

"But if we pack," the woman reasoned, "we will be ready. What if Moses says that we are to leave tomorrow? We should get ready now."

Josh did not counter her reasoning. And so, for the rest of the day, in spite of the darkness outside of their walls, the Hebrew families began to consolidate their belongings and pack them for travel. I wanted to pack my things to leave, too—to go home. I wondered how long it would be before Josh would let me go back to reality.

Without the sun to measure our day, our hours dragged by. But soon I learned to gauge the passage of time by the sound of the camp's hourly ram's horn blasts. The hours were announced by certain elders who monitored the camp's official water clock—a device comprised of two bowls set in place one above the other. Water from a hole in the top bowl dripped slowly into the bottom bowl, and when the top bowl emptied, an hour had passed. Others in the camp set and reset their *family hour bowls according to the elders' announcements which ended at bedtime and resumed early in the morning.*

On our second day of darkness, I became aware of a commotion somewhere in the camp. Not long after, word arrived that a message from Moses and his brother Aaron was being relayed from family to family. Some of our group's leaders went to hear and bring back a report.

In late afternoon, Josh and I joined others at Asher's door for a broadcast of Moses' announcement. By the light of a lamp hung at the entrance, Asher called out, "Our wives were right to begin to pack. Moses and Aaron tell us that in five days we will move out of Egypt. By then the darkness will have ended."

The crowd cheered.

"Finally!" I said loud enough for Josh's benefit. "Enough of this darkness."

Asher's face flickered in the flame of the hanging lamp. "Don't cheer just yet," he cautioned. "Moses warns that there is a tenth plague to come. And the tenth plague is the one that will convince Pharaoh to let us leave."

"This plague," Asher said, "will be a terrible one—worse than all of the others. And you need to be alert and carefully observe everything Moses has relayed to us."

I glanced at Josh, who ignored me. I knew this part of the story—a story I had always found overly dramatic and overly written. But now, in the middle of the darkness, I found myself listening closely to what Asher was passing along to everyone.

"Our God," said Asher, "is going to send an angel of death at midnight on an appointed day. That angel will visit every home in the land of Egypt to kill every first-born son and every first-born male animal. Even we, the Hebrews, will not be free from this judgment."

With alarm, I stop reading. "Uncle Chad is a first-born!" I whisper. "He could be in danger."

But Cricket refuses to entertain my panic. She urges, "You've got to read more, Alexander. Don't stop."

Then she adds, "You know that your uncle doesn't die or he wouldn't have been able to write all of the later entries in the journal."

I know that she's right, of course. I'm getting too caught up in the story and I'm not thinking straight. I have to read how Uncle Chad escapes.

*June 27, 2015 continued*

> *"No!" people whispered in alarm. Gasps passed throughout the crowd. "Surely God is not going to bring death to us, too!"*
>
> *Asher shouted more loudly. "I'm not finished!" he insisted. "Listen to me!"*
>
> *The crowd hushed and stared.*
>
> *"Moses says that you are not to fear," he declared. "God has given some very specific instructions that can save our people. But you must listen and carefully do everything I tell you. It is important! Ignore these words at your own peril."*
>
> *Every ear strained to catch his words as Asher leaned in. "Here is what you are to do."*
>
> *"Each household," said Asher, "must select a perfect year-old male lamb or goat and bring it into your house. There, you must care for it as a pet until you are given instructions to slaughter it for your family's supper. This will be your last meal in Egypt before you follow Moses into the desert."*
>
> *"Note," Asher added, "that if your family is too small to eat the whole animal, you must arrange to share the meal with another family."*
>
> *Asher continued, "On the announced day (which will be very soon), you will slaughter that perfect lamb at the twilight hour. Drain its blood into a basin and roast the whole animal on a spit over a fire. Also prepare bitter salad greens and make fresh bread without yeast. Gather into your house everyone*

*who is to eat the meal. Tell them they must wear sandals and a belt, and they must tuck up their skirts as a reminder that they will soon be marching out of the land. Each man should also keep his walking stick close by. Your guests must be prepared to spend the night.*

*"After everyone has assembled inside, take a bundle of hyssop branches and dip it into the blood you drained earlier from the lamb. With the hyssop as a brush, smear the blood across the sides and top of the doorframe of the house. Once the doorposts are painted, no one is to go in or out of the dwelling until morning.*

*"Then, you are to eat the evening meal. Anything that cannot be eaten must be burned before morning.*

*"Again, remember that no one is to leave your house; it is vitally important for everyone to remain inside."*

*Asher pointedly cast his eyes around the crowd to emphasize his point. Only after everyone nodded that they had heard him did he continue.*

*In a voice grown ominous, Asher said, "You will understand why it is important to be shut safely inside, because at midnight God's angel of death will pass through all the land of Egypt. He will be terrible to behold! He will see the homes with blood on the doorposts and will not enter them. The blood will be a sign. The angel will not bring the plague of death on the blood-marked houses; he will pass over them. Those without the blood will not be so fortunate. The angel will enter every unmarked home, whether those within are Hebrew or Egyptian or any other race, and the angel will kill every firstborn son and firstborn male animal he finds."*

*At this, I heard murmurings and saw fear in the eyes of first-born children. They clung fearfully to their parents. And I saw dread in the eyes of first-born adults. Asher's words served as a powerful incentive for every family to follow God's instructions to the letter.*

*Asher now said, "After the angel has passed through Egypt, the land will be filled with mourning. There will be death in the huts of the poorest slaves and in the homes of the highest officials of the land, even to the family of Pharaoh. Daylight will dawn, but the mourning of death will draw down its own night. Everyone in the land will know that the Hebrew God has done what he has warned, and all of Egypt will implore us to leave. At noon our exodus will begin. Moses will lead us out of Egypt."*

*Instead of celebrating their coming release, everyone remained sobered by the seriousness of the plague. Asher asked if anyone needed him to repeat the message, and everyone told him no. Every word he had spoken was burned into their minds. And his message was exactly what I knew to be in the biblical account.*

*Then, to my surprise, Asher invited Josh and me to be under the protection of his roof and to eat the specified meal with his family.*

*"There are only two of you," Asher said, "and you will not be able to eat an entire lamb by yourselves. My family would be honored to have you join us. We have already brought our lamb into the house."*

*Josh accepted the invitation on our behalf, and Asher blessed us when we left to go to our hut, guided by a newly lit torch.*

———◆———

"Wow!" I tell Cricket. "Now we're getting to the good stuff. At least this part of the story is exciting."

Because I am caught up in the tale's suspense and want to know what happens, I am ready to read more. But Cricket stops me with a sharp cry. "Alexander! It's already six o-clock! You have to go!"

"Oh, no!" I gasp. "My mom will have words if I'm late for supper. I should have been paying attention to the clock."

Hero dances around my feet as I hurriedly gather my things. I quickly pet him goodbye, and I remember to tell Cricket, "I'm not sure that I can come tomorrow. I'll text you." Then I run out the door to climb onto my bike and pedal home like mad.

# Chapter 6

## The Exodus

For two days I am stuck at home. I can't get away to Cricket's house because Mom's sister and her family have come for the weekend.

I can't even get a half-hour alone in my room to peek ahead at the story in Uncle Chad's journal. My every waking minute is spent in entertaining my seven- and nine-year-old cousins. For the most part, Lennie and Aiden aren't bad kids, but they get into things. Nobody's taught them the meaning of *keep your hands off my stuff.* I can't keep them from toying with my solid-fuel rocket model.

In desperation I gather some supplies from Mom so I can show the boys how to make paper-tube rockets and set them off with Alka-Seltzer™ tablets. Instantly I become Lennie and Aiden's favorite (and only) cousin, and my dad whispers in my ear, "Clever tactic, son. Just one more day."

Lennie makes a second rocket with little supervision and sends it over the crabapple tree. And then, when Aiden begs Lennie to help him make a third rocket, Lennie's big-brother air of superiority kicks in and I don't even have to point out where to cut or glue. But I still can't retreat to my room.

Mom saves the day with a double batch of her world-famous triple-chocolate brownies, and I get to sit for a few minutes. (The brownies are *world-famous* because Mom sent them overseas when her brother, Roger, was in the Air Force.)

Finally, very early on Monday morning, I am able to wave goodbye to our visitors, and I watch with relief as their car disappears down the road. At last I can text Cricket: *I'll be there after school.*

I rescue my rocket model from Mom's and Dad's bedroom, where Dad wisely suggested I hide it for protection. Tonight, I'll have to clean up the remains of two long days of Lenny and Aiden. But for now, I have just enough time to pack the journal and some brownies for after school.

———◆———

Cricket laughs when I tell her about trying to keep Lennie and Aiden occupied over the weekend. Then, before we open Uncle Chad's journal, I help her take bites of one of Mom's triple-chocolate brownies. Hero sees us snacking and begs for a bite too, but I tell him *no*; I know that chocolate is harmful to dogs. Instead, Cricket calls for Marlene Grace to bring him a couple of dog bones.

Finally, we are ready to visit Uncle Chad in the desert. I open the journal and begin to read.

*July 1, 2015*

> *The sun, which had returned yesterday—after Moses had been summoned by Pharaoh—stirred an uneasy thanks in everyone because word had also come that today was the day to kill the lamb and smear the blood. Nervous energy fueled the compound as families completed the many tasks they had been told to perform for their safety. Fathers trembled in fear that if they made a single mistake, the angel of death might visit their house.*
>
> *Surprisingly, however, there were a few people who actually dared to take no precautions. These few were convinced that God's angel would not harm Hebrews—in the same way that the Hebrews had escaped previous plagues. I heard one man shout the slogan, "If God's angel can see the blood on the door posts, he can also see that we are Hebrews. He won't harm us. God is only out to punish the Egyptians. You'll see."*
>
> *I listened to both sides of the argument with mixed emotions. I had to admit that before the darkness had fallen, I had doubted the historical veracity of the plagues. But my experience over the three days of darkness had shaken my doubts. If I was in a dream, it was the most realistic and complex nightmare I'd ever experienced. And if somehow it wasn't a dream, I didn't know what to think. True to my nature, I questioned the need for all of the elaborate spiritual procedures Asher had prescribed, but in the end, I was not willing to put my life on the line to flout those instructions. After all, I was the first-born of the Tennysons. I did not want*

*to die. I confess that I was relieved when Josh agreed for us to join Asher in his home. I was sure that Asher would take all the proper precautions, especially regarding the blood on the doorposts.*

*And so, Josh and I ate lamb with Asher's family. And as much as we tried not to dwell on it, we ended up talking about what was to come. Asher and his sons burned the leftover food after the meal, and we nervously checked the window shutters and the locks on the door. Then we made a pretense of retiring. No one undressed. We simply pulled blankets over ourselves and laid quietly waiting for midnight.*

*By the dim light of an oil lamp turned low, Asher monitored his water clock and marked the number of times the water dripped out of the hour bowl and into the lower reservoir. I too counted every time the bowl was refilled. I had never dreamed that I might be trusting an ancient water clock in a matter of life and death.*

*Outside of our desert-brick walls, the night reminded me of the utter darkness of the last three days. No doubt the Egyptians, including the inhabitants of Pharaoh's palace, had stumbled in that darkness and had cursed the Israelites. (How could it be that the god of the Hebrews could defy Ra, the sun god who ruled light and darkness?)*

*Finally, the last drop of the last hour-bowl before midnight fell into the receiving bowl below it, and we all held our breaths.*

*At first there was no sound outside. But within seconds, a scream sounded from one of the worker's huts, and everyone in Asher's house raced to peer through the cracks of the shuttered windows. Then another cry pierced the night, and another. But no one from our house dared open the door to investigate. The instructions from Moses had been explicit about that.*

*Relit oil lamps glowed ominously in the huts filled with wailing. Doors unmarked by blood were thrown wide, and families inside spilled into the street. Draped over their arms were dead children who they lifted up to heaven with pleas that the lives be returned. They cursed God for betraying them.*

*A pounding on our door startled us. Asher held out his arms to hold us back from opening the door. "The instructions from Moses were specific," Asher said. "No one is to come in or go out until morning."*

*Distraught friends continued to pound on the door and entreat us to let them in. It was hard to listen and not respond. But Asher was adamant. And as we peered out the cracks in the shutters, we learned that Asher's precautions were keeping us safe. Another home like ours, with the doorposts painted, had opened up and let in those who begged for safety. And within minutes, a new wail filled the night. The home that had allowed entry had, in that moment, lost a firstborn son.*

*Asher wept. We all wept. How could anyone not weep at such tragedy?*

*"All over Egypt, families are suffering," Asher mourned. "Even Pharaoh's house is not immune. Our God will be heard!"*

---

The journal's description of the first-born deaths stuns me and brings tears to Cricket's eyes. I whisper, "Uncle Chad could have died!"

To her credit, Cricket doesn't hassle me about the contradiction between my reaction and my previous assertion that the journal is pure fiction.

Instead, Cricket murmurs, "Yes, but God protected him, just as he protected the obedient Hebrews."

For a moment more, I let myself relive the events I have read. And now, I pick up the journal to read on.

*July 2, 2015*

*With the dawn, Asher threw open the shutters and the door and we ventured outside. We could hear the sounds of mourning, but we also heard rejoicing from those whose households had been passed over by the death angel.*

*As a sobering reminder to us, Asher found a small number of dead sheep in his fold—all first-born males. The work of the night angel had been thorough.*

*While we stood in the middle of the street praising God for our deliverance, we noticed a cloud of dust approaching on the road from the city. Someone was coming.*

*"What if it is Pharaoh's troops sent to punish us?" a man wailed. "What if he blames us for all of the first-born deaths?"*

*If it were Pharaoh, we had no time to flee. The women and children in the camp scattered, and the men stood resolutely to face whatever was to come. But when the travelers drew near, all worries and forebodings changed into welcomes.*

*"It's Rachel and Sarah!" cried Asher. His daughters and hundreds of other Israelites rode in from the palace and from elsewhere in the royal city—all with loads on their shoulders or accompanied by heavily laden donkeys.*

*"So, it is true that you have been let go!" cried Asher. "And is this all of the gifts you said that your mistresses have given you?"*

*Rachel told him, "Yes! Our masters and mistresses have sent us away; they want us to leave the land. They are afraid of us and our God. They fear what God might do next if Pharaoh doesn't let us go. The donkeys and the loads we bear are gifts to take with us. The givers want to be in our favor and in the favor of our God."*

*"And," said Sarah, "I've brought my mistress and her children. They want to go with us and worship as we worship."*

*"Yes," the mistress and several other Egyptians confirmed. "Please do not leave us here to suffer more judgments for the sins of our pharaoh."*

*Asher hesitated at first, but then he welcomed Sarah's mistress and many other Egyptians who sought acceptance.*

*As the new arrivals moved forward into the camp, noisy shouts rose from behind them. "Come!" loud voices called. "Come and receive our gifts!"*

*Asher and other leaders walked back to respond. With an unaccustomed respect, a large contingent of Egyptians with horse-drawn carts and loaded animals addressed the Hebrews.*

*"We have come with gold and silver and fine linens," a spokesperson announced. "Please accept our gifts to help you leave our country. And please leave soon on your journey, before we all die at the hand of your God."*

*At first only a few Hebrew youths scrambled to collect the treasures that were dumped onto the ground, but soon everyone surged forward to glean the wealth that the Egyptians pressed upon them. Some of the Egyptians left animals and carts, as well as the gifts they had borne. And once the gifts were offloaded, the Egyptians turned and left.*

*Before the givers could change their minds, those in the camp quickly lugged the gifts into the safety of their huts. As I watched, I doubted that any of the hundreds of thousands of Hebrew families in Goshen would leave Egypt empty-handed. Even I, a stranger from another time, was handed one of the bags. "Carry this," Josh ordered, and I took it from him. I was surprised at the bag's weight, but it was manageable and I shouldered it.*

*Now, cheers resounding throughout the camp announced, "It's Moses and Aaron!" With cries and applause several of those among us met them with, "It's a miracle! We're rich! You should see what the Egyptians have brought us." In a giddy dance the men and women encircled the two figures who stood smiling at their jubilation.*

*When Moses finally raised his staff to quiet them, Aaron announced that it was time to pick up their belongings and treasures and leave. Without delay, Moses and Aaron strode right through the crowd and out into the desert. The eager parade that formed behind them sang praise to God with every step. Sheep, goats, and cattle were released and herded, and nothing was left behind. Marchers guided their piled carts and burdened beasts away from their shabby homes. Little by little Goshen was abandoned. Those who had been slaves joyfully followed their emancipators and never looked back.*

*Josh and I watched and waited for the end of the throng. Then I reshouldered my bag of treasure and took a somewhat stooped step toward the crowd. But Josh held out his arm to stop me.*

*"We have to go back, now," he said. And before my mind registered what he meant, Josh lifted the stone from his necklace and clicked it against mine. In an instant, lighter than air, Josh and I were caught up into the clouds. Higher and higher we flew. Below us, the departing Israelites shrank to a wave of antlike creatures that spread over miles of the desert. And then the exodus became too small to see. Josh and I raced on, through the stars and past the moon, and we streaked our way back to the Earth that I knew. I saw my planet expand and rush toward us, and I experienced the old feeling of impending doom. But as before, when the ground raced up to demolish us, we fell into a profound slow motion. Down through the ceiling we melted, and my sandals connected solidly with the linoleum of the kitchen floor we had left only days before.*

# Chapter 7

## The Gold Serpent

"This is no *journal*," I announce firmly to Cricket as I close the cover. "I think Uncle Chad was writing a *story* for some reason. I admit that it is interesting, but the premise is too far-fetched for me. I like stories that are real, don't you?"

Cricket doesn't answer. Instead, with a frown she asks, "Alexander, do you believe in God?"

"What?" I'm caught off guard by her question, and I wonder what this has to do with whether or not Uncle Chad's journal is a work of fiction.

Cricket repeats, "I was wondering if you believe in God."

"Well, of course, I believe in God," I answer quickly. "Doesn't everybody?"

"No, not everybody. It sounds like your uncle questioned God's existence."

"I guess it depends on what you think God is," I answer. "Uncle Chad is a scientist. He believes that things have a rational explanation."

"So, why," asks Cricket, "do you suppose your uncle wrote a story about supernatural things?"

I shrug. "To explain them away scientifically, I suppose. The title on the journal is *Proof*—perhaps the proof is that there is a natural explanation for the mythological stuff he's writing about. We just haven't read far enough yet."

"I see," says Cricket, and I can tell that she disagrees.

"Are you saying that you believe in the odd darkness and the people dying who don't follow all the rules? And what about that business of flying through time?" I ask. "That's not logical."

"Sometimes things aren't logical," Cricket replies, and then she asks, "Do you know the stories from the Bible very well?"

"Not well," I admit to her. "When I was small, I went to Sunday school, so I know a little about Moses and David and Daniel. But my family doesn't go to church anymore. And as I've grown, I've come to realize that many of the Bible's stories are like Santa Claus and the Easter Bunny."

Cricket emits a peculiar, "Hmm," and then asks, "But what if the stories are true? And what if you could go back in time and see them as they are happening?"

"You can't be serious," I insist.

Surely Cricket isn't saying that she believes in time travel and magic stones. But what is she trying to say? She seems to know something about the stone necklaces and the mysterious Josh character that may have a bearing on Uncle Chad's story.

I say, "Tell me about your stone necklace and what you know about this Josh person," but Cricket shakes her head. "I can't share that right now," she says.

Before I can object, Marlene Grace taps on the bedroom door to invite me for supper.

"Alexander, would you like to eat some homemade pizza with us? If so, I can call your parents and see if it's all right for you to stay. The pizza is coming out of the oven in five minutes."

The interruption delays getting answers from Cricket, but staying for supper may give me a chance to probe, later.

"I love pizza!" I say.

---

During supper, I'm surprised to learn that Marlene Grace and her husband William know about the journal. Cricket has told them how I found it and that we're reading it. But it seems that she has not told them specifically what's in it.

"Journals can be interesting," William says. "I have a journal that my Grandpa Joe left me. He was the first in my family to go to college. His journal contains what he remembered of all of his father's stories about his days as a plantation slave and what it was like after the Emancipation Proclamation was signed. The journal traces our family's move to the North and how Grandpa Asa got his first paying job as a handyman for a lawyer. The lawyer taught him to read, and Grandpa Asa made sure that his son, Joe, went to school and then to college. I might never have known the story if Grandpa Joe hadn't written it down. That journal is one of our family's prized possessions."

I try to tell William that Uncle Chad's journal is a little different. I tell him that the one Uncle Chad has penned is not a real journal but a story written in the form of a journal. I explain, "It's an interesting story but it's definitely fiction."

Marlene Grace and William look surprised, and Cricket hurries to say, "It's a special treasure for Alexander because it's in his uncle's handwriting. And Alexander is sharing with me what his uncle has written."

William replies, "That is special. And even though it may be fiction, I'm sure you're gaining insights into your uncle that you may not have had before."

William's comment is truer than he knows. I would never have imagined that Uncle Chad would write a story like the one he has penned.

◆━━●━━◆

After supper, Cricket shares again that she isn't ready to reveal more about her necklace. I can't imagine a more appropriate time, but I try to respect her decision.

"Let's read some more of the journal," Cricket suggests. And since I can stay at her house for a little longer, I shrug and open to where we left off.

*July 3, 2015*

> *It was the wee hours of the morning when I floated to the floor of my kitchen and looked around. Nothing had changed. Everything seemed exactly as it had been when I had left. And I was alone. I had no idea where Josh had disappeared to.*
>
> *Moreover, in my hands was the flap of the bag of Egyptian valuables that Josh had thrust at me when treasures were being handed out in Egypt.*
>
> *I started when I saw it. Was I still dreaming? I must be. There's no other way to explain how I happened to have this bag with me in my house.*
>
> *But the gold and jewels felt solid as I examined them. No matter how much I pinched myself, I could not make them dissolve into the fancy of my imagination. I knew without a doubt that they would still be there in the full glare of daylight.*
>
> *So, what was I supposed to do with a bag of gold I could not explain? I had to put it out of sight before Alexander or others arrived to see and question it. The only safe place I could think of was my attic crawl space. No one would stumble across it there.*
>
> *In the dark (I was afraid to turn on the light and be seen through the windows by a passing neighbor) I pulled out the ladder from the kitchen closet and dragged the jewel bag down the hall. I then carried the bag slowly up the ladder*

*and through the attic opening in the ceiling of my bedroom closet. I also whipped off the rawhide necklace and tossed it into the attic's depths. I wanted no reminders.*

*But even with the bag out of sight, it haunted me. I sat for a long time in my workshop caught between sleep and wakefulness. Finally, I pulled out a blank journal and began to write down everything I could remember. Strangely, every detail, every thought I had processed, and every scene I had pictured came to me as clearly as if I were reliving it.*

*And as I wrote it down, I was able to let it go. Little by little my present, my real life, finally broke through. Although day had dawned and I had work to do, I slept—without dreams.*

*July 4, 2015*

*When I awakened, I was relieved to find myself alone. No Josh. No strange chase through space. No mythological Israelite illusion. Just me in my bedroom, in my house, alone.*

*I fixed and ate breakfast, and I walked with my cup of coffee through the house and back to the kitchen. I stacked my dirty dishes on the counter, and I returned to the bathroom off my bedroom to brush my teeth and get dressed.*

*And in the bathroom the dream possessed me again, because in the mirror I saw that the rawhide necklace with its black, smooth stone was once again around my neck and no longer in the attic where I had flung it!*

*As if it were a poisonous snake, I yanked the necklace over my head and threw it onto the bed. And then I snatched it up again and raced for the ladder. I climbed back through the ceiling of the bedroom closet and threw the necklace farther into the dark. "And stay there!" I cried. Then with knees shaking I climbed back down.*

*My whole body trembled, and I sat on the edge of the bed with my face in my hands. Why couldn't I put this craziness behind me? Why couldn't I shake this dream?*

*It was almost noon when I changed clothes, poured another cup of coffee, and left the house. I wandered around the block and saw children setting off strings of firecrackers and sending up clouds of small smoke bombs. I hadn't remembered that it was the Fourth of July.*

*When I returned to the house, my nephew was waiting on the porch with his parents. I had forgotten that we were going to launch one of Alexander's rockets today. It was a relief to have something normal to concentrate on.*

*I appreciated Alexander's company and his excited chatter about the rocket. We hooked the launch pad to the garden hose and I stood with my brother and his wife as they recorded Alexander's accomplishment.*

*As the rocket lifted off, I laughed. And for one delightful moment, I forgot the dream.*

———◆———

I let the journal fall back as I remember that launch day. "I can't believe that Uncle Chad has included me and my rocket launch in his story," I say. "It doesn't seem like much now, but to a ten-year-old, that launch was a milestone. And the best part was that I knew Uncle Chad was proud of me."

I sigh. "I really miss him."

"I know," Cricket murmurs.

I sigh again and resume reading.

*July 5, 2015 continued*

*Help! Why can't I make this nightmare go away? Although I slept in the living room and booby trapped the hallway to make sure I didn't sleepwalk, I found the rawhide necklace around my neck again this morning. It seems that I cannot throw it away or (I suspect) destroy it. For some reason, I must wear it. And I dread that Josh might return and click his stone against mine.*

———◆———

When I turn the page to read more of Uncle Chad's story, I find the next page blank. Although there are more entries in the book, there is a gap—a large gap—before *March 17, 2016*. Nearly a year.

While I wonder about the blank pages, Cricket suddenly asks, "How would you feel about another trip to your uncle's workshop?"

"What? Now?"

"Sure. Why not? If we hurry, we can be there before you have to go home. There's something we should see."

Cricket tells Marlene Grace and William our plans, and they nod. "Just don't be too late," Marlene Grace warns. "It's getting dark and it's a school night, you know."

When the front door opens, Hero leads the way.

———— • ————

Cricket says nothing about what she wants to see at Uncle Chad's house. I don't like letting myself in at this time of day, but I turn the key in the lock. The kitchen feels cold and unwelcome as I turn on the overhead light. I want to hurry to the workshop where the old familiar clutter is distracting, but Cricket stops me.

"Before we go to the workshop," she says, "can we check something, first?"

I let her pass me and start down the hallway. After she passes the guestroom, I know she is going to Uncle Chad's bedroom—and the attic crawl space.

"There's nothing there, you know," I declare, but Cricket doesn't stop.

"It won't hurt to check, will it?" she asks over her shoulder. I have no good argument. I know that Cricket won't be satisfied until I peer into the attic depths and prove that the space is empty. But I am angry at having to check.

I march back to the kitchen closet and yank out the ladder. Then I drag it with more force than necessary to Uncle Chad's room. Hero wisely keeps a good distance until I have set up the ladder in the bedroom.

Then, even as I huff and start up the rungs, a tiny part of me wonders what I will do if I find something up there.

When I push aside the overhead cover, it's obviously too dark to see anything. Without explaining, I climb back down and fetch a flashlight.

When I climb again, I find it even harder to keep my heart from pounding and my hands from shaking.

As Cricket watches, I stick my head through the opening and point the flashlight. Immediately I breathe a sigh of relief. The attic is empty!

"There's nothing here," I call down, and to show that I'm being thorough I scan the insulation recesses once more.

"Are you sure?" Cricket asks, and before I tell her again that it's empty, I catch a glint of something just out of reach. It's not the bag—it's too small. Just something tiny. Maybe only a nail.

"Wait a minute," I call down, and I straddle two of the attic's skinny wooden floor beams to gingerly slide myself toward the little reflection. I try not to think that if my knee slips, I'll crash through the bedroom ceiling.

Then, as I feel carefully between the insulation and the floor beam, I let my fingers curl around a small, hard item. With it clutched in my fist, I begin a careful retreat.

Halfway back to the ceiling opening, my elbow wobbles and the flashlight clatters through the attic opening. It falls all the way to the floor. Cricket cries out, and I carefully finish my descent.

When I reach the bottom of the ladder, Hero celebrates my return. I fight the temptation to look and see what I've retrieved; I wait to open my hand until Cricket can see it too.

Now, under the overhead bedroom light, I slowly uncurl my fingers and flatten my palm.

Instantly, Cricket exclaims, "Wow!" And I echo her astonishment.

Our attic discovery is a tiny, coiled gold snake with jeweled eyes. "It's a ring!" Cricket murmurs. "An ancient ring, like nothing I've ever seen."

I agree. The ring is the work of a master craftsman, and there is no doubt that it is from another age.

"It must have fallen out of the treasure bag," Cricket theorizes, and I frown.

"What treasure bag? I saw no treasure bag."

I'm sure there are other explanations for the ring in the attic. After all, Uncle Chad has been on many trips where he could have found such an item. And the discovery of the ancient ring doesn't answer my real question: *Where is Uncle Chad?*

# Chapter 8

## Suspicion

We show the ring to no one. I take it home and start to put it in the bottom of the rocketry box in my room. It's a place I'm fairly certain that my mother will not invade in her housecleaning but that is easy for me to access whenever I want. I check the little snake's ruby eyes before hiding it.

"Where did you come from?" I whisper to it. "I wish you could talk and tell me where to find Uncle Chad."

Then I put the ring away and sigh. Perhaps tomorrow afternoon's journal pages will reveal more clues.

———————•———————

*March 17, 2016*

> *The young man at my door was a typical college student. "Lawrence Traeger," he said.*
>
> *I'd never had a student apprentice before, but since a new program at the university offered apprenticeships, I had decided to take advantage of it. I could use the help, and the student could gain knowledge and earn credit for working on my projects.*
>
> *According to the university, Lawrence was in his final year of a dual major: Master of Science in Archaeological Studies and Master of Arts in Science Writing. His field work in archaeological studies had been completed and he was intent on finishing his science-writing degree by the end of May.*
>
> *"Dr. Tennyson, I can't thank you enough for taking me on. I'm one of your biggest fans, and I consider it a great honor to complete my apprenticeship under your direction and supervision. I've read every one of your articles in* Armchair Science *and in other science journals."*

*I thanked Lawrence for his flattery and invited him into the kitchen for a cup of coffee so we could become better acquainted.*

*Steady brown eyes, rugged jaw, dark hair pulled into a ponytail, work shirt, and blue jeans. Easy to talk to. We should get along just fine.*

*After our coffee, I gave Lawrence the tour: kitchen, living room, workshop, and two bedrooms—all on one floor. The workshop used to be a sun room, but I had long ago filled the space with tables and equipment for experiments and demonstrations. Lawrence seemed comfortable in the room, which satisfied me that he wouldn't take a lot of breaking in. I pointed out a small make-shift desk with a file cabinet that I had created for him, and he off-loaded several things from his backpack.*

*The rest of his backpack went into the guest bedroom. "This is your room during your apprenticeship," I told him. "And the bathroom in the hall is all yours. I have my own bathroom off the back bedroom."*

*Lawrence smiled. "Thanks. This is definitely better than I've had on my field digs. This is first-class!"*

*"Take it easy and settle in," I offered. "We can start work tomorrow."*

*"Oh," Lawrence said, "I don't have much to unpack— just what's in the backpack. So, if you have anything you need me to do this afternoon, I can start right away."*

*I laughed. An eager beaver. I hoped I could keep him busy!*

*March 19, 2016*

*Like clockwork, each weekday afternoon at 3:45 I expect to hear Alexander's knock on the front door. Rain or shine, my nephew rides his bicycle here after school to spend time in my workshop. I see so much of myself in the boy. At eleven, I was also driven by curiosity to study science and explore the world. I wanted proofs and facts of how things worked and why. Alexander learns quickly and easily grasps concepts that some, who are years his senior, have struggled with. And I believe that one day Alexander will do great things.*

———◆———

Embarrassed by Uncle Chad's praise, I stop reading. But because I know that Cricket is watching, I hurry to continue reading.

*March 21, 2016*

*Today I gave both Lawrence and Alexander the rundown on my next project—a demonstration of fractal growth patterns in algae. I handed each a sheet of paper with their instructions for setting up the growth equipment and creating some photo-worthy results. The algae patterns they grow for me will accompany my article on fractal design in the universe. Because Alexander knows where to find my equipment, Lawrence follows his lead. I can tell that the two of them are going to get along.*

*April 29, 2016*

*I've moved my journal. It is no longer in my desk drawer.*

*Two weeks ago, I discovered evidence that, overnight, items on my desk had been disturbed. It had to have been Lawrence's doing. Although he attempted to return everything as it had been—to cover his tracks—I could tell things weren't right.*

*What disturbed me most was to find that he had been through my desk drawers and had been reading this journal. I have always left bits of paper as markers in various pages of the journal, but morning after morning I found one or two markers on the floor under the desk. Lawrence had carefully replaced the journal in the drawer, but he had failed to notice the missing markers.*

*Then yesterday, when I had to pick up some things at the hardware store, Lawrence made an excuse not to go with me. I suspected that he wanted to be left alone in my house, and I knew why. I pretended to not be concerned with leaving him, and I ran my errand. But when I returned, I saw that the ladder in the maintenance closet had been moved. I said nothing, but last night, after I heard Lawrence snoring and knew he was asleep, I crept down the hallway and brought the ladder to my room. As quietly as I could, I climbed with a flashlight to check the attic crawl space and found the treasure satchel gone. Lawrence was still snoring when I replaced the ladder and returned to my room.*

*I wondered if I should confront him and search his bedroom, but I worried that he might became belligerent. I thought of calling the police, but I didn't know how to explain how the jewels and gold had come into my possession. I couldn't prove they were mine, and I knew the police wouldn't believe my story. I decided my best course of action was to bide my time and steal my treasure back.*

---

At this declaration in the journal, Cricket stares with her mouth open. Then she whispers, "The pirate treasure! This is where Lawrence got his so-called pirate treasure!"

"What?" I ask. I haven't made the same connection that she has, so she explains. "Pretending to find buried treasure was a clever way for Lawrence to disguise his theft of your uncle's treasure."

"Do you think so?" I ask. I suppose that it could be true. Perhaps Cricket is right. But even if she is, how does that figure into Uncle Chad's disappearance? We need more information. Perhaps Uncle Chad will give us more in the next pages of his journal.

*April 30, 2016*

*When Alexander arrived after school, he and Lawrence accepted their assignments as usual, and while they worked, I excused myself to use the restroom. But instead of going to my room, I slipped into the guestroom. I had only minutes to find the satchel, and after a rapid, methodical search, I found it!*

*Just as quietly as I had entered the guestroom, I retreated to my own room. It was hard to be quiet as I stole the treasure back, but I managed. And, at this point, I had the dilemma of where to re-hide the bag. I didn't want to return it to the attic, and I was afraid Lawrence would find it under the bed. I finally went into my bathroom and locked the door. I flushed the toilet to cover the noise of opening the bathroom window, and I carefully dropped the satchel into the bushes below. I was pleased to see that the bag fell down into the back of the bush and could not be seen. Satisfied, I closed the window, ran some water in the sink as if I were washing my hands, and returned to the workshop. I had no idea if Lawrence would miss the bag tonight or if he would confront me about it. I would have to take that chance.*

*May 1, 2016*

*Lawrence didn't say a word about the treasure at breakfast, but I knew from his demeanor that he had discovered the bag missing. Lawrence was quieter than usual all day, and we spoke only as needed to conduct our business.*

*The strain of the secret made it difficult to work, and I made several mistakes. I even had to do our main experiment over for the day.*

*Alexander's visit supplied the only bright moments to the afternoon.*

---

"I remember that day!" I cry. "It's the only time I've seen Uncle Chad mess up. We had to do one of the big experiments twice."

Hero hears the excitement in my voice, and he stands and wags his tail. I pick him up and his tongue swipes the side of my face before I go back to the words in the journal.

*May 2, 2016*

*Lawrence left for a few hours in the morning with little explanation. I didn't offer to drive him, and he set off on foot. I had thought that perhaps the strain of our secret had become too uncomfortable for him and he needed some time away. His absence gave me time to regroup. I checked to make sure the bag was still safely hidden under the bushes. I didn't want to move it. Lawrence would complete his apprenticeship on May 25, and I decided the treasure could wait until then to find a new hiding place.*

*May 5, 2016*

*After two days of grunted acknowledgements and bare civility, Lawrence surprised me at breakfast this morning. He openly admitted that he had taken the bag. "And you've taken it back and put it somewhere," he said.*

*Then Lawrence sat back in his chair with a smug air. "That journal has disappeared too," he said. "And I can see why. Very interesting reading. I'm not sure how it works, but it seems that your onyx stone is a key to something otherworldly—a time transport of some sort. And a great way to get rich."*

*Then Lawrence leaned forward and pulled an object from his pocket. My mouth flew open! What he set on the kitchen table was another onyx stone necklace.*

*At my dumb-founded expression, Lawrence grinned. He said, "You didn't know this other necklace was in the bag, did you? I doubt that you ever looked inside that bag before you tossed it into the hole in your closet. At least I looked in it."*

*Then Lawrence laughed and stood. With the treasure-bag necklace in his hand, he lunged toward me, and I could tell that he was intent on clicking his stone against the onyx stone I wore. I fought him and, in the struggle, his stone necklace fell under the table. Lawrence scrambled to retrieve it, but by then I had taken hold of a cleaver from the knife holder on the counter. Lawrence backed away. "Careful, old man," he said with respect for my weapon. "I just wanted to take a little trip and get some gold."*

*I brandished the cleaver menacingly. "Leave this house!" I shouted, and I backed him to the door. He huffed and clenched a fist, but he thought better of it and escaped out the door and disappeared off the back porch.*

*I've written of this encounter, because I fear that he will return. I have a premonition that if he succeeds in clicking the two onyx stones, we will be borne away—to where I do not know. I don't know what to do or who to turn to. My story won't make sense to anyone. I wish that the mysterious Josh would return. Perhaps he could take care of this.*

*As I have written before, I am hiding this journal so that Lawrence cannot find it.*

———— • ————

I turn the page quickly, but there are no more penned pages and no more words for me to read. The rest of the journal is blank.

With wide eyes, I whisper, "And then Uncle Chad disappears. The End."

# Chapter 9

## Impossible Possibilities

The abrupt conclusion to the journal leaves me feeling empty and my mind all twisted up. Even as fiction, the story in the journal is disturbing. The picture it paints of Lawrence is so dark that if it is true, I wonder if he killed Uncle Chad. I clench my fists.

Cricket, however, calls out loudly to get my attention. "Alexander, please listen to me," she insists, and I manage to pull my focus back to her.

She declares loudly, "I think there's more to the story. I think your uncle was right about Lawrence returning to the house. Lawrence probably broke in while Dr. Tennyson was sleeping, and he clicked his stone against your uncle's. If he did, the stones did their job and transported Lawrence and your uncle back to the ancient desert among the Israelites."

"That," says Cricket, "explains why your uncle didn't take his glasses with him."

I blink at this thought. I'm still hazy about what is real and what is fictional in the journal. I struggle to follow Cricket's scenario.

"And once Lawrence and your uncle landed in the past," she says, "something happened that made Lawrence tear off Dr. Tennyson's necklace and return home alone. I think he left your uncle stranded."

My heart constricts. What if Cricket's right?

"Alive or dead?" I ask, and Cricket doesn't know. "Alive, I think," she says.

"But you don't know!" I say.

And then I object to all that she has been saying. "I don't agree with your premise," I declare. "You're basing everything on a tale that isn't logical and makes no sense. I don't even believe that the snake ring came from the time-transport. Uncle Chad has been on lots of digs in the Middle East and could have brought the ring home from any of those. Who knows?"

I jump off the bed and start for the door.

"Where are you going?" Cricket asks.

"It's my turn to check on something," I say. "You can come if you want."

---◆---

Cricket, Hero, and I make our way to Uncle Chad's house. I don't bother to get the key, because this time, we're not going inside. Instead, I push Cricket through the grass to the far end of the house. It is easier for me to push her than for her to maneuver herself over the yard. When we get across the lawn, I wade through the bushes under the bathroom window and ignore how the twigs scratch my legs. Hero thinks it is great fun.

Cricket knows what I'm looking for. She knows that I'm trying to disprove the journal. But it doesn't work.

Instead of finding nothing in the bushes, I find the bag of ancient gold and jewels exactly where Uncle Chad wrote that he had put it.

Still desperate to discount the fantasy, I latch onto a new theory. Could this all be part of a game? Could Uncle Chad have devised his story to be an elaborate treasure hunt? And if so, why? And what did his disappearance have to do with it?

I quickly outline my idea to Cricket. "We're doing a good job of following the clues," I tell her with a nervous grin.

And in keeping with my treasure-hunt theory, I tell Cricket that I'm sure the items in the treasure bag are mere tokens for whoever follows the clues. To prove it, I drag the bag a few feet out into the yard and whip open the flap. But what I find proves me wrong again.

The gold and gems packed inside Uncle Chad's bag are obviously real. They are not cheap game trinkets. There is absolutely no doubt about their authenticity. To Cricket's credit, she says nothing. I sit down, hard, on the ground and try to make everything settle in my brain.

I have no more theories to disprove the journal's accounts. As much as I don't want to accept what Uncle Chad has penned, I have to believe the physical evidence sitting before me. And I have to believe that Cricket is probably right about Lawrence being a thief and a traitor. I picture Lawrence's face as it must have looked when he confronted Uncle Chad, and I am repulsed.

It angers me to recall how coolly Lawrence showed up at the scene of the crime after what he had done. And I can't believe that Lawrence acted so innocent while we kept him in our home. If only the traitor were here, I would confront him and beat him with my fists. I would run him to the nearest police station and make him confess.

But who would believe my story? I can see that Lawrence has won. And Uncle Chad may be lost forever.

"Now what?" I moan. Hero pushes his nose between my fingers as I hold my head. He licks my chin, but I don't even bother to pet him.

Cricket tells me, "Don't give up, Alexander."

"Why not?" I cry. "We have no way to bring Uncle Chad home."

"You don't know that," Cricket says.

And before she can finish speaking, I toss back an exasperated reply. "So, what do you propose? Magic beans or a wave of the hand? We have no way to travel back in time. If your far-fetched scenario is correct, Lawrence has all of the necklaces."

Cricket calmly interrupts. Quietly she says, "Stop ranting, Alexander. Lawrence doesn't have every necklace. He doesn't have *my* necklace."

Her words stop me, cold. I recall the day I asked Cricket about her necklace and why she had a stone exactly like Uncle Chad's. On that day, she had not answered me, except to say that she had not known anyone else had such a necklace. But now, after all that we have read, I realize there may be more to the coincidence than what she has yet revealed.

"Your stone?" I murmur tentatively.

"Yes," she says.

Because I may be expecting too much, I'm almost afraid to ask, but I do. "Are you saying that your stone can take us back to Uncle Chad?"

"Yes, and no," Cricket answers, and I mutter in my frustration, "That figures."

Cricket starts to explain. "My stone is like Uncle Chad's in that it is a transport stone."

"Right," I mutter. "But you need two stones to travel, and Lawrence has all the other stones."

Cricket is done babying me and she hollers, "Stop it, Alexander! You've given up before we've even begun." Then, like a drill sergeant to a new recruit, she barks, "And you can't leave that bag sitting here, either."

I have nearly forgotten the treasure at my feet. Glumly, I bend down to move it. Hero can't sit here guarding it forever.

"Get that sack onto your bike," Cricket orders. "You need to take it home and hide it."

At her direction, I walk my bicycle around the house. Because of the weight of the sack, I have to empty and refill the bag a little at a time so I can get it onto the bicycle seat and lash it firmly.

"I'll have to walk this home," I grumble. "It'll tip if I try to ride it."

Then I add, "If I can get home without dumping it, I think I can hide it in our garage with some stuff Mom made me clean out of my room. Just wish me luck that Mom and Dad don't see it before I can unload it."

I'm still sullen when I walk Cricket to her house and set off for my own home. When I arrive, I slip into our garage unnoticed and unlash my cargo. It is heavy, but I manage to get everything unloaded, and I push the sack into my junk corner and hide it behind a box. Later, I also drop the serpent ring into the bag, so that all of the treasure is together.

After that, concentrating on my homework is nearly impossible. All I can think of is the treasure in the garage and the impossibility of rescuing Uncle Chad.

———————◆———————

As I lie in bed with sleep far away, it dawns on me that one of Cricket's earlier assumptions about Lawrence is wrong. She had said that Lawrence was trying to palm off Uncle Chad's treasure as pirate treasure from his yard. But that can't be right. Since we have Uncle Chad's treasure, Lawrence's so-called pirate treasure must have come from somewhere else. I now suppose that he could very well have stolen it from the past. And if he did, it may be one more proof that he left Uncle Chad behind—perhaps in great danger.

How can I ever sleep again? I am convinced that we have to find Lawrence. We have to make Lawrence give us Uncle Chad's necklace so we can rescue Uncle Chad.

———————◆———————

I'm frustrated that Cricket isn't listening when I burst in after school and announce that we need to hurry and track down Lawrence.

"It's vital that we find him!" I declare. "Finding Uncle Chad's treasure under the bathroom window has convinced me that Lawrence's treasure wasn't Uncle Chad's. Lawrence's treasure has to have been stolen from the past, and that means you were probably right: Lawrence has left Uncle Chad stranded with the Israelites. And if we want to rescue Uncle Chad, we have to get his necklace back!"

I now present a dozen ideas for finding and forcing Lawrence to turn over the necklace. But despite all of my passion, Cricket remains preoccupied. She doesn't even look at me. Instead, she casually breaks into my discourse and asks me to fetch all of her blue jeans from a bottom dresser drawer.

Without a break in my incessant monologue, I drop to one knee to fulfill Cricket's request. As I pull out the drawer, I blabber on with details for yet another possible pursuit of Lawrence. Then I slip my hands under three pair of blue jeans, draw them out, and stand up again.

As I turn to place the jeans on Cricket's bed, I hear something fall onto the floor. Without missing a beat in my Lawrence litany, I offload the blue jeans and go back to pick up whatever has fallen.

Suddenly my voice trails off and my jaw drops. I see Cricket smiling as I stare at the object on the floor.

"Y-y-you have a second necklace!" I manage to stutter.

"Yes," says Cricket. "I've been trying to tell you that, but you've have been so obsessed with telling me your plans for finding Lawrence that you haven't let me speak. I figured the only way to get you to listen was to let you see my second necklace for yourself."

I accept her reprimand, and I apologize. "I'm so sorry, Cricket. I've been really unbearable, haven't I?"

"You could say that," she chuckles. "But I understand."

"So," I say, "does this mean that we can go and get Uncle Chad?"

Cricket nods. "We can certainly try."

I stare again at the necklace that I've picked up from the floor, and a torrent of questions runs through my thoughts.

"Have you used the stones before? Have you been to Egypt? Will your stones take us right to Uncle Chad? Do we need more stones if we have three people to transport? When…"

Cricket slows me down. "One question at a time," she says. "Yes, I've used the stones. No, I haven't been to Egypt. Yes, I think we can get the stones to take us to the same place and time that your Uncle's stones did. And no, we shouldn't need additional necklaces for the rescue."

Now I ask, "So, when can we go?" And although I'm ready, right now, to click the stones, Cricket shakes her head.

"There are things we need to work out," she says. "We have to plan and take certain precautions before we go anywhere. And we need some help."

I ratchet down my impatience, but I can't keep from insisting, "We need to hurry! It's already been such a long time."

Cricket says, "I know." And then she tells me, "The first thing we need to do is to tell Marlene Grace and William."

In astonishment, I question, "Are you sure? What will they think of all of this?"

"You may be surprised," Cricket responds with a twinkle in her eye and the twist of a grin.

———————•———————

I am indeed surprised at how well Marlene Grace and William accept our story. William pats me on the back, and Marlene Grace lights up with excitement. Neither of them questions anything we've shared. It is obvious that they know all about the onyx-stone necklaces. And I suspect that they have taken time-travel voyages before.

"What do you need us to do?" Marlene Grace asks Cricket, as if it is the most natural thing in the world to plan a trip into the ancient past.

Cricket replies, "I believe the onyx stones will take us to the Exodus march. And I propose that all four of us join that march with the Israelites. If we go as a family, we may be less conspicuous. We can blend in, and it will give us time to look for Alexander's uncle."

"Good idea," agrees William.

I look at William, a neatly dressed, tall, and impressive man, and I try to imagine him arriving in the middle of a desert march of ancient Israelites. Built like the ex-marine he is, William will not be easy to disguise. Neither, for that matter, will Marlene Grace, who is not a small woman.

"We need proper costumes, of course," Cricket says, and Marlene Grace's face lights up.

"I think I know what we need and just where to find them," she says. "We can raid the costumes and props from the church Christmas pageant. William was a splendid shepherd last year. And there should be staffs, walking sticks, and shoulder bags to go with the tunics, robes, and headdresses. All we need to provide are leather sandals. Do you have a pair of sandals, Alexander?"

I tell her that I do. And I repress a laugh at the thought of the four of us traipsing through the ancient desert in Christmas pageant garb.

"We'll need lots of food," declares Marlene Grace. "I'll pack some olive oil, salt, crackers, cheese, dates, dried beef..."

"And cookies?" William suggests.

"And cookies," says Marlene Grace. "But we need to be careful about what they see us eating."

"We'll need lots of water, too," William says. "I'll get some canteens that we can camouflage inside some fabric pouches."

"I'll pack a bedroll for each of us," announces Marlene Grace.

"Wait," I say. "A bedroll? How long do you think we're going to be away? Do I need to warn my parents?"

I'm confused. The idea of having to spend the night has never occurred to me.

Marlene Grace is quick to answer. "It's up to you if you wish to tell your parents. But the plan is to leave tomorrow after school and return late Sunday afternoon—unless we find your uncle sooner."

Then she says, "Can you ask your parents if you can spend the weekend with us?"

I assure her that I can. But I still can't imagine needing that much time to find Uncle Chad.

William sets me straight. He explains, "The transport may not take us directly to your uncle. If that's the case, it may be difficult to find him in a day. After all, there were between 600,000 and two million Israelites leaving Egypt."

"Two mill...?" I am stunned. For some reason I have been picturing a few thousand people, like a crowd at a high school ball stadium. But now it sounds like we'll be wading through miles of people. If so, how will we ever find Uncle Chad?

"But," says Cricket, "if we don't find your uncle this weekend, we can always go again."

The scope of our mission is suddenly daunting. My vision of us flying in and rescuing Uncle Chad and flying home the same day has been dashed. And what if Uncle Chad isn't even there? We're making a lot of assumptions.

# Chapter 10

## Friday

When Friday, the day of our departure, finally arrives, Marlene Grace has an early supper for us. I force myself to eat despite the butterflies in my stomach. Everyone but me is calm. Marlene Grace even takes time to wash the dishes before we put on our travel outfits.

I feel like I'm going to explode if I have to wait much longer.

When we finally dress and face one another in the living room in our tunics, robes, and sandals, I see that Hero is going, too. The little terrier has been stuffed into Cricket's shoulder bag and all I see are his little white head and russet ears poking out, eyes bright with anticipation.

"Hero's traveled before," Cricket explains. And, somehow, I am not surprised that even a little dog knows more about stones travel than I do.

I pinch myself, just to make sure this is all really happening.

Marlene Grace finishes filling our food pouches. "I've given each of you an apple," she says, "but you can't let anyone see you eat it. There were no apples like this in the Egyptian desert."

I notice that Marlene Grace isn't the only one packing contraband items. When she isn't looking, I see William toss into his bag some matches, a flashlight, a small length of rope, and a gadget-filled pocket knife. With a finger to his lips, he warns me to keep our secret. I reassure him with a nod and a nervous grin.

I look our group over and decide that, all in all, we appear pretty authentic. But it occurs to me that Cricket is in a wheelchair. No one in ancient Egypt will have a wheelchair, so how is that going to work? Will William carry her? I'm sure these three have encountered this before. That's probably why Cricket wants Marlene Grace and William to go with us.

I don't ask.

"Time for last-minute instructions," Cricket says, now. "This is important because we've never traveled with four people."

She explains, "As you know, we have only two onyx-stone necklaces—the one I'm wearing and the one we've given Marlene Grace to wear. Because there are four of us, it will be vital that we be connected. Every person must be touching someone who is wearing a stone. And you must be holding your travel packs. When we return, there will hopefully be five of us. But as long as each person is touching someone with a stone, we'll be fine."

Cricket looks from person to person and ends with me. "Are we ready?"

William holds Cricket's hand, and I grip Marlene Grace's hand tighter. I draw a breath and hold it. But we go nowhere.

That's because first, before we do anything else, William prays. It has been a long time since I've heard anyone pray, and I had not realized that William was so religious. I bow my head.

"Lord God," William says, "You know our mission, and You have provided the means to accomplish it. Guide us and bring us all back safely, including Dr. Tennyson. We thank You for Your journey's mercies. In Jesus' Name, amen."

I open my eyes and wonder if there will be more delays. But apparently, we are now ready.

Marlene Grace steps forward and pulls her stone toward Cricket's necklace. And the instant the stones touch, I gasp: the floor drops away!

The four of us rise, weightless, and pass like ghosts through the ceiling. As if I'm on a carnival ride, I holler, "Woo-hoo!" and from somewhere behind me, I hear Cricket laugh.

Everything Uncle Chad has written in his journal about his onyx-stones adventure is happening—and with near-explosive force. The clouds rise to meet us, the atmosphere thins and we enter space, and our speed increases exponentially.

We are truly on our way!

We leave the Milky Way and streak past streams of stars toward our target. The tiny planet we approach expands so quickly that, like Uncle Chad, I fear crashing into the surface. From Uncle Chad's accounts I know that we will not crash, but I shudder anyway and close my eyes. Only after the impossible featherlike landing kicks in do I allow myself to breathe, and then we drift like autumn leaves onto the dusty night floor of a vast desert plateau.

My first impression is one of stillness. It is like awakening in the middle of the night when all is hushed. The Israelites camping across the plateau before us are asleep.

And then I hear a rumble, and I see, high above us on the peak of a nearby mountain, fiery lightning flashing through a shroud of foreboding clouds. A hapless landing on that peak could have been deadly. It is good that we have landed safely on the plain.

And, speaking of safety, I now take stock to see that Cricket has arrived safely in William's arms.

But Cricket is not in William's arms. I see that, instead, her atrophied limbs have been transformed, and Cricket is standing!

What Uncle Chad has written is true. Josh had told Uncle Chad, *You won't need your glasses*. And in the same way, I see that Cricket doesn't need her wheelchair. It is a miracle!

I stand beside her and survey the panorama of the sleeping Israelite camp. It is unlikely that anyone has seen us arrive, or if they have, we have appeared to them as mere elusive clouds or passing shadows. Flocks and herds and hundreds of thousands of tents and campfires blanket the area for as far as the eye can see. And in the distance, set off by itself on the opposite side of the camp, a curious towering fire burns a hole from the ground into the sky.

Because I am shivering, the fire looks inviting. I have not expected such cold temperatures at night in the desert, and I wish I had brought my coat. Cricket's teeth are chattering, too.

Thankfully, William has hurried to gather an armload of sticks, and he lights a fire with one of his secret matches. We warm ourselves before we unroll our backpacks to snuggle under our blankets.

"Are we really here?" I ask out loud, and Cricket replies, "Yes, Alexander, we're really here."

"I'm afraid," I say, now, "afraid that we won't succeed. What if, even after all of this, we don't find my uncle?"

"But we will," Cricket assures me. "It may take a little while, but I believe we will find him."

I'm glad that she can't see the tears in my eyes. I want so much to succeed and to have Uncle Chad come home.

By the time we roll out our bed rolls, I find that I am ready for sleep. My eyes have grown heavy, and the covers are inviting.

I don't remember falling asleep, but I do recall wandering in my dreams on a hillside with shepherds and a flock of bleating sheep. And when I awaken in my Christmas pageant costume in the morning, I question briefly if I'm still dreaming. But then I remember our mission and where we are.

And when I sit up, I stare. Around us are thousands of people, awake and slowly walking the sun-dried ground. They're bent and searching for...a lost contact lens?

"They're gathering breakfast," Cricket explains. "Manna. See it spread over the plateau?"

My thoughts turn, again, to Christmas. Like snow, a mantle of white paints the desert floor, but unlike snow, each flake is a bit of food. I swipe the ground with my fingers and lick the sweet, wafer-like treat.

"What is it?" I ask. And Marlene Grace chuckles.

"That's the same question the Israelites asked when they first saw it. They asked *Manna?* which means *what is it?*"

"And," Marlene Grace says, "whatever it is, the Bible says that we must each collect three meals' worth for today. Bring your allotment to me and I'll mix the morning portion with our cooking oil to bake some warm cakes over the fire."

Marlene Grace hands me, in a closed fist, a plastic bag to hide inside my satchel. I accept it in the same secrecy with which she gives it. "Put the manna in the bag," she advises, "or you may have a mess."

I obediently stuff the plastic bag inside my satchel and begin to fill it. Marlene Grace, William, and Cricket do the same. And I watch Cricket, as I work. My friend is not the same girl trapped in a useless body and confined to the wheelchair we have left behind. I've never seen her this way. How different she looks without her disability—vibrant and alive.

William catches me staring and grins.

Thankfully, my embarrassment is interrupted. A toddler wanders into our campsite and engages Hero in a noisy game of tag. Between fits of barking and giggling, the child lisps in perfect English, "Here, doggie! Here, doggie!" until his mother calls, "Come along, Caleb."

In a flash I realize that I'm hearing ancient Israelites speak in a language I can understand. And it dawns on me that we are experiencing the gift of universal language that Josh had bestowed on Uncle Chad. Without it, our mission would be doomed. No matter how authentic our Christmas pageant costumes might make us look, our speech would have marked us as strangers and caused everyone to shun us.

Cricket realizes the miracle at the same time that I do, and she whispers, "Isn't it beautiful that we can understand and be understood?"

The full import of how we got here, where we happen to be, and how we are able to converse suddenly attacks my reason, and I feel faint. I've never fainted in my life, but now my legs wobble beneath me.

"Steady, son," William advises, and he catches me before I fall. "Onyx-stones travel can take some getting used to," he says. "Don't think about it so much. Your brain hasn't caught up to your body yet."

Then William says, "Don't feel badly about being a wobbler. I'm a former marine and I froze up like a stick on my first transport. And Marlene Grace never opened her eyes until halfway through the stars. Cricket's the brave one!"

"I can see that," I say. "She's amazing."

William grins. I am embarrassed again, and I quickly turn my focus to Uncle Chad. I concentrate on wondering what he might be doing at this very moment, and I ask William what he thinks.

William says, "He's probably feeling the same morning sun warming his back that we do. And he probably sees the manna on the ground beginning to melt and dissolve in the heat of the day. Hopefully he has all of his manna collected, and we'd better hurry and finish gathering ours before it is all gone."

I take a few steadying breaths and let William guide me back to where I can collect my food. I don't want to spend long in this menial task of food-gathering. We have other work to do. I want to hurry and eat our breakfast so we can begin our search.

# Chapter 11

## The Search Begins

"Uncle Chad! Uncle Chad! It's Alexander. Where are you?"

I shout the words over and over. William booms out the message, too. And although we've passed hundreds, perhaps a thousand, people, few of them take any notice of us.

Frequently we stop to drink from our leather-wrapped thermoses and to catch our breath. That's when William and I wet our headdresses—a trick we learned by watching other men as they rested from the heat. Earlier I had been tempted to pour a gallon of my precious drinking water over my head, but I didn't dare waste it. When we saw a man wet his headdress, we copied him and found that it helped. Likewise, the women dip their scarves in a few drops of water and dampen their faces and necks.

As we sit, we remove our sandals and rub our feet. Instead of the sand dunes I had thought we would be trudging through, the wilderness surface is rocky and hard. There's just enough dirt on the surface to support a surprising number of tough little trees and a great deal of scrub grass for the camp's sheep, donkeys, and cattle. And there's just enough grit to infiltrate our sandals and irritate our feet. I'll be surprised if we don't all have blisters before long.

Marlene Grace taps her sandals upside down on a rock, and William and I pick sand and dirt from between our toes. Cricket asks for help to wipe the soles of her feet, and Marlene Grace obliges with a growing frown. With a cluck like a mother hen, she announces, "These cuts on your feet will follow you home, child. We can't have that."

Then Marlene Grace stops in front of William and throws out her hand. With a stare at her husband she says, "William, give me that pocket knife you're not supposed to have here."

In surprise, William doesn't deny that he has the knife. He simply digs in his bag and produces it. But he whispers, "How did you know?"

"Because I know you, William Jeffries Fox," Marlene Grace whispers back. "I know that you can't live without that knife. And I had little doubt that you brought it with you."

Then she adds, "And I'll bet you brought that flashlight, too."

With eyes wide, William exclaims, "Woman, you scare me."

"Nothin' to it," Marlene Grace sniffs with a toss of her head. "I can read you like a book."

Now William smirks with a grin. "And it's a favorite edition, right?"

Marlene Grace's eyes dance. "The best," she says. "Now give me that knife."

William palms it to her so no one can see what he's not supposed to have in this millennium. And as we watch, Marlene Grace makes a cut in each of our costume hems. She then begins tearing fabric until each of us has lost about three inches of our tunics.

"Now, sit next to me, Cricket," Marlene Grace instructs, and we watch Marlene Grace wind some of the fabric loosely around Cricket's feet.

She says, "Let's see if this helps protect you from cuts and blisters."

"Socks!" I exclaim, and Marlene Grace chuckles.

"They're not perfect," she says, "but it should help a little."

When she wraps my feet, I tease her. "Won't your church wonder why their Christmas costumes are shorter than last year?"

"Don't you worry about that, young man. I'll sew some new hems before I put the garments back. And I'll put them through the washing machine, too."

"Good thing," William quips. "I forgot to pack my deodorant."

"Me too!" I say.

And Marlene Grace orders, "Keep your arms down, men!"

In our shortened and sweaty garments, and with our feet wrapped inside our sandals, our chuckling foursome sets off again. The morning shade on the western side of the mountain stays just out of reach.

———◆———

No one takes much notice of us as we bawl out our cries. We are a mere distraction in their busyness. And especially busy in this area are a great cluster of wood workers intent on converting desert logs into tent frames and domestic furniture.

Their ancient axes and adzes and saws and hammers are not that different from the hand tools of our day, and William slows his pace to check on some of the work. In a partially isolated area on the periphery he spies some high-quality work and he motions for us to follow him.

"Look at this beautiful workmanship," he says. "See how carefully they've measured and dressed these planks? Every board is identical and perfect. Plus, the carpenters have crafted mortise and tenon joints that are textbook, and they've done it without modern tools!"

Cricket shakes her head. "What are *mort...*?" And William is prepared to explain.

William carefully slides two finished boards from a neat stack about chest high, and he points out how each board has been designed to connect to the other. "These rectangular-shaped holes in the long edge of this board have been cut to match the rectangular tongues you see protruding from the edge of this other board. The holes are *mortises* and the matching tongues are called *tenons*."

"And," William tips the board on its end and continues, "the two tenons protruding from the bottom edge of each board are designed to fit into holes in a couple of heavy silver bases—like those sitting over there. When all of the boards and bases are fitted together, they will create walls over which tenting materials can be thrown."

"And if I'm right," he says, "this is acacia wood, and each board is exactly 15 feet tall, two feet wide, and nine inches thick. In all, there will be 48 such boards and 96 silver bases. And the boards will each be overlaid with gold and have gold rings attached through which gold-covered wooden crossbars will slide to stabilize the walls."

"How do you know all of this?" I ask, just before a gruff voice surprises us.

"Is there something wrong here?" demands a man wielding a large hammer.

"N-no, friend, not at all," William stutters uncomfortably. William offers a weak smile. "We were simply admiring your work."

The man doesn't return William's smile. Instead, he scolds, "Go and admire someone else's work. These boards are not to be trifled with; they are for God."

William withers a little, mumbles an apology, and turns to restack the boards he has displaced.

The man then pointedly inspects the stack to satisfy himself that nothing has been marred. Finally, he stalks wordlessly back to his tasks, and William bustles us away from *God's work area*.

"Sorry about that," William mumbles when we are far enough away.

To help break the awkward tension, I ask, "How do you know so much about carpentry?"

"Easy," he responds. "My dad's hobby was cabinet making. I grew up watching him work on the weekends. He would have loved seeing all of this, especially some of these old tools."

"And," says Marlene Grace, "my dad, the preacher, would have loved to have seen the boards for the Tabernacle."

"Is that what those boards are for?" I ask.

"I'm pretty sure," says William. "Everything fits the description in the Bible."

"I've only seen a picture of the Tabernacle once, in Sunday school when I was a little kid."

"It'll be a grand sight when it's done!" William declares.

"Who knows," says Cricket. "We might get to see it before we're done."

William glances quickly at me before he answers her. "But maybe not. The Bible says that the Israelites were camped for two years at the base of Mt. Sinai and that the Tabernacle is constructed and dedicated before they move on. From the look of things, I'd guess that these people have been camped here for a year or so, but there's a lot more to be done to finish the Tabernacle."

I get the point of William's observation and why he countered Cricket's speculation. After all, if we are here to see the finished Tabernacle, it will mean that we will not find Uncle Chad for a long time.

Cricket gets the point, also, and quickly backtracks on her comment. "Of course," she says, "we'll probably never see the Tabernacle. But it is exciting to think that we've seen how some of it was crafted."

"True," says Marlene Grace. "I never realized, before, how the boards were designed to fit together."

I have to admit that it has been interesting to watch the work and to hear William's explanations. But I hope we're not still here when the sacred tent is finished.

***

If we had known that we were heading into the furnace district, we might have skirted it. Instead, in the hottest part of the day, we find ourselves where things are intentionally made even hotter. In a long rocky section set apart from the woodworking area, sweating men force air through leather bellows to stoke coals in scores of clay-walled kilns and many more stacked-stone furnaces. The coals have to reach extreme temperatures to fire pottery and to melt gold, silver, and copper.

Kiln observers hover over the impressive three-foot pottery kilns, and smelters check their furnaces which are thicker and three times taller than the pottery kilns. One of the gold workers tells an inquiring William that after about six hours of smelting, a tapping hole will be unplugged near the furnace bottom so that the slag impurities can drain and the pure molten gold can flow into a series of waiting molds. An army of metalsmiths will work the cooled metal into elaborate candlesticks, food vessels, and basins for the Tabernacle.

William comments to us that, "Nearly everything relating to the Tabernacle is gold or to be overlaid with gold. Even the curtain hooks are pure gold, and the acacia wood boards that we saw earlier will be overlaid with gold."

I comment, in turn, "And to think that all of this gold was given to the Israelites by the Egyptians."

William doesn't know what Uncle Chad has written about the gold, or that I've read about it. He exclaims, "Why, yes! That's exactly right! That's what the Bible says."

Cricket smiles.

We continue to press on. "Uncle Chad!" I call out more loudly, now. But unfortunately, Uncle Chad is not in the furnace district.

◆

Finally, the western shade of the mountain affords the relief we have been seeking. Fresh water collected in man-made cisterns at the mountain's foot fills our camouflaged thermoses, and we dampen our faces and necks. It feels good to sit without the sun beating down and sapping our strength.

From our resting place, we look out on a tangle of spinners, weavers, and embroiderers who have wisely set up work, here, to take advantage of the afternoon shade. In contrast to the male-dominated industries of carpentry, kiln-work, and metalsmithing, most of the workers around us are women and children. And Marlene Grace directs our attention to the unusual ancient weaving looms.

"My mom's mama worked an old loom to make rugs and table runners and placemats," she ways, "and I was always fascinated by it. Later, in college, I learned some history about ancient looms, like these.

"These standing looms are called *vertical-warp* or *warp-weighted* looms. Unlike the sitting looms of our day, the *warp* (vertical) threads of these looms simply hang loose, and special clay or stone beads tied to the thread bottoms keep them taut."

Around the looms, children and other women chatter as they twirl and toss *drop-spindles*—elongated spools that twist flax fibers into linen threads.

The final toss of each spindle is into a dye vat where it lies drowning and absorbing the strong blues, purples, scarlets, or other thread colors that appear on the looms and in the needles of a cluster of skillful embroiderers.

The brilliant reds produced in one vat catch my eye and I ask, "What makes this red dye so bright? Does the color come from a plant?"

"Let's ask someone," suggests Marlene Grace, and she steps aside and engages a woman who is stirring red threads in a vat. The smiling woman invites us to sit, and her curious children quickly encircle and pet Hero.

"The brightest of the red dyes," the woman explains, "comes from the crimson worm." She reaches into a nearby basket and pulls out a handful of dried insects. "These are the adult form of the crimson worm."

She explains, "The worm encases itself in a cocoon, and once the female insect hatches, she attaches herself to the desert oak to lay her eggs. When she does that, she produces a red stain. Harvesters scrape hundreds of the female insect bodies from the trees, and we dry them until it's time to boil them for the dye."

"So," I say, "it isn't the worm itself that produces the dye?"

"No," the woman says. "The dye comes from the adult when she lays her eggs."

Cricket examines the dried insects in the woman's hand, and the dyer pours them from her hand into Cricket's hands. "Keep them, if you like," she says, "but don't let them get on your clothes. Even though they aren't yet boiled, they can stain." To demonstrate, she holds out her red hand.

Instantly, Marlene Grace opens one of her empty plastic-lined food bags. "Let's store them here," she hurriedly suggests. And she wipes Cricket's palm. For all of her fuss, I know that when we get home, Marlene Grace will help Cricket add the crimson-worm bugs to her framed insect collection.

After thanking the dyer and extricating Hero from the children who call out their goodbyes to the *puppy*, I am relieved to be back on our search. We hurry on through this area because there are so few men. And no matter how widely we range or how many times we call out, there is no response to our cries.

"Uncle Chad, where are you?" I plead as the afternoon sun wanes. How I wish we could have quickly found him and returned home. In all of our time here, we've barely made a dent in canvassing the camp.

"Don't get too discouraged," Cricket sympathizes. "We're not finished yet." And to lend more encouragement, she yells out Uncle Chad's name even more loudly.

By nightfall, however, without a single response to our cries, we have to stop.

# Chapter 12

## The Pillar of Cloud and Fire

As we eat our evening manna cakes, I notice how much closer we are to the tower of fire that sits on the far edge of camp. Its mesmerizing flames continue to burn a hole into the sky.

"What is that?" I ask.

"That," says William, "is the presence of God leading his people. When the pillar moves, the people move. When it stays, the people stay. It is a pillar of fire by night and a pillar of cloud by day."

"A pillar of cloud? I haven't noticed that," I say. I guess I've been too preoccupied with searching faces and taking in all of the activities around us.

And then it dawns on me... "But wait," I say. "I thought God was in Heaven and that he was invisible— until Jesus came."

"Ah," says William. "It is true that God is in heaven, but he is also here. He can be many places if he chooses. And God can take on any form. He first appeared to Moses as a burning bush that never burned up. He has sometimes appeared as an angel that looks like a man. And he is in the lightning storm on top of Mt. Sinai. But he is also in the fiery and cloudy pillar."

"Didn't you say that God is going to come and live in the Tabernacle, too?" I say.

"Yes," says William. "That's what he promised Moses."

I sigh. "I wish that God would help us find Uncle Chad."

William answers gently, "But God is helping you, Alexander. We're all here because God has arranged it."

"But," I protest, "we've been here for a day and a half and haven't found him."

"But that doesn't mean God isn't at work," William says. "We just need to be patient and trust him."

Then William suggests, "It's kind of like when we're very young and our family takes a long trip in the car. Our parents know how many hours the journey will take, but we're too young to grasp time, so we just keep asking, 'Aren't we there, yet? Aren't we there, yet?' To us, the trip seems endless and we're impatient to have it done. But then we arrive in Disneyland. And, in our excitement, we forget how long it took us to drive there. In the same way, God knows the plan and the timetable for our journey, and we need to trust that we will get there at just the right time."

I manage a smile. I guess I am acting like a little kid. I do want to bypass the car ride and skip straight to the destination. This journey into the ancient past is rich in information about life in Bible times, and I should be thrilled to see it. I should be thankful to God for bringing us here. God must be awfully tired of hearing me whine, "Aren't we there, yet?"

———— • ————

The next day, we search all morning with no success. And then, per William's suggestion, we finish our lunch and cut a search swath straight through camp, toward the pillar of cloud. William knows that I've wanted to see the cloud up close before we leave. After all, it's not every day that one gets to see God in any physical form.

The closer we come, the more I am awed by the size of the towering whirlwind. And we discover that the swirling mass of luminescent mist is not silent. Its tornado-like roar is a statement of force and power. I can't imagine how much more frightening it must be to stand near the cloud in its fiery state at night.

I am disappointed, however, that even though we can now see God in one of his many forms, he remains elusive. There is no sense of one-on-one with the God of the cloud. There is no way to approach him any differently than we've been doing with our prayers.

We turn away to search a few hours longer. Then someone in the crowd shouts. "Look! It's Moses, back from the mountain!"

People all around us practically stampede to see. In the confusion, children are snatched to their parents' shoulders to avoid accidental trampling.

With their advantage of height, Marlene Grace and William peer over the heads of their shorter neighbors. I see nothing, even on tiptoes, until Moses and his companion climb to the top of a rock and lift their staffs to quiet the crowd.

"After tomorrow's Sabbath," Moses announces, "we need to clear the Tabernacle area of brush and debris. We need to sweep it clean so that we can move any finished frames and other materials to their proper places. We still have much construction to do, but we also have much done. The work is progressing well, and the details are being well-attended to. It is pleasing in God's sight."

Now Moses lifts his hands toward Heaven and leads the people in a prayer of blessing to God.

I must confess that my curiosity overtakes my devotion, and I sneak a peek during the prayer. Moses commands attention, but I am also drawn to the pillar of cloud that seems to glow brighter as the words of praise pour out to God. Then, when Moses finishes his prayer, all of the people thunder an *Amen*.

In the middle of their shout, I whisper my petition. Perhaps if I tack it onto Moses's prayer God will be more inclined to hear me. "God," I cry, "please help me find Uncle Chad."

———◆———

When Moses and Aaron pass through the throng and out of sight, and all the crafters and workers return to their tasks, I wonder if Moses and Aaron are on their way to spread the word to other parts of the camp. If so, it will take them a long time to reach everyone, as we well know. But William observes, "Did you see the runners, the young men who sped away to share the announcement to the various tribes?"

I didn't notice them, but I do think it makes sense. Runners will no doubt get the message to other runners who can spread it quickly. I only wish that runners would take up our cry, too.

We trudge on. And when work around us stops for the night, Cricket suggests that we wait to eat supper until we get home. I am grateful for the extra time to search. Perhaps an extra hour will make the difference. But it doesn't.

After an hour, we finally stop, and, when I sigh my disappointment, Cricket promises, "We'll come back. We're not finished."

Our little group looks weary as we draw together in a secluded spot to prepare for transport. We have walked untold miles and it has been hot. Even Hero is ready to leave. He paws for Cricket to lift him into her shoulder bag.

Cricket picks him up, and I watch her rub her cheek against the terrier's fur and scratch his ears. It is a simple exchange between pet and owner but one that Cricket will not be able to do when she returns home. At home, she will take up her unfeeling body again. But why? Why does God always return Cricket to her disability? Why doesn't he simply heal her?

I push the thought away. I can't afford to be critical of God right now. In case he can hear my thoughts, I want to be on good terms with him. He knows where Uncle Chad is, and I need to believe that he's working on helping us find him. I just hope that God is more patient with me than I am with him. I want immediate results, like the little kid in the back seat of the family car. And God keeps saying, "Not yet."

"We will come back," Cricket promises again. "You'll see. We're not quitting."

We join hands, now, and William prays. "Lord God, thank you for keeping us safe and for keeping Alexander's uncle safe, wherever he is. Help us as we return home to manage those things You have for us there, and please bring us back soon to continue our mission. We pray that when we return, we will find Dr. Tennyson. In Jesus' Name, amen."

When we lift our heads, Marlene Grace clicks the stones together, and, like shadows in the desert, we disappear.

# Chapter 13

## Juggling Two Worlds

"It's a quarter to six!" Marlene Grace cries the minute our toes reach her carpet. "Alexander, you need to change clothes and get home for supper."

I know I should hurry but I'm sluggishly caught in the time warp between my body and my brain. William gently removes the bedroll from my back, and Marlene Grace thrusts my blue jeans, cell phone, and T-shirt into my hands and steers me toward the bathroom.

Before I take a step, I ask, "Didn't Moses say that the Sabbath was tomorrow, Friday evening?"

"Yes," says William. "And the work to clear the Tabernacle ground was to start the day after."

"But..."

Cricket answers before I can finish my question. "You're noticing that we left the Israelite camp on Thursday evening but the date on your cell phone says it is already Sunday evening here."

"Yes," I say. "I'm having trouble keeping things straight."

"But that's how onyx-stones journeys are," Cricket says. "The stones aren't tied to time in the same way we are."

"But it's confusing," I say. "And it's frustrating to have to leave the past before we finish our task."

Marlene Grace and William agree, and William says, "It is too bad that we have to break up our searches. But we can do it. We aren't done yet."

"Besides," William continues, "we couldn't have searched on the Sabbath anyway. No one is to work or travel on the Sabbath. The Israelites would be observing a day of rest. We would have had to sit, and you would have been frustrated."

It's true. I would have resented every wasted minute. It is better to be home and to plan on another trip, soon.

Even so, I find it hard to let the ancient world go. Uncle Chad is there, and the images of the Israelite camp linger in the forefront of my mind.

I get to my house a little late, but Mom doesn't mention my tardiness. She just welcomes me back and asks if I had a good time. Dad smiles from across the table.

As we pass the food, I compare the meal spread before us to what I've been eating for the last two-and-a-half days. The closest thing to manna I see is the pile of mashed potatoes liberally smothered in butter. My mind tugs me back to the desert, and for just a second, I imagine Uncle Chad walking past us in a crowd. He doesn't hear me calling, and I lose him again.

I force my attention away from the daydream when Mom asks me a question.

"Alexander, you look like you've been in the sun; you have a sunburn. Did you and Cricket's family spend time outside?"

I nod. "Yes, we did. We visited some very old friends and walked outside a lot."

"Well, I'm glad you got exercise, son," Dad says.

"Yeah, it was great, Dad. As a matter of fact, I was wondering if I could have a couple of days next weekend, too. They've invited me to go on another trip to the country with them. What do you think?"

Mom shrugs, and Dad says, "As long as you get your schoolwork done, it should be fine."

"It's nice that they've invited you," Mom assures me. "Cricket is a good friend to have, and I'm sure she appreciates your company."

"She's an interesting person," I reply. "We have a lot of similar interests. She's really smart, you know."

Later, I overhear Mom tell Dad, "I'm glad Alexander has something to take his mind off your brother for a change. I've been worried about his never-ending preoccupation with Chad's disappearance."

I shake my head. If only Mom knew!

———— • ————

Before I shower and change clothes for bed, I text Cricket to say that I can spend next weekend on our search. She texts back, *Great. By the way, your manna supper is still here.*

I reply, *OK. I may eat it tomorrow after school.*

She responds, *OK. See you.*

I put the phone away and pull out my pajamas to wear after I'm clean. In the bathroom mirror I see the pink of my sunburn, and I smell the smoke of campfires in my hair. In my mind's eye, I see Cricket, Marlene Grace, William, and me unrolling our beds so we can settle in. And I stare off to where the bright tower maintains his fiery sentry. Somewhere in that camp Uncle Chad is readying himself for bed, and I assume that he is wondering what is happening back home.

Now, for some reason, my anger boils up against Lawrence Traeger. In contrast to my image of Uncle Chad consigned to the harsh conditions of an ancient desert, I picture Lawrence lounging on a yacht that was paid for with his so-called *pirate treasure*. How unfair! My stomach tightens as I imagine Lawrence surrounded by stewards in crisp white jackets who murmur, "Here's your glass of wine, sir. Will there be anything else?" In my vision, Lawrence summarily dismisses his servants from his presence, heaves a satisfied sigh, and surveys the sky as if the stars belong to him.

I growl my frustration. Does the man have no conscience? Does he even care that he's abandoned Uncle Chad to the rigors of a Bedouin existence far away from his family? Why did he do it? Uncle Chad was good to him, generous and willing to help him complete his university degree.

I cannot reconcile the two images: one of Uncle Chad wandering in the desert and the other of Lawrence basking in his fortune. I wonder if I will ever encounter Lawrence and have the opportunity to accuse him of his crimes.

"Sleep tight, Lawrence Traeger," I mutter, "because one day I may topple your world as you have mine."

———◆◆———

I'm still angry and out of sorts in the morning. My foul disposition threatens to ruin my day. Mom chastises me at breakfast when I say barely a word.

"Alexander Tennyson, I don't know what's gotten into you this morning, but you'd better straighten up before you leave this house. There's no excuse for your rudeness. Do you hear me?"

"Yes, ma'am," I mumble. "May I be excused?"

"If you're ready to act civilly, yes."

Dad adds, "And tell your mother you're sorry."

"Sorry, Mom," I say without looking at her.

I am sorry; I do dislike how I feel and how I've been acting. I wish I could explain to Mom and Dad why I'm cross, but it's too complicated, right now. I can't wait for the day when everything will be put right.

———————•———————

At Cricket's house after school, Marlene Grace shows me my supper allotment of raw manna, poured from my travel pouch into a bowl on the counter.

She says, "I was sure it would be rotten this morning. The Bible says that the Israelites were to collect only enough for the day. Anything hoarded until the next day would be rancid. But I find the manna from our bags is still fresh. It's puzzling, don't you think?"

Then Marlene Grace's eyes widen. "I have it!" she cries. "To keep the Israelites from working on the Sabbath, God let them gather twice as much manna on the day before. And manna that was collected before the Sabbath would keep overnight. I think this manna doesn't know that we're back in a future time. It was collected in the past on the day before the Sabbath!"

Having solved her own puzzle, Marlene Grace asks me to tell Cricket that our manna cakes and strawberry jam will be ready in a few minutes. "We have to eat the manna today," she says. "It'll all go bad by tomorrow."

"Sure," I say, and I start for Cricket's room.

I think how impossible it is to keep everything straight between the present and the past. Even the manna is confused.

———————•———————

"How are you doing?" Cricket asks. "Did you sleep okay?"

"I did get to sleep, eventually," I reply. "My thoughts kept me awake. I keep reliving everything we've seen and done, and I can't forget that we were in the desert only hours ago."

Cricket nods. "I understand. Time travel does play with your mind. We're used to a linear world where time flows in only one direction. We shouldn't be able to hop back to former times or leap into the future. I'm not fully used to it, either. And I've given up trying to explain the mystery of the onyx stones. I thank God for what they have taught me, but I don't understand why they've been introduced into my life and not the lives of everyone."

Cricket reflects, "Before Josh clicked my onyx stones for the first time, I had never given time's constraints much thought. But then, Josh suddenly whisked me away from the present and into the future."

I blink in surprise. *The future? Surely not!* Travel into the past is tricky enough. But travel into the future is to travel into events you will live again. I don't think I want to know my future. I don't want to foresee tragedies, even if they are sprinkled between triumphs.

But Cricket makes me see her journey differently. She says, "My first onyx-stones adventure happened at a time when I believed I had no future. The accident had cost me my family and my body. And, for a long time, due to swelling in my head, I was also blind."

"I remember that you said that it was like the plague of darkness, only it was just you that experienced it," I say.

"Yes," she says. "After the crash, it took several weeks for my eyesight to return. More than anything else, I hated being blind. You can't imagine what it's like to not be able to see *or* feel anything. I wasn't even sure that Josh was real when he first showed up. But Josh kept me sane. He kept talking to me, and he fed me pancakes every morning. And then one day he placed the stone necklace around my neck and clicked his stone against mine, and he took me away to a distant time not yet come. And on that trip, I was healed, and I came alive again!"

"So, on your trip to the future, the blindness and quadriplegia left you like it did on our trip to ancient Egypt?" I ask.

"Yes," says Cricket. "And the stones took me to a terrible time. There I saw other people living in persecution and tragedy. And I began to see life through their eyes. And what I saw astounded me. Those oppressed and poverty-stricken people had a faith in God and his promises that overrode their immediate difficulties. They were hungry and in hiding, yet they pressed forward with a hope and belief that God was faithful and trustworthy.

"And one day, I got to see their whole planet changed. On that day God's blessings were so overwhelming that all of the old was forgotten. Jesus came and lived with them, and life was so beautiful that I was tempted to stay there and never click the stones to return home. But then I felt the love of Jesus guiding me back to Marlene Grace and William. And I wasn't sad. And I love them and I know, without a doubt, that when my time comes to leave this earth, I will rejoin Jesus, my family, and my End Times friends in that happy place forever."

I ponder what Cricket has said. Her view of the future is not what I was expecting. I have never considered God's involvement in my life in the way that Cricket sees it. She sees God and his son, Jesus, as kind and loving, and she trusts them in everything. Cricket expressed no fear of the God of fury we saw on the mountain or the pillar of fire in the ancient desert. I wonder if I will ever see God as she sees him.

# Chapter 14

## Fire in the Stone

With five school days until we return to our search in the desert, I stumble through math and science and push myself through the paces of PE. Some of my classmates ask where my mind is, because I seem distant. I shrug and laugh. They wouldn't understand if I told them.

When the last school bell signals freedom for the weekend, I leap from my desk and race home. I drop off my books and rush to kiss Mom goodbye.

"Have a good visit, son," Mom says, and I feel guilty that I can't tell her the truth about what I'm doing. I know that if I do, she and Dad will think I'm suffering from delusions and forbid me to go. I can't afford that. The only thing they will understand is when they see Uncle Chad walk through the door. And I'm going to make that happen!

"Did you pack your toothbrush?" Mom asks, and I refrain from rolling my eyes. What an oddity a toothbrush and toothpaste would be to the ancient Hebrews!

"Love you, Mom," I tell her, and I see her surprise when I hug her for a second time. Then I climb on my bike, and I pedal like the wind.

The pile of travel gear on the Fox's living room floor has grown. Marlene Grace and William have added a new pack to our transport supplies—a lightweight tent to replace our ropes and sheets.

"William promises to carry it for us," Marlene Grace says.

I'm torn by the idea of a tent. It tells me that Marlene Grace and William think we will, once again, spend more than a day in our search for Uncle Chad. With a tent it will be more comfortable, but I'm impatient to have this venture over with quickly.

"Looks great," I say with an attempt at enthusiasm.

I also battle my impatience with eating supper before we leave. But I know it is for the best. We will not have manna for our meals until tomorrow.

Marlene Grace shoos us out of the kitchen for a few minutes while the burgers finish cooking. "Why don't you children run along until I call you," she says. "And the same goes for you, William."

William dutifully heads for the living room, but only after sneaking a handful of potato chips. Cricket and I start down the hall toward her bedroom.

"She always calls us *child* or *children*," I comment quietly.

Cricket grins. "We'll always be children to Marlene Grace, even when we're forty. It's her way of saying she's the adult and in charge. She means no harm by it, and I have come to find it comforting."

"Oh, I'm not saying it's a bad thing," I hurry to say. "It just seems odd to me."

Hero rubs against my leg to remind me that I haven't petted him in the last five minutes, and when I reach down to give him a scratch, he swipes the side of my face with his tongue.

Cricket wants my attention, too. With her smile she guides my eyes to a new hanging on her wall. Above her desk I see a neatly typed half-page description framed with a red smear and a collection of adult crimson worms. "I did some research on the worms and Marlene Grace framed it," Cricket explains, "and Marlene Grace helped me to mount the insects. Yes, that's Marlene Grace's red thumbprint in the corner."

Cricket chuckles. "Marlene Grace really tried to keep the dye off herself, but she didn't succeed. And when you see her later, you'll see that her thumb is still stained red. William teases her about it."

"Well, the display looks great," I say, "and it's something that not just anyone in Heatherton has on their wall."

"You're right about that," laughs Cricket. "I doubt that anybody in Heatherton even knows what a crimson worm is."

As I let my mind wander back to the dye vats in the Hebrew camp, Cricket interrupts to ask, "Alexander, would you do me a favor; would you please slide my stone so that my necklace will hang straighter?"

"Of course," I say, even though I think the necklace looks straight already. I make a show of pulling down the stone so that the ribbon is definitely evened out.

"How does that look?" I ask after turning Cricket toward her mirror.

"Fine," she replies. But then she says, "Now, could you remove the necklace and put it on the dresser for me?"

I look at her as if she's asked me to stand on my head. "I just straightened the necklace," I object. "And now you want me to take it off?"

"Correct," she affirms.

I decide that there must be a point to this exercise, even though I can't yet see it. I obediently bend over and reach for the necklace. But I stop. Three times I stretch out my hand, and three times I have to pull it back.

"What's wrong?" Cricket asks.

"I'm not sure," I say. "For some reason, the necklace is hot. Don't you feel it? Is it burning your neck?"

When she tells me no, I try once more to remove it.

"That thing is red hot!" I exclaim. I stare as she calmly sits there.

"Not to me," says Cricket. "The stone is as cool as ever against my throat."

I check and see that she's right; there are no signs of redness or burning anywhere on her neck.

"Is this some kind of trick?" I quiz.

Cricket smiles. "No. No trick. But it is an important property of my necklace that I thought you should know."

"Oh, yeah? What's that?"

Cricket explains. "You see," she says, "my stone cannot be removed. While the necklace may be adjusted and touched, such as when I'm getting dressed, it reacts very differently whenever anyone tries to take it off. Somehow, the stone knows the difference between a casual brush and an intent to slip it off my neck. It reacts protectively when it is threatened. No one can take the necklace from me, not even Marlene Grace or William."

I reply skeptically, "That doesn't make sense. Marlene Grace had no problem putting on and taking off the necklace that she wore on our trip. I've even seen William slip it over her head."

"I know," says Cricket. "But there's a difference between my necklace and that one. You see, even though the necklaces look alike, they are not the same. Mine is a master necklace and is unique to me, alone. It was Josh who put my stone around my neck, while the other stone was simply left for me and others to use.

Then she says, "I didn't realize this property of my stone, at first. I learned it by accident and over time. My first lesson came on my initial onyx-stones journey. That's when an evil woman tried to steal my necklace. She had no sooner wrapped her fingers around the stone, than she dropped it and screamed that I had burned her. Because I had done nothing, I had no idea what she was talking about. I was just glad that she hadn't succeeded in taking the necklace.

"Then, much later, back home, I asked Marlene Grace to take off the necklace and put it away for me. She reached for it, as you've done, and I was surprised when she told me she couldn't take the necklace off. She insisted that the stone was suddenly too hot to handle. I doubted her because I felt nothing unusual—the stone was still cool at my throat. I also doubted her because she had touched the stone hundreds of times before this. It was impossible not to touch it when dressing me or adjusting the chin rig on my wheelchair. But this time, Marlene Grace would not budge; she refused to touch it.

"It was only then that I remembered the woman from the first incident. She and Marlene Grace were very different people, but the one thing they had in common was their intent to remove the stone from my neck. I told Marlene Grace the story, and she and I decided to perform an experiment. We learned that if Marlene Grace simply meant to adjust the necklace or brush against it to fix my collar, she had no problem. But if she reached for the necklace with the idea of removing it, the stone radiated a heat too intense for her to perform her task. It became clear to Marlene Grace and me that my stone must never be removed."

"Hmm," I reply. "So, you're saying that you've never had the stone removed from your neck?"

"Only once," says Cricket. "Josh removed it, once, and later replaced it."

Cricket turns her chair to face me when she says, "Alexander, I think that your Uncle Chad's necklace is similar to mine. Remember how he could not get rid of the necklace? He took it off and threw it into the attic, but in the morning, it was back around his neck. It wouldn't stay gone."

"Right," I say.

Then Cricket continues. "But the secondary necklace that Lawrence found in the treasure bag is different. It's like the necklace that Marlene Grace has worn. It isn't imprinted to any person in particular. And yet, both the master necklace and the secondary necklace are needed for transports to take place."

I can see that Cricket is right. The imprinting of the master necklace is a unique property of certain onyx stones. It's an amazing property—almost as amazing as the stones themselves.

I wonder, now, if I can touch the necklace. Cricket suggests that I erase from my mind the idea of removing the necklace and simply tell myself that I am only going to adjust it, as I did earlier. Inch by inch I move my hand toward the stone. And finally, I grasp it in my fingers. I shake my head in wonder.

"Who would ever have guessed such a thing?"

Cricket smiles. "The reason I wanted you to know about the master stones and their defense response," she says, "is because I think it explains Lawrence's burned hand."

*Lawrence's burned hand?* My head snaps up. In a flash I know what Cricket is saying.

"You think that Uncle Chad's necklace burned Lawrence!" I tell her.

Cricket nods. "Makes sense, doesn't it?"

"But..."

"But you want to know how Lawrence managed to return to the present without Uncle Chad," Cricket says.

And she's right. If the stone burned Lawrence's hand, why hadn't he let go of it? If he had, perhaps Uncle Chad would be here now.

"That same question puzzled me," says Cricket. "And I finally concluded that something truly traumatic must have happened for Lawrence to grab that necklace and not heed its burning."

In alarm, I ask, "But wouldn't he have thrown the necklace away?"

"Possibly," says Cricket. "But what if he couldn't throw it away? What if the burning stone remained stuck in his hand?"

That thought spins in my head for a minute before I cry, "Serves him right! If he hadn't forced the transport to begin with, Uncle Chad would be here!"

But then the rest of the awful truth hits me. "So, where does that leave Uncle Chad? If something terrible made Lawrence panic and override the stone's warning, did he leave Uncle Chad in danger? What if...?"

Cricket stops me. "We can't go there," she says. "We don't know what happened. But I, personally, think Uncle Chad is fine."

"But you don't know!" I cry.

Cricket hurries to answer me. "I think he must be fine because otherwise the onyx stone wouldn't keep telling me that we need to rescue him."

Now, I'm confused. What is she saying? I ask, "What do you mean that the onyx stone talks to you?"

Cricket answers, "I can't explain it, Alexander, but the idea of going back to the desert to find your uncle wasn't my idea. It was God's. He's the one who controls the onyx stones. And he's the one who gives me dreams or puts thoughts into my head about using the stones."

I shake my head to make sure I'm hearing her right. "So," I say, "you're telling me that you can't just click the stones any time you like and go anywhere you want?"

Cricket smiles. "No," she says. "If I were to try that, it would probably end up in a disaster like the chaos Lawrence created."

Her mention of Lawrence stirs my anger again. Why couldn't Lawrence have left the stones alone? Why did he have to make a mess that Uncle Chad and my family have to pay for?

# Chapter 15

## Return to the Desert

In our freshly laundered and newly hemmed Christmas pageant costumes—including some newly sewn soft chamois booties to line our sandals—Cricket, Marlene Grace, William, and I once again set foot on the hard-packed desert floor. And in that odd way of stones time-keeping, it is not the approaching Jewish Sabbath when we arrive, even though we left Cricket's house on a Friday. And the Israelites are no longer at the foot of the mountain.

Instead, ahead of us at some distance, the Hebrews are marching behind the bright pillar of cloud. We move quickly to catch up with them and are thankful when the falling sun causes the company to slow. We finally pass through the crowd's perimeter, after wading through the herds that straggle behind the travelers, and we push toward the center of the camp to pitch our brand-new tent. William figures that from the center of camp we can spiral outward in the morning to make best use of our search time.

When William stops, we unload our supplies and set to work on our campsite.

With nightfall, the far-off pillar explodes into fire. The tower's flaming wings rise spectacularly into the heavens. William strikes one of his secret matches to start our fire, and since we don't have manna to bake, we guardedly chew on Marlene Grace's homemade cookies and warm ourselves until bedtime.

———◆———

In the morning, by our fire in the middle of the Israelite camp, we supplement our breakfast manna with cheese from home. Because we see that goat cheese is plentiful around other campfires, we eat our cheese openly.

As we eat, I ask, "Have these people had cheese all along? If so, why did they complain that they were starving? Didn't they have milk and flocks of animals? Why did they need God to provide manna?"

Marlene Grace suggests, "I think the people seldom ate their flocks."

"That's right," agreed William. "They were more valuable for milk and cheese and wool—and a certain number of sacrifices. And although we see large herds here, if you divide them by the number of people, you will probably find that each family has only a few animals.

"I think the biggest worry of everyone was grain. Without grain they couldn't make bread—their daily staple. And as the Promised Land seemed farther and farther away, they feared their supplies would run out. Manna was God's answer to their fear. With manna, God demonstrated that He could provide for them."

"And it tastes good," I say.

"Yes," agrees William. "It does taste good. And the Bible says that, at times, God sent quail for the Israelites, too."

William's knowledge of these things amazes me.

Marlene Grace confides that William studied up before this trip. "He's read everything he could find about the Exodus, life in the desert, and details about the Tabernacle."

"It's true," admits William. "I wanted to be prepared. I didn't want to be caught short in case we get to see the Tabernacle constructed on this visit."

Indeed, William's hopes seem to be rewarded when word comes that we will be camping here for an extended period. William claps his hands, and his eyes shine as he exclaims, "That means the Tabernacle is likely to be erected, here!"

To add to his excitement, shortly after we finish breakfast and set out from our central location, we come across a flat spot, about one-fifth the size of a football field, that is being swept clean. William recognizes the boards being stacked at one end of the field—scores of boards that are now all overlaid with gold.

"The shorter boards and their bases," William says, "are for the curtained fence that will outline the Tabernacle courtyard. The finished courtyard will be seventy-five feet wide, a hundred-fifty feet long, and seven-and-a-half feet high."

Cricket gives me a sideways glance and grins. I think it means that she feels like I do, that William sounds like the smart kid in class who wants to share everything he knows. But in this case, what William is sharing is interesting. I don't mind listening. William's eyes sparkle with the expectation of seeing the courtyard and the Tabernacle materialize.

But then, unexpectedly, William stops cold and puts out his hand to stop us. "Wait!" he commands sternly.

With eyes widening in fear, William frightens us, too, when he declares, "We have to leave this place!"

He hisses, "We shouldn't be here. We need to move away from the center of camp quickly!"

"Hurry!" he urges us.

Without questioning, Cricket picks up Hero, and we stick close as William leads us away from the cleared field.

"What's wrong?" Cricket asks. "Where are we going?"

In between breaths, William explains, "I've made a mistake. I shouldn't have settled us in the center of the camp. We can't be anywhere near the Tabernacle ground. Since our last visit, things have changed. The Tabernacle has now been dedicated, and the Levites have been set apart as the only ones who can touch or care for it—certainly not Gentiles, like us! Not even the other Israelite tribes can trespass on the ground it will occupy without being put to death. And the Tabernacle is always set up in the center of the camp. The Levites settle immediately around it, and the other tribes are to settle around the Levite perimeter in designated locations. I inadvertently put us in the middle of the Levite clan, and we don't belong here. We could be killed!"

We hurry faster, now, and William adds, "But don't worry, Alexander. Your uncle isn't likely to be among the Levites. We don't need to search their company."

At the moment, that is the last thing on my mind!

———◆———

When, in our haste to vacate the forbidden area, we come to a kind of no-man's land—a wide path that separates the Levites from everyone else—we cross it, and William finally lets us slow our pace. Cricket sets Hero back on the ground and he sticks close to us.

William heaves a sigh of relief. "I was afraid the Levites would discover us and accuse us of defiling them or the Tabernacle in some way," he says.

"We would have had a hard time explaining ourselves and we might have been stoned, on the spot."

Then William says, "Even if we hadn't been killed, our mission would have been ruined. If we want to find Alexander's uncle, we can't afford to arouse the least bit of suspicion."

The idea of messing up our mission shakes me. As far as I know, this is our only chance to find Uncle Chad. I don't think I could stand it if we couldn't keep looking.

"Thank you for getting us out of there," I murmur.

"I'm just sorry that I didn't figure it out sooner," William says dejectedly. "I've scared you all, and me. And it wasn't necessary."

Marlene Grace comforts him. "You did great, honey," she says. "Without you, we never would have known we were in danger. Thank you for doing your homework." She gives him a big hug, and I see tears in William's eyes.

Cricket hugs him too, and when she does, I realize that this is the first time I've seen Cricket show affection for William. The big man melts under it.

I decide that William might be large and imposing, but his heart is over-sized, too. I have always tended to see him as more marine (he was a marine once) than as a well-dressed exotic car dealer. But there is no doubt that he happens to be deeply in love with his wife and his dependent.

Because Cricket's hugs are only possible when she's on an onyx-stones journey, I note that the treasure of them is not lost on William.

———◆———

It is mid-morning when our big, soft-hearted leader sets us on a spiraling clockwise path around the Levite area. He outlines his plan.

"Imagine yourself as a fly on a big apple pie that the baker has sliced into eleven pieces," William says, and he draws a pie-face in the dust. "We're here," he says, and he points to a spot just outside of the center of the pie.

"The pie center is the Levites," he says. "We're just outside of that area." He gives a wry smile.

Then William tells us, "If we walk in a small circle around the center of the pie, we will cross each pie piece until we come back to where we started. Each pie piece represents a different tribe, so when we finish our first circling, we'll have visited all eleven tribes—we've already visited the twelfth by accident."

Now William moves his pointer to make a wider circle, concentric with the last one. "This circle," he says, "will be our next pass through the tribes. And we'll continue widening our circle until we either find Uncle Chad or reach the crust on the edge of the pie."

"Do you know which tribe we're in now?" I ask, and of course William is prepared.

"Yes," he says. "We are here." He points to a pie piece on his drawing. "This is where Judah always camps. They are always due east. And as we march clockwise, we will pass through the tribes of Zebulun, Simeon, Reuben, Gad, Manasseh, Ephraim, Benjamin, Asher, Dan, Naphtali, and Issachar."

William is triumphant in his knowledge, and we commend him. After we take one more look at William's pie drawing, William asks, "Are we ready to go?" and we set out to follow his plan.

Hero seems to anticipate our route, and he trots a few steps ahead of us. Cricket and I follow him, and Marlene Grace and William stroll behind us.

Our calls for Uncle Chad are largely ignored, as before. But we are able to catch occasional glimpses of the raising of the fifteen-foot-tall Tabernacle roof frame. Because of his height, William usually sees the views first and points them out for us. Because Cricket is the shortest, he lifts her up so she can see what the rest of us are oohing and aahing over as we stand on tip-toe.

The acacia-wood roof beams with their gold overlay reflect brilliantly in the midday sun as they outline the sacred tent's form. We also see the many drapes that cover the beams. The lower portion of the Tabernacle is hidden from view, however, because of the seven-and-a-half-foot tall curtain that fences the Tabernacle enclosure.

As we break for a late lunch within the tribe of Manasseh, William shares more of his Tabernacle knowledge.

"It's too bad," he says, "that we won't get to see the Tabernacle interior, but I'm thrilled that we have seen as much as we have. Do you remember the first roof covering that was laid down—that exquisitely embroidered blue, purple, and scarlet linen?"

"Yes!" exclaims Cricket. "I recognized it as the beautiful fabric we saw being woven and embroidered at the foot of Mt. Sinai."

"Yes," says William. "And although its beauty has been covered over with another drape, it will not be totally hidden. It will be visible from inside the Tabernacle as it rests over the gold-covered ceiling beams."

"I can almost picture it," Marlene Grace murmurs. "Gold and all of those rich colors!"

"If we are lucky," says William, "we'll see the linen being covered over by a plain fabric of undyed goat's hair, and then over that we'll see a layer of rams' skins dyed red."

"Crimson-worm red," I say, and William smiles. Marlene Grace lifts her still red thumb with a grin.

"The final layer," William says, "is blue—blue-dyed sealskins."

"Sealskins?" I exclaim in surprise. "Where would the Israelites get sealskins in the desert?"

William chuckles. "I knew you'd ask. I had that same question when I was researching. And I learned that because of the sealskin's waterproof properties, the hides were well-supplied throughout the ancient world. The skins were in demand for footwear and to keep tents dry. Traders from the coasts supplied them throughout nearly every country. The Israelites may have even brought skins with them, or they might have purchased them from the occasional Bedouin trader on his way to market in Egypt. We know that the Israelites could pay a good price for the merchandise, and I like to think that the Bedouins would take tidbits of news to the Egyptians about their former slaves."

"I hope we get to see the sealskins," I say. "Who would have thought!"

Hero is the only one not interested. His eyes are on Cricket's hand as she slips him a bite of cookie.

———◆———

At one point in late afternoon we do see the sealskins on the Tabernacle roof.

Marlene Grace wonders, "Do you suppose that now that all of the coverings are on the Tabernacle, that the inside furnishings are in place, too?"

"It's possible," says William. "I've been smelling meat cooking. And that means that the Levites are performing the required sacrifices that will precede the installation of the Ark of the Covenant into the Holy of Holies. Then God's Spirit can fill the Tabernacle as it did under Mt. Sinai before they left the mountain."

"I have a question," I say. "Does that mean that Moses will talk to God from the Tabernacle, like he did on the mountain?"

"Yes," says William. "When the Tabernacle was first dedicated at Mt. Sinai, God's Spirit came to rest inside the tent, between the wings of the two cherubim decorating the cover of the Ark of the Covenant. Moses would then visit God there. And wherever the Israelites go, now, God's cloud and fire go with them and his glory fills the Tabernacle when it is assembled."

No wonder the curtains are high, I decide. And no wonder the Tabernacle coverings are layered. They not only protect the interior, but they hide everything that is happening inside. If the God from the mountain is somehow in the Tabernacle, it must be a scary place to enter.

───────◆───────

By early evening, we have passed through the tribes of Ephraim, Benjamin, Asher, Dan, Naphtali, and Issachar. Cricket has been carrying Hero for over an hour. His little legs have grown tired.

When we arrive again in the tribe of Judah, we stop to build our campfire and eat. It is a relief to relax.

But just as we finish eating, we become aware that everything in the camp has suddenly become still. We stop our conversation and Hero pricks his ears.

The normal clatter and subdued chatter of families around their campfires has died. There is no sound. All noise—yes, *ALL* noise—in the camp has died away. It's as if everyone—all two million people—are holding their breath.

Then suddenly, as one, all two million Israelites rise to their feet. Cricket whispers, "It's the cloud! It's moving!"

She's right. The pillar of cloud from the edge of camp has lifted from the desert floor and is moving in our direction. Its towering mass passes high over the tribe of Judah, and its wind flaps our tent and robes and nearly snuffs the campfire.

"It's heading for the Tabernacle," William murmurs.

Sure enough, the cloud passes over the Tabernacle courtyard, and with measured deliberation it comes to rest over the Holy of Holies of the sacred tent. All eyes are fixed on the whirling mass of wind.

And then, as if the sight of a tornado settling over the Tabernacle's sealskins is not dramatic enough, the cloud suddenly bursts into its fiery form. The transformation, although expected, is nevertheless startling, and we cry out in spite of ourselves.

The pillar's flames now rise higher than ever before. They seem to scorch the floorboards of heaven.

And yet, miraculously, the fire does not consume the tent beneath it. And although the flaming pillar is now in place, no one in the camp moves. It is not until we hear the sound of the Tabernacle trumpets that the people relax. The trumpets are the signal that the spectacle is over and we can retire for the night.

Has Uncle Chad seen this awesome display, too? And is he as afraid as I am? Even inside our tent and under my blanket, I cannot erase the image of the towering pillar of cloud and fire hovering over the gold-gilded Tabernacle in the center of camp. I feel like God is suddenly too close and I need to hide, but where?

———•———

In the morning, even though the fiery tower over the Tabernacle has returned to its cloud form, it is impossible to ignore. Every eye in the camp can see it as we eat our manna breakfast. The cloud remains clearly visible as Cricket, Marlene Grace, William, Hero, and I set off again in search of Uncle Chad.

I try to ignore my uneasiness and the feeling of being watched every moment by the God of the cloud. I concentrate on searching the hundreds of faces before me and calling out my message.

Sometimes little children follow us and mimic my calls, as if it is a game. And they call to Hero: "Hello, puppy! Come and play!" But no one else pays us any attention.

Today, our path takes us past women rocking babies and milking goats. We see men working at a more leisurely pace than on our first onyx-stones journey. Some simply sit in circles and share news and wisdom while children race about them playing games and squealing with laughter.

William says, "It's nice to see the camp so relaxed. The rush to complete the Tabernacle is over, the cloud has settled, and there is time now for normal activities and family."

I note that the leisurely atmosphere is the same no matter which tribe we pass through. We are the only ones driven by a sense of urgency.

I try not to resent our stop for lunch at midday. I know that although William seems to never tire, Cricket and Marlene Grace have to rest. Even Hero takes a little nap in our shade.

William informs me that we are in the midst of the tribe of Reuben. "We've covered a lot of territory, today," he says. I don't say it, but I wish we had been able to cover more.

I'm grateful when Cricket finally stands. "We should get moving again," she says. And she shoulders her bag and rallies the rest of us to follow her.

At day's end we eat supper somewhere within the tribe of Benjamin, and from there we watch the pillar of cloud burst into its flaming tower. As tired as I am, I resent that the day has ended and we have to sleep.

"I wonder what Mom and Dad are doing," I tell Cricket before we leave the fire. "I miss them. I wish I had told them what we are doing, but I know it would complicate things. We need to find Uncle Chad and get this over with."

"I know," Cricket sympathizes, and she adds, "And I can only imagine how much your Uncle Chad has missed you. He's been away for a long time."

Even Hero senses my mood. The bright-eyed terrier lifts my hand with his nose. *Pet me,* he is saying. *It will help.* And I do stroke his fur and I do feel a sense of comfort.

Then, just before we all get ready to go to bed, Cricket tells me, "Don't forget to pray, Alexander."

I know that she and Marlene Grace and William have been praying all along, and I'm grateful. But somehow, I have trouble forming the words that I think will make God hear me.

At last, William and I spread out our bedrolls next to the fire (we've left the tent for Cricket and Marlene Grace tonight). Because I can't sleep,

I wait until I hear William's light snore. Then I roll over to face the tower of fire, and I whisper, "God of the fire and God of the cloud, I do not doubt Your power and Your might. You must know that I fear You. And yet I feel that I have to lift up my request. I am here only because I need to find my uncle. I don't know why You have allowed such difficult things as his disappearance to happen, and I am trying to believe that You have power to fix it. My request must seem very small, which is how I feel in Your presence. But Cricket, Marlene Grace, and William believe that You care about everything. And because that may be true, and because I am, at this moment, the closest to You that I'll ever be, I ask for Your help to find Uncle Chad soon."

And then, because I am uncomfortable with addressing this all-powerful God, I decide that I need to thank Him for listening. Only then do I allow my weary eyes to close in sleep.

# Chapter 16

## Marlene Goes into Action

I awaken under the burden that this is our last search day before we have to leave again. I want to race through our meal and hurry through the crowds. Cricket and the others know how I feel, and we quickly eat and gather up our things.

But as we prepare to head out, Hero suddenly stiffens and growls. His ears perk to full alert, and Cricket touches my arm in concern. Then Hero runs, and Cricket cries, "Hurry! We have to follow him. Hero hears something important."

William immediately scoops dirt over our fire. In case it is Uncle Chad that Hero hears, I fly faster than the others through the zig-zag of campsites. The barking dog is barely in sight. Cricket is close behind, and William and Marlene Grace bring up the rear.

We catch up to Hero at the edge of a large gathering just as he dashes between the feet of those in the crowd and disappears. And now we can hear what he and the by-standers have heard.

A woman screams, "She's choking!" "Help us!" a man cries. And the woman pleads pitifully, "Oh God, please save her! My baby can't breathe!"

In a flash, Marlene Grace bulldozes past me with a speed and force that I haven't known she possessed.

"Make way!" William shouts behind her, and he clears the path for us to follow her.

"I can help!" Marlene Grace bellows. And the crowd gives way.

Cricket and I duck through the holes that William and Marlene Grace have made, and we burst suddenly out of the crush of people and into an open fire circle. There, a distraught mother rocks her child and keens her despair.

Marlene Grace marches to the woman and announces firmly, "If you let me have her, I think I can save her."

The surprised mother blinks at the large woman who has appeared out of the crowd. And in a kind of desperate awe, she timidly lifts her little girl's body. I watch, spellbound, as Marlene Grace expertly wipes the inside of the child's mouth, feels the little girl's pulse, and listens for her heartbeat. Then Marlene Grace turns the child so she is facing out, and with her thumbs, Marlene Grace presses sharply into the child's diaphragm, twice. On the second application of force, a piece of food flies from the little girl's throat and lands in the dust. Marlene Grace instantly kneels and applies mouth-to-mouth resuscitation.

At first it seems that Marlene Grace's efforts might be too late. But after a long minute, the child's color returns and her fingers move. Hero licks her tiny hands, and when the little girl gasps, Marlene Grace sets her up and pats her on the back. Marlene Grace encourages the child to take deep breaths. And when the little girl has recovered, she sees her mother and lifts her arms with a cry of "Mommy!" And the crowd cheers.

Word of the miracle flies beyond the mass of onlookers like ripples on a pond, and everyone begins to dance with joy.

Marlene Grace rises to her feet, and the little girl's father bows before her. "Thank you!" he cries. "Are you a prophetess?"

"No, no," Marlene Grace hurries to say. "Just someone who has seen this kind of thing before and knows what to do."

"God has surely sent you!" the mother insists. "You and your family must stay and eat with us. Even the little dog."

Marlene Grace consents to sit for a while, but she tells the mother that we've already eaten and we can't stay long. "We're on a search," Marlene

Grace explains. "We have lost someone in the journey and have not found him yet. So, we need to continue looking."

"Who have you lost? A child perhaps?"

"Not a child. An elder. An uncle. We call him *Uncle Chad*."

"And you have not seen him for a while?"

"No. We lost track of him and have been separated for a very long time. And there are so many people."

The father now stands, and with determination in his voice, he says, "You must not worry anymore. My family—my brothers and I—will help you search. We will go to the leaders of each tribe. We will find him! You have saved my child, and we can do nothing less for you."

With a new spark of hope, I am expecting that the man and a couple of his brothers will guide us to the various tribal leaders, but I am wrong. The man calls out to the whole crowd that a man named *Uncle Chad* needs to be brought here to find his family. We are to remain here and wait.

Before the father leaves us, William hurries to explain that Uncle Chad will recognize the name of *Alexander*. "Uncle Chad will come with you if he hears Alexander's name."

And so, the crowd passes along the message, and soon everyone is bent on the mission. The only people remaining with us are a few women and children and the restored child and her mother. We are told again to wait; Uncle Chad will be brought to us.

Cricket makes Hero stay, and she and Hero sit next to me while we wait.

———◆———

It is agonizing to sit, but my heart beats with hope. Perhaps Uncle Chad will be here soon. Cricket sits with me, and I know she understands my flip-flopping emotions.

Hero has left my lap to wriggle and play with the recovered little girl, who laughs and chases after the terrier as if nothing has happened to her. And her mother wipes endless tears of joy.

A relative of the girl's parents brings goat cheese and precious honey for us and insists that we eat some. Another woman brings a beautifully embroidered vest for Marlene Grace that just barely fits around her ample form. Other gifts appear: a colored sash, an embroidered scarf, a brass mirror, a pouch of herbs, gold earrings, and an alabaster-carved bottle that holds a powerful perfume.

"I hope they find Uncle Chad soon," Marlene Grace whispers to William, "or we'll need a pack animal to carry all of my gifts!"

No sooner has she said this than someone comes leading a donkey strapped with two empty baskets. "This animal can carry your tent and goods," the owner says. "He is yours now!"

My eyes grow large. I whisper to Cricket, "How are we going to transport a donkey home?"

And the gifts keep coming. Carved items and jewelry. A flask of oil and a gold cup.

When I see the cup, I am certain that Lawrence Traeger's pirate treasure has come from these people. He must have snatched it and brought it back with him. I find it ironic that while he was intent on stealing his booty, we are being showered with the same treasures as gifts. And I wonder how we will explain our gifts if we take them home. Unlike Lawrence, we can't say we discovered them in our backyard.

The morning passes slowly. When noon finally comes, we consume our midday manna, along with cheese and goat's milk provided by our hosts. And I'm embarrassed when parents instruct their children to fan us with their scarves in the heat. I feel like royalty—like a royal prince sitting under palms waved by a host of servants. But I don't want to be sitting. I don't want to be pampered. I want to be with those who are searching. Sitting here is a waste of our onyx-stones time.

The afternoon sun moves with deliberate slowness and relentlessly counts off our precious hours. I heave a frustrated sigh and am starting to wonder how we will extricate ourselves to make our trip home when I hear shouting. Word is passing through the crowd that, "Uncle Chad has been found!"

Cricket and I scramble to our feet, eager to see if it is true. I can't wait to catch sight of Uncle Chad's face.

First, however, partiers with tambourines, flutes, and singing pass us in waves. It seems that Uncle Chad is being ushered to us by a parade. Even the children abandon their fanning posts to race into the celebration.

At one point, the partying crowd thins, and I hold my breath to see four men in their midst riding on donkeys. But celebrants press forward again on every side and I can no longer see the riders. I wonder if one of them is Uncle Chad.

"He is here!" the people chant. "He is here! Uncle Chad is here for his Alexander!"

When I finally get a clear look at the mounted men, I peer anxiously into their deeply tanned and bearded faces. I wish they were closer so I could be sure. And then I see him!

Actually, he sees me first, and the grin on his face is so wide that I cannot mistake him despite the unfamiliar facial hair, the impressive turban, and the real robes (not Christmas pageant costumes).

"Here is your Alexander!" the people shout now. "The boy you had lost!"

I grin back at the man who is found, and I run. Uncle Chad slides from his donkey and catches me up in his arms. With tears and sobs, we cling to one another, and the people around us celebrate our reunion with more dancing and louder singing. Everyone pats our backs repeatedly and crushes us with hugs and kisses. I fear we will be suffocated. And Cricket picks up Hero so he won't be stepped on. The little dog, in his own celebration, lavishes his mistress with kisses.

Between my sobs, I cry over and over, "It's you! It's really you!"

And over the noise of the celebration, the only words I hear from Uncle Chad are, "How did you ever...?"

# Chapter 17

## Supper's Getting Cold

Uncle Chad and I have virtually no time to talk because of the singing and dancing that accompanies our reunion. And the celebration is long. It is a relief when the crowd finally says goodbye and people begin to make their way back to their own campfires.

It is then that Uncle Chad excitedly asks how we came to be here. "Did Lawrence bring you?"

"No," I say with a decided shake of my head, and Uncle Chad sighs.

"I doubted it," he says. "As time passed, I gave up on the possibility that Lawrence would return for me."

But then Uncle Chad asks, "So how did you come? Are you stuck here, too?"

The wistfulness in his voice makes me sorry that we haven't explained sooner. As happy as he is to see us, it is clear that he also fears we have been tricked and are now trapped with him.

I want to set his mind at ease, but before I can explain, I am startled by a faint but unmistakable *ching!* from within my shoulder bag.

"Oh, no!" I murmur in alarm. "It can't be!"

"It can't be!" I repeat, as I feverishly dig through the contents of my bag. When my fingers finally curl around the familiar rectangular form and pull it out, Cricket and Marlene Grace gasp. I hurry to grab the edge of my Christmas pageant robe and drape it over my head so I can read the screen of my cell phone without being seen.

*Where are you?* the message on the phone says. *Supper's getting cold.*

"It's my mom," I whisper. "What do I tell her? We aren't going to be able to leave here for a while."

Marlene Grace has recovered from the shock of seeing the cell phone, and she calmly suggests, "Tell her we're sorry but we were delayed in returning from our trip, and tell her we promise to get you home within a couple of hours. Also tell her that we'll make sure you get supper."

I key in the message, and Mom replies, *I wish you would have told me sooner, son. But it is good to know you are okay. Be safe and we'll see you soon. Say hi to Cricket and her family. Love you!*

I type in my *Love You* reply and quickly stash the phone back into my bag.

"Can you believe that phone worked?" Cricket cries. William, Marlene Grace, and Uncle Chad are incredulous, too.

I hang my head. "I can't believe I forgot to leave it behind."

But then I say, "It has come in handy, though. We are going to be here for a while."

And then I giggle. "But what a reason to be late for supper! I can't wait to tell Mom and Dad our story and let them see Uncle Chad."

Uncle Chad's eyes fill with tears. "Is my brother doing well?" he asks, and I assure him that Dad is fine and will be excited to see him.

"So, we are going home?" Uncle Chad asks, just to be sure.

"Yes, we're going home," I tell him.

With eyes still glistening, Uncle Chad says, "I can't believe it, after all this time. I had resigned myself to living here among the Israelites the rest of my days. And I missed all of you terribly! What I missed most was not being able to say goodbye and explain what was happening."

"But," I say, "you did leave clues."

"You found the journal!"

"Yes. And I found Cricket and Marlene Grace and William."

I introduce my friends, and I explain how Cricket has an onyx-stone necklace of her own. Cricket lifts her stone from under the collar of her robe, and Uncle Chad shakes his head in wonder.

"I never knew there were more necklaces!" he exclaims. "It's all so new to me and so unbelievable."

"It was Cricket's idea to come here and search for you," I say. "And this is our second trip; there are so many more Israelites than we anticipated. We searched and searched. And if something unusual hadn't happened this morning, we might still be looking for you."

"But," Cricket breaks in, "we will have to tell you that story, later. It is very important for us to make our way to the edge of the camp so we can escape without creating a furor."

"And we have so much stuff to carry with us!" William exclaims, pointing to all of the gifts the Israelites have given us, including the donkey that is befriending Uncle Chad's donkey.

Marlene Grace organizes our packing, and we load everything onto our new four-legged burden bearers. We thank the healed little girl's family and wave goodbye, giving the impression that we are going back to Uncle Chad's campsite, even though it is dark.

As we make our way through the retiring compound, I match my step to Uncle Chad's, and person after person calls out their thanks to Marlene Grace for saving the child.

Little by little we wind our way to the outskirts of the settlement, and we find a sufficient outcropping of rock to hide our disappearance.

"But what do we do with all of this stuff?" William asks. "We can't take this back with us. How will we explain it?"

"And we have to leave the donkeys behind," Marlene Grace insists firmly. "I won't have them landing in my living room."

We laugh. But she's right.

Uncle Chad comes up with the solution. "We need to leave the treasures behind," he says. "We should bury everything right here, at the base of this rock. It will be easy to dig because sand has drifted here.

"And," says Uncle Chad, "pull out your phone again, Alexander."

He orders me to send a message to Cricket's cell phone back home. "Just say that we're on our way, or some such thing. The message doesn't really matter."

I do as he says, but because Cricket is here, I wonder why.

Then Uncle Chad recruits William and me to dig in the sand beside the rock. Hero helps. Although the sand is loose and easy to scoop, it takes several minutes before we have a good-sized hole. Now, Marlene Grace and Cricket help us roll our pile of treasures into the cavity.

"Keep nothing," Uncle Chad advises. "Put all of the treasure in there."

We do as he says, and we smooth the sand back over everything.

"What about the donkeys?" I ask.

"Turn them loose. They'll go back to the herd; they'll be all right," says Uncle Chad.

Cricket helps Hero crawl into her shoulder satchel, and with the stars shining overhead, we look back at the camp. The pillar of fire burns above the Holy of Holies of the Tabernacle, and all across the desert, campfires burn low. The only sounds are the occasional moos and bleats of contented beasts. The Israelite company is asleep.

In the quiet, and nearly invisible in the dark, we stand in a circle and hold hands as William prays: "Heavenly Father, thank you for helping us find Alexander's uncle. Thank you that You have preserved Dr. Tennyson among the Israelites. Go with us now, as we journey home. And help us to resume those things that You have for us there. We lift our praise to You for your might and love and faithfulness. In Jesus' Name, Amen."

In the smallest of whispers, I add my own thank you to the God who has heard my prayers: "Thank you that Uncle Chad is coming home!"

Cricket smiles at my happiness and grips my hand. She offers her other hand to Uncle Chad. William slips his fingers into Marlene Grace's, gives her a kiss, and pulls her close. Marlene Grace returns his kiss just before she clicks her stone against Cricket's. And when she does, we join the stars in the sky.

# Chapter 18

## At Last

I don't take my eyes off Uncle Chad as we soar through the universe. Flying home with him is the fulfillment of everything I have longed for, for so long.

The minute our feet sink into the carpet of Cricket's living room, I drop to my knees and sob. Uncle Chad is finally here! My nightmare is over, and he is safe.

Hero has wriggled out of Cricket's satchel, and he licks my tears. Marlene Grace and William lift me up so Uncle Chad can grip me in his arms.

"My dear boy!" Uncle Chad cries into my shoulder. "I never thought I would be home. And I never thought I would see you and your parents again. It's like waking up at the end of a long, convoluted dream."

"But it's real," I say. "You really are home."

And Uncle Chad weeps.

It is several minutes before Uncle Chad and I can collect ourselves and begin to deal with our new reality. When his eyes clear, Uncle Chad notices Cricket in her wheelchair.

"My dear!" he cries, "I had no idea!"

Cricket smiles. "It's okay. You couldn't have known."

"You're a very brave girl," Uncle Chad declares.

"And this whole rescue plan was Cricket's idea," I tell him.

Like a nobleman to a princess, Uncle Chad lifts Cricket's listless hand and places a kiss on her finger tips. "I can't thank you enough, young lady," he says. "You must tell me the whole story, soon."

"But not right now," Marlene Grace interrupts gently. "We're back in real time, now, and Alexander has to go home. The question is, are you going to go to Alexander's place tonight?"

Uncle Chad's eyes twinkle. "Of course, I'm going with Alexander. I can't wait to see the expression on my brother's face!"

"Dad won't believe his eyes," I predict. "And we'll probably be up all night talking about everything that has happened."

"But what has happened?" Uncle Chad asks. "I'm still unclear about so much of the story."

Cricket answers, "That's understandable. We have a lot to tell you, and you have a lot to tell us."

"And," she says, "Alexander's parents know nothing at all! They have had no idea of where you were or of our rescue mission. This is all going to be a shock to them, I'm afraid."

"Cricket's right, of course," I say. "Everything that we did happened so fast and with so much guesswork, that my parents were left out of it. I didn't think they would believe it, so I was afraid to share. After all, I barely believed the whole idea of time-transport, myself, at first. It's going to be hard to explain it all to them, I'm afraid. They're going to think we're all crazy!"

Uncle Chad nods. "You're probably right. I know my brother. And Gwen will never believe all of this."

Marlene Grace has been listening, but now she offers a suggestion. "What would you think," she says, "if we all got together and told the story, once, for everyone to hear—from start to finish? We could perhaps meet for supper tomorrow. I'd be happy to have everyone here, if you like."

"That's a great idea," says Uncle Chad. "That way, we won't have to repeat ourselves over and over. And everyone will know what everyone else has done. I say, let's do it!"

"I agree!" I say. "I'm sure my parents will come. They need to hear everything from the very beginning to the very end."

"Great," says Marlene Grace. "I'll get things together. Let's plan for six-o'clock."

"Okay," I say.

Now William offers, "I'll drive Alexander and Dr. Tennyson to Alexander's house. I imagine that you'll spend the night there, Dr. Tennyson. And tomorrow, your brother can take you to check out your house."

"What? My house? Do you mean that my house has not been sold?" Uncle Chad asks in surprise.

"Oh, no," I tell him. "Dad has refused to believe you wouldn't return, and he's kept up the payments and your lawn care. Everything inside is just as you left it. Except..."

I explain that Cricket and I have moved the treasure from under the bathroom window, and Uncle Chad guffaws.

"You are going to have to tell me that story, too," he cries. "I can only imagine!"

Marlene Grace thrusts my jeans and T-shirt into my hands and points me to the bathroom. "You need to get changed, child," she directs, and I text my mom that I'm on my way.

"We'll put your bike in my trunk," says William. "I'll drive you and your uncle home."

# Chapter 19

## The Bearded Man

When I let myself in the front door, I call for Mom and Dad. They are surprised to see William, and are even more surprised to see a bearded man standing with us in a strange robe and sandals.

"Welcome," my dad starts to say before he looks fully into the stranger's face and realizes it is Uncle Chad. Dad stiffens in shock, and then pulls his brother to him.

"How...? Where...?" he cries. "Thank God, you're back!"

My mother stands stupefied and watches the men hug. Then she understands the truth and her hands fly to her face.

"I can't believe it!" she exclaims. "After all this time!"

"I never gave up hope," Dad declares. "And I've kept your house for you."

"Thank you, Jonathan. I'm sorry to have worried you."

"But where have you been?" Mom chides.

"I've been in the Middle East. Unexpectedly transported. And then delayed, as you know."

"But couldn't you have called or written so we wouldn't worry?" Mom insists.

"Not really," says Uncle Chad. "It's hard to explain, but I was totally out of communication."

"You look like you've been living in a desert," Mom observes now.

"That's right, I have."

"On an archaeological dig or something?" Dad asks.

"Kind of like that, I guess. Let's just say that I learned a lot about ancient Egyptians and Israelites while I was away."

Then Uncle Chad adds, "And I didn't have any way to get back home."

Now Uncle Chad changes the subject. "But Jonathan, you look like you've done well while I've been gone. And Alexander has grown!"

Dad gives a brief overview of how his work has expanded and how much I've missed my after-school visits to Uncle Chad's workshop to help arrange scientific experiments.

"That boy rode his bicycle past your house every day while you were gone," Dad says, and Uncle Chad looks surprised.

"We'll have to start our experiments, again," Uncle Chad says to me with a wink.

"You aren't planning to go home tonight, are you?" Dad says. "There's no food at your place. You should stay here and we'll start you off with a good breakfast in the morning. Then we can buy groceries and take you home. I'll take the day off work. Insurance can wait."

"That will be wonderful," says Uncle Chad, "and I need a shower and a change of clothes."

"No problem," says Dad. "But first, let's see what Gwen can whip up for us in the kitchen. We can munch on something while we talk. Can you stay also, William? You're welcome, of course."

William has been standing in the background, watching us. But now he steps forward.

"Sorry," he says. "This evening is your time with your brother. I need to get back home."

"Of course," Dad says. "I understand."

"But," says William, "I've been instructed by my wife to invite all of you to dinner tomorrow night so we can share the story of Dr. Tennyson's return—and so he won't have to keep repeating it."

Dad starts to say, "Wonderful, what time...?" But Mom interrupts.

She suggests, instead, that we all meet at our house. "We'd love to have everyone here," she insists. "Do you think your wife will mind?"

"I'm sure it will be okay," says William. "The idea is to have us all get together. Doing it at your house will be fine. I'm sure that Marlene Grace will be in touch to see if there is something that she can bring for the meal."

"Wonderful," Mom says. "Is six o'clock, okay?"

"Perfect. I'll tell Marlene Grace and Cricket."

William turns to leave and Dad shakes his hand, and for a brief moment I see that Dad is curious about how William has been involved in Uncle Chad's return. But he says nothing. Instead, Dad repeats, "I look forward to hearing the whole story tomorrow. We'll expect you at six."

After William departs, Mom drags us to the kitchen and asks if we're hungry for a sandwich or a piece of cake.

"Both!" says Uncle Chad. "Whatever you've got."

Mom pulls out plates and food and listens to some of the story that Uncle Chad briefly shares. I notice that he skillfully skirts the questions that require a deeper understanding and that will take some explaining beyond the natural course of things. There will be time enough tomorrow to share the full truth and to explain the unexplainable.

———◆———

Going to school has never been so hard. I do not want to leave Uncle Chad, but I have to. After breakfast I give him and my parents a hug, and I trudge reluctantly to my bicycle.

At school, I am too euphoric to concentrate on math and history. And I smile so often that my science teacher comments on my good mood.

"It's nice to see the frown gone from your face, Alexander," Mr. Green says, and my grin deepens.

"My uncle has returned," I tell him. "My uncle who was gone for two years."

"Really!" Mr. Green exclaims. "How wonderful. I recall reading about his disappearance not long after it happened. Where has he been all of this time?"

"The Middle East," I say. "He's been living with some people in the desert."

Mr. Green makes no attempt to hide his surprise. "The Middle East! Whatever for?"

"I'm sure he'll write about all the things he's learned, soon," I say.

"That will be interesting. I look forward to reading about it when he does," Mr. Green replies. And before he moves on with the lesson, Mr. Green says, "You certainly have an interesting family, Alexander!"

———•———

By the time school lets out and I get home, Uncle Chad has shaved and is wearing his own clothes and glasses. He looks once again like the uncle I knew before his disappearance.

He and Dad have stocked his house with food and have verified with the police and the bank that Uncle Chad is back. At the bank, he signed to unfreeze his funds.

Uncle Chad tells Mom and me how the police peppered him with questions. "The detectives acted as if I am not me. But they finally marked my missing person's file as resolved," he chuckles. "After all, I'm right here."

Dad adds that Detective Gorman never did get a satisfactory answer as to why Uncle Chad had gone to Egypt in the first place without telling anyone—and without his glasses. And Uncle Chad was pretty vague about how he returned to the U.S. "I thought Gorman was going to put Chad in jail just because he didn't tell his plans to anybody ahead of time. But Gorman closed the file, anyway."

"The detective asked three times if I worked for the CIA, and I didn't lie," says Uncle Chad, "but I didn't dissuade him of the idea, either." Dad looks at his brother as if he believes he might truly be in the secret service.

"Now, Jonathan," Uncle Chad replies to Dad's raised eyebrow. But he says nothing more.

Then Uncle Chad reports, "For lunch, I made Jonathan drive me through McDonald's and I ordered a couple of Big Macs, two large fries, and two Cokes." With a wink to me, Uncle Chad says, "Manna can get really monotonous."

Mom fusses in concern that Uncle Chad has swathed himself in sweaters and two pairs of socks against the November cold. But I am not surprised. After so much time in the desert, his body is not prepared for the oncoming winter.

Dad points out that Uncle Chad's new shoes are in a larger size, too.

"It's all of that walking in sandals," Uncle Chad tells him. "My feet have spread out."

"Wasn't it hard to walk with sandals in all of that sand?" Mom asks.

"Ah," says Uncle Chad. "You hold a common misperception of the desert. You see, not all deserts are vast dunes of sand like you see in certain movies. Most deserts are sun-dried, hard-packed earth with a thin surface of sand and grit. There are certainly some sand-dunes in areas where I traveled, but most of the land is hard-surfaced and allows for a bit of desert plant life—scrub trees, wisps of desert grass, and the like. It might also surprise you to know that not all desert temperatures are in the nineties around the clock. At night, the temperature can get as low as twenty-five degrees."

"Really!" Mom exclaims. "I had no idea. You'll have to tell us all about what you've seen. I hope you took lots of photos."

My head drops to hide my amusement, and Uncle Chad swallows a grin. It is definitely going to be an interesting evening! I can hardly wait for Cricket and the Foxes to get here.

<hr />

After feasting on Mom's pot roast and mashed potatoes, the seven of us move to the living room for the *Uncle Chad story hour*. Even Hero seems ready to hear from his spot on Cricket's lap.

When we grow quiet, Uncle Chad looks around the room. Then he declares, "It is a relief to be back. I wasn't sure I would ever see my family again. And yet, after two long years, here I am."

He smiles. "There is much to tell you. And I know that my story is going to be difficult for some of you to grasp. But you need to know what has happened, and I assure you that every word is true."

Uncle Chad now holds up his journal, and Mom and Dad look at it with curiosity. Uncle Chad explains, "I am going to start by reading to you from this journal. It gives the background you need in order for the rest of my story to make sense. Only Alexander and Cricket know what is in these pages. And I am thankful that these children did not treat my words lightly. If they had, I would not be here today."

Mom and Dad give Cricket and me a half-smile and act as if Uncle Chad is probably exaggerating and giving us special praise and credit for some reason. With a little shrug, I smile back.

Now Uncle Chad prefaces his reading with, "It all began on June 22, 2015 with a break-in."

"A break-in?" Dad stops adjusting the throw pillow on the sofa. "Is that what this is all about?"

Uncle Chad holds up his hand. "Don't rush me, Jonathan. You'll understand when you hear the story."

Uncle Chad proceeds to read his account of the breakfast visits by Josh and about his first onyx-stones flight. Dad impatiently frowns and demands, "What is this? This is preposterous."

Uncle Chad acknowledges Dad's comments and says, "It sounds crazy, I know, but bear with me. There's a lot more, so fasten your seatbelt."

Mom and Dad roll their eyes as Uncle Chad describes making bricks with the Israelite slaves, tells of the unexpected darkness, and then relates the awful story of the first-born deaths. But they begin to pay more attention when he introduces Lawrence Traeger into the story and reports on Lawrence's theft of the treasure from the attic.

Dad's eyes narrow when Uncle Chad steals the treasure back from Lawrence's room and hides it in the bushes. And Mom gasps in dismay when Uncle Chad defends himself during the ensuing confrontation.

"You threatened Lawrence with a meat cleaver?" she cries.

"To protect myself," Uncle Chad admits. And he reads the final journal entry: *"As I have written before, I am hiding this journal so that Lawrence cannot find it."*

When he stops reading, Mom asks, "That's it? That's the end?"

"That's where the journal ends, Gwen. But it's not the end of the story," says Uncle Chad. "There are two more years to cover." Uncle Chad sits back.

"As I feared," he continues, "Lawrence came back and clicked the onyx stones together while I slept. I awakened in mid-transport to find myself being swept into the past. Unfortunately for Lawrence, we landed in broad daylight in the middle of the ancient Israelites, I in my pajamas and Lawrence in his modern street clothes.

"Needless to say, we caused quite a stir. Lawrence panicked and tore my necklace from my neck and ran screaming through a bunch of startled women. Those who pursued him reported that he dashed into a tent and disappeared. No one ever saw him again. I knew he had returned to the present and left me stranded."

Dad starts to interrupt, but Uncle Chad pushes on with his account.

Uncle Chad says, "I don't know what would have happened to me if Asher hadn't recognized me as the man who spent the Passover in his home. Asher assumed that Lawrence had robbed me, and he gave me clothes and took me in. And I lived with his family until my rescuers brought me home."

When Uncle Chad pauses, Dad shakes his head. "Do you really expect us to believe this?" he protests.

And Mom says, "Why don't you just tell us what really happened."

I know that Mom and Dad are never going to accept the story, and so, I interrupt. "Mom. Dad," I say. "There's something you need to see. Can everyone come with me for a minute?"

Uncle Chad is the first to stand, and Hero and I lead the group from the living room to the kitchen and out the door into the garage.

William helps Cricket down the one step from the kitchen. When everyone is gathered, I rummage in the near-dark under the bare overhead bulb. I pull out and set aside my experimental water-powered engines and my dust collection: the things Mom made me clear out of my bedroom. And from behind those boxes, I drag out a heavy leather bag that Hero recognizes with a wag of his tail.

Instantly Uncle Chad exclaims, "That's my treasure bag!" He hurries forward to help me pull it into the light. In the center of the garage, he opens the bag and its contents spill onto the floor.

Mom gasps. "Is that real gold? Are those real jewels?"

Dad asks, "How did you get this stuff, Alexander?"

"From the bushes at Uncle Chad's house," I say.

Dad shakes his head and starts to ask more questions, but Marlene Grace breaks in. "Excuse me," she says. "But this is a whole new story—one that I think is going to take more time than we have left, this evening.

"I've learned a lot, tonight, that I didn't know, and I want to hear more. But this is a school night and it's getting late. We can't stay. We need to get Cricket home to bed, and I'm sure you want Alexander to get a good night's rest, too. So, why don't we plan to continue our story-telling tomorrow night? We'll fix supper at our house, and we can hear how Alexander got the treasure and became involved. We can save up our questions so everyone can hear the answers. What do you think?"

Mom and Dad are dying to hear my story, but they reluctantly agree.

I know they will press me for answers before I go to bed, and I hope I can stall them until we get together again. I will tell them that not even Uncle Chad knows what I am going to share. That may help them understand why I'm waiting.

"Is six o'clock all right?" Marlene Grace asks. Everyone agrees to the time.

Marlene Grace and William help Uncle Chad move his Egyptian gold to the trunk of their car, and Uncle Chad announces how nice it will be to wake up in his own bedroom in the morning.

With a wink to me, he adds, "And after breakfast, I'll need to re-hide my treasure!"

Mom and Dad wave a dazed goodbye, and our guests pull out of the driveway and are gone.

Mom and Dad are fairly quiet. I imagine they are still a little stunned by everything they've heard. And surprisingly, they don't press me for information.

I know they are curious and even concerned about what they don't know. And their hugs are warmer, and Mom's goodnight kiss is dearer than before tonight's initial revelations.

# Chapter 20

## Mom Has a Conniption

How I would love to ride my bicycle to Uncle Chad's after school, just like I used to. But, tonight, I can't. I need to go home so I can go with my family to Cricket's house for supper. I can hardly wait for Mom and Dad and Uncle Chad to hear my part of the story.

---

Uncle Chad and Hero meet us at Cricket's front door as if the house is theirs, and Dad and Uncle Chad clasp shoulders again, still caught in the wonder of being reunited. Uncle Chad grips me too and says, "My fine nephew, who saved my life!"

I don't look up to see Mom's and Dad's reaction to his comment. They don't yet know the part I played in Uncle Chad's rescue. But they are beginning to sense that it was more than just token involvement.

I see that tonight Marlene Grace wears her onyx-stone necklace, and Mom comments on how it matches the one around Cricket's neck. I doubt that Mom has made the connection between these necklaces and the ones Uncle Chad has told us about. But she'll understand the significance soon.

Dinner drags a little, but dessert flies by. And then we move to the living room. There, I find myself at the center of attention and with Marlene Grace announcing, "Tonight, Alexander will share how his uncle's bag of treasure came to be hidden in his family's garage. You can begin whenever you wish, Alexander."

"Yes, ma'am," I say. I sit a little straighter and take a deep breath before I say, "It all started with my rocketry program."

Mom raises her eyebrows, and I continue. "As you know, Mom and Dad, I finished assembling my solid-fuel rocket kit not long ago."

Uncle Chad shouts, "Bravo! Good to know, son!"

I grin at his pleasure in my accomplishment, and I go on. "As Uncle Chad knows, the next step in the program is to produce a written report that covers assigned subjects in a specific format—a format that is outlined in the official rocketry guidebook. For a long time after Uncle Chad's disappearance, I put off writing this report because that guidebook was in Uncle Chad's workshop. I'm ashamed to say that I couldn't bring myself to enter Uncle Chad's empty house to get it.

"But finally, I asked Cricket to go with me. I got the spare key from under the paving stone and went in the back door. My plan was to go straight to the workshop, get the book, and leave. But when I retrieved the rocketry book, I found another book packed inside the box with it. I recognized Uncle Chad's handwriting in what appeared to be a journal, and Cricket and I decided to go to her house to read it. Before we left Uncle Chad's workshop, I also tucked Uncle Chad's photo under my arm to take home."

While my listeners wait, I open my book bag and pull out Uncle Chad's photo. I set it on Marlene Grace's coffee table, and Uncle Chad grins when he sees it. Then I resume my story.

"You've already heard from Uncle Chad what he wrote in the journal. Like you, Dad, I questioned the fantastic parts that Cricket and I read.

But, little by little, I found that I believed the story—especially after we found the treasure in the bushes, exactly as Uncle Chad had described."

"And then," I say, "Cricket pointed out something that I had missed. She showed me that in his photo, Uncle Chad was wearing an onyx-stone necklace like the one mentioned in the journal."

"See the necklace?" I say, and I pass Uncle Chad's photo around the room.

When Mom sees the picture, she exclaims, "Why, it's the same necklace that Cricket and Marlene Grace are wearing."

"Yes, it is," I say. "All three necklaces are onyx-stone necklaces and all three have properties like those Uncle Chad described in his journal."

Mom shakes her head, and Dad frowns.

"And," I continue, "Cricket shared that she knew how the stones worked. Plus, she speculated that Lawrence might have used the stones to transport himself and Uncle Chad to ancient Egypt. And she suspected that Lawrence had come back alone and left Uncle Chad stranded."

"Smart girl!" says Uncle Chad. "That's exactly what happened."

"What an awful thing to imagine!" Mom murmurs.

I continue. "And Cricket suggested that we set up a plan to use her onyx stones to visit where Lawrence had left Uncle Chad."

Dad interrupts. "Are you going to tell us some more fantastic stories about time travel?"

Uncle Chad defends me. He says, "I thought the idea was fantastic, too, Jonathan, until it happened to me. And I'm a scientist!"

Dad sighs. "I don't get it, but I'll listen." He motions for me to go on.

"Well," I say, "Cricket told Marlene Grace and William about the plan, and they agreed to go on the adventure with us."

Silence.

Mom and Dad turn to stare at the Foxes, who politely smile back. Mom and Dad look again at each other and shake their heads. But they remain quiet while I continue my story.

"Cricket, the Foxes, and I collected supplies for our journey. And I got your permission, Mom and Dad, to spend the weekend with Cricket's family. Then, Cricket, the Foxes, and I changed into robes and sandals, clicked the necklace stones together, and went to the desert among the ancient Israelites."

At this, my mother lets out a squeak. "So, the weekends you spent with the Foxes were spent on preposterous journeys to a desert in the past?"

"Yes, Mom," I say. "I'm sorry I didn't tell you and Dad the whole truth. But I wasn't sure myself that it would happen."

Dad's lips are set in a firm line, but he puts his arm around Mom and says quietly, "It's a bit much to believe. But let's listen."

By now, Uncle Chad is sitting forward in his chair, and he encourages me to continue. "You must remember that I've not heard this part of the story. Do go on, Alexander," he encourages.

And so, I continue. "When the four of us—and Hero—arrived in the Israelite camp, we searched and searched among as many people as we could, but we couldn't find you, Uncle Chad. Our weekend ended, and we had to come back. We went again on the next weekend, and on the last morning of that trip, Hero led us to a little girl choking on some food. Marlene Grace rushed in and saved her."

"Yes," says Cricket. "Marlene Grace did the Heimlich Maneuver and mouth-to-mouth resuscitation."

"Really!" exclaims Uncle Chad. "I'll bet that brought you some attention!"

Marlene Grace smiles and explains, "I'm a nurse by profession. I just did what any nurse would do."

"Yes, but it would seem like a miracle to that girl's family and friends," Uncle Chad says.

"You're right," says William. "It did seem like a miracle to them, And all of the Israelites who saw Marlene Grace save the child's life started giving us all kinds of gifts."

I couldn't resist interrupting, "You should have seen the stuff they gave us! It was like Uncle Chad's treasure!"

"But the important thing," William says, "is that when the people heard that we were searching for someone who was missing, they wanted to help us. They scattered and spread the word that we were looking for Alexander's Uncle Chad. And just before we had to come back home, they found him! And they brought Uncle Chad to us on a donkey!"

Dad laughs. "That I would like to have seen!"

"I'm sure I was a sight," Uncle Chad chortles.

"And all of this," says Dad, "is why you were late getting home on Sunday night?"

"Yes, Dad," I tell him.

Suddenly, Dad looks from me to his long-lost brother. I see that he realizes we've been telling him the real story. I watch the conflict play over his face, and then I hear Dad's broken cry, "I don't understand it all, but I'm glad you're back, Chad."

Mom still isn't sure. She grips Dad's hand tightly and says, "It all sounds frightening! If I had known, I never would have let Alexander go!"

Marlene Grace takes Mom's other hand in hers and says, "You would have been proud of your son."

Cricket echoes her sentiment. "Alexander was very brave and determined."

"And we're back, aren't we?" Uncle Chad celebrates. "It's a miracle, but I'm here!"

And Uncle Chad's presence is the one fact that no one can decry.

"Yes! You are finally home!" Dad exclaims. "As hard as the story is to believe, we can't deny that you have returned."

Now, Uncle Chad quiets us. "And there's more to tell," he says. "Although it might seem that this is the end of the story, it is far from the end. But, because there's so much more that you all need to hear, and because we need more time, I invite you to come to my house tomorrow night for supper."

Dad immediately says, "We'll be there."

"And," Uncle Chad tells Mom, "you don't need to bring anything, Gwen. I have it all taken care of."

Although I know that Mom and Dad are bursting with questions after tonight's revelations, they manage to keep them under control for a little bit longer. I do overhear Marlene Grace whisper to Mom, "Call me tomorrow, Gwen, if you want, and we can talk."

I smile. If anyone can convince Mom (and Dad) about the truth of what we're sharing, it will be Marlene Grace.

———◆◆———

At home, Mom pulls me into an extra-long hug. I'm almost too tall for her to gather into her arms like she used to when I was a kid, but I know that tonight she needs to mother me, and I let her.

"It scares me to imagine that you were so far away and I didn't even know it!" she chides.

"I'm sorry, Mom." Then, I apologize to her and Dad for not telling them the truth about the past two weekends.

Dad shrugs it off with, "It's pretty far-fetched, but look at how it all turned out. Sounds like quite an adventure!"

Mom gives Dad an exasperated look. "It's foolhardiness," she says. "If there's a grain of truth in all of it, just think of what could have happened."

To me, she says, "What if you hadn't come back? What if you had become stranded in the same way Chad had? What then? How would we have ever known what happened to you?"

Now, I confess to her that, before each trip, I left Uncle Chad's journal under my pillow, along with a note explaining what I was trying to do with Cricket and the Foxes. "I knew it wouldn't make complete sense to you and Dad," I say, "but I hoped it would help if something did happen and I couldn't get back."

I pull out the note and hand it to Mom.

"Oh, Alexander!" she cries, and she squeezes me so hard I have to gasp for air.

# Chapter 21

## Pizza at Uncle Chad's

I've never eaten a meal in Uncle Chad's dining room, but tonight he has spread the table with a white cloth and put out dishes and silverware just like Mom does. There are ice cubes in the glasses and a large homemade salad sitting in the center of the table. Soft drinks and several delivery pizzas wait on the sideboard. Marlene Grace and Mom comment on the arrangements, and Uncle Chad whispers in my ear, "Bet you didn't think I could impress your mother, did you?"

After dinner, Uncle Chad urges us to move into the living room. And there I am surprised again. I have never seen anyone sit in Uncle Chad's stuffed chairs or on his sofa. But tonight, the floor lamps are lit and there's a bouquet of fresh flowers on the coffee table. And Uncle Chad says, "Now we can continue the story we had to cut short last night."

He puts his hands on his knees and says, "Tonight, I'd like to talk about Lawrence.

"Jonathan graciously texted me this morning with the link to the *USA Today* article on Lawrence's supposed pirate treasure discovery, and I found the article to be very interesting. I wonder, however, is there anyone here who believes that Lawrence found that treasure in his back yard?"

"I don't," says Marlene Grace. "Nor I," says William. And I'm surprised when Dad says, "I did until the other night." Mom still looks unsure.

"But where did Lawrence get his treasure?" I ask. "At one time I believed that it was your bag of gold, but your treasure was still in the bushes at your house. So, where did Lawrence get his treasure?"

Uncle Chad sits back. "I believe," he says, "that when Lawrence tore away my necklace and ducked into that empty tent, he stumbled upon the bag of treasure. There were many such bags in the tents of the Israelites. Then he clicked the stones and returned home with it."

"That scoundrel!" Dad growls, and I'm starting to think that Dad is finally believing our story. I'm sure of it when Dad says, "And what you probably haven't heard is that after Lawrence abandoned you, he took your car and was gone for a couple of days. When he returned, he said he didn't know that you were missing. And then he had the gall to stay with us while the police finished up the forensic work at your place."

Mom frowns. "I still have a hard time believing that that nice young man has done everything you say he has. He was so pleasant and polite when he was in our home."

"Why wouldn't he be pleasant?" Dad exclaims. "He'd just gotten away with a theft that would set him up for the rest of his life!"

Mom insists, "Even so, I would think his conscience about Chad would be eating him up. How can anybody do such an awful thing and not feel guilty?"

"But he's paid a big price for it," Cricket interjects.

"Yes, he has!" I say.

Mom and Dad look confused, and Cricket explains, "Lawrence burned his hand so badly that he may never be able to use it."

"Wait," Mom says. "Are you saying that his burn wasn't from a grease fire? That's what he told us."

"Actually, Mom, there's a better explanation," I answer. "We think

Lawrence burned his hand when he stole Uncle Chad's necklace and left him behind."

When Mom and Dad give me a blank look, I say, "It's like this: the necklace burned him."

Dad raises an eyebrow and Mom looks at me, still without understanding.

Marlene Grace comes to the rescue. "It will be easier to show them," she suggests. And I remember Cricket's demonstration.

"Of course," I say. "Mom, could you remove Cricket's necklace and set it on the coffee table?"

"Of course, dear," Mom says, and she reaches to pull the necklace over Cricket's head. But immediately Mom draws her hand away. "I can't touch it!" she cries. "It's red hot!" Then she jumps up and starts to run to the kitchen. "We have to hurry to get some ice! Cricket's neck is being scorched!"

Marlene Grace hurries after Mom and brings her back. "No, Gwen," she says. "Cricket's all right."

"But...!" Mom sputters. Dad runs, now, to remove Cricket's necklace. But he, too, pulls his hand back. He even tries to force his hand to touch the necklace through the pain, but William stops him.

"It's okay, Mr. Tennyson!" William shouts at him. Startled at the yell, Dad jumps back.

"I'm not being burned," Cricket insists. "Honestly! I'm fine."

"But..." Dad objects.

"That's what we're trying to show you," William says. "The stone is hot to you *but not* to Cricket. It's only hot to people who want to remove it from her neck. See?"

William lifts Cricket's necklace to show that her neck is not being burned.

"How can you touch that thing?" Dad cries. "It's searing hot."

"Not for me," William says, "and not for Cricket."

"But..." Dad sputters. Dad reaches out, again. And again, he fails to touch Cricket's necklace.

Now Cricket turns to me. "Alexander, would you please adjust my necklace so that the stone hangs straight?"

I reach out my hand, and to my parents' astonishment, I am able to adjust Cricket's necklace without harm.

Mom reaches out again, but again she has to draw back her hand. "I don't understand," she says.

Now, Cricket explains. "The stone didn't harm Alexander because he wasn't trying to remove the necklace. Alexander only meant to adjust it. If he had meant to lift the necklace over my head and take it off, he would have found the stone hot to handle, just as you have."

I tell Mom, now, "Try to touch it again, Mom. But first erase the thought that you are going to remove the necklace from Cricket's neck. Instead, tell yourself that you are simply going to reach over and adjust its position, like I did."

Mom is afraid to try, but Dad reaches out. And this time, he is able to slip the stone slightly to one side and then return it to its proper place. "It's cool to the touch!" he exclaims in astonishment. "It isn't hot at all."

"But," Mom sputters. And then she too reaches out and slides the stone without harm.

Uncle Chad joins my mother in her wonder. "I never knew this!" he exclaims. "That does explain why Lawrence fled screaming with my necklace."

"Yes," says Cricket. "Certain necklaces cannot be removed. Your necklace, Dr. Tennyson, and mine, are similar in this respect."

Uncle Chad pauses with his finger over his lips for a moment. Then he says, "You know, you must be right. Although the stone didn't burn me when I took off the necklace at my house, it wouldn't let me throw it away. It kept returning to me."

"But," puzzles Uncle Chad, "why doesn't the other necklace burn those who wear it and remove it?"

Cricket explains the difference between the master and secondary necklaces and Uncle Chad nods. "I understand," he says. "And that is why you suggest that Lawrence burned his hand when he tore my necklace from around my neck. He would have had no idea that he would be burned."

"Exactly," says Cricket. "And his hand has never been the same since."

"So," says Uncle Chad, "the boy has paid dearly for his gold. I'm sorry about that. Perhaps his stolen treasure can pay for some medical help."

Dad objects to Uncle Chad's compassion. "Lawrence deserves his punishment," Dad says firmly. "In fact, he should pay more for his crime! We should turn him in!"

Uncle Chad shakes his head. "No, Jonathan. No one in law enforcement will believe anything we say. The whole world will think we're crazy if we press charges on the only evidence we can give. I'm afraid that Lawrence will never go to trial on any of this."

"Then, it's too bad you can't transport Lawrence to ancient times and leave him there," Dad spits, and I'm surprised at the vehemence of his anger.

"That would only make us as bad as he is," Uncle Chad says.

Dad grimaces. But suddenly Dad sits forward. "I just realized something else," he says. "I just realized how the desert-sand footprints got on your bedroom rug!"

Everyone but Mom and I stare until Dad explains about the forensics report on the desert-sand footprints found on Uncle Chad's bedroom rug. "I see, now, that those footprints were there," says Dad, "because that's where Lawrence returned from his villainous trip without you!"

Like Dad, I picture Lawrence landing on Uncle Chad's bedroom rug with his sack of stolen gold, and I murmur, "And now Lawrence is back and he's rich."

"But you're also back, Chad," Dad points out. "Do you suppose that Lawrence will be worried to learn that you're here?"

Uncle Chad considers the thought for a moment and then says, "I imagine it will shake him up a little. He'll be wondering how I managed it. And he'll be wondering if I'm going to show up on his doorstep and bring his stolen world to ruin."

"So, are you going to ruin him?" I ask.

"No, Alexander, I'm not. I know that vengeance is not sweet. Vengeance just makes your insides ugly, and I choose not to live like that. I gave it up, long ago. And now, God has seen fit to restore me to my home and my family. It's only fitting that I leave Lawrence's punishment in God's hands."

"That sounds noble," Dad says. "But I don't like the idea of Lawrence getting away with his crimes."

"Me either," I mumble. I want Lawrence to pay. Uncle Chad isn't the only person he has hurt.

———•————

Uncle Chad now squelches further talk about Lawrence. "Enough," he says. "Let's move on. I have something else for us to discuss—something positive."

"You see," he announces, "I've decided to submit an article to *Armchair Science* on the subject of *The Treasures of the Exodus.*"

"And," he adds mysteriously before we can react, "I plan to center it around a particular archaeological find, if I can pull it off. It will be a feat extraordinaire, known only to all of you in this room."

With our curiosity piqued, we sit expectantly, awaiting an explanation. But, instead, Uncle Chad asks, "Alexander, do you have your cell phone with you, this evening?"

"Of course," I say.

"Great! Bring it to my workshop. Come on, everyone. Follow me."

Eager for clues to Uncle Chad's mystery, we obediently traipse down the hall after him. In his workshop, folding chairs have been set in a semicircle behind his desk. From our seats we can view his laptop screen.

"This computer may not be the latest in modern technology," Uncle Chad admits, "but it will do." He's right about its age. Over the last two years, a lot has changed in the design of personal computers. His laptop is an older model that still has ports and even a DVD slot, into which he feeds my phone chip.

"I've already downloaded Cricket's phone chip," Uncle Chad tells us. And we watch as he pulls codes from my phone chip and performs a series of complicated online tasks.

Within minutes, Uncle Chad breathes a triumphant, "Aha!"

"Now," he asks, "do you remember, Alexander, that before we left the rock in the desert to come home, you sent a text from your cell phone to Cricket's phone, back here?"

"Sure," I say. "Just like you told me to."

"Well," says Uncle Chad, "it worked as I hoped it would. See these numbers on my screen? These are GPS coordinates for that rock."

"What?" I exclaim.

"Yes," Uncle Chad says with a satisfied smile.

"That's amazing!" Cricket cries. "You're saying that you've managed to get a Global Positioning Satellite fix from a prior millennium when satellites hadn't even been imagined!"

"Yup," says Uncle Chad.

Now William exclaims, "I get it! You're saying that you've established the location of the rock where we buried the treasure!"

"Exactly," says Uncle Chad. "I'll admit that I wondered if it would work. And I've had to do some fancy figuring. But if Alexander hadn't accidentally brought his cell phone on that trip and received his mother's text about supper, it never would have occurred to me to try it."

"Theoretically," he says, "the phone transmission shouldn't have happened. But somehow, the stones' magic has a way of playing with time dimensions that I can only guess at. And it created the possibility for this."

Mom and Dad are confused. They look at us without understanding.

Uncle Chad points to a satellite image on his screen and says, "This is what that area of the desert looks like today."

"I see a lot of sand," Cricket says. "And our rock has grown smaller."

"It just looks smaller," says Uncle Chad, "because, over the years, sand has buried it."

"How deep do you suppose it's buried?" William asks.

"Well, the rock we left was probably twenty feet tall," estimates Uncle Chad. "And my guess from this satellite photo is that it is now about ten to twelve feet tall. It's hard to gauge without a point of reference, but I'll bet that I'm right."

"Do you suppose that what we buried under that rock is still there?" I ask.

"That, my dear boy, is the real question. We have no way of knowing if our things are still where we left them. But," he says with a twinkle in his eye, "I plan to organize an archaeological expedition to find out and hopefully dig it up!"

"You're really going back?" asks Cricket.

"Absolutely," says Uncle Chad. "Why not?"

"But how will you get to the site?" Marlene Grace asks.

"Oh, I plan to involve some experts," says Uncle Chad.

At last, Dad is catching on. "You're going to lead an expedition to dig up a treasure that you put there, thousands of years ago?"

"Yes, Jonathan. A real archaeological dig, with real archaeological experts."

"So... You're not going to dig up the stuff to get rich?"

Uncle Chad laughs. "No, Jonathan. Not in the way you think. I just need someone to find it, so I can write about it."

"But who's going to drop everything and go on a wild goose chase just because you say so?"

Uncle Chad concedes, "You've got a point, Jonathan. My problem is that there is no reason for anyone to dig at that location. No building foundations to find. No ancient city or pyramids. That rock is between the modern city of Dahab and the port city of Nuweiba, in the middle of nowhere. My challenge is to convince my archaeological friend Dr. Ibrahim to check it out."

"Isn't Dr. Ibrahim the man you worked with on the article about the pyramids?" I ask.

"Good memory, my boy! Ibrahim and I got on well."

"But how can you convince him to look at that spot without revealing that you've been there?" Cricket asks.

"That is a consideration," Uncle Chad says, "but I think I can do it. I think I can tell the truth without giving away the real truth. For example, it's not unusual for Bedouins or other desert travelers to find items that stir interest in a dig. So, I plan to take something from my treasure bag to Ibrahim and tell him I've traced it from the hand of a desert wanderer to our rock location."

"And," says Uncle Chad, "I'll say that for two years I lived with desert dwellers who helped me trace one of the possible Exodus routes. And I'll say that I know a spot with anthropological promise that is related to the Exodus. Ibrahim will be intrigued. Right now, there are no archaeological finds that prove the Exodus ever happened."

Cricket asks, "So, you think that your suggestion will be enough to convince Dr. Ibrahim to check out the site? Will you go with him?"

"I've known Ibrahim to make significant finds on less evidence than this," says Uncle Chad. "And I'd love to go along and hear Ibrahim's special radar go off at the rock's location and see the expression on his face when he discovers what I hope is still there."

"But most of all," Uncle Chad says, "I'd like my family to fly to Cairo with me when I convince Ibrahim to do the dig."

Uncle Chad's proposal catches us by surprise. Dad blinks for a minute, not sure that he's heard his brother correctly.

Uncle Chad tells him, "I know your passports are in order, Jonathan, because of your cruise last spring. And it won't cost you anything. I'll pay for your Egypt tickets. What do you say?"

"Say yes, Dad!" I cry. "You and Mom can see where we found Uncle Chad."

"Yes, you should go!" William says.

"It'll make a great trip for all of you," says Marlene Grace.

I can see the spark of adventure glowing in Dad's eyes, but Mom is not convinced. She's never been much of a traveler and hates to fly. Dad turns to her and says, "Say *yes*, Gwen. It will be a great family adventure. I know you don't like flying, but..."

Mom hesitates. "I'm not sure," she says.

"It's the opportunity of a lifetime," Dad urges, and Mom catches the earnestness in his voice.

Mom looks at me, and my heart leaps when she says to Dad, "I'm not going. But you two can go."

"I don't like leaving you behind," Dad objects, but Mom says, "I'll expect you to keep Alexander safe. I'm staying here."

It's no use trying to change her mind, and Dad reluctantly agrees that he and I will go.

Uncle Chad gives Mom an out: "You can always change your mind, Gwen, and come with us." But I doubt that Mom will change her mind.

I just pray that she doesn't change her mind about Dad and me going so far away.

143

# Chapter 22

## Preparations

When I finally make my first after-school visit to Uncle Chad's house following his return from the past, I am surprised to find Cricket and Hero already there. Cricket and Uncle Chad have been discussing something, and Uncle Chad tells me, "Cricket's a smart girl!"

"That's why we're friends," I reply. And Uncle Chad says, "I heartily approve!"

Cricket tries to hide an embarrassed grin at our compliments.

"I wish Cricket could go with us to Egypt," I say. But Cricket shakes her head.

"It wouldn't work, Alexander. I'd keep you from doing things you will need to do. My physical requirements are too great. I wouldn't be walking, you know."

Of course, she's right. Traveling with the onyx stones is unique. Climbing aboard an airplane to go overseas with a wheelchair would not be the same. No matter how handicap-friendly sites might profess to be, they will be restrictive.

"It isn't fair," I say, but Cricket replies, "I'm fine with it, Alexander. My life is not boring. Plus, you'll tell me everything when you get back."

"I will," I promise. "Maybe I'll keep a journal."

Uncle Chad chuckles. "It's been done before, you know."

"I know," I laugh. And then I ask, "After our trip to see Dr. Ibrahim, will we all go on the expedition?"

Uncle Chad declares, "Perhaps. But that may be at a much later date. For now, let's concentrate on the first trip and how to convince Dr. Ibrahim to invite us on a second trip."

Uncle Chad reaches under his desk and tugs out his treasure bag. I help him lift it to the desktop.

"Right now," Uncle Chad says, "I'd like you two to help me decide which artifact to show Dr. Ibrahim. What do you think?"

Uncle Chad pours the full contents of the bag over his desk. Gold plates and gold cups, jeweled hair combs, brass mirrors, gold and silver earrings, necklaces, loose jewels, and a few blocks of gold in various measures vie for our attention. I touch everything, including a gold cup like the one in Lawrence's *USA Today* photo.

"How about this?" I ask.

Uncle Chad nods and approves. "Good choice, Alexander. I think this would pique Ibrahim's interest. Its design and gold composition will affirm its period authenticity, and it will hopefully hint at similar treasure to be found."

Uncle Chad asks me to hold the cup while he stuffs everything else back into the sack. I watch in puzzlement when he drags the treasure across the room and hides it under the far workshop table and behind my old rocketry box.

"Why not?" he says. "No one found the journal back there."

I have to agree. My leftover rocketry materials are of little interest to anyone but me. It makes a perfect hiding place.

"Now," says Uncle Chad, "you two young people need to be on your way. Suppers are waiting."

When he shoos us out the door, I don't mind. I know that this will not be the last time I will see my remarkable uncle. I walk Cricket to her house, and then I head for home.

———◆———

Preparing for our present-day trip to Cairo proves to be more complicated than preparing for our time-transport to ancient Egypt. In fifteenth-century B.C., I didn't need a toothbrush or five pair of clean underwear, and I didn't need to guard my passport so I wouldn't lose it. Nor did I have to sit strapped in the same seat and unable to move for hours on end.

I used to think that taking a trip in an airplane was the most exciting thing in the world. But after my experiences with the onyx stones, I am impatient with modern air travel. Its novelty has lost its luster. Once aboard the plane, our flight will last nearly eleven hours. How I wish we could just click some stones and be there.

And yet, for all the inconvenience, I appreciate one thing about the long flight. Unlike travel with the onyx stones, Dad and Uncle Chad and

I have time to talk. I've hardly ever spent time with the two men together. Today I feel included, grown up.

The flight attendant brings sodas and packaged cookies, and we sit forward with our seat trays down. I remember the cookies that Marlene Grace always packed for our onyx-stones transports, and I wish these in-flight cookies were more like hers.

As we munch our sugary treats, Dad asks his brother, "Chad, while you were with the Israelites, did you learn anything special?"

My ears perk. What might Uncle Chad share that he hasn't already told us?

When Uncle Chad sets down his soda and its ice cubes rattle, he stares at it for a second, and then he says, "Jonathan, I learned so many things that I'm not sure where to begin."

He pauses. "Perhaps the greatest thing I learned is the one thing I least expected. I have always been so certain of myself, but these experiences tore away my confidence."

"I've already told you some of it," he says, "such as when I could find no rational explanation for the regional and selective aspects of the plague of darkness. And that plague forced me to consider that the next plague would happen exactly as predicted and that all first-borns would die. I was frightened because I was a firstborn!

"Fortunately, I was taken in by someone who followed all of the safety requirements assiduously. And I cried secret tears in the morning when I learned that I had been passed over and was safe.

"And then, when Josh whisked me back to the present with an unexplainable bag of Egyptian gold, I struggled to reorient myself. Two realities were colliding in my brain, and one of them was impossible.

"I hid the bag and the necklace in the attic and was determined to never look at them again. But my plan failed. In the morning, the necklace was somehow again around my neck. With fear and anger, I threw it again into the attic.

"And then, that night, I slept on the sofa —after I had placed several kitchen chairs in the hallway leading to the bedroom. I even pushed the dresser in front of the closet door. Surely, I would wake up from sleepwalking if I encountered all of that mess. I glared at the barricade, and then I did one more thing. I opened the container of foot powder from my bathroom and sprinkled it all across the pathway from the living room to the chairs in the hallway. If I set one foot on that path in the night, I would see evidence of it in the morning. Finally satisfied, I let myself go to sleep.

"But in the morning, the necklace was back, and I was staggered to see that not a particle of foot powder on the floor had been disturbed. Plus, the chairs and the dresser remained exactly as they had been placed the night before. I had not walked in my sleep. The only other explanation was not possible. And yet, I could not deny that there was some force at work over which I had no control."

Uncle Chad stares out the airplane window, but I know he is not looking at the clouds. "And then," he says, "Lawrence found the journal and believed it all to be true. And Lawrence became a tool in the next step of my lesson.

"When Lawrence abandoned me in Egypt, I had no choice but to march with the Israelites. I stumbled along in sorrow that I would never see my family again, but my companions sang songs and cheered as they put distance between themselves and Pharaoh's slavery. I understood their joy, but I could not join in.

"And then, their songs died. Word spread that the Egyptian army was behind us and would overtake us by nightfall. The news could not have come at a worse time. Having reached an impasse, we had planned to backtrack in the morning. But now, with no way to retreat, we were trapped.

"Mountains stood hard at our backs and water lay immediately in front of us. We had nowhere to go. And unlike what I had always thought of the Red Sea crossing story, what I saw before us was not a shallow reed bed. Instead, we were stranded at the edge of a very deep sea—an impossible four-to-five-mile-wide torrent of water that could neither be waded nor swum."

"Five miles wide?" Dad interrupts in surprise.

"Yes," says Uncle Chad. "By my best estimation, the sea at this point was at least five miles wide."

"And," says Uncle Chad, "the Hebrew people began to wail and accuse God of leading them here to die. Why had His pillar of cloud and fire led them into a dead-end trap?"

My head perks up. "I saw that tower of cloud and fire!" I exclaim. And Uncle Chad nods.

"Of course, you did, Alexander," he says. "That same pillar of cloud and fire was in the Israelite camp when you came to rescue me."

My dad's expression is hard to read when I confide, "I was afraid of it," and Uncle Chad admits with a loud whisper, "So was I!"

"And yet," says Uncle Chad, "for all of the pillar's great leadership, we were in terrible trouble. Night was coming on. Had God changed his mind about the Promised Land? Was he going to let everyone die or be taken back to Egypt? Where was the mighty God of the plagues, now?

"And then it happened! With a dramatic roar, the great tower of cloud that had stood at the front of our company rose into the air. We gaped in astonishment as the cloudy pillar whirled its way from before us to behind us, whipping at our clothes and sending our things flying. And it came to rest like a stalled tornado between us and the approaching army. Perhaps God was going to fight for us, after all!

"But instead of fighting, the pillar did something else. Exactly as the Bible stories have said would happen, the mighty cloud burst into its nightly flames. And our scouts reported that while we had the light of the flames before us, the Egyptians had the darkness of night over them. And without light, the Egyptians could not advance. For the moment, we were safe.

"And then, another miracle transpired. I watched as Moses stepped to the edge of the sea and dramatically raised his staff. He stretched his hand over the waves. And a great wind rose up and howled over the water. It continued its tempest for hours, way into the night. And in the wee hours of the morning, long before dawn, we found that the wind had miraculously pushed up all of the waves into two giant heaps. Between the waters' two walls lay a bare path, straight to the opposite shore.

"We watched Moses stride out into the dry pathway that had formed. 'Follow me!' he called. And with fear and wonder, we fell in line after him through the supernatural canyon.

"Walking between the walls of water was terrifying. The waves rose so high that we knew we would be doomed if the wind stopped holding them back. We wondered if the water would remain in place long enough. After all, five miles is a great distance for one man to cover in a few hours, and we were a company of two million.

"Ours was not a sprint by a bunch of stripped-down, athletic young men. We were parents with little children, elderly people dependent on canes, pregnant women set on donkeys, and vast herds of sheep, goats, and cattle. Although we hurried, I estimate that it took us three to four hours to cross from one shore to the other. We carried everything we owned. Every person was weighed down with belongings: tents, tools, clothing, cooking gear, food, oil, wine, and bags of gold, silver, copper, and bronze from the Egyptians. Many could not run; they could only plod. Imagine yourself strapped with a huge backpack and trying to rush your similarly burdened grandmother and grandfather and your toddlers and grade-school children over rocky, uneven terrain and then up a slope to an opposite shore. And although the fiery pillar threw light from behind to light our path, the sky overhead was dark and the wind continued to roar in our ears.

"Then, just as the last of our party and herds was climbing onto the new shore, the morning sun rose and began to dissolve the blackness that had blinded the Egyptians. Their generals could see that we had escaped. The walls of water remained in place, and, finally, the generals gave the order to advance. The frightened Egyptian army began to race through the watery canyon after us. We watched in horror as they drew closer and closer. Was God going to do nothing?

"And then, as if in answer to our cries, the pillar of fire on the shore we had just left suddenly morphed back into its roaring cloud and lifted up. While we watched, the tornado passed over the heads of the awed Egyptian army. The sight and sound panicked the horses and the horsemen, and the army's chariots overturned and their wheels fell off. We cheered as the horses ran away. And as the army fled on foot toward our shore, we saw Moses raise his staff again and call for the walls of water to collapse. And they did.

"I've never seen such a sight! The thundering, collapsing water that covered the Egyptian army also shook our shore and threw us to our knees. The towering walls crashed back together in the center of the sea and also splashed in a race of waves to the shore that threatened to carry us away, too. Only the mighty wind of the pillar of cloud that now stood with us kept the waves pushed back. Not a single Israelite was lost as the sea swallowed up the entire army of Pharaoh.

"And in that miracle moment, something inside of me broke. Every one of my old ideas about God were shattered in one instant. I could no longer dismiss Him. And as the Israelites broke into singing and dancing over their rescue by the mighty *I AM THAT I AM*, I sang too. Yes, me!—the man who had relegated God to the world of myths. I now acknowledged and praised the God who had, before my very eyes, performed a miraculous feat like no other. And I will never be the same."

Dad nods slowly. He struggles to accept his brother's story. I, on the other hand, am transfixed. I have been to the ancient desert, and I can believe every word.

# Chapter 23

## Cairo

I manage to sleep only a little on the flight. Although eleven hours is a long time, it is difficult to nod off when you are soaring on the wings of adrenalin in anticipation of an adventure. But even so, Uncle Chad has to awaken me as the plane banks on its approach to the Cairo International Airport.

"Look there," he says and points.

He wants me to see the Giza pyramids before we land. Through my window I see them looking just like they do in the postcard pictures. But Dad and I marvel at how close they are to the city.

"I have always thought the pyramids were way out in some isolated area of the desert," Dad says.

"It is a surprise, isn't it?" says Uncle Chad. "I couldn't believe it the first time I saw it, either. But that Giza site is just a forty-minute taxi ride from downtown Cairo."

Beneath us, the city streets and the buildings of modern Cairo stand in stark contrast to the cluster of ancient pyramids casting their shadows on the sand. And as I survey the scene, I know that Uncle Chad has seen this area as it was when the pyramids were still young. How many ancient landmarks have been buried since then, beneath millennia of sand and centuries of concrete and cars?

"We may not get to visit Giza on this trip," Uncle Chad apologizes, "but I promise that one day we will."

"And can we ride camels when we do?" I ask.

"I don't see why not," Uncle Chad chuckles.

Once the plane lands and we disembark, I see a man opposite the boarding ramp waving wildly in our direction. Uncle Chad waves back. "It's Ibrahim!"

We quickly pay for the use of a luggage cart to transport our bags—especially Uncle Chad's heavy ones—to a waiting car. Then Ibrahim's rapid-fire questions keep Uncle Chad busy while Dad and I gawk at the street sights on our way to the hotel. After we check in and drop off our bags, we are escorted to Dr. Ibrahim's headquarters, one block from the Egyptian Museum of Antiquities.

"The place hasn't changed a bit," Uncle Chad quips as we step into an eclectic jumble of ancient artifacts. Books and loosely defined piles of paper occupy every tabletop, and a clutter of archaeological oddities possesses every open spot on the floor at the edges of the room. Squeezed in, just in front of Dr. Ibrahim's desk, are three folding chairs. My chair brings me eye-level with the tightly bandaged face of a mummy, and Dad blinks nervously in the stare of a stuffed hooded cobra.

"I imagine that you're all thirsty after your trip," declares Dr. Ibrahim. Ice tinkles into our glasses as an aide pours soft drinks.

Ibrahim tells Uncle Chad, "It is good to see you here again, my friend. I hadn't heard from you in such a long time, and suddenly you show up with something you want to show me."

"Yes, it has been a long time," says Uncle Chad. "And, yes, I've brought a little treasure connected to a journey that kept me away in the desert." Uncle Chad rummages in his travel case as he says, "This artifact may entice you to consider a digging spot—the one for which I sent you coordinates. I have reason to think that this spot could yield anthropological evidence of the Hebrews passing that way on their exodus from Egypt."

Uncle Chad sets his gold cup on a corner of the desk, and although Dr. Ibrahim attempts to maintain a detached composure, a gleam in his eyes gives him away. I can tell that he is impressed and excited by what he sees.

Ibrahim picks up the cup and turns it over in his hands. "Very likely fifteenth century B.C. Egyptian," he appraises. Then he asks, "And did you say that you think there may be more artifacts near where this was found?"

"You can call it an educated hunch," says Uncle Chad, "but I think the spot has real promise. Of course, you are better equipped than I to determine such a thing."

Dr. Ibrahim rubs his chin and leans back in his chair. "And what's in it for you? Another *Armchair Science* article? Or a book, perhaps?"

Uncle Chad steeples his fingers and smiles. "Possibly both."

Now Ibrahim polishes the gold cup with his sleeve. "It is intriguing. You say this was found on the assumed exodus route *after* Mt. Sinai, right?"

"Right," says Uncle Chad. "Does that mean you're interested?"

"I think so. When would you want to go?"

"Sometime before April. I hear that the area gets too hot after that."

Dr. Ibrahim grins. "Actually, I have a group going to Nuweiba Beach in two days. That's about 90 miles from your coordinates. Or is that too soon?"

My heart leaps. Uncle Chad looks at Dad, and Dad looks at me. Then Dad says, "Why not? It's Christmas vacation, isn't it? And if we're late getting back, it's for a good cause—something educational, right?"

I can't believe my good fortune. No doubt, Mom will have a conniption when I miss getting back in time for school, but it'll be worth it! A chance to go trekking into the desert with Dad and Uncle Chad doesn't come along every day. I'm ready for the adventure. I only wonder if we'll get to ride camels.

# Chapter 24

## Into the Sinai

The first leg of our trip to the desert is by plane. In preparation for our mission, Dr. Ibrahim gathers the desert clothing and equipment we will need, and we check out of our hotel. At the airport, we board our flight for Sharm-el-Sheikh at the southern end of the Sinai Peninsula. We will stay overnight at Sharm-el-Sheikh's grand resort hotel, and our tickets for home have been changed to fly out of Sharm-el-Sheikh in three days instead of out of Cairo in two. Dad has given Mom all the details about our delay so she won't worry.

Sharm-el-Sheikh's resort is plush. What a place to vacation, if only we had time! But we have to rest before tomorrow. After a swim and supper, Dad, Uncle Chad, and I catch up on our sleep.

At eight in the morning, a convoy of SUV's (not the camels I had hoped for) sets out on the main road to Nabq and then on toward Dhahab. From there we will detour to the northwest and blaze our own off-road trail for about twenty miles.

Mid-morning, Dr. Ibrahim announces, "We're here!" and our lead vehicle rolls to a stop.

Although the landscape reminds me of our final transport with Uncle Chad, everything looks different, even our rock. I would not have picked it out of a lineup. It has shrunk and its base has been swallowed up in thousands of years of drifting sand.

Dad, Uncle Chad, and I watch from under a hastily improvised shade tent while Dr. Ibrahim's crew verifies the exact coordinates for the search and sets to work arranging the ground-penetrating radar equipment and its computer readout.

"This exercise is good practice for our newer crew members," Ibrahim declares. "This is their first hands-on assignment. What they practice here will be helpful on our originally scheduled survey outside of Nuweiba, next."

As Ibrahim hands out instructions to his students, Uncle Chad explains the exploration process for Dad and me. "The equipment will emit and receive ground radar pulses," he says. "The pulse reports will be converted by the computer into three-dimensional images that will let us visualize what the equipment sees below us. It's really quite a marvel. The technique works well even through hard surfaces."

"But," Dr. Ibrahim interjects, "it can produce a lot of false-positives. It is tempting to interpret vague images into what you want to see, when nothing is there. So, don't get your hopes set too high."

The crew continues to work while Dr. Ibrahim tells us about the Nuweiba site and what he'll be looking for there. "You know," he says, "some people think that the Red Sea crossing took place at Nuweiba on the Sea of Aqabar and not on what most people consider the Red Sea at all. We'll check out some possible clues there."

Then, before Ibrahim can elaborate, one of the computer-technicians shouts, "Got something!"

"Already?" exclaims Dr. Ibrahim.

From my first glance at the screen on the computer, I can't make out what I'm supposed to be seeing. But Dr. Ibrahim and Uncle Chad both whoop. "Look at that!" Uncle Chad exclaims. "How far down would you say that is?"

"Only about twelve or thirteen feet," guesses the technician with a shrug. "Easy dig, though. Most of it is drifted sand against the rock."

"Hassan!" calls Dr. Ibrahim, and a crew member raises his head. "Bring some shovels and rope buckets."

Uncle Chad, Dad, and I exchange knowing glances as the men sling dirt and sand away from the point of interest. It is hot work and the sand keeps sliding down and refilling their hole. When the pit is finally wide enough and about ten feet deep, the workers take more care; they begin to scoop sand with their hands into the rope-tied buckets that others have been pulling up to take the sand away.

"I feel something!" shouts one of the men, and together the crew quickly uncovers the objects beneath their fingers. A photographer is lowered, now, to capture a first glimpse of the find.

I can see that the sacks that had once held our ancient thank you gifts have disintegrated, but the tokens at the bottom of the sandy pit endure. Each object is swept clear and photographed in place. Then each is pulled to the surface and photographed again from all angles with size markers and description cards. Everything is meticulously documented under Dr. Ibrahim's strict scrutiny.

"Another gold cup!" Ibrahim cries. "Just like the one you showed me, Chad. And look at these necklaces! This is definitely Egyptian loot."

He pats Uncle Chad on the back. "Good job, my friend!" he says. "Good job!"

One of the workers lets me handle a jeweled necklace. "What do you think, boy?" he asks in broken English. "Do you like it?"

I nod vigorously, and the worker laughs.

Uncle Chad pounds me on the back. "Well, Alexander," he says, "we did it!" And only I and Dad know exactly what he is referring to.

Eventually, every artifact is carefully boxed and labeled and stacked in the hold of our SUV. Satisfied that his crew has uncovered everything from the pit, Dr. Ibrahim now suggests testing more of the ground. "Just to make sure we haven't missed anything else," he says.

The radar imaging equipment is repositioned several times with no result, and the crew starts to pack up. Uncle Chad lingers over the original hole with his hands in his pockets and casually asks, "Have you checked the backside of the rock?" The crew turns to see Dr. Ibrahim's response.

"Hmm. Not a bad idea," says Dr. Ibrahim. "Maybe we should check there. We have time."

The crew shrugs and sets up their equipment once more. It is obvious that they feel it to be a useless exercise, but they comply. What they don't know and haven't seen is that while they were surveying and digging in the front of the rock, Uncle Chad was secretly burying the contents of his original bag of treasure on the backside of the rock. I had suspected something of the sort when I had seen Uncle Chad stealing off, earlier, with his heavy suitcase.

When the radar reveals the second cache, the technician whistles in astonishment. "We almost missed this!" he exclaims. "And it's shallow. Good call, Dr. Tennyson!"

Shovels once again shift the sand and free the ancient gold from its hiding place. "Amazing!" says Dr. Ibrahim. "There's even another gold cup!"

Now Ibrahim speculates, "I wonder why all this treasure was buried around this rock. Perhaps someone hid the stuff with the intent of returning this way and using it in trade. Or perhaps the owners were being pursued and needed to lighten their load. We'll never know, I guess."

I try to remain low-key as we listen, and I note that Uncle Chad nods sagely as if Dr. Ibrahim's ideas could be reasonable answers. How Ibrahim would laugh if we told him the truth. He would never believe it!

In the middle of processing the new find, Hassan calls out, "Dr. Ibrahim, come quickly!"

Ibrahim hurries and bends over the hole to see what has caused the stir. When Hassan points to what he has seen and not yet extracted, Dr. Ibrahim draws in a breath and his eyes grow large.

"What is it?" Uncle Chad asks.

"It's an inscribed piece of clay—a fragment of a tablet. In Hebrew, I think!"

"Are you sure?"

"I'll know more once the photographer finishes and I can pick it up."

The photographer takes the hint and quickly records the clay piece. The minute he backs away, Ibrahim drops flat and stretches until he can gingerly pick up the artifact—and its other half, which he discovers right below it. We encircle Ibrahim to inspect the clay pieces he displays in his palms.

Ibrahim's voice trembles. "It is definitely Hebrew," he declares. "A transaction receipt, I think, a sale between Hebrews. I'll know more when I can examine it properly."

"Is it significant?" Uncle Chad asks.

Ibrahim nods with awe in his voice, "It is a possible proof that Hebrews did pass through this area. And if this Egyptian treasure was in their hands, it may help corroborate part of the exodus story."

Uncle Chad grins and nods, and Dad and I smile at one another. I can't help but wonder if Uncle Chad secretly planted the tablet among his treasure. Or was it in his bag all the time?

After Ibrahim carefully catalogues, wraps, and boxes the clay pieces, he places them in his personal travel case and not with the other artifacts. Ibrahim barely notices as the crew dismantles the equipment. His little pieces of clay hold more fascination for him that all of the gold we have dug up today.

"That tablet has a story to tell," Ibrahim says to Uncle Chad. "I can only imagine the man who inscribed it and why he left his bag of valuables here. Don't you wish you could go back in time and see him?"

"We could certainly learn a lot on such a trip," Uncle Chad replies solemnly, before he sneaks a secret wink to me. I grin but say nothing.

Our few hours here have gone quickly, and yet much of the day remains. Ibrahim and his crew will return us to Sharm-el-Sheikh and then go on to Nuweiba to begin their second survey.

Uncle Chad doesn't think they'll find much in Nuweiba, but he doesn't discourage them. "Half of the fun of archaeology is speculation and the search," he murmurs to me.

As we leave the rock behind, I recall the last time Uncle Chad and I took our leave of it. How strange it seems to say goodbye a second time in a completely different millennium. When I close my eyes, I can almost see the sleeping Israelite camp spread over the desert in front of us, guarded by the pillar of fire rising into the night sky. And I can see a couple of donkeys turned loose and trotting back to their herd.

I tuck that vision back into my memories and open my eyes. And although I am still in a strange country, thankfully I am back in my own time and I am in the company of my Dad and my Uncle Chad.

———◆———

From the resort, I text Cricket and Mom about our success, and I can almost hear them shouting: "Wonderful news!"

Mom texts back, *I'm so glad you're coming home. And I'm glad you're safe.*

Cricket texts, *You'll have to tell me all about it when you get back! Can't wait!*

"Great fun, huh?" Dad says when I tell him what Mom and Cricket have written.

Like me, Dad has loved every minute of our adventure. I've never seen him happier.

———◆———

"So, Chad," Dad says at 35,000 feet on our return flight, "did you plant that tablet at the rock with your treasure?"

"I confess that I did," Uncle Chad admits. "But it is part of a bona fide tablet from the Hebrew exodus. When I was among the Israelites, I came across it on the ground and put it into the pocket of my robe. Then when I got home and changed into my modern clothes, it fell out on the floor (that's when it broke). I stuffed it into my treasure bag in hopes that one day I would be able to offer it for discovery. And that is exactly what has happened. I hope that Dr. Ibrahim will be able to decipher it and decide that it doesn't discount the biblical story. I plan to include mention of it in my *Armchair Science* article."

Uncle Chad's comment reminds me that he has promised to include Dad and me in his article, too. "After all," he said, "you were part of the discovery expedition."

I can't wait to see the published article. Won't my classmates and friends be surprised when they see me in the magazine?

Dad and Uncle Chad continue to talk, and I listen even though my eyes have a hard time staying open. I am tired, and the droning of the engine does nothing to keep me awake.

Before I fall asleep, however, I manage to hear references to the brothers' childhood and things that I have never known. Of course, I knew that they grew up on a family farm, but I have seen the farm only in photos. And I barely remember their parents because I was in the first grade when Grandpa died from a heart attack and in the second grade when Grandma died from cancer.

I keep my eyes closed as they talk, but I rouse when I overhear Dad mention Uncle Chad's girlfriend. *A girlfriend?* As I listen, I learn that someone named Cynthia broke off their dating relationship when Uncle Chad left for college. Uncle Chad sadly recalls how she married someone else.

"I loved her," he admits. And Dad says, "You would have been good together. I'm sorry you never found anyone else."

"What I miss most," says Uncle Chad, "is that I've not had children. And I want to thank you, Jonathan, for letting me spend time with Alexander. He's a great kid, a lot like me when I was younger, and I enjoy his company."

Then Uncle Chad adds, "I believe that, one day, you and Gwen will be very proud of his accomplishments. Alexander's curiosity will take him far."

With my eyes still closed I bask in his praise, and I hope that I can live up to what Uncle Chad thinks I may one day become.

# Chapter 25

## It's Not Over

Of course, Mom wants to hear everything about our venture, and Dad and I nearly trip over our words to describe all that we experienced.

"Did you ride a camel?" Mom asks.

"No," I reply. "The expedition had SUVs."

"We didn't need camels," Dad says. "It was exciting without them. Egypt is not only a land of mystery, but we had our own mystery to play out. And Dr. Ibrahim never knew that our treasure location came from coordinates established three thousand years ago when Alexander forgot to leave his phone behind and you texted him."

"I guess I did have a small part to play in all of it, didn't I?" Mom purrs with a pleased grin.

"You sure did!" Dad affirms.

"Well, I'm glad you had a great time," Mom tells us. "I worried only a little."

Dad gives her a hug. "You wouldn't be you, Gwen, if you didn't worry a little."

———•———

Now that we're back home, my old after-school pattern returns. My bicycle automatically heads for Uncle Chad's house.

But today, I see Dad's car in Uncle Chad's driveway. When I ask if something is wrong, Dad shakes his head and smiles. "Since I had to meet an insurance client on the next street," he says, "I decided to stop here before going back to the office. I'm learning to take advantage of certain opportunities and not take them for granted like I used to."

"Plus," says Dad, "Chad has been showing me all of your rocketry models and certificates. I haven't seen some of these since you launched them."

He tousles my hair—something he hasn't done in a long time—and he says, "I had nearly forgotten how much you've accomplished. And now you're almost ready to launch your last model in the youth category."

"Yes," I say. "I just have to finish my report, and then Uncle Chad and I can launch it."

Dad picks up the rocket from my previous launch, and he points to the photo and my certificate.

"I remember this one from two years ago, or so," he says. "It was pretty spectacular, but I hear that the new launch will be ten times better."

"At least ten times," says Uncle Chad. "This one has a solid-fuel cell and will really perform."

Dad raises his eyebrows. "Well, your mother and I will certainly have to be there with our cameras. We may need a full video of this one!"

"You won't be disappointed," says Uncle Chad, and he pats my shoulder.

It feels good to have Dad *and* Uncle Chad, the two most influential men in my life, affirm my achievements and encourage me. I want to make them both proud.

Before Dad turns the front door knob to leave, he says, "You know, I think the three of us should take in a ballgame or something, soon. Don't you?"

"Yeah!" I say.

"Great idea!" agrees Uncle Chad. "The Three Tennysons take on the world."

I stand taller and lift my chin. Today, I am one of the guys!

———•———

After Dad leaves, I settle in at one of Uncle Chad's workshop tables with my I-pad, and I work on my rocketry research paper. Uncle Chad is busy writing, too, and the workshop is unusually quiet. Since Uncle Chad's upcoming article is about our trip to Egypt and not about some physics proof, there are no experiments to create or projects to photograph.

"My article should appear in the May issue of *Armchair Science*," says Uncle Chad. And he grins when I reply, "And I'm going to order twelve copies!"

"I hope that's enough," he quips.

"If not, I'll order some more," I say. "I want everybody to see it."

"You just want everybody to see your picture in the magazine," Uncle Chad teases. And it's true.

We work in silence for an hour or so, before Uncle Chad's cell phone rings.

When he answers, he clowns a frown and mouths the words, "It's your mom!"

"Am I in trouble?" I whisper—although I can't imagine what I've done that might upset Mom.

Now Uncle Chad laughs. Into the phone, he says, "Thanks, Gwen. I'll be sure to watch," and he hangs up.

"No, you're not in trouble, Alexander," he admits. "Your mom was just calling to tell me to watch the six o-clock news. Evidently, the national station has been running a tease to promote an interview with Dr. Ibrahim about an exciting new archaeological find in Egypt. Your mom thinks we might be mentioned, and she's excited about it."

"Wow!" I say. "Won't that be neat?"

"You bet," says Uncle Chad. "So, you'd better not be late getting home tonight. You want to make sure you see what your friends will be seeing!"

He's right, of course. And I text Cricket to make sure that she and the Foxes watch, too.

———◆———

The television is never on at our house during meals. But tonight's meal is an exception. This evening we're all eating on TV trays in the living room, and Dad is recording the program so we can watch it again.

"Here it is," Dad says, and he turns up the sound.

"Tonight," says the interviewer, "we are coming to you live from Cairo, Egypt, to tell you about a significant discovery by prominent Egyptologist Dr. R. G. Ibrahim. We'll let Dr. Ibrahim tell you what he has found and why it may be important."

The camera pans slowly over our treasure and settles on Dr. Ibrahim seated behind his desk.

"Good evening, Dr. Ibrahim," the interviewer says. "What we're seeing is an impressive display of recently discovered ancient Egyptian gold and treasure. Can you tell us a little bit about it?"

"Certainly," says Dr. Ibrahim. "What you are seeing here is the result of a dig not far from Dhahab at the southeastern tip of the Sinai Peninsula—a dig precipitated by a tip from the noted *Armchair Science* magazine writer, Dr. Joseph Chadwick Tennyson, of the United States."

Uncle Chad's picture appears on the screen. In the photo he is flanked by Dad and me at the base of our rock.

"Woo hoo!" Dad shouts. "There we are!"

Mom presses her hands together and coos, "And aren't you handsome! My two men!"

Dr. Ibrahim continues. "Dr. Tennyson had been researching the biblical exodus of the Hebrew people from Egypt in Fifteenth Century B.C. And during his research, he developed an educated hunch that this spot might prove productive for a dig. Following his coordinates, my crew and I set up our ground-penetrating radar equipment and uncovered the artifacts that you see here."

The interviewer now asks, "Aside from the gold and other precious items, what else did you find?"

Dr. Ibrahim replies, "We found this clay tablet."

Ibrahim points to the tablet for the camera to feature. "As you can see," he says, "it isn't glamorous or decorative. It is a simple piece of clay inscribed in Hebrew."

"So, it isn't inscribed in Egyptian?" prompts the interviewer.

"No. One might have expected that to be the case. But instead, this little tablet records a transaction between two Hebrews, and the exciting thing is that it references a contribution of gold for the creation of curtain hooks for the Hebrew Tabernacle. Now, as you may know from biblical accounts, the Tabernacle was a Hebrew tent of worship, constructed after the Israelite exodus from Egypt began. The Tabernacle was designed to travel with the Israelites as they made their way to the Promised Land."

"So, this is a significant find?" asks the interviewer.

"It certainly is!" declares Dr. Ibrahim. "To date, this is the only artifact in existence that corroborates an aspect of the exodus account found in the Bible. Until now, there have been no definitive discoveries to validate the historical truth of that monumental event—a pivotal moment in the history of the Jews."

"Well, that is exciting," says the interviewer. "I had no idea that the exodus event was in doubt. I have always thought there must be a lot of historical proof for the story. But you say that this is the first, ever."

"Yes," says Dr. Ibrahim. "And once again—as is often the case—archaeology supports something recorded in the Bible that scholars have long debated."

"All right, then," says the interviewer. "This has been interesting. I wish we had more time. Perhaps we will have you on again, at a later date, to share more historical proofs from the sands of the Middle East. For now, thank you, Dr. R. G. Ibrahim, for sharing with us about your intriguing discovery. I understand that these items will soon be on display for the public to view."

"That's right," says Dr. Ibrahim. And as the camera once again pans the array of treasures, including the inscribed clay tablet, Dr. Ibrahim reports that all of the items from the find will soon be on display at the Egyptian Museum of Antiquities in Cairo. "And," he says, "the clay tablet will be available for examination by qualified experts who can help to further verify its authenticity."

When the interview ends, Dad and I sit grinning like Cheshire cats, and Mom says, "Well, there'll be no living with you two, now."

"You're right, Mom," I say. "We're famous!"

At almost the same time that the house phone rings, my cell phone *chings*. Dad runs to answer the phone call from Uncle Chad, and I pull up Cricket's text.

*It was fun to see our treasure again!* Cricket writes. And I tell her, *I only wish you could have been there with us.*

Cricket writes back, *I was there for the important part—the rescue of your uncle. That's enough for me.*

She's right that her trip with me to the past was the most important of all my trips. Nothing will ever compare with that. But I do cherish my modern trip with Dad and Uncle Chad, including the way our gold was rediscovered. And now, because of our part in Ibrahim's expedition, Dad and I share a little of Uncle Chad's fame. Hopefully, some of my school friends saw my face in the photo during the television interview. That story and my image in that photo is the closest I will ever come to sharing my adventures with them.

# Chapter 26

## Believing Without Having Seen

More and more often I find Dad at Uncle Chad's when I arrive after school. Today, I walk into the workshop to hear the two of them discussing again the miracles that Uncle Chad saw during his time with the Israelites. I slip into the room and sit quietly at the worktable as they talk.

Dad says, "I envy your experiences, Chad. I can see how God became real to you after you saw such astounding things. I just wish that I had been able to see all of that, too. I've tried several times to do the religious thing, but it has never seemed real to me. Gwen and I went to church for a while after one of Alexander's friends invited him to Sunday school. And we heard the usual stories of David and Goliath and Moses in the bullrushes. And we celebrated Christmas and Easter. But I could never make God and Jesus feel real. Maybe if I saw the stuff you've seen, I would *get it*. It's a shame that God doesn't flash around a few of those really spectacular miracles, today, so that people like me could believe in him."

Uncle Chad smiles and shakes his head. "Jonathan, I disagree with you. History doesn't support your theory. Instead, the record shows that the effect of miracles doesn't last for long. The plagues of Moses' day are a good example. Those plagues—ten of them—were sent to convince the pharaoh to let the Israelites leave Egypt. And yet, we read that Pharaoh refused to believe and listen to God. Even Jesus, who did hundreds, perhaps thousands, of miracles in his lifetime, was called a charlatan by the religious leaders of the day. And they killed him instead of believing that he was sent from God."

Then Uncle Chad asks, "What miracle do you think that God could do, today, that would convince you and the world to believe in him?"

Dad shrugs, and Uncle Chad shares, "All my life I've ignored the numberless every-day miracles that were right in front of my face. I simply refused to allow the existence of anything that I couldn't explain or control. As a scientist, I studied the stars and never once asked who made them. I labored to explain the diffusion of light that makes a sunset beautiful but never once gave credit to the artist who made the sunlight. I dissected mummies and recovered ancient bones but never once worshipped the life-giver. I simply ignored the idea of God. Thank God, the onyx-stones journeys made me wake up to how wrong I've been."

Dad sighs. "I want to believe, but how do you make that leap to trust that God is real and that all of this is true?"

Uncle Chad answers, "You're right that it is a leap—a leap of faith. It wasn't easy for me, or even for the people of Jesus' day, to put it all together, either. But when they did, it changed their lives forever. Thousands shared the truth they came to know, even though it often cost them their lives."

Dad says, "But it had to have been easier for them to believe if they had seen Jesus and seen his miracles and seen him alive after the resurrection."

"True," says Uncle Chad. "Seeing is often believing. But in John 20:29 Jesus says to Thomas, *'Because you have seen me, you have believed; blessed are those who have not seen and yet have believed.'*

"You and I, Jonathan, don't need to take a journey into the past with onyx stones in order to believe. We can believe what's in God's Word, and we can respond to the promptings of his Spirit."

Dad replies, "I guess that I want to believe, but it's not easy."

Uncle Chad nods. "It isn't always easy. But Romans 10:9 promises, *That if you confess with your mouth, 'Jesus is Lord,' and believe in your heart that God raised him from the dead, you will be saved.'*

Dad is silent now. But from my quiet corner of the room I whisper, "Jesus is Lord."

# Chapter 27

## A Cry in the Night

The day that every student counts down to has finally come—the last school day of the year. Summer vacation begins tomorrow. And I am particularly excited because our May issues of *Armchair Science* have arrived. Mom has stacked eleven copies on our living-room coffee table with page eleven open on the top copy. That's the page where Dad and Uncle Chad and I grin at the camera. The twelfth copy is in my book bag to take to school. I plan to shamelessly shove my picture in front of everyone in the hallway, the cafeteria, and every one of my classes.

— • —

At school, Mr. Green's response to the *Armchair Science* article is the most satisfying.

At the end of science class, he says, "As I've said before, Alexander, you have the most interesting family. Thank you for sharing with us about your Egypt trip." (Needless to say, my embellishments to the class about our adventure have made the forays of Indiana Jones pale in comparison.)

Still riding high after the last bell rings, I ride quickly to Uncle Chad's workshop where he and I hold up our magazines and dance a little jig. Next, I race to Cricket's house, where she and Marlene Grace pore over the article and read every word. I leave the magazine with them so they can show it to William. "I have more copies at home," I say.

But when I get home, I find that only five issues remain on the coffee table. Dad has taken a few to work, and Mom has broadcast the story to her friends. I pull one copy from the diminishing stack and put it in my desk drawer so it won't disappear too.

Later, before I turn out my light to sleep, I flip through Uncle Chad's article and smile at our picture. My eyelids close and my reminiscence dissolves into a dream. In it, I am smiling down at a cache of treasures peeking through ancient sand exactly where we buried it thousands of years ago. Dr. Ibrahim's mouth is hanging open in amazement, oblivious to the knowing glances passing between Uncle Chad, Dad, and me.

But then in my dream, the arid desert oddly fades and I shiver. I am cold and alone in the dark. A curtain has been drawn and I can't see where I am. Wherever it is, something is wrong. A desperate voice pleads for help—a voice that I feel I should recognize, but I can't. The voice belongs to a face that refuses to materialize.

In my dream, I shudder, and I will the nightmare to go away.

— • —

In the morning, the vividness of the dream is still with me. I drown it with extra syrup on Mom's traditional first-day-of-vacation breakfast—a strawberry-and-whipped-cream waffle with an egg, hash-browned

166

potatoes, four crisp bacon strips, and a tall glass of fresh-squeezed orange juice. Savoring the first few bites makes me feel better.

Mom is passing more hot syrup when the telephone rings. Dad answers, and I can tell by his response that the caller is Uncle Chad. It sounds as if something is wrong.

I hear Dad say, "Are you sure you want to do that? When are you leaving?" Then Dad announces firmly, "I'm going with you, you know."

When the call ends, Dad announces, "Gwen, I'm driving with Chad this afternoon to North Carolina to check on Lawrence Traeger. Chad has it in his head that Lawrence needs him. I don't get it, but Chad is insistent. We're leaving right after lunch, so I need to call the office to postpone a few things. I don't know how long we'll be gone, but I'm not letting Chad visit that man alone."

Dad's face is set like stone.

Suddenly it comes to me that the pleading voice in my dream was Lawrence's. I blurt, "That's who I dreamed about last night!"

I explain. "I had a dream and I couldn't sleep because I kept hearing someone crying for help. He sounded desperate and it bothered me. And I realize now that it was Lawrence."

Dad peers at me over the breakfast table. "Did you overhear anything Chad told me on the phone?" he asks.

"No. I could only hear what you were saying."

"That's right," Mom confirms. "That's all I could hear, too."

Dad sits back and stares. "I ask because those are the exact words Chad said to me. He said he'd had a dream that compelled him to go to Lawrence and help him."

Mom looks at both of us. "Well, we're all going," she says. And my dad starts to object.

"Yes, we're all going," Mom repeats. "I had the same dream."

Dad throws his hands in the air and admits that he too dreamed the same dream.

"I don't know what's going on," Dad mutters. "I don't understand it."

———◆———

When Uncle Chad sees all three of us at his door, he cocks his head and asks, "What's this?"

"We're all going with you," Dad says.

"That isn't necessary," Uncle Chad protests. "The whole family doesn't need to go. And for that matter, Jonathan, you don't even need to go."

"Oh, but we're going," Mom replies. "You don't understand. We've all had the same dream."

Uncle Chad looks at her without understanding. "What?" he asks. "What have you dreamed?"

Dad describes our visions, and Uncle Chad stares.

"What is going on?" he murmurs.

"I don't know," Dad says, "but you're not going to meet Lawrence alone. After all he has done to you, you can't be too careful. You don't know what he'll do if you show up by yourself. And if he is in trouble, you don't owe him a thing. He doesn't deserve it."

"No, he doesn't deserve it," agrees Uncle Chad, "but something is wrong, and I can't do to him what he did to me."

"Do you even know where you're going?" Dad asks in one last-ditch effort to dissuade him.

Uncle Chad opens the back of his SUV and nods for us to pile our overnight bags inside. "Somehow, I do," he says. "It's as if there's a homing device in my head. I can't explain that either. And something tells me we have to hurry."

Uncle Chad climbs behind the wheel and backs quickly out of the drive.

———◆———

Pushing the speed limit, we make our way from Ohio through West Virginia and into Virginia. Our only stops are for drive-through sandwiches, bathroom breaks, and fill-ups. We eat in the car, and Mom, Dad, and Uncle Chad catnap between their turns at the wheel. Mom drives part of the way through Virginia, and when it gets dark Dad takes over. He drives the rest of the route through Northern Virginia and onto US-158. Then he continues onto the Outer Banks highway.

I have never seen a long ribbon of highway bounded by water like the Outer Banks drive. At times it seems like we are riding on top of the moonlit water. But we speed on.

Uncle Chad then steers us to Ocracoke. There we wait in the dark for the first ferry to Swanquarter on the mainland. The ferry departs at 6:51, and we sleep through the crossing.

Following a hurried drive-through breakfast in Swanquarter, Dad relinquishes the wheel to Uncle Chad. "I don't know how you know where you're going," Dad says. Uncle Chad murmurs, "Neither do I. But, somehow, I know every twist and turn of this road as if I've been here a thousand times."

After barely ten minutes on Route 264, a gravel road beckons, and after the first turn, it winds back into the woods. When we are presented with a choice of several dirt driveways, Uncle Chad steers unswervingly onto one and drives down a long lane. At the end is the cabin pictured in the *USA Today* article about Lawrence's pirate treasure. Dad marvels aloud that Uncle Chad could lead us here with no address and no map.

The car rolls to a stop, and we stare at the place for a minute. The cabin sits on a couple of acres of poorly tended ground. Only a small patch around the cabin has been cleared, and even that is overgrown. An impressive stack of firewood rises beside a detached garage, and when no one answers our knock on the cabin door, Dad confirms that there is a car in the garage. Uncle Chad now tries the door knob and finds the cabin unlocked.

"Good," says Mom. "I need to use the bathroom."

After calling and announcing ourselves, we step inside and see that, unlike the yard outside, the cabin is tidy and well kept. Lawrence appears in a photo on the mantel with an elderly man, so we know we're in the right place. A cold pot of coffee sits on the counter, along with a used cup and saucer. But other dishes have been washed and stacked in a drainer.

Uncle Chad checks the kitchen cupboards. "The refrigerator, freezer, and cupboards are stocked," he reports, "so, Lawrence should be here."

"We'll wait," Dad says. "He might have taken a boat out for a couple of hours."

"I'll be outside," I say. "I need to stretch my legs." It has been a long ride in the car and I am ready to unwind.

I text Cricket and give her the briefest idea of where we are and why. I can't give her much more because I'm not sure myself what our trip means.

As I stride through the knee-high grass, I scare a rabbit and startle a small snake. And because I happen to remember that Lawrence supposedly found his treasure in a crumbled old well in the yard, I pick up a long stick to test the ground ahead of me. I don't want to fall into something that the weeds are hiding.

Ahead, through the leaves of several trees at the back of the yard, I can see flashes of sunlight sparkling off the water of Pamlico Sound. I can't see well enough to tell if Lawrence is out there in a boat, but it doesn't look like it. I walk closer and stand on a ledge where the yard drops off.

Again, I scan the water through the trees that line the lower shoreline. My search is interrupted, however, when the edge of the ledge I'm standing on begins to sink. Just in time, I scramble back to solid ground. Stones and earth fall away from where I had been standing. Tall grass hides the edge of the ledge, but I can hear stones falling below. My heart pounds at the close call. And then I hear a cry.

"Help me!" someone moans from under the drop-off. "Is someone up there? Please help me!"

"Where are you?" I shout.

"Down here. I'm hurt."

"I'll get help," I yell. "I'll be back!"

With all the speed I can muster, I race to the cabin and burst through the door.

"Dad! Uncle Chad! I think I've found Lawrence. You need to help!"

"Whoa! Slow down," Dad says. "Where is he?"

"There's a drop-off at the back of the yard. I think he's fallen down there. I can hear him, but I can't see him. The edge is too crumbly so I can't look. We need a rope or something."

"More than a rope," Uncle Chad says. "We'll use the winch on the front of the SUV. I have a harness and some straps, too."

Uncle Chad races to start the car and follows my directions across the yard toward the ledge. He stops before he hits the soft ground, and as the SUV engine idles, Dad pulls on a pair of work gloves.

Uncle Chad attaches the winch harness to its cable hook, and Dad inserts his legs into the leather loops. He then stuffs some extra leather straps into his belt. And after Dad grabs the cable firmly, Uncle Chad engages the winch motor. The cable unwinds and Dad steps backward, toward the drop-off point. With a sudden cry of surprise, Dad's feet slide away and he hangs in mid-air.

"Hold on!" Uncle Chad calls.

"I'm okay," Dad calls back. "It just surprised me. You can let me down, now, slowly."

Little by little, the winch cable unwinds from the spool at the front of the SUV.

"More!" Dad calls. "A little more. A little more. Okay! That's it. Now give me a minute."

Dad announces loudly that Lawrence is unconscious. "I'm going to strap him to me so you can bring us up together. Can the winch handle that?"

"Yes!" calls Uncle Chad. "I'm more worried about the ledge holding up than the winch. Let me know when you're ready."

"Now," yells Dad. "Pull us slowly."

The winch engages, the SUV shudders, and the cable begins to rewind. The steel rope slices through the loose dirt and sends more stones over the drop-off edge. I wonder if the entire ledge is too soft to make the rescue, but then the line scrapes on rock and the cable begins to raise its precious cargo.

When Dad's head appears, Uncle Chad calls out, "I'm sorry, Jonathan, but we have to drag you across to a more stable spot. Hang on!"

To protect Lawrence and to keep him off the ground, Dad lies on his back with Lawrence on top of him. When the winch stops, Dad's shirt is torn and his back is bleeding. Mom and I hurry to release both men from the straps and the harness.

"Your back looks awful!" Mom cries, but Dad asks, "How is Lawrence?"

"His leg looks broken, and he's passed out. We need to get medical help quickly," Uncle Chad says.

Mom dials 911. The dispatcher assures us that someone is on their way. "Can you stand in the driveway turnoff so our EMTs know which drive to take?" he asks.

Uncle Chad turns to me, "Come on, Alexander. Let's go and flag down the ambulance."

———◆———

"Your friend is in shock," the EMTs say, after they slide Lawrence into the emergency vehicle. "He's lucky you found him when you did. We'll engage the siren, and you can follow us."

In Uncle Chad's SUV, we follow the racing ambulance to a Plymouth hospital about an hour away.

# Chapter 28

## Grace

Dad answers the hospital's admitting questions and is relieved to learn that the hospital computer already has Lawrence in its database. "Everything's here," the admitting receptionist says, "even insurance details. I just need your information now, so we can treat you, too. We're really busy, so I'm going to assign you to the same emergency bay as Mr. Traeger. You'll both be treated there. Bay Three, on the right." Dad and I go to the bay, but Mom and Uncle Chad stay in the waiting room.

"I'm surprised that Mr. Traeger was able to call for help," the ER doctor says. "He's very lucky you came when you did." Then he asks Dad, "Is he by any chance accident prone? I see that he was admitted last year with a sprained elbow. And his hand looks like a burn from an industrial accident."

"He's not accident prone that I know of," Dad says. "The burn is old. He told us his hand was burned in a grease fire a couple of years ago."

The doctor gives a sideways glance. "A grease fire, huh? I doubt it."

To the nurses, the doctor says, "Get Mr. Traeger cleaned up and ready for some X-rays of his leg and spine. And one of you needs to stay and help me take care of this guy, too. He looks terrible. We need to pick some gravel from his back."

Lawrence is wheeled away, and the doctor and one of the nurses turn their attention to Dad. After they patch him up, I bring Mom to the bay. Together we lead Dad out to a waiting room chair.

"Every muscle is stiff," Dad whimpers, and Mom tells him, "You look terrible."

Because he can't lean back in the chair, Mom pulls Dad's head onto her shoulder. "Close your eyes, dear," she says. "Just rest. If they're taking Lawrence for X-rays, we may be here for a while."

When another family enters the waiting room with carry-out sandwiches from the cafeteria, I realize we haven't had lunch. Uncle Chad says his stomach is growling, too, and he asks Mom and Dad if they want us to bring sandwiches.

The other family in the waiting room tells us to hurry because the cafeteria closes at 1:30.

———— • ————

At three o'clock, a nurse tells us that Lawrence is on his way to surgery. "After recovery, he'll be taken to Room 355," she says. "You can wait for him in that room if you like, or I can call you once he is out of recovery. It may be several hours."

Dad gives the nurse his cell phone number and we go to sit outside the hospital entrance on a quiet, sunny bench. The fresh air and the bright colors of the entrance-area flowers offer a welcome change from the drab interior and the hum of hospital activity.

Like me, Uncle Chad is tired of sitting. "Want to go for a walk?" he suggests, and we amble along paths that wind through the hospital gardens.

"Bet you never thought you'd be stuck in a North Carolina hospital at the start of your summer vacation, did you?" Uncle Chad asks.

"Nope," I say. "And I'll bet you never thought you'd be in North Carolina to save Lawrence's life."

"Nope," Uncle Chad replies. "That was the farthest thing from my mind."

After a moment, I ask, "Why do you suppose we all dreamed about Lawrence needing help?"

Uncle Chad looks at the sky. "Because of grace," he says.

I look at the sky too and ask, "What's grace?"

"Grace, my boy, is something God set in motion when he sent Jesus to earth," says Uncle Chad. "It is a gift—something that is totally impossible to earn. And that gift involves a chance for forgiveness and starting over. Sin has a strangle-hold on each of us and robs us of life and its fulness. So, Jesus, who was God's perfect and sinless son, gave his life to free us from sin's power and to open the way for us to be reborn—to start fresh is God's eyes."

Now Uncle Chad looks at me over his glasses. He says, "Lawrence needs forgiveness and a new start. And I have to follow God's example and give him my forgiveness."

"So, you forgive him, just like that?" I ask. "After all he's done?"

"Especially because of what he's done. We all need forgiveness and grace for something."

"I have to think about that," I say.

Until I saw Lawrence hurt and broken, I had wanted revenge. I had wanted him to pay for his treachery. Even now, I want him to admit to his crime and hear how much he has hurt me and my family.

But I don't know what I'll say when he finally wakes up.

———◆———

Long after supper, Lawrence is delivered to Room 355. He arrives sound asleep and with his leg in traction and in a cast. His head is also bandaged.

"He's doing all right," the nurse assures us, "but he's on pain killers that will keep him drowsy. He may not make a lot of sense when you try to talk to him. And he will sleep a lot." Then she suggests, "Since it's getting late, why don't you go home and get a good night's rest? You can see him in the morning. We'll take good care of him, I promise."

Uncle Chad agrees, and we collect our things.

We are just about to leave when Lawrence opens his eyes. In his drugged stupor, he sees Dad and he frowns. "No," he mumbles. And he closes his eyes again. "I'm sorry. I'm sorry," he whispers. But then he is once more asleep.

Lawrence's reaction makes me think about what Uncle Chad has said. Is Lawrence in need of our forgiveness? How will he react when his drugs begin to wear off?

———◆———

Back at the cabin, we're so tired that we can barely get ourselves ready for bed. Uncle Chad stretches out on the sofa and I curl up in a sleeping bag on the rug. Mom and Dad take the spare bedroom, and we leave Lawrence's bed unused.

In the morning my dad's grumpiness makes it plain that he didn't sleep well. "I never sleep on my stomach," he complains.

"But you're learning," Mom says. "It's going to take a while for those cuts to heal."

Over eggs, milk, and toast—things from Lawrence's larder that we will need to replenish—Dad asks Uncle Chad, "Does it strike you as odd that Lawrence is living here and not somewhere fancier and more modern?"

"In keeping with his fortunes, you mean?" Uncle Chad asks.

"Right. Why isn't he in some big city with a penthouse or a mansion?" (*Or a yacht,* I think, when I remember my dream about him with all of his onboard servants.)

Uncle Chad says, "I believe that Lawrence is in hiding, or is at least avoiding people."

"But," Mom says, "with his money couldn't he hide somewhere expensive, more comfortable?"

Uncle Chad suggests, "I am going to guess that he stays here and out of the limelight because he's caught up in guilt."

"I should think so!" Mom exclaims.

"But who is he afraid of seeing?" Dad asks. "As far as he's concerned, there's nobody who knows what's happened."

"Nobody but himself. It's enough that he knows. And he can't face you, Jonathan."

"Me?"

"Yes. You and Alexander. I think what he's done haunts him. Even though he thinks you'll never know what happened, he knows that he's wronged you. He took me away from you. And it eats him up that he can't confess it. After all, who would believe him?"

Dad nods. "You could be right. But if he's feeling guilty now, how will he feel when he discovers you're back and learns that we know everything he's done?"

"I've thought of that," says Uncle Chad. "That's why I've stayed out of sight since we found him. I've made sure that you, Jonathan, are the one he sees—not me. If he wasn't in bad shape, I might have shown myself, straight out. But in this condition, I don't think he can take the shock. There will be time enough for us to reveal me and my story."

And Uncle Chad stays at the cabin in the morning when we leave again for the hospital.

# Chapter 29

## Lawrence Awakens

When we enter Lawrence's room, we see that he is still sleeping. But he is not alone. Bent over the edge of his bed and holding his hand is an attractive young woman who smiles when she sees us.

"Are you the people who found Lawrence?" she asks.

"Yes," Mom says. "It was quite by chance."

"I'm glad you did. My name is Laura. I work at The Captain's Diner in Swanquarter, and I'm a friend of Lawrence's."

"It's good to meet you," Dad says. "I'm Jonathan and this is my wife Gwen and my son Alexander."

Then Dad explains, "We came to Swanquarter on a surprise visit to Lawrence, but I guess the surprise is on us."

"I'm sorry it turned out this way," Laura says. "But if you hadn't come, Lawrence might not have made it. We might have found him too late. It was a full day before I began to miss him at the diner. And I just happened to overhear an ambulance driver mention at breakfast that Lawrence was in the Plymouth hospital. I made a quick trip here this morning because I have to be at work in a couple of hours and I didn't want Lawrence to be here all alone."

I try to imagine Laura serving tables at the diner. It helps that lying with her purse is a folded pale green apron that matches the ribbon on her pony-tail.

"Hopefully, you can come back," Mom says. "It sounds like Lawrence would like that."

"Oh, I will," says Laura. "I want to encourage him. He's always so depressed. I hope this accident doesn't make it worse. I just keep praying."

Mom says, "That's good, dear. He can use all the help he can get." Mom's tone holds a tiny note of sarcasm but I doubt that Laura has heard it.

"I hope you can cheer him up," Laura says.

"We'll try," replies Mom, and Laura smiles and leaves.

Lawrence remains asleep. A nurse peeks in from time to time, and we watch television with the sound turned low. The hours pass at a snail's pace.

---◆---

At lunchtime, on our way to the cafeteria, Dad places a call to Uncle Chad. "Lawrence is still sleeping," he reports to him, "and we're on our way to find some food. How are you faring?"

Dad listens to Uncle Chad's reply and chuckles. "You always were fond of grilled cheese sandwiches."

Now Dad listens again and we hear his responses. "Uh-huh. Sure. Well, we've met a friend of Lawrence's. Laura works at a diner in Swanquarter and was here when we arrived this morning. She's gone now because she had to get back to work."

Dad listens and then replies, "No, I didn't ask Laura if she knew of any relatives. I can ask the hospital for a contact name, but I doubt that they'll share it with me—HIPPA laws, you know."

Then Dad replies again. "Sure. I'll try that. Talk to you later, Chad."

After he hangs up, Dad starts thumbing through some online resources on his phone. "Chad suggested we take a peek at the grandfather's obituary for a list of surviving relatives."

"Good idea," Mom says, and she looks over Dad's shoulder as he reads the obituary on his screen.

"Kellen H. Traeger, 87," reads Dad. And then he says, "But the only living relative seems to be Lawrence. Everyone else who's listed has preceded Kellen in death, including Lawrence's parents."

Mom frowns. "His parents?"

I am surprised too. And although I'm still angry at Lawrence, I'm also sad that he seems to be without family. I'm glad that Laura is his friend.

---◆---

At about one-thirty I walk into Lawrence's room while the others dally in the hallway after our lunch. Lawrence groggily turns his head and sees me.

"You're awake!" I cry, and I haven't thought about what his response might be until I see the terror in his eyes.

"No!" he cries. "No!" And he begins to thrash about and tangle the traction equipment.

Nurses rush in past Mom and Dad and force Lawrence back against the mattress. "You have a broken leg, Mr. Traeger," they declare loudly. "You cannot get out of bed."

Lawrence continues to fight them but is unsuccessful. The nurses force him to lie back, and they end up strapping his arms and other leg so he cannot move. Now, only his head is twisting in defiance. His eyes are squeezed shut and he is grinding his teeth. "No!!!" he howls. And before we can say a word to him, another nurse rushes in with a sedative. Within seconds Lawrence melts calmly into a drugged sleep.

"What happened?" the nurse asks.

"A nightmare," Dad says. "I think we surprised him in the middle of a nightmare."

What Dad says is partly true. We are his nightmare, and I wonder if we'll ever be able to talk with Lawrence.

———— ◆ ————

Laura arrives around three o'clock and finds us napping and Lawrence still sleeping. She's disappointed that she can't talk with him.

"I hope he'll rouse before I leave at eight," she says. "I want to cheer him up. I had to pull some strings to switch my dinner shift to the breakfast and lunch shift."

She takes Lawrence's limp hand and says, "I wish you could have known Lawrence's grandfather. He could make everyone—even Lawrence—laugh at his stories. And he loved playing at being a fishing guide for vacationing anglers. We all miss him, but especially Lawrence. I've been worried about Lawrence since Kellen died."

I look at Laura's worried face and at the man lying in the bed in front of us, and I can't recall Lawrence ever being depressed. If anything, he was a bit of a practical joker and enjoyed teasing me while we set up experiments in Uncle Chad's workshop. The closest I ever came to seeing Lawrence solemn was after Uncle Chad disappeared and we were all caught up in worry.

Was Lawrence suffering from a guilty conscience, as Uncle Chad has speculated? I do wonder.

Mom asks Laura if she has known Lawrence long, and Laura replies, "About a year. I met him when he moved here several months before Kellen died. I guess that when Lawrence was a kid, his family visited here each summer and Kellen taught him to fish. Lawrence told me how much he always looked up to his grandfather. And then Lawrence's mother left (she ran off with a dentist back in Pennsylvania), and Lawrence and his dad would come to the cabin alone. Lawrence told me that his dad never got over the divorce and that when Lawrence went off to college, his dad walked out of his shoe store and never came back. They found his body several miles away along the highway and nobody ever learned what happened to him. That was the beginning of Lawrence's depression. And his melancholy overwhelmed him when his grandfather died. Lawrence simply holed up in the cabin and never went anywhere."

"We had no idea," Mom murmurs.

We all look at Lawrence's broken body in the hospital bed and see a side of him we never knew. I still envision the jokester I had prepared projects with and the smug traitor who betrayed us, but now I also see a lonely, disappointed man.

"Tell me again how your family happens to know Lawrence," Laura says. And Dad answers.

"Lawrence came to Ohio a little over two years ago. He was finishing a degree in science-writing that would complement his other degree in archaeological studies. My brother, Chad Tennyson, writes for *Armchair Science* magazine and agreed to let Lawrence live and work with him while he gained the on-the-job credits he needed to graduate. But then, my brother mysteriously disappeared."

"Oh!" Laura cries. "Another person who dropped out of Lawrence's life!"

I wish we could correct Laura's view of things and tell her that Lawrence was the reason for Uncle Chad's disappearance, but Dad merely clears his throat and continues.

"No one knew where Chad went or what happened to him," Dad says. "Lawrence remained at our house for a short time during the missing person's investigation. Then he returned to the university, and we lost track of him after he graduated. We just happened to see the *USA Today* article about his Swanquarter pirate-treasure discovery, and we were happy for his good fortune and assumed that he was on his way to life among the rich and famous. It was a surprise to learn that instead of living it up in the Bahamas or somewhere equally wonderful, Lawrence has been staying in Swanquarter in his grandfather's cabin. We decided to look him up and were able to find the cabin the other day. But Lawrence wasn't home. Since his door was unlocked and the truck was in the garage, we thought maybe he'd gone to visit a neighbor or gone fishing for a while, so we waited. And then Alexander was exploring the back of the yard and found the ledge that had broken off. He heard Lawrence's cry for help and realized that he had gone over the ledge. Fortunately, Chad has a winch on his car, so we hauled Lawrence up to safety and called an ambulance. And you know the rest."

"What a blessing that you came when you did!" Laura says.

Dad nods and looks down. I'm sure he's wondering, as I do, what Laura will think when she hears the full story.

---

In the evening, just before seven o'clock, Lawrence opens his eyes. "You came," he murmurs to Laura, who sits beside him.

"Of course, I did," she reassures him. "We're friends, right?"

Lawrence smiles, and Laura pats his hand.

"I got kind of banged up," Lawrence says. "I can't believe I fell."

"I understand you fell down a drop-off?" Laura asks.

"Yeah. The leading edge of the ledge in my backyard broke off. I wasn't expecting that."

"You're lucky that your friends came along," Laura says.

Lawrence looks confused. "You didn't find me?"

"No. Your friends, here, found you."

Lawrence turns his head and sees Dad and me. His pulse rate rises on his monitor, and his eyes grow large. A nurse quickly steps into the room.

"Is everything okay?" she asks.

"Yes-yes, I'm fine," Lawrence stutters. "I was just surprised by something, that's all."

The nurse nods and moves on.

"Glad you're doing better," Dad says. "We were worried about you."

Lawrence lowers his eyes. "Thanks."

Then Lawrence says, "So, you're the ones who found me?"

"Yes. We were on our way to give you a surprise visit, and you weren't home. Since it looked like you might not be far away, we waited. And Alexander decided to explore the yard; he's the one who heard your cry for help."

Lawrence manages a small smile. He turns to me. "So, I have you to thank?"

"Yes," I say. "I found you, but Dad is the one who went over the ledge to get you winched up."

Lawrence nods as if trying to remember. "I'm afraid things are too hazy about all of that. But I'm glad you got me to the hospital."

Laura informs him, "The nursing staff says you have a serious compound fracture and you have a lot of bruised bones—plus a bump on your head and a couple of bruised spots on your back. They tell me the doctor says you'll recover fully, but it's going to take time."

Then she adds, "And you will do everything they tell you; I'll make sure of it."

Lawrence grins. He says to me and Dad, "This little woman is the only reason I'm sane, today. At least I think I am. She prays for me all the time."

"Somebody has to," Laura says.

Then Lawrence asks Dad, "Tell me again why you came to visit me. How did you know where I lived?"

"The *USA Today* article," Dad says. "It said you found your treasure at your grandfather's cabin in Swanquarter. We thought we'd see if we could find the cabin."

"Hmmm." Lawrence lowers his eyes. "I've thought about you guys a lot. Sorry I haven't kept in touch. A lot of sad memories."

"Yes," says Dad.

And then I'm surprised when Dad offers, "Did you know that Chad is back?"

Lawrence fights to maintain his composure, and he says, "Yes, I-I saw the news reports about his Egyptian discovery. You must be very happy."

"Oh, we are!" I say.

"I-I am surprised," Lawrence says. "After all this time..."

"It's good to have him back," says Dad. "And he's enjoying getting back to his work and writing."

"He-he's a good man," Lawrence murmurs.

"And a very forgiving man," Dad says.

Immediately tears fill Lawrence's eyes.

A nurse catches him crying when she comes to replace his saline drip and dispense his medications. "Hey!" she offers jovially, "No crying on this floor. The doctor will think we've been beating you! You look like it, you know."

"And," says the nurse, "visiting hours are just about over. So, y'all better say your goodbyes and skedaddle. I'll be taking it from here."

# Chapter 30

## How?

In the morning, without Laura present, Uncle Chad joins us in Lawrence's room. The minute Lawrence sees him, he bursts into tears. A nurse comes to check, and Lawrence tells her, "It's okay." And Dad explains, "Just a reunion from a long time ago. This is my brother, Dr. Tennyson."

"A doctor?" the nurse replies.

"Not a medical doctor," Uncle Chad explains.

"Well, it's nice to meet you. Just don't upset my patient too much, okay?" The nurse is serious, but she smiles when she leaves.

Lawrence's eyes continue to fill, and he refuses to look at Uncle Chad. "I-I'm sorry! I'm so sorry!" he murmurs. And Uncle Chad shakes his head.

"What's done is done," Uncle Chad says. "And all has ended well. I accept your apology. And you need to know that I forgive you."

Lawrence cannot hold in a sob. "I don't deserve your forgiveness," he says. "And I've hurt your family."

"Ah, but I have learned a great deal from my experience," says Uncle Chad. "You needn't cry. I learned so many good things. My experience opened my eyes to insights I never would have gained in any other way. So, you need to know that I'm actually grateful for what happened."

Lawrence sputters, "But-but I don't understand how…"

"How I got back to the present?" Uncle Chad finishes his question.

"Yes. Because I know that the necklaces are still at the bottom of the ledge. I saw the coffee can still there after I fell, so I don't understand how…"

"We'll cover all of that soon," says Uncle Chad. "But Laura will be here any minute, and we don't want to spoil her visit. We'll talk after she leaves."

Lawrence nods. Quietly he says, "Thank you."

———— ◆ ————

By the time Laura arrives in the afternoon, there are no more tears. We've left the chair next to Lawrence's bed for Laura, and she takes Lawrence's hand and squeezes it.

"This man is Dr. Chad Tennyson," Lawrence tells her. "I'm glad you're able to meet him. He's a world-famous science writer, and with his help I finished my science-writing degree a few years ago."

Laura turns her surprised eyes to Dad. "Is this the brother who disappeared?"

"Yes," Dad says. "He was gone for two years, but he's back now. Turns out, he was living with some desert dwellers in the Middle East and had no way to communicate with us. Now that he's back, he's writing about his experience and what he learned."

"Ah," says Laura. "Sounds mysterious and exciting."

Uncle Chad's eyes crinkle into a smile. "It was, my dear. Mysterious and exciting."

"And," says Uncle Chad, "I could use a snack from the vending machine down the hall. Anybody want to join me?"

It is impossible to miss that he wants us to go with him and leave Lawrence and Laura alone.

We get up and follow him and say that we'll be back in a little bit.

———— ◆ ————

We stay away for about an hour, wandering the halls and inspecting the hospital gardens while sipping soft drinks and coffee from the vending machines.

When we finally return, we hear laughter. Laura is in the middle of a story about one of her customers, and she and Lawrence are giggling.

"Don't let us interrupt," says Uncle Chad. "We can take another turn around the hospital if you two need more time."

"Oh, don't be silly," Laura chuckles. "This is a story you'll like, too."

And she backtracks to bring us up to the point she was getting ready to share with Lawrence.

"...and then Cecil saw the sheriff's deputy walk past the window, and he was sure he was going to be found out, so he ducked under the table. I decided Cecil must be finished eating, so I cleared the booth and started for the kitchen. When Deputy Loomis saw the empty booth, he slipped in opposite the seat that Cecil had just occupied. I tried to act natural when I came back to the booth to take the deputy's order. I also managed to slip Cecil's bill under the table. As I poured Deputy Loomis's coffee, Cecil slipped me his money and mouthed the words, 'keep the change.' By then, everyone in the diner was snickering and staring at the booth, and Deputy Loomis was getting uncomfortable with the attention. Loomis whispered, 'Do I have something on my face or the back of my shirt that I should know about?' I put on my most innocent look and told him I didn't see a thing. He finally asked me to make his meal a *to go* order. 'I'll eat at the office,' he said, and I brought his packaged lunch to him. Everything would have been fine, except that as I turned away, the deputy's sleeve caught a fork and swept it off the table. When Deputy Loomis gallantly reached down to get it for me, he came face-to-face with Cecil under the table! 'You!' cried Loomis. And Cecil nearly knocked himself out getting out from under the booth. Loomis, however, was faster and had handcuffs on him before Cecil could turn around. Then the whole diner broke out in applause. Loomis took a bow, and he led Cecil out the door while reading him his rights."

"Bravo!" cries Lawrence. "It was about time Cecil got caught." Lawrence continues to laugh until he looks up, and when he sees Uncle Chad, he realizes that he too has been *caught*. His laughter trails off, and he covers it with a cough.

"Are you okay?" Laura asks.

"Yes. Yes, I'm fine," Lawrence insists.

Uncle Chad realizes the problem and hurries to relieve the awkward situation. "What kind of food do you serve at that diner?" Uncle Chad asks Laura. "We might stop in there and let you wait on us, one of these days."

"Depends on whether you're interested in breakfast, lunch, or dinner," Laura answers, and she fluently rattles off the favorites for each meal.

"Plus," she says, "you might be lucky enough to see Deputy Loomis.

I'd introduce you to Cecil too, but he won't be out of jail for a while. He has multiple counts against him for stealing his neighbors' chickens."

We laugh again, and Laura shares more stories about Swanquarter and her customers. I feel like I know each person and would have no trouble picking them out from the diner crowd—all the way from the mayor down to the owner of the bait store.

When it is finally time for Laura to leave, she gives Lawrence a peck on the cheek and says good bye. Lawrence clings to her hand as if unwilling to let her go. And when she leaves, the sunshine leaves the room.

————— • • —————

At noon we bring our lunch from the cafeteria so we can eat with Lawrence. And Mom mentions Laura.

"I like her," Mom says. "She's bright and cheerful."

"Yes," says Lawrence. "I'm lucky to have her for a friend. It's a cinch I don't deserve her."

"Maybe not," says Uncle Chad, "but don't let her get away."

Lawrence sighs. "She won't want to stay when she finds out what kind of person I really am."

Lawrence starts to lapse into a distraught apology, but Uncle Chad quickly interjects, "You don't know Laura's reaction. All of us have things in our past we're not proud of. But we move on. We learn from our mistakes, and we become better people."

Lawrence protests, "You keep saying that, but I don't deserve forgiveness for what I did. I'm glad you were rescued, but it doesn't erase my guilt."

"But the harm from your action is less now that I've been rescued, wouldn't you say?" Uncle Chad replies with a raised eyebrow.

"But I had no part in your rescue," says Lawrence. "I don't even know how it happened."

"Ah," says Uncle Chad. "I think it's time for you to hear a wonderful story."

Uncle Chad settles back in his chair, folds his hands, and says, "My rescue. Page One."

Then he says, "The beginning of my rescue started when Alexander found my hidden journal."

Instantly Lawrence lowers his head.

"I knew you were reading my journal," Uncle Chad tells him, "and I recognized the danger it posed to you and to me. I hid the journal away, but it was too late. I could tell that the poison of the onyx stones' power had already begun to tempt you. You were drunk with the idea of visiting the past and gaining easy wealth, and you didn't see the danger. I tried to send you away, but I also knew you would return. And you did. When I awakened from a dead sleep to find myself among the ancient Israelites, I knew you had clicked the stones. Then before I could get you to click the stones again and come home, you tore that opportunity away. I watched you run away with my necklace, and I didn't see you again, until now."

Lawrence can't look at Uncle Chad. His eyes are closed.

"For two years I lived in hope that you might come back for me," says Uncle Chad. "But with the passing of every day my hope melted away, and I mourned my family and my other life. Then, eventually I came to grips with where I was and how I needed to live out my days among the Israelites."

"But," Lawrence insists, "I did try to come back for you. You may not believe it, but I did try. But the stones wouldn't let me."

He shakes his head at the memory.

"I do believe you," says Uncle Chad. "I learned recently how my necklace burned your hand. I'm even surprised that you were able to get back to the present without more damage to yourself."

Lawrence looks at his hands and heaves a huge sigh. His words come quickly, now, as he explains, "I did plot to click our stones and fly to the past with you. But I hadn't planned on stealing your necklace after we got there. It all happened so fast!"

"I don't know what I had expected," Lawrence continues, "but the trip through time was horrifying to me. And when we got there, I wanted to hurry and undo what I had done. But in my disorientation and fright, I pulled on your necklace too hard. And when the necklace broke off, it burned so deeply into my hand that I couldn't let go of it. It burned right down to the bone. I wasn't in my right mind, and I ran. Because people were chasing me, I ducked into a tent and hid in a corner. And there, right in front of me, were bags of Egyptian treasure—exactly what I had made the onyx stones trip to find. I heard noises outside, and I quickly looped the bag's ties around my good arm and clicked the stones. As I had hoped, the bag rose into the air with me. But I paid a heavy price to bring it home. The stones continued to punish me, and I screamed in pain through the universe. It was impossible to let the stones go. Even if I could have released them, I was petrified of being stranded in space and unable to go forward or backward. I had no choice but to let the stones melt my flesh!

"Only after I got to your house and stuck my hand into your freezer was I finally able to let go of the necklace. But by then my hand was a melted mess. I grabbed my treasure bag and drove to the university hospital with a towel full of ice wrapped around my burn. At the hospital the doctor was convinced that I had been handling nuclear material. I just let him believe whatever he wanted as long as he fixed me up. When I finally brought your car back, I found the investigation underway for your disappearance. I hated that I couldn't tell anyone the truth. But how could I explain? No one would have believed my story. I stayed with your brother's family for a couple of weeks and then I left. I couldn't keep up the lie, and I imagined that you were dead. The only person I could flee to was my grandfather."

Uncle Chad nods. "You couldn't have known I was still alive," he says. "No one knew until Alexander and his friends found me."

"But how?" Lawrence asks. "How could they find you without the necklaces?"

Lawrence's eyes are filled with disbelief.

"It was a miracle," admits Uncle Chad as he pats my back. "And it all started in October. Alexander and his friend Cricket visited my workshop and happened to stumble upon where I had hidden my journal. And the two of them read my story, including my final entry that said I was hiding the journal from you and that I had fended you off with a meat cleaver."

Lawrence winces and barely whispers, "I'm so ashamed!"

"Thankfully," says Uncle Chad, "the children believed the whole story. And not only did they believe it, but Cricket revealed to Alexander that she also had a history with onyx stones."

Lawrence blinks his astonishment. "Someone else has onyx stones, too?"

"Yes, it's true," says Uncle Chad. "And because of her experiences with them, Cricket was able to deduce what had happened to me. She and Alexander then recruited Cricket's guardians to help mount my rescue."

"Really!" Lawrence breathes. "I never dreamed..."

"Nor did I," says Uncle Chad. "But I am here!"

Now Lawrence fidgets uncomfortably. Looking down, he admits, "I knew you were back. And it scared me. I saw your photo with Dr. Ibrahim in the news report, and I couldn't imagine how you had returned. You had no necklaces—or so I thought. But I remembered what you wrote in your journal about not being able to throw away your necklace, and I wondered, *did the necklaces magically return to you? Or were they still in the coffee can I had thrown over the ledge in the yard?* I had to know. That's why I ran to the ledge and was peering over. And that's when the ledge broke off and I fell. And I thought I was going to die."

"But we found you, and you're on the mend," says Uncle Chad.

"I know," says Lawrence, "but I still don't understand how you came to be in Swanquarter. Why did you come, and how did you know I was here?"

"It wasn't too difficult," says Uncle Chad. "Your picture was plastered all over the *USA Today* several months ago. We read about your grandfather's cabin and your pirate treasure."

"Pirate treasure, humph!" Lawrence spits bitterly. "You know very well that that treasure came from ancient Egypt. I never showed it to my grandfather. But I did try to tell him once what I had done. He couldn't grasp it though, and I never mentioned it again.

"Then when Grandfather died, I lost the last of my family and the last sane person in my life. And I wanted to run away. I stupidly decided to fake how I found the treasure so I could sell it to a state museum. But their evaluators didn't believe it was Blackbeard's, and they kept putting off acquiring it. Plus, news of a pirate find drew treasure rats from everywhere. I found them digging in my yard in the middle of the night or whenever I went into town."

"So, you're not rich?" I ask.

"Rich? No. I'm the poorest man that ever lived."

"But don't you still have the treasure?" I ask.

"Yes, but it's of no use to me. It's behind a pile of junk in the garage. I can't sell it easily and I don't have enough money to run away without selling it. Besides, I know that running away will not solve my problems. My guilty heart will just follow me wherever I go."

"But it doesn't have to," says Uncle Chad.

Lawrence laughs bitterly. "That's funny, coming from you," he says. "I can't deny anything, now that you're back."

"Just because something can't be denied doesn't mean that it can't be forgiven," says Uncle Chad. "After all, God knows everything, but even He has provided a path for forgiveness."

"God? You, talking about God? Those are words I never thought I'd hear from your lips," Lawrence says. "You're the scientist who only believes what he can prove."

"Or what he has seen," says Uncle Chad. "And I've seen more than enough over the last two years to convince me that the God of the Bible is real."

Lawrence considers this for a moment. "You were close to believing all that stuff when you experienced the things you wrote about in your journal."

Uncle Chad nods. "And I've seen more—enough to convince me that the Old Testament accounts are not just the myths I used to believe them to be."

Lawrence shakes his head. "I guess that's good for you. But that stuff is all in the past. If God exists, where is he today when you need him? He seems to have stopped caring about people a long time ago."

But Uncle Chad challenges him. "I think you're wrong. He seems to care about you."

"Ha!" Lawrence laughs. "Is that why I'm all broken and lying here in a hospital bed?"

"Yes," says Uncle Chad. "You're being taken care of in a hospital because of God's intervention."

"Oh, not so fast," says Lawrence. "People end up in a hospital automatically when someone finds them hurt. God didn't have to lift a finger to make that happen."

"Oh, but he did," says Uncle Chad. "You wouldn't be in the hospital if we hadn't found you."

"So, you found me and brought me here. What's God got to do with that?"

"Everything."

That answer has come from Dad, and Lawrence looks surprised.

"God had more to do with it than you know, young man," Dad says.

"Like what?" Lawrence says. "All I see is that you came to my house, Alexander heard my cry, and you got me to a hospital. What's so unusual about that?"

"Nothing, except for how and why we came to your house."

Lawrence looks at Dad with impatience. "You keep hinting that there's something I don't know. Spit it out! What's so unusual?"

Uncle Chad answers. "Don't flatter yourself that we came all this way to spend our vacation in Swanquarter. In truth, we had no intention of coming here."

"So, why did you?"

"Because," says Uncle Chad, "we all had a nightmare—we all had the *same* nightmare. And in it, we heard you crying in the dark for help."

Lawrence looks shocked.

"And when we realized that we had all had the same dream, we felt compelled to come. And even though we didn't know where you were, God guided us here. We drove thirteen hours on the strength of our shared dreams and a kind of homing device that told us where to drive."

Lawrence is struck dumb. He looks at us in disbelief.

"That's not possible!" he says.

"Nor is time travel," says Uncle Chad.

And the awe of how we were led to Swanquarter to save Lawrence electrifies him as it had electrified us.

# Chapter 31

## Full Confession

It's nearly dark after we eat our drive-thru supper and finally get back to the cabin. Dad has been unusually quiet on the drive, and he surprises us now as we pull in. "There's something I want to do," he says. "Come with me."

Dad leads us across the driveway to the garage and we follow him inside. When he starts to inspect the piles of fishing gear and debris in the corners and along the walls, we know that he is looking for Lawrence's bag of treasure. We join in the search. And after we move dozens of tools and useless old car parts, we find it.

With a little hesitancy, Dad bends to open the bag. "I guess he is telling the truth," he says. "I just can't imagine that he hasn't found a way to sell this yet."

Uncle Chad reminds Dad, "To sell this kind of treasure, except in certain circles of billionaire buyers, you have to explain where you found it. Lawrence's tale about it being pirate treasure isn't convincing enough for legitimate buyers of antiquities."

"It's a shame that he stole it," says Mom, "but it's also a shame that he can't sell it."

Uncle Chad watches while Dad replaces the sack to its dark corner. And Dad says, "I can see now why you took your treasure to that desert rock to get rid of it. It's too bad we couldn't have taken Lawrence's treasure, too, and put this whole mess behind him."

"True," says Uncle Chad. "The only rightful place for these items is in the past."

Now Uncle Chad chuckles. "It will be interesting to see if we can get it there."

"Wha...?"

Mom and Dad react in surprise.

"Surely you don't mean that you're going to fly back to Egypt and hide this bag and let Ibrahim dig it up," says Mom.

"And," says Dad, "tell me that you're not talking about taking it back in time, right?"

Uncle Chad smiles. "I have to admit that from time to time things pop into my head that even I wonder about." And he says no more on the subject. My imagination is already running wild.

———◆———

In the morning at the hospital, Laura dances into the room with a magazine. "Look at what I found in the hospital gift shop!" she cries. In her hands is the May issue of *Armchair Science* opened to page eleven. I know that she is clueless as to what really happened on our expedition, but she is excited, nevertheless.

"What a wonderful adventure!" she exclaims. "Look at you, Alexander! Did you have fun?"

"Oh, yes," I say. "I got to fly to Egypt with Uncle Chad and my dad. It was great!"

"How lucky you are," Laura says. "I've never been outside of the United States. I would have loved a trip like that."

Uncle Chad smiles. "Maybe one day we could arrange a trip and take you with us."

"I would love it," Laura says. "You would come too, wouldn't you, Lawrence?"

"Sure," Lawrence says quietly, as if he doesn't believe it will happen. And he adds, "As long as we take an airplane."

Laura smiles at the odd remark, but the rest of us know exactly what Lawrence means. Mom shifts uncomfortably in her seat. She's beginning to realize that something is brewing. Something is going to happen.

———————•————————

Mid-morning, Lawrence's doctor visits his patient. We politely bow out of the room and head for the cafeteria for a snack. Only Laura remains to hear what the doctor says.

When we return, Lawrence's traction equipment is gone, and Lawrence gives us his news.

"The doctor says it could take from three to six months for my leg to fully heal. And the hospital is making arrangements for me to go to a nursing facility for that time. It's a cinch that if I went home, I couldn't fend for myself."

"Too bad you don't have a wife to take care of you," Uncle Chad teases with a twinkle in his eye.

And on his cue, without a smidgen of proper restraint, I blurt, "Yeah. You could marry Laura and then you could stay home."

Lawrence coughs, and a bright flush rises on Laura's cheeks. Uncle Chad chuckles and says, "Not a bad idea, Alexander."

Lawrence mumbles, "Well, I may need to take that under advisement."

"You like her, don't ya?" I prod.

"Yes, Alexander, I like Laura a lot," Lawrence admits in a voice that says, *enough, please.*

"Well, then," I reply with a shrug, and Mom shushes me.

Now Lawrence laughs. "It's not that simple, Alexander. I'm not sure Laura would have me. I don't have much to offer a wife."

To the surprise of all of us, including Lawrence, Laura replies, "You may not believe this, Lawrence Traeger, but I would be happy to marry you, broken leg or not—if you'll have me, that is."

Lawrence is stunned and his reaction is delayed. Uncle Chad urges, "Well, say something, man!"

Lawrence finally stammers, "Y-you know I love you, Laura. And I would be honored to have you as my wife..."

Laura accepts his words as confirmation, and she leans in and kisses him.

I interrupt. "Does this mean you won't have to go to a nursing home?" I ask.

Lawrence stutters. "Uhhh, that might be rushing things," he says. "We're only engaged; weddings take time."

"Not necessarily," Laura says with a shrug. "My family, including my minister father, lives only two hours north of Swanquarter. And you could get Dr. Tennyson and Alexander to stand up for you."

"I-I just need some time," Lawrence stutters, and Laura takes pity on him.

"We can always wait if you prefer," she assures him. "Either way, I'm not going anywhere."

Lawrence nods gratefully. "I feel badly that I don't have a ring to give you. All of this has come up rather suddenly."

"I'm not worried," says Laura. "I'm marrying you for you, not a ring."

"Well," interrupts Uncle Chad, "you two can work that out later, but for now, may I be the first to offer my congratulations!"

Laura beams with contentment, and we all move in with our hugs of congratulation.

---

Laura arrives before we do in the morning, and she has brought a half-dozen thickly frosted cinnamon rolls from the diner. When we enter the room, we dive into them.

"Thanks, Laura!" I exclaim. "These are great!"

The box quickly empties and we're still licking our fingers when Laura notices that the cinnamon roll on Lawrence's hospital tray has not been touched.

"Not hungry?" Laura asks. "Is something wrong?"

"Yes and no," Lawrence says quietly. His tone of voice makes us all stop talking.

"What's wrong, Lawrence?" Laura asks. "Have I done something?"

"No, Laura, you could never do anything wrong. It's me. I'm the one who is wrong. And I'm afraid I'm going to hurt you."

Laura reacts in alarm as Lawrence continues.

"Laura," he says, "I love you so much that I can't let you marry me until you know all about me. There are things in my past that you need to know. Things I'm ashamed of. Things that could hurt you."

Mom puts her fingers on her lips as if to keep herself from interrupting. And Laura squeezes Lawrence's hand.

"Please bear with me," Lawrence says. "I have to confess to you a story that you will find difficult to believe but that you need to know."

The room is quiet now except for Lawrence's nervous swallows before he begins.

"It all began a little more than two years ago when I started to work with Dr. Tennyson. He was good to take me on while I earned my final university credits. I'm ashamed to say that I betrayed that trust by snooping through his private papers. And one day, I uncovered a journal that changed his life and mine. You see, in his writings, the doctor documented something I had believed was impossible—an episode of time travel."

Laura looks at Uncle Chad in puzzlement, but Lawrence continues and assures her that he is telling the truth.

"It is indeed possible to travel in time," Lawrence says, "and I believe that one day it will be commonly known. But Dr. Tennyson's assertion astounded me as it does you. He wrote how he had initiated a time voyage with the help of two transport stones that took him back into the ancient past among the Israelites as they were leaving Egypt."

"Oh my!" breathes Laura. And I see what looks like disbelief twist her lips into a tiny smile.

"And," says Lawrence, "Dr. Tennyson described how, before the Israelites left, the Egyptians showered them with gold and riches. I read those notes with interest and incredulity. How could a man of science write such things?

"I would have dismissed it except for one more detail that Dr. Tennyson included in his notes. He wrote that he had brought back a large bag of that treasure and had hidden it in his attic. I laughed at first. But then on a lark, I decided to check it out. I had only to peek into his attic. One look and I could prove that the whole story was simply fiction.

"But it didn't work out that way. To my amazement, the bag was there! And when I saw it, I went a little crazy. I stole it."

Laura sucks in a breath. "Oh, no," she whispers.

"Oh, yes," says Lawrence. "I'm a thief. Plus, one of the bags contained a transport stone, and with it in my hand, I became obsessed with taking an onyx-stones trip to the past to get more gold. I don't know if I mentioned it, but two onyx stones are required for a transport, so I knew that I would have to take Dr. Tennyson and his stone with me.

"That presented a problem, because I was not supposed to know anything about Dr. Tennyson's journal or the necklaces or time travel or treasures. I tried to bide my time until I could figure out a strategy and get him to confide in me and invite me into his secret.

"But it all went wrong. Dr. Tennyson discovered my theft. And when I told him I had another onyx stone necklace and that I intended to use it to force a transport, Dr. Tennyson fought me and chased me with a meat cleaver from his house."

Laura gasps and bites her knuckles.

"Yes, Laura," Lawrence says. "It's not pretty. I was like a crazy person. I was determined to get back into that house and get my way. And I did.

"I sneaked in while the doctor was sleeping, bent over his bed, and clicked my stone against the one around his neck. To my surprise, the result was immediate. Dr. Tennyson and I rose up through the roof and into the skies. We stormed past the moon and the stars and flashed like lightning through the universe. And then we arrived back at this planet as it was three thousand years ago. I won't lie; the trip was terrifying!

"And even more terrifying was that instead of landing in some isolated spot as Dr. Tennyson had always done on his earlier trips, we landed smack dab in the middle of a crowd of ancient people who instantly closed in on us. Needless to say, I panicked, and I could only think of undoing everything and going back home.

"With Dr. Tennyson still half-asleep, it was up to me to click our stones together again, and I yanked his necklace toward mine. But I yanked so hard that his necklace broke off in my hand, and then I ran. With hundreds of men pursuing me, I zig-zagged through the camp and threw myself into an empty tent. And there, in the tent, was the treasure I had come seeking! I immediately clutched the bag and clicked the transport stones. And, within seconds, my treasure bag and I were deposited back in Dr. Tennyson's bedroom.

"But I didn't arrive unscathed. Dr. Tennyson's stone burned my hand. All the way home, that red-hot necklace melted my flesh, and only after I thrust my hand into Dr. Tennyson's freezer could I release it."

With tears streaming down her face, Laura lifts and kisses Lawrence's crippled hand. But Lawrence slowly pulls it away and continues.

"It took me awhile to realize that by leaving the past in the way I had, I had left Dr. Tennyson stranded. I suddenly loathed the gold I had stolen. My only thought was how I could return and bring Dr. Tennyson home. But the transport stone wouldn't let me touch it again. Its fire was hotter than before. I could not make the trip back to get Dr. Tennyson. I hated myself. I knew I was not only a thief but also a coward and a traitor. And perhaps I was also a murderer."

"No!" Laura whispers.

"Then," Lawrence says, "When I knew that Dr. Tennyson would be missed and I would be questioned, I left town to remove suspicion from me. I drove the doctor's car to the university hospital and got treatment for my burn. When I returned, I told everyone that Dr. Tennyson had loaned me his car, and I pretended not to know that the doctor was missing. (Who would have believed me if I had told them what I knew?) Then I ran away to stay with my grandfather. I threw the transport stones over the ledge in the yard, and I tried to cash in on my stolen gold by pretending it was pirate treasure. I wanted to run away. But antiquities experts wanted answers I couldn't give, and I disgustedly stashed the bag in a corner of the garage, where it remains today. And I became the recluse that you know, my dear Laura."

"You poor thing," Laura starts to say, but Lawrence stops her. "There's more," he says.

He tells her, "I recently saw Dr. Tennyson's photo on television. The newsman said that Dr. Tennyson had just come from an archaeological discovery in the Middle East, and I couldn't believe it! I couldn't imagine how he had been able to return. I ran to the ledge in my yard to see if the stones were still there, and that's when I fell. I cried out for help, but no one knew where I was.

"And then I awakened in the hospital and learned that Alexander, his family, and Dr. Tennyson had brought me here."

"Thank God," Laura whispers.

Lawrence sighs. "And this, my dear Laura, is the man you think you want to marry: a man who is a thief and a traitor. I don't deserve you. Heaven knows, I need you and I love you, but I have no right to claim you. As much as it hurts me, I release you from our engagement. I cannot hold you to a life with a man who cannot be trusted."

With his head bowed nearly to his lap, Lawrence can no longer look at Laura or any of us. My eyes look down too. I don't want to see Laura's face if she decides to break the engagement.

And then Uncle Chad speaks. "Lawrence, I forgave you a long time ago. Now it's time for you to forgive yourself."

Lawrence barely speaks. "I don't know how you can forgive me. I ruined your life and the lives of your family for two long years. And I am sorry!"

"But we do forgive you," Mom says. And Dad nods in agreement.

"I forgive you too," I say, and Lawrence looks up with tears in his eyes. "Thank you!" he whispers to me.

"And I forgive you," says Laura. "And I have no intention of letting you out of your proposal." She leans over the edge of the bed and kisses Lawrence tenderly.

# Chapter 32

## The Coffee Can

"We're going to have to go home soon," Dad says during supper back at Lawrence's cabin. "I have to get back to my job."

"Yes," says Uncle Chad. "We should leave. Laura will take care of Lawrence now."

"But we need to come back for the wedding," Mom says. "Can you get your business straightened out so we can come back for a couple of days at the end of the month?"

"I should think so," Dad says. "My secretary and partner already have things pretty well under control. I just don't want them to think they don't need me."

"I doubt there's any real danger in that," Uncle Chad chuckles.

Then Uncle Chad says, "You know, before we go, I'd like to take Lawrence's boat for a ride. What do you think?"

"Sure!" I say. Dad is more hesitant, but he agrees.

"Well, what about tomorrow morning before breakfast?" Uncle Chad asks.

"Before breakfast?" Dad asks.

Uncle Chad answers, "Sure. Wouldn't you like to see the sunrise over the Sound?"

"I guess so," Dad shrugs. And Mom says, "Why don't you guys go out, and I'll have breakfast ready when you get back?"

"Splendid!" says Uncle Chad. "If we get up around five, we could be on the water by six."

I don't think I have ever gotten up by five o'clock in my whole life. "You'll have to wake me," I suggest. And Uncle Chad laughs when Dad asks for a wakeup call too.

———————•◆•———————

In the morning, I'm dressed but hardly awake when we pull Lawrence's truck out of the garage and hook up the boat and trailer. Soon we make our way down the drive to the turnoff marked with a sign that says *To Boat Launch.*

The boat glides smoothly into the water and the engine purrs to life. When Uncle Chad comments that we need to hurry, I ask, "Where are we hurrying to?"

Uncle Chad's eyes twinkle. "We're going to take the water route to Lawrence's lot. From this level we can explore what's underneath the ledge."

"But there's nothing there to see," Dad says. "Believe me, I've already been down there."

"I know," says Uncle Chad, "but I think there is something to see."

"The coffee can?" I ask.

Dad shakes his head. "You two think those necklaces are down there, don't you? Haven't you been through enough nonsense without going in search of more?"

Uncle Chad says, "Are you saying that it doesn't intrigue you just a little, Jonathan?"

Dad doesn't answer.

By now, the sun is peeking over the horizon and its rays glitter the top of the waters of the Sound. As we putt along, even Dad admits that it's beautiful. "But," Dad says, "Everything on the shore looks the same. I don't see how we're going to pick out Lawrence's lot from any other lot."

"And that, Jonathan," says Uncle Chad, "is why I planted a red flag on the ledge before we left. Just let me know when you see it."

Seconds later, a spot of red appears through the trees. "There it is!" I cry. "There's Lawrence's land!"

Uncle Chad quickly steers the boat to shore. We tie up to a tree and pull ourselves up the bank. Only fifty feet from the water's edge, Lawrence's ledge rises above us and we are soon exploring the undercut. Dad points to the footprints from his rescue and he shows us where Lawrence lay after his fall.

"And," says Dad, "this pile of debris is from the edge of the ledge when it crumbled. These stones are from up there." He points to the overhang. "I'm surprised that the whole thing hasn't come down. It isn't really safe under here."

Uncle Chad kicks at the pile of fallen stones and inspects another pile of debris a few feet away. When he stoops, I ask, "Is that Lawrence's coffee can?"

Uncle Chad lifts the can and removes the lid. Together, we peek inside, and I am disappointed. There is only one necklace.

"Why is there only one?" I ask. "Lawrence said he threw both necklaces down here."

"He did," says Uncle Chad. "This one returned to me of its own accord the day we pulled Lawrence up the ledge." Uncle Chad lifts his necklace from under his shirt.

"But you never said anything!" I exclaim.

"No. I decided to keep it hidden for a while."

Uncle Chad hands the coffee can to Dad. "You can take that necklace out of the can, if you'd like, Jonathan."

Dad hesitates but finally does reach in and gingerly extracts the necklace. He inspects it carefully.

"It looks very ordinary," he says, "like an ordinary polished stone. There's not much to it, is there?"

"Put it on," suggests Uncle Chad, and Dad instantly drops the necklace back into the can.

"Oh, no!" Dad says.

"Nothing will happen," Uncle Chad declares, "unless you bring that stone into contact with the stone I'm wearing. It's perfectly safe, I assure you."

Dad hesitates and then picks out the necklace and haltingly pulls it over his head. As he does so, I see his hands tremble.

Uncle Chad murmurs gently, "If you're worried about creating a problem with the stone, just tuck it inside your shirt. That will keep it safe."

Uncle Chad does the same with his stone, and Dad copies him. As I watch them, I am sure that a time is coming when the stones will come out and come into contact, and our lives will change.

"Okay, let's go," says Uncle Chad.

Our mission has been accomplished. We traipse back through the brush to the boat and make our way back to the cabin. Mom is waiting with our breakfast, and I wonder if Dad will tell her about his necklace.

Mom stares at the necklace around Dad's neck. Uncle Chad shows her his onyx stone as well, and Mom whispers, "You're not going away, are you? Please tell me you're not taking Jonathan and Alexander!"

"Gwen, Gwen! Don't worry so," Uncle Chad soothes. "We have no plans to return to the exodus. And if it makes you feel any better, I can keep both necklaces."

"N-No," Dad interrupts. "I'm okay wearing this one. It's safe where it is."

Mom's eyes plead. "I just…"

Dad answers her, "I know. You're worried. But I swear I won't let anything happen to take us away from you."

Mom dabs her eyes with a tissue, and Dad pulls her into his arms.

"I don't know what I'd do if I lost you two," Mom says.

"I know, dear. It's okay."

I hear Dad's words but I see the look on Uncle Chad's face, and I know we'll be going away soon.

# Chapter 33

## Laura's Home

"I hope you don't mind that we borrowed your boat," says Uncle Chad when we see Lawrence and Laura at the hospital.

Lawrence looks surprised. "Catch any fish?" he asks.

"No, no fish. We went in search of something else," says Uncle Chad, and he lifts the stone necklace from under his shirt.

Laura, who has never seen any of the necklaces, whispers, "Is that one of those stones?"

"Yes," says Uncle Chad, and I know that Laura is envisioning all of the things she's heard.

Lawrence closes his eyes and sighs. "I wondered if you would ever retrieve that can," he says. "And it appears that the stone has settled down and hasn't burned you."

"No," says Uncle Chad. "The stone doesn't burn its owner."

At that, Lawrence opens his eyes. Uncle Chad explains, "My stone is a master stone that can't be removed without consequence."

Lawrence rubs his maimed hand. "And I assume you found the other necklace, too?"

Dad reveals the necklace around his neck, and Lawrence murmurs, "And that necklace doesn't burn you?"

"No," says Uncle Chad, "no more than it burned you when you wore it. It's a secondary necklace and not a master stone. Anyone can wear that one."

Lawrence emits a bitter laugh. "I hated those necklaces when I got back. I dropped them into the coffee can and weighted it with rocks to throw into the Sound. But the fire of the necklaces burned right through the can and into my hand. I was afraid I'd burn a hole in the boat before I could get out onto the water. I finally grabbed a shovel and a pair of oven mitts. I put the coffee can into the shovel and gripped the handle with the oven mitts and, even like that, I barely got the can over the backyard ledge. The shovel handle burned me right through the pot holders. I never want to bother with those necklaces again. I hope you take them home with you."

Dad and Lawrence tuck the stones back under their shirts.

"Speaking of home," says Uncle Chad, "we will be leaving in a couple of days. Laura wants us to help move you into her house before we go. And I understand that a home-health nurse will stay with you and take care of you while Laura works."

"Yes," Laura confirms. "The nurse will stay until the wedding at the end of the month when I take a leave of absence. I hope that all of you can come back for the wedding."

"Of course," Mom tells her. "We wouldn't miss your special day for anything."

Laura and Mom discuss the wedding details, and I wonder again when our onyx-stones journey will begin.

---

Laura's home is larger and brighter than Lawrence's cabin. With three bedrooms and two baths, her house is well-suited for a live-in nurse. Laura has taken moving day off, and we help her and the nurse arrange things so that Lawrence's wheelchair can maneuver through most of the house.

"We'll stay here after we're married," Laura tells us. "And we'll probably sell the cabin."

"But not until I'm well enough to clean out and save the memories I want to keep," says Lawrence.

"Of course," Laura concurs. Then she says to us, "And you can all stay at the cabin when you come for the wedding. It's too small for my family; they'll stay at the motel overnight. I'm anxious for you to meet them."

"Sounds perfect," say Uncle Chad."

"We'll hold the wedding here in the yard," Laura says. "That will be easier for Lawrence."

"And I want you, Alexander, and you, Dr. Tennyson, to stand up for me, if you will," says Lawrence.

"Of course!" says Uncle Chad, and I nod my yes.

I've never been to a wedding, let alone taken part in one. But I know I'll be all right, because Uncle Chad and Dad will be there, too. And later, in the car on the way back to Heatherton, I wonder what I'll be expected to do in the ceremony. I hope I don't have to say anything!

# Chapter 34

## A Return to the Past

The fact that, except for answering *I do*, men have few responsibilities in weddings can be hard on guys, especially kids like me. Only one of Laura's cousins is my age, and the two of us watch for what seems like hours in our best clothes as a no-nonsense band of women fusses over ties being just right and bows and lace being straightened. One woman races around pinning corsages and boutonnieres on the wedding party, while another, a stern-faced woman, gives last-minute instructions on where we are to stand and when. Mom wipes a smudge from my chin, and Uncle Chad and I get into place to make our entrance under the flower arbor when the music cues us.

And then, after all that waiting, the ceremony begins and ends faster than my last rocket launch. In less than a half-hour, Lawrence and Laura are finally married and Laura pushes Lawrence's wheelchair down the aisle and into the receiving line. Once again, we stand and wait, shaking hands and smiling as people pass us on their way to kiss the bride and shake Lawrence's hand.

And then, I'm stuck again. The photos require that we wait while everyone else goes inside to eat hors d'oeuvres. The photography session is taking longer than the ceremony itself!

I am just wondering if anyone is getting hungry when Uncle Chad slips me a piece of candy. Of course, Mom sees and frowns. "Don't get any of that chocolate on your suit," she warns.

When we finally get to join the others at the dining tables, there are little speeches and lots of clapping before we can eat. I'm ravenous by the time I get to fill my plate.

It's all worth it, though, when Laura bends down to give me a kiss and Lawrence pats me on the shoulder. "Good job, Alexander!" Lawrence says. "I'm so glad you were here."

They look happy, and I'm glad. And I will soon be back in my comfortable clothes and be able to breathe again without worry. So far, I've managed not to spill anything. Let's hope I can make it all the way!

———— •◆• ————

Because the big honeymoon has been planned for when Lawrence is well again, the couple remains at home. And back in our civilian clothes, we're invited to return the next day for lunch. Laura and Lawrence, Laura's family, and my family gather on the patio to chat and say goodbye over hot dogs and hamburgers. While the grownups talk, Laura's cousin Billy and I explore the small sliver of beach at the far end of the yard. We skip stones, largely in silence, until someone calls for Billy to come and leave with his family.

"Hey, man, nice to meet you," Billy tells me before he answers his summons. And after a flurry of hugs and kisses and lots of well-wishes, Laura's family sets out on their two-hour drive home.

"We should be going, too," Mom offers. But Laura insists that we stay. "You're easy company," she says, "and we can relax a little longer. Let's just sit on the porch, okay?"

The breeze is soft, and we lazily chat and watch the pelicans and gulls wing their way over the portion of the Sound that we can see.

"How's your book on the exodus coming along?" Laura asks Uncle Chad. "I can't wait to read it."

Dad says, "Chad will make it interesting. He has a knack for engaging average Joe's like me. I'm better at selling insurance. Chad and Alexander are the ones who live, eat, and breathe science and history."

"And Lawrence is good at it too," says Uncle Chad. "I hope he plans to resume his calling. Maybe I can convince him to collaborate with me on some new projects. When he's better, we could even take a few trips."

Lawrence looks surprised, and Laura immediately declares that if Lawrence travels, she's coming too.

She says, "I want my family to someday see a picture of Lawrence and me in a magazine, just like your picture in *Armchair Science*." She waves her hand as if reading a huge billboard announcement: "'Laura and Lawrence Traeger stand beside Queen Whombody's tomb in Wherever after a bold new discovery with Dr. Chadwick Tennyson.'"

Uncle Chad laughs. "That's not so far-fetched," he says. "Who knows what adventures might await us? Jonathan and Gwen could come too. I've always thought that Jonathan could use more excitement in his life. He certainly seems to have enjoyed our expedition to Egypt."

Dad grins, but Mom frowns. I, of course, hope the trips will be during school vacations so I can go, too.

So far this morning, Lawrence has said little, but now he thanks Uncle Chad. "I'm overwhelmed by your offer, sir," he says. "I don't feel worthy of your generosity, but I appreciate it. It's a cinch I can't keep living off what's left of my grandfather's inheritance. I'm going to have to do something soon to support my wife."

"And, who knows?" says Laura. "You may help Ibrahim dig up another treasure in a far-off desert!"

I smile. Laura doesn't know the real story about Ibrahim's treasure hunt. Nor, for that matter, does Lawrence. But Lawrence does seem to have an inkling about that special discovery.

My suspicion is confirmed, when Lawrence says, "I have some questions about Ibrahim's treasure find."

"Oh?" says Uncle Chad. "What's puzzling you?"

"Well, I don't mean to doubt his find," says Lawrence, "but some of that treasure looks awfully familiar."

Uncle Chad's eyes twinkle. "It should. You've seen it before."

"What?" says Laura. "How can Lawrence have seen those ancient artifacts before?"

"Easy," I say, "because it's the treasure that Lawrence stole from Uncle Chad."

Laura looks lost.

"But," Uncle Chad interrupts, "those items were only part of the treasure that Ibrahim uncovered. The rest is from a stash buried there over 3500 years ago by Alexander and his friends."

Now Lawrence is confused.

"You see," says Uncle Chad, "you don't yet know the full story of my rescue. We haven't told you how Alexander and his friends acquired their own treasure in the rescue process. Right, Alexander?"

"Right!" I say, and at Uncle Chad's urging, I explain.

"It happened on the last day of our search among the Israelites," I say. "We had just finished breakfast and Cricket's dog Hero began to bark. He took off running, and we had to follow him."

"Wait," says Lawrence. "Your friend Cricket had a dog with her?"

"Yes," I say. "Hero is Cricket's dog."

I start to go on with my story, but Lawrence stops me again. "I'm sorry, but I'm not clear on the dog. Are you saying that the dog is from the present?"

"Yes," I repeat. "Hero is Cricket's dog."

Lawrence looks incredulous. "So, you're saying that you took a dog with you on your time-transport journey?"

"Oh, yes," I say. "And not just any dog. Hero has time-traveled before."

Lawrence shakes his head in wonder. "You're kidding, right?" he says. "I can't imagine how an animal would handle whizzing through space. It was terrifying enough for me, let alone for an animal."

Then Lawrence repeats, "And you say that Hero helped to rescue Dr. Tennyson?"

"Yes," I say. "Hero led us through the Israelite camp to where a little girl was choking. And Cricket's guardian, Marlene Grace, rushed in and performed the Heimlich Maneuver and mouth-to-mouth resuscitation. Afterward, the girl's family helped us find Uncle Chad and showered us with gold and other presents."

"And," Uncle Chad shares now, "before we came home, we buried the gifts they gave us."

Lawrence shakes his head. "You didn't bring the stuff with you?"

"No," says Uncle Chad. He looks straight in Lawrence's eye and says, "we didn't bring it home, because, as you have learned the hard way, it isn't easy to explain treasure from a time transport."

"But," asks Lawrence, "how did you ever find it again? How were you able to lead Dr. Ibrahim to that spot? That was thousands of years ago."

"True," says Uncle Chad, "but we had something in fifteenth century B.C. that most people didn't have. Right, Alexander?"

"Yeah," I say. "I wasn't supposed to have my cell phone with me, but I did. And it beeped."

Lawrence throws up his hands. "This story is getting wilder and wilder!"

"Yeah," I say, "but it's true. Mom texted me to find out what time I'd be home for supper. (She didn't know I was in the ancient desert.) I heard my phone *ching* in my shoulder bag and dug it out."

"And the text came through?" Lawrence exclaims.

"Yes, it did," says Uncle Chad. "By all of the science I know, it shouldn't have happened. But that message came through on Alexander's phone. And once I knew that it was possible for messages to pass from the present to the past, I assumed that messages could also pass from the past to the present. So, I had Alexander send a return message that allowed us to pinpoint that rock again, later."

"No!" says Lawrence. "You don't expect me to believe that when you got back to the present you got a GPS lock on a location from thousands of years in the past?"

Uncle Chad beams and holds out his hands. "It's true!" he says.

Lawrence shakes his head and turns to Laura. "Can you believe this?"

She shakes her head, too, and smiles. "All of this is incredible to me," she says. "I still can't get over that time-travel is possible!"

Now Lawrence asks, "So, I suppose that after you got back to the present, you set up your elaborate scheme to fly to Egypt and persuade Dr. Ibrahim to search in a place you knew held the artifacts and gold?"

Uncle Chad grins his response.

"And," says Uncle Chad, "you guessed the other half of the story. I did take my own treasure bag on our flight to Egypt, and I buried it at the back of the same rock so that Ibrahim's crew would find it, too."

"So," laughs Lawrence, "Ibrahim's crew got two treasures for the price of one."

"Exactly," says Uncle Chad.

Lawrence exclaims, "Unbelievable!" Then he turns serious and sighs, "I wish I could get rid of my stolen treasure that easily."

Uncle Chad's lips slip into a mischievous grin. "I was hoping you might entertain something like that," he says, "because I have a plan."

"A plan to go back into the past?" asks Laura. And before Uncle Chad can answer, Mom tips forward in her chair and glares at him. "I knew it!" she says.

"Gwen, Gwen," Uncle Chad soothes. "You haven't even heard what I have to say."

He calmly tells her, "Remember when we all had the same dream about Lawrence? Well, I've been having a dream that keeps repeating itself. It first came to me when my necklace came back to me, and it is always the same dream. It doesn't tell me much, but we are all in it—including you and Lawrence and Laura. And all I really know is that we take Lawrence's treasure with us, and we travel back in time. And somehow, we learn who to give the treasure to. And once we've given it away, we come home."

"That part I like," says Mom. "We all come home. None of this getting stuck so that nobody knows where anybody is!"

"Right, Gwen," says Uncle Chad.

"So," Dad asks, "are you saying that we'll all take this journey together? Laura and Lawrence, and Alexander, and even me and Gwen?"

"Yes, if you're up for it."

"I don't think so," says Laura. "How can Lawrence possibly go into the past with a wheelchair?"

"Easy!" I cry. "He won't need it."

"That's right," says Uncle Chad. And quickly, Lawrence jumps in to say, "Yes, I remember! People who are on the onyx-stone journeys lose their physical impairments. Right? Dr. Tennyson didn't need his glasses. And Cricket, who is Alexander's paraplegic friend, didn't need her wheelchair. She was healed while on the trip."

"Exactly," says Uncle Chad. "Lawrence's leg will be good as new the minute we click the stones together. His wheelchair will be left behind and will be waiting for him when he gets back."

"But how can that be?" Laura asks. "Who ever heard of such a thing?"

Uncle Chad guffaws. "And who ever heard of time travel with a couple of ordinary-looking stones?"

"I guess you're right," Laura grins.

I finally ask, "When do we go? Is it soon?"

Uncle Chad answers, "We could go anytime. Next week or tomorrow— or even right now. We just need to pick up Lawrence's treasure bag."

"Then it's settled," Dad says. "Alexander and you and I can go to Lawrence's garage, right now, and pick up the treasure."

Mom blinks and her mouth opens, but nothing comes out.

* * *

When we return from Lawrence's cabin, Laura and Mom watch as we tug Lawrence's treasure from the back of the SUV and carry it to the patio. Eager to catch a glimpse of the gold, the two women loosen the ties and peek inside.

The treasure sparkles, and Laura gasps.

"We've brought some other stuff, too," says Uncle Chad, and Dad helps him retrieve a bulging plastic leaf bag from the car.

"This is soft but heavy," Dad says. "What's in here, anyway?"

Uncle Chad unties the top and dumps the contents on the ground. "Clothes!" he says. "We can't go into the past in the clothes we're wearing."

"That's right!" I cry. "We all wore Christmas pageant costumes when we went to ancient Egypt. But these aren't Christmas pageant costumes."

"No," laughs Uncle Chad. "But they're similar."

Out of the pile he pulls a wrinkled brown bathrobe and hands it to Dad. "See if this fits you, Jonathan."

Then he digs into the bag again and says, "I think I have something for everyone."

"Where did you get this stuff?" Dad asks.

"The Swanquarter rummage store when I was in town for gas, the other day."

"Of course!" cries Laura, and she begins to dig through the clothing in the bag, too. She and Uncle Chad pass around six or seven old robes and some other thin garments that Uncle Chad suggests can be cut up for headdresses. There are also several fake-leather shoulder bags and various worn leather sandals.

The sandals immediately remind me that we need socks. With Laura's help I round up a couple of chamois and explain how Marlene Grace had sewn them into protective socks. Uncle Chad remarks on the "genius of those things!" and pulls another chamois from the back of his SUV. His chamois is large enough to make two socks, instead of just one sock per chamois. When the two pair are finished, we insist that they go to Mom and Laura.

Although Mom has been hesitant about the idea of going on a time-travel journey, she gets caught up in trying on the costumes and creating socks. She and Laura whip up some socks for the rest of us from tan sheets. Then she and Laura iron everything and cut out headdresses for us to try on.

Uncle Chad laughs at the ironing. "Those wrinkles are going to come back real fast," he says. But Mom insists, "That may be, but we're going to start off looking half-way nice."

"Will we need food?" I ask.

Uncle Chad chuckles. "Spoken like a growing boy! Always hungry."

"Well, we might be gone more than a day," I suggest, and I describe Marlene Grace's disguised plastic baggies filled with sandwiches and fruit.

"Not a bad idea," Uncle Chad admits, and Laura and Mom disappear to the kitchen to assemble something similar.

"And cookies!" I call in to them. "Don't forget cookies."

Lawrence laughs, now. "We're definitely going to be more prepared than I was!"

When I mention thermoses for water and ice, Uncle Chad produces them. "Thank you for reminding me," he says. "I almost forgot I had these."

He instructs Dad and me to fill them at the sink. "Put in lots of ice," he calls after us.

"Matches!" I say, next, and Uncle Chad raises his thumb. "Good call. I wish I would have had those with me while I was living in the desert. I did manage to trade with a Bedouin merchant for a couple of pieces of flint."

"And pocket knives and rope," I suggest, as I picture William with his knife and short coil of rope.

Over the next couple of hours, we try on our desert clothes, arrange headdresses, make belts, and cut draw-string bags to camouflage the thermoses and baggies of food. Then we pack everything into our shoulder bags.

Laura passes out handfuls of salt-water taffy. "Homemade," she says, "left over from the wedding favors. We might as well take it along." I stuff my costume pockets and put one in my mouth.

"And," Mom says, "Laura and I have packed a medicine kit and some safety pins."

Uncle Chad cautions, "Just be careful with some of those modern things and with the matches. People didn't have that stuff in the past, and we don't want to make anyone think we're into black magic. We could be hanged, stoned, or drowned."

With our sleeping blankets rolled up with some sheets for tenting, we're nearly ready. Now, Uncle Chad divides the treasure from Lawrence's bag of gold.

"Take what you can comfortably carry in your satchel," Uncle Chad says. "This stuff is heavy, and you don't want to be so burdened that you can't move about easily."

He's right that the gold is heavy, but when it is split among us, it is manageable.

Once we're totally outfitted, we look at ourselves in the mirror. Laura giggles. "We look like a hodgepodge of rummage." But Uncle Chad assures us that we, "don't look too bad for where we're going."

"And where are we going?" asks Dad.

"I don't know exactly," says Uncle Chad. "But from the impressions in my visions I think we're dressed correctly."

"So," I ask, "are we ready to go, now?"

Dad puts his hands on my shoulders as if to keep me from levitating, but Uncle Chad replies, "I think so."

Mom's eyes dart between Uncle Chad, me, and Dad. She asks, "What do we do now?"

Because I know that Mom is scared, I put her hand into Dad's, and I take his other hand.

"We join hands," I say. "Each of us needs to be connected to someone who is wearing one of the stones."

"Exactly," says Uncle Chad. "Make sure you're holding the arm or hand of Jonathan or me."

Laura and Lawrence grip Uncle Chad's arms. Then Uncle Chad pulls out his stone and moves it toward Dad's necklace.

"Hold tight," he says. And with a simple click of onyx, he sets our journey into motion.

"God help us!" breathes Laura, as all that has been our reality begins to slip away.

---

When we pass through the ceiling, Laura cries out again, and Lawrence reassures her. "It's okay," he says, "this isn't even the scary part!"

Up and up we float, and Mom whimpers to see the house grow small below us and the clouds draw near. I see her tightening her grip on Dad's hand. "Are you okay, Alexander?" she cries, and I hurry to reassure her that I'm fine. I see her wide-eyed attempt at a smile, but I also see excitement on her face.

"We're going to go faster, now," I advise her. And almost instantly we gain speed and shoot into the atmosphere. Mom's voice turns to awe as the blue of the sky begins to give way to a blanket of stars set against the deep jet-black of space. The moon and sun are only after-thoughts as we begin to soar faster and faster through galaxies and swirling black holes. And we seem to be heading for oblivion, except that one small speck continues to grow in front of us.

"There's Earth!" I cry. "That speck is where we're going."

"But we just came from there," Laura says.

"But it's not the same Earth that we left," Lawrence tells her. "What's ahead is an Earth in the past."

Faster and faster we hurtle, and the tiny blue planet increases exponentially in size. The orb's surface flies up at us, and when we seem doomed to disintegrate in a collision with the approaching ground, Mom, Dad, and Laura scream. But in that very instant, that unreal change to slow-motion catches and holds us only a few feet from the surface. We hang weightless for a second. And then we descend and land as softly as butterflies on flower petals. And we are not alone.

It is late afternoon, and we are at the tail-end of a large caravan making its way along a hard-packed dirt road. Fortunately, no one has seen us arrive. And I notice that the travelers in front of us wear robes not that much different from our own. Everyone is headed for the entrance to a walled city.

Then I notice that Mom and Dad are frozen in place with their eyes tightly closed. They don't seem to realize that we're safely on the ground. A tiny cry tells me that Laura's eyes are open, however. She has seen Lawrence standing and walking. "You're well!" she cries into his shoulder, and he pulls her tight. "Yes," he says, "I'm healed! Just like I will be in a few weeks back home."

I encourage Mom and Dad to open their eyes. "We're safe," I assure them, and I give Mom a hug. She clutches me, and when she opens her eyes she cries, "It's true! We're safe, Jonathan!"

"But where are we?" Dad asks. And Uncle Chad replies that he thinks we are about to enter Jerusalem.

"And we need to hurry," he says. "We have to get through that gate before it closes."

# Chapter 35

## The Wrong Place

We are the last travelers through the massive gate in the city wall. Those ahead of us disperse quickly in different directions, but most of them head south along a double-walled passageway that Uncle Chad thinks ends at the marketplace in the center of the city. We follow a contingent of merchandise-laden donkeys and camels.

As we enter the market, we are assailed by new smells and sounds—a confusion of foods, spices, sweat, and raucous hawkers. And Mom exclaims, "I can't believe that everyone speaks English!" Uncle Chad briefly explains about the gift of universal language.

"Buy your figs here! The best you will find!" "Bread! Freshly baked bread! Enough for your whole family!" "Lamb for supper! And cheese. Goat cheese!"

Other vendors hawk knives and linen and oils. But one vendor's cry, above all the others, draws my attention. "Sealskins! Waterproof sealskins!"

the turbaned camel-owner cries. "Stay dry in the rainy season! Quality skins from the southern sea!"

*Sealskins!* Instantly I picture the final layer that was draped over the Tabernacle roof in the Sinai wilderness. Blue-dyed sealskins! William had told me from his research that sealskins were not as rare in the desert as one might think. And now I see that he was right. I will have to tell him!

As we wander through the confusion, we are aware that evening will be upon us soon, and we need to decide where to settle. I can tell that Uncle Chad is surveying the area for the best spot. Lawrence asks, "Should we look for an inn?"

Uncle Chad considers this for a moment but decides that we should stake out a place on the outer edge of the market, instead.

"If we stay at an inn," he says, "we'll have to pay with some of our treasure, and I don't want to reveal our wealth. It's too dangerous. We don't have coins. It would be like trying to pay for a candy bar back home with a diamond ring."

We begin to work our way to the far edge of the marketplace. As we do, I notice that we are heading toward a wall topped with a parapet and festooned with flags flapping in the breeze. Soldiers in shining helmets and breastplates stand guard at the wall's gates.

"What is that?" I ask Uncle Chad, and he suggests that it is Herod's palace.

"Herod the Great," he says. "From what I've studied of Jerusalem, it seems that we are in his period of history. The corridor we followed after entering the city gates was bounded on one side by the city wall and on the other by the Temple wall."

"Oh, my!" cries Laura. "Do you think we'll get to see the Temple while we are here?"

"Perhaps," says Uncle Chad. "We may catch a glimpse if we happen to pass when the gate is open. And we could enter the outer courts, but no further. We are strangers and foreigners, and the sacred grounds of the Temple are protected from people like us."

Uncle Chad's comments make me think of when William hurried us away from the Levite camp and away from the Tabernacle grounds on our mission to rescue Uncle Chad.

"Does the pillar of cloud and fire stand over the Temple like it did over the Tabernacle?" I ask Uncle Chad, and he simply answers, "No. Not this Temple," and he offers no explanation.

It's too noisy to hear a longer explanation, anyway, because we are passing through an especially busy part of the market. The vendors here are bold and insistent. Mom and Laura keep shaking their heads as merchants approach them to buy trinkets and foods. The women haven't learned not to gawk, and their curious stares make the vendors think they are interested in buying.

When the number of vendors finally dwindles and the crowd thins, we are as close to the palace as the guards will allow. "Let's set up our camp here," Uncle Chad says, and he arranges our site in a small circle. "Put our goods and shoulder packs in the center," he says, "where we can watch them."

Other market visitors have also camped here, and we have visitors squeezed in on either side.

Mom is a little uneasy and asks, "Do you think we'll only be here for the night?"

"I wish I could tell you, Gwen," Uncle Chad says, "but my dream wasn't specific on how long or exactly where we would be. But I think we will know when it is time to move and where it is that we should go."

Because Dad knows that Mom is uncomfortable in this close setting, he turns her attention to getting the camp set up. "Gwen, how should we arrange our tent and our bedding?" he asks. "If you'll tell me the best way, I'll lay things out." Mom begins to oversee the arrangement of our things, and once the tent (more of a lean-to than a tent) is set up, she seems less nervous.

Now the sun disappears behind the city walls, and I realize that I am hungry. I also know from our visits to the desert at nighttime that it may grow cold. We need a fire. Uncle Chad knows it too, and I hear him grumbling to himself, "I knew I forgot something."

"What's wrong?" I ask.

"We don't have firewood," he says. "Nothing to burn with my wonderful twenty-first century matches!"

"Don't worry," I tell him. "I'll find some wood." But I can't.

Searching for firewood inside of a city proves to be much different from collecting wood from the desert. Dad and I manage to gather only a few scarce twigs and tufts of grass and bring them into our little camp circle. Just as darkness falls, Uncle Chad strikes one of our secret matches and lights our meager pile of kindling. The pitiful, smokey little fire offers almost no heat for Mom and Laura. We all huddle close together under our blankets and pass around our sandwiches. Uncle Chad, Dad, Lawrence, and I sit back, away from the fire, so that Mom and Laura can benefit from the little bit of heat.

"I had no idea that it would get cold here," Mom says. "We're in a desert, for Pete's sake!"

"I agree," says Laura as she shivers. "I thought it would be hot around the clock, like it is during our summer." Lawrence rubs Laura's hands to warm them, and Dad rubs Mom's fingers. I'm wishing I had my mittens.

Suddenly I feel an unfamiliar hand on my arm.

"I mean no disrespect," a voice whispers in my ear, and I turn to see a young man about my age. "But I wonder if I might light my stick at your fire."

"Of course," I say, and I take the stick he holds. I scoot forward to put it into our little blaze. Once it holds a healthy flame and glow, I hand it back. The boy nods his thanks and disappears into the darkness.

I am still thinking about the boy when, after a moment, I feel his hand on my arm again. And this time he offers me a small armload of firewood. "To thank you for helping me light my fire," he says. "This is for you."

"Why, thank you!" I exclaim in surprise. "Thank you very much."

"Yes! Thank you," Laura calls after him.

The young man bobs his head and turns to leave, but I stop him. "What is your name?" I ask.

"I am Aziz," he says. "A friend."

"And I am Alexander," I tell him. "Thank you again, friend."

The boy nods, bows, and backs away into the dark.

"How nice of that young man to share his firewood with us," Mom says, and Uncle Chad agrees.

"Alexander has made a friend," says Dad. "Alexander lit a stick for the boy to take to his own fire, and the young man returned the favor by sharing his firewood with us."

"Actually," says Uncle Chad, "there is a little more to it than that. That young man saw that we had no firewood, and he devised a way to ask us for something. Only then did he offer us some firewood.

"You see, that is the way of these people. If anyone sees a need, they not only offer to fill it, but they first request something of you. That way, you will not feel obligated or shamed because of your poverty. Your young friend must have seen you scavenging for twigs and tufts of grass, and he realized that we had no firewood. So, he asked for a start for his fire and then he provided us with the firewood we need."

"How interesting," I say. "What a polite way to offer help to someone! I want to remember this when I get home and see someone who needs help."

As we warm ourselves by the new fire and finally slip under our bedroll covers for the night, I wonder if the helpful young man sees us enjoying his gift.

---

In the morning, the shouts and calls of the marketplace begin early, and we eat our fruit and cookies amid the loud chorus of cries that call for buyers to stop and sample the various wares on display.

When I stand and stretch, I see camped next to us the boy who gave us the firewood. Aziz has drawn a bucket of water from somewhere and is offering it to four thirsty donkeys. He disappears and returns several times with more water for a couple of goats and four camels. While the animals drink, he looks in our direction and waves to me.

Aziz's entourage is large, perhaps twenty people. Two distinguished men and their guards sit outside the door of a small tent, and they are attended by a host of cooks and servants who watch them eat before they sit down to their own breakfast. While the noblemen smoke their long thin pipes and confer with one another, Aziz eats with the servants and soon returns to his duty with the animals.

Mom is urging us to straighten up our camp and roll up our beds, but Uncle Chad moves slowly. He does not seem to be in a hurry for us to break camp. As I sit waiting for instructions on what to do next, I notice that the two distinguished gentlemen from next door have disappeared. Perhaps they are in their tent or have gone shopping in the market. I decide that they are away from the camp, because the servants are relaxed and I even hear some laughter.

I ask Uncle Chad if we are staying here for a while. "Do I have time to pet one of Aziz's camels?" I ask.

"Go ahead, my boy. Go and talk with your young friend."

Aziz sees me coming, and he leaps to his feet and bows. He asks, "Is there something you require?"

"I-I mean no trouble," I say. "I simply wondered if I might pet your camels."

A surprised grin crosses Aziz's face. "You wish to pet the camels? Have you never petted a camel before?"

"No," I say. "I have never been close to one before."

Aziz stifles a laugh so as not to offend me, and he says, "Well, person-who-has-never-touched-a-camel-before, please feel free to touch these." He puts out his hands as if directing me to the animals, and I step forward cautiously.

"Just be careful," he warns. "They spit."

"They spit?" I say.

"Yes, they spit if they do not like you."

"Oh. Then I hope they like me."

Aziz reaches into his pocket and produces a small handful of figs. "Give Shazad this. Shazad likes figs."

I take the sticky figs and hold them flat in my palm as I approach the first camel.

At first the haughty animal turns his head away, but the scent of the figs soon draws him back. Shazad looks at me and decides to ignore me as he accepts my gift. While he savors the tidbit, I reach out my other hand and stroke his neck a couple of times. The animal shivers as if my hand brings him discomfort, and I stop.

"This one is Jasmina," Aziz tells me. "She is more friendly. But she does spit sometimes."

Aziz produces another token of figs for me to offer, and Jasmina looks me straight in the eye and takes the food. When I pet her, Jasmina doesn't shiver my hand away. I am able to stroke her several times.

"I think she likes you," says Aziz. "It is a good thing to have a camel like you."

I smile. "Thank you," I say, and I produce two pieces of Laura's homemade taffy from my pocket. "These are for you," I tell him.

Aziz seems pleased that I have a gift for him, and he takes the candy with a smile. He sniffs it first and turns it over. When I show him how to untwist the waxed paper wrapping, he looks at the candy and says, "I have never seen such a thing."

"It is sweet," I say. "I hope you like it."

Aziz sniffs the candy again, and this time, he takes a tiny nibble from the edge. He rolls it over his tongue and his eyes light up. He says, "Yes. It is very sweet! And mysterious. What is it called?"

"Taffy," I say. "It is common among my people."

Aziz pops the rest of the piece of taffy into his mouth and lets it dissolve on his tongue.

"I like taffy," he says. "Very different, and very good."

Then Aziz asks, "Now that you have petted the camels, do you also want to pet the donkeys or the goats?"

"No," I laugh. "I have petted donkeys and goats before."

"Very good," Aziz says.

We stand without speaking for a minute, and then Aziz asks if I want to sit down. I accept his invitation and lower myself to the ground beside him. Together, we sit and watch the people at the market.

"See that fat man, there?" Aziz directs. "He's cheating the people who buy from him. He puts his finger on the scale to make the wheat weigh more than it does. Watch."

Sure enough, I see the man pressing on the scale as he weighs the flour.

"And that man with the dark turban? He removes one of his dried fish as he bags them up for his customers. They should not cheat," Aziz says.

"Are any of them honest?" I ask.

"Some are honest, I think," Aziz says. "For example, that man. The one in the tattered coat with the little girl. He trades honestly. Sadly, some of his customers take advantage of him by bargaining for less than he can afford to sell. And he needs to make the sale, so he lets them do it."

"You have a sharp eye," I tell my new friend. "I would not have noticed."

"I see many things that people don't think I see," Aziz says. "For example, many people in this land do not respect my princes because they come from far away, like you. They call them *strangers* and *gentiles* and avoid physical contact with them. But my lords are good. Without them,

I, and most of the others in our camp would still be in debtor's prison. An unscrupulous man in our village cheated us and threw us into jail. Kaysan and Najib, who had also had dealings with the swindler, had him arrested, and they secured our release. Then, because I and my friends no longer had any money, our redeemers offered us jobs. We have joyfully served them ever since. They are generous and honorable men, and we have traveled far with them."

"Why are you in Jerusalem?" I ask.

"We're here on a mission," Aziz says mysteriously. "My lords have studied the skies and they know that the God of the Earth has written a message in the stars that a great event has taken place in this land."

"What kind of event?" I ask.

Aziz whispers, "A God-child has been born!"

"A God-child?"

"Yes, a king of the Jews. And Kaysan and Najib have gone to the palace to pay their respects and offer their homage to the new king."

*A new king. A God-child.* The words swirl in my brain. I know this story! At least part of it—as much as I can remember from my Sunday school teachings. And before I think, I say, "But I think the new king is in Bethlehem, not Jerusalem."

Aziz looks doubtful. "But this is the king's palace," he says. "What is Bethlehem? Is it a great city also?"

I realize that I need to stop talking. I don't know enough to give the right answers. I wish that Uncle Chad were here. He would know.

Because I don't want to mislead, I simply say, "I am probably wrong, my friend. Don't pay attention to me."

Then I stand and say, "I should get back to my camp. I enjoyed petting the camels, and I am glad you liked the taffy."

"Yes, I like the taffy," Aziz grins. "I like sweet things."

"Me too," I say, and I bow and retreat as I have seen Aziz do.

He bows back, and he says goodbye.

# Chapter 36

## The Right Place

When I return to our camp, I am surprised to see a donkey, a bag of feed, and a load of firewood.

"Chad has been shopping," Dad tells me.

"Yes," says Uncle Chad. "I happened to find a money-changer, and I took a chance on presenting him with a ring from our treasure. It was the smallest thing I had, and he was able to provide me with coins in exchange—coins we can spend without drawing attention."

"Do you mean that the donkey is ours?" I ask.

"Yes," he says. "He can carry our firewood and bedding and even some of our shoulder bags."

Then Uncle Chad asks, "Did you enjoy petting the camels and visiting with your friend?"

I excitedly try to tell him what I have heard from Aziz and what I suspect. "Aziz is with the wisemen!" I blurt.

"Yes, I imagine you could call his masters *wisemen*," Uncle Chad replies.

"No, you don't understand," I say. "His masters are *the* wisemen."

Laura asks, "Alexander, do you mean that you think they are the wisemen we associate with Christmas?"

Uncle Chad exclaims now, "Aha! I see! You think these men are on their way to see the Christ child."

I nod, and Uncle Chad strokes his chin. "I wonder," he says. "Perhaps they are!"

I reply, "Aziz says that his masters have followed the stars to Jerusalem and that they are looking for a new king, a God-child. Doesn't that sound like Jesus?"

"Yes. Yes, it does," Uncle Chad murmurs, now. "And to think I almost missed it. I had placed our arrival at a later time, and I ignored the clues.

"In the market, I overheard gossip that foreigners were on their way to honor Herod's newest child. The story elicited guffaws because there were no new children. And if there had been, Herod would have already killed them. He killed everyone he considered a threat to his throne.

"I knew about Herod's murderous nature, and I simply chalked up the merchants' gossip as just that, gossip. But you, Alexander, have made me realize that I should have paid attention. You recognized the connection!"

"I only wish that I remembered more of the story," I sigh. "When Aziz told me that his gentlemen believed the stars were directing them here to Jerusalem, I carelessly corrected him and said that the new king was born in Bethlehem and not Jerusalem. And then, when Aziz asked how I knew this, I didn't know how to answer him. I don't know enough of the story. I was hoping you could tell me more in case Aziz asks. Aziz says his lords went to the palace this morning to congratulate Herod."

"Hmmm," says Uncle Chad. "Their visit to Herod is a mistake, but it is one that we cannot and should not try to correct. It is through their visit that Herod learns about Jesus' birth. And true to his nature, Herod immediately identifies the child as competition. He knows that the *Messiah* is to be a universal ruler. The Bible says that when Herod asks the Temple scholars where the Messiah is to be born, they cite the words of the prophet Micah and tell him Bethlehem. Herod cunningly instructs the wisemen to find the child and to send word so he can come and worship, also. But of course, once Herod learns where Jesus is, he plans to kill him. The Bible says that, fortunately, God sends a dream warning the wisemen not to return to Herod, and they go home by a different way. When Herod learns of their deception, he orders the death of every male baby born in Bethlehem in the last two years. Jesus would not have escaped, except that God intervenes and sends an angel to warn Joseph to take his wife Mary and the baby to Egypt where they are safe until Herod dies."

"How awful!" I say. "Shouldn't we warn the wisemen, now, before they go to Bethlehem?"

Uncle Chad shakes his head sadly. "No, Alexander. We are not here to change what the Bible says. We are here to learn from it. We cannot and must not try to change history. God is in control, just as the Bible says. God will send the wisemen dreams and he will send an angel to warn Joseph, so that no harm will come to Jesus. Sadly, we cannot alter the deaths of babies as ordered by Herod. Herod has to live with that sin before

God, forever. If we try to change anything in the story, I believe we will be returned home immediately and will not be able to complete our mission."

"But what is our mission?" Lawrence asks.

Uncle Chad replies, "We will know it when the time comes. I believe that God will guide us."

---

We notice that the wisemen return from the palace in mid-afternoon, and in the subsequent stir of their arrival back at their camp, I see Aziz bob his head when instructions come to him. I see him hurry to the camels and begin arranging their saddles and driving gear. He doesn't yet outfit the animals, but he is ready for whenever the command comes, and it seems that it will come soon. Others scurry throughout the camp to prepare supper and make the wisemen comfortable.

"I believe our neighbors will be leaving in the morning," Uncle Chad observes. "They seem to be preparing."

We follow the activity in their camp as we build our fire and eat our supper. When the evening chill sets in, Dad adds another stick of wood and stirs up the embers.

As I watch the flames lick the wood and spit sparks into the darkness, I wonder at the miracle of wisemen following a star across a continent to worship the one that Aziz calls the *God-child*.

I ask quietly, "Doesn't it seem odd that while nobody, right here, knows about God's Son being born, these travelers, from so far away, know about it?"

Dad murmurs, "I've been thinking the same thing. Unlike me, with access to hundreds of Bibles that spell it all out, these strangers have had so little to go on. And yet, they have believed and have put their belief into extreme action. I'm beginning to see how foolish my doubts have been."

Uncle Chad smiles at his brother, and I can see that my dad has come to believe.

Now, before our conversation can continue, Laura suddenly calls out, "We have visitors!"

Uncle Chad leaps to his feet and bows to the men who have appeared. The rest of us scramble to our feet as well.

"Welcome to our camp," says Uncle Chad. "I am Chadwick Tennyson.

Won't you please accept our hospitality? Come, sit here by the fire. Laura and Gwen, could you bring some of the pressed dates I bought at the market? And perhaps some taffy?"

I note that we look like peddlers in rags next to our richly garbed visitors. But they seem to take no notice. The taller man nods his thanks to Uncle Chad and the two men sit.

"I am Kaysan and my companion is Najib," the man says by way of introduction. "If it please you, sir, we will not stay long, but we have a question that perhaps you can answer for us."

"Of course, my friends," Uncle Chad says with another bow. "What information do you seek?"

The shorter man speaks now. "Our stable boy tells us that perhaps you have similar interests to ours. He says that you know of a new king in Bethlehem. Is he correct in what he says?"

Uncle Chad nods. "Your young man speaks truth. We are indeed aware of a new king in Bethlehem—a child who was born to be Messiah."

Uncle Chad's words spark an excited chatter between our visitors. I can only make out a few words before Kaysan turns back to Uncle Chad and says, "We have been surprised to arrive in Jerusalem and find that no one knows about the birth of a new king. We were certain we would find the new king at the palace. Instead, we learn that not even the present king knows of the event. Herod's own learned men suggest that we try Bethlehem. But you—you have said that you know already about the child in Bethlehem. How can this be?"

Uncle Chad is careful with his reply. He says, "All of the signs in the heavens tell us that at this time God is doing a great thing. And we have searched the words of the prophets and find that Bethlehem is spoken of highly by Micah in his Messianic message. And so, we believe that Bethlehem is where this great thing has happened."

Najib speaks now. "We too follow the heavenly signs. And we thought we had arrived, but we believe now that we must adjust our course for Bethlehem. In the morning we will check the stars again before they disappear, and if they agree, we will set out. A new morning star has guided us from the time we left our home, a thousand miles away, and we will confirm by it if we are correct in going to Bethlehem. Our assumption that Jerusalem was our destination was wrong. We erred because, as we drew close, it seemed logical that the king would be here. We assumed that we had arrived and we stopped testing the guidance of the star. Now we have seen our careless mistake, and we will be more cautious."

"Of course," says Uncle Chad. "It is good to follow the guiding star in this."

Uncle Chad's words please Kaysan, and he says, "Sir, if it would please you, we would like for you to join our caravan and go with us to Bethlehem. We will leave tomorrow before the sun drives the stars away. Would you find such an invitation agreeable?"

Uncle Chad bows lower than I've ever seen him bow, and he says, "We would be honored to travel with you to visit the new king. We will be ready to join you in the morning."

"Very well," says Kaysan. "It is our pleasure to have your company and to talk with you along the way. And now, we will leave you to prepare for your rest. May your sleep be guarded by the Almighty."

Kaysan and Najib bow and return to their camp.

———◆———

Before morning can lighten the skies, we eat our breakfast, and Dad, Uncle Chad, Lawrence, and I go to visit the wisemen's camp. There, we are invited to sit where Kaysan and Najib are observing the stars. I notice, again, the contrast between our shabby dress and their rich robes. Even the servants of the wisemen are dressed better than we are. But to our hosts, it doesn't seem to matter.

We watch the wisemen hold out a rod to measure between the horizon and various stars in the sky. And one extra-bright star receives special attention. Kaysan and Najib also reference the writings of a scroll and of a map painted on a large piece of parchment. They discuss their findings with Uncle Chad, and I know that they are determining our current position and how to navigate to where the large star is guiding.

Lawrence and Dad remain seated at the wisemen's fire circle. They also stare at the sky, but I hear Lawrence whisper to Dad, "I've never followed the stars before. I have a rudimentary knowledge of the constellations and how to navigate by them, but I have never had to do it."

Dad whispers back, "I can barely find the North Star and the Big Dipper."

I say nothing. Like Lawrence, I have memorized the major stars and constellations. And because of my interest in space travel, I know something about celestial navigation. But everything I know depends on computers to compute the angles and do the math.

Now, Najib puts down his star stick and turns to us. "Watch," the stargazer says. "Even after the other stars fade, that one light will remain. That is the star that has guided us, even into the daylight hours. Like the planet Venus at times, it is bright enough to hold its own against the overpowering light of the sun. And when we move, the star goes before us."

"It is a special star, indeed," says Uncle Chad. "And it is an honor to follow it."

At that, Kaysan says, "So, my friend, is your company ready to travel?"

Uncle Chad stands. "Yes, we are ready."

Within minutes, we pass through Jerusalem's southern gate toward our goal, about six miles away.

Kaysan, Najib, and two men armed with gleaming, curved swords ride in the lead, on camels. A few long-legged attendants keep pace with them, and we follow closely after. A few personal attendants walk behind us, and Aziz and the pack animals, including our donkey, bring up the rear with the last of the servants.

For the first mile, we keep up fairly well, but we are out of shape. As we begin to lag behind, the party stops, and Najib sends one of the long-legged men back to the rear of the entourage. Within a few minutes, the man returns with four bare-backed donkeys.

The man bows to Uncle Chad. "My lords wish you to accept the backs of the donkeys for your ease of travel."

I know that I have seen these donkeys bearing burdens, as does our donkey, and I look back to see Aziz and others now carrying bags that had once been on the backs of the beasts we are to ride.

Uncle Chad accepts the offer, and he helps Mom and Gwen onto the long-eared mounts. With two donkeys left and four men, a decision needs to be made.

Uncle Chad offers, "I would be happy to walk, if you will walk with me, Jonathan. That will allow Alexander and Lawrence to ride. What do you think?"

Dad objects. "I think that Kaysan and Najib would like you to ride and keep up with them so you and they can talk. I will walk, and I propose that Alexander walk with me. Lawrence can ride with you."

Lawrence objects now. "I will only ride if we change off in a little while. We can take turns."

"Very well. Good idea," says Uncle Chad.

The new arrangement does help us move faster, and as we travel along the road, I see Uncle Chad in conversation with Kaysan and Najib. Only after Dad and Lawrence have each ridden, am I allowed to mount the fourth donkey, and I move ahead on his back quickly so that I might be able to hear some of the conversation between Uncle Chad and the wisemen.

Other travelers along the route cast curious stares at our odd party— not only at the regal bearing of the camel-riders, but also at the wrinkled and somewhat disheveled companions conversing with them from lowly donkeys.

I hear Najib explaining, "That star was not visible in our home sky until a little over a year ago. And its brightness could not be ignored. We knew that it meant something special, and we searched the prophecies of our ancestors to see what it might portend. We felt particularly led to several references about the Jewish Messiah—a Messiah that ancient Jewish wisemen like Isaiah wrote about. And we studied them and memorized them. We even memorized an oracle from the prophet Balaam to Balak, the ancient king of Moab, that refers to *a star that will come out of Jacob* and *a scepter that will rise out of Israel.*

"Isaiah says of God's servant, the Messiah, that he will not only *restore the tribes of Jacob* but he will also *be a light for the Gentiles* and *bring salvation to the ends of the earth.*"

Najib says, "Such words warmed our hearts. They told us that even though we are not numbered with the Jews, the Almighty One provides for us, too. We want to honor this king, this representative of God, this God-child. You cannot imagine how exciting it has been for us to realize that we are living in the days that were prophesied. How could we not come and worship!"

Kaysan adds, "The only thing we had missed was the prophecy of Micah. We were instructed by Herod's wisemen and priests who quoted for us that *the ruler from old, from ancient times* would be born in Bethlehem.

We believe that those words are sent from God to guide us the rest of the way on our mission."

As I listen, Kaysan and Najib lift their voices in a psalm, and as their voices rise in praise of the Almighty One, the bright star remains in the sky—bright enough to be seen even in the light of day. And I can almost see it moving slowly as we move, with the sun rising and threatening to overpower its light.

---

The star has held its own against the daylight as we have traveled, but as we approach Bethlehem—at what I guess to be around ten o'clock in the morning—the star slips behind a broad bank of unwelcome clouds. An irritated Najib cries out, "We are so close, and now we have to wait!"

Just inside the city gate, Najib and Kaysan dismount, and Aziz hurries to the well to draw water for the animals. Dad and Lawrence help Mom and Laura down from their donkeys, and the four of them settle beneath a small, lone tree. Servants pitch a hasty two-sided shade tent for Kaysan and Najib, and Uncle Chad and I sit with them.

Like Najib, Kaysan also deplores the timing of the cloud cover, but he calms Najib. "Soon, the clouds will pass," he says, "and we can complete our search."

Najib sighs. "I know, but I hate to be sitting here and doing nothing."

Najib fidgets like a toddler in church, and it is uncomfortable to watch him. I am antsy, too, and I excuse myself by saying that I need to check on our pack donkey.

I needn't have bothered, of course. Aziz has already removed the packs from the little animal's back and left water for him. I see that he has also tended to the donkeys that Mom and Laura have ridden. Although I don't sit, I linger near enough to overhear Laura commenting on how much Bethlehem looks like the Christmas card images she has seen.

"Yes," Mom agrees, "except that in the Christmas pictures it is always night and the shepherds and wisemen are gathered around the manger."

Mom says, "Do you suppose that we will see the baby in the manger, today?"

Laura smiles and shakes her head. "I think we are too late," she replies.

"Too late? What do you mean?" Lawrence asks. "We're here with the wisemen, and they haven't seen Jesus, yet. So, we can't be late!"

"Oh, but we are," Laura declares. "The Christmas cards conveniently depict the wisemen beside the shepherds on the night that Jesus was born, but that's not what the Bible says. It is true that there were shepherds beside the manger, but there were no wisemen until much later. Matthew says that the wisemen found Jesus at a *house* and not at the inn."

"Really!" Mom exclaims. "I never knew that!"

"Yes," says Laura, "and from what I've read, it is thought that Jesus might have been as much as two years old when the wisemen visited. Sadly, that idea comes from the fact that Herod orders all male Bethlehem children two years old and younger to be killed."

"But," Laura hurries to say, "I do believe that we will soon see the Christ Child. After all, that's where we're headed, today."

Dad sits up, now.

"You're right!" he says. "I haven't really thought about what we're doing. We *are* going to see Jesus, today, aren't we?"

Mom murmurs, "It all seems so different from what I've always imagined."

Lawrence moves close to Laura.

"I agree," he says. "This trip is the most remarkable thing I've ever experienced! I'm not saying that I haven't experienced time-travel before, but I am saying that this time I feel what Dr. Tennyson must have felt when he first visited the past—before I messed it up for him. He wrote in his journal how all of the things he had thought of as myths seemed real all of a sudden. And after I abandoned him and he was present for the mighty miracles of the Exodus, he became a believer in God. Now I find myself walking in the company of wisemen whose story was recorded two thousand years ago. And I see them searching for a *God-child*, the *king of the Jews*, because they've read it in the stars. And here we are in Bethlehem, the very place that the Bible says was the birthplace for God's Son. How can I not believe?"

Laura smiles and snuggles into his shoulder. Then she says, "And we're going to see Jesus, together."

The cloud cover remains overhead, obscuring the star from our sight. When I see Aziz with the camels, I wave, and he calls for me to come and join him.

"We are nearly there!" he exclaims. "When the clouds leave, we will surely see the Child!"

I agree. "Yes, I believe we will. And your journey will be ended."

Then I ask, "What will you do after you have seen the Child? Will you stay?"

Aziz cocks his head. "I don't think so. I think that my lords plan to return home, to take the news back with them."

"It's too bad you can't stay and watch the Child grow up and fulfill His mission," I reply.

"True," says Aziz. "But my lords are not young men. By the time the Child is grown, they will be too feeble to return and tell what they have found."

I have not thought of that. And I realize that it is probably true that they could not return to their homeland after many years.

Now, with mischief in his eyes, Aziz asks if I want to sit on Jasmina for a minute. "It might be your only chance," he whispers. "No one is paying attention."

Aziz quietly commands Jasmina to kneel so I can mount, and I quickly climb into the unusual saddle. When Jasmina rises, I gulp, because on the camel's back I sit higher than I have expected. I guiltily glance around from my high perch to see if anyone notices my brief dream-come-true. Aziz taps Jasmina, again, to lower me, and I slip out of the saddle with a little giggle. Finally, I've been able to ride a camel, if only for a few seconds!

Once I'm down, Aziz whispers conspiratorially, "Now, you-who-had-never-petted-a-camel, you can say that you have ridden one!"

I thank him and pet Jasmina and give her some figs before Aziz and I sit.

Once we are settled, I ask Aziz about something that has been bothering me. I ask if he has noticed the man in the striped turban, who sits a short distance away. "He's watching us," I say, "I'm sure of it. Whenever I turn his direction, he looks away—as if he doesn't want us to know he is spying on us. I saw him again, while I was sitting up high on Jasmina."

Aziz nods his head solemnly. "So, it isn't just my imagination," he says.

"I have noticed it, too. That man has followed us from Jerusalem. And I think he is the same man I saw coming and going out of Herod's palace when we were there."

These words send a shiver up my spine. I recall Uncle Chad's story of Herod wanting to find Jesus so he could kill him.

"I don't like that man," says Aziz. "I don't like that he is following us."

"Neither do I," I say. But I am careful not to reveal all that I know. I remember Uncle Chad's warnings about changing history.

"I just wish we could make the spy stay here and not follow us to where the Child is," I say.

"Me, too!" exclaims Aziz.

Then Aziz laughs. He turns to me and whispers, "I have an idea for slowing him down!" He whispers his idea in my ear, and I laugh.

When I return to sit with Uncle Chad and the wisemen by their shade tent, I try not to peek at Aziz and give him away. But I know that he is stealing a pot of honey from the food supplies on one of the donkeys. And I know that if he is successful, he will dump the pot over the spy and race away before he can be caught.

A loud commotion suddenly tells me the deed has been done. Every eye turns to the roaring man now covered in honey from head to toe. I peer anxiously in the direction of our camels and catch sight of Aziz tossing off a dark cloak and coming to where he can watch the scene with us. We shake hands behind our backs and laugh with everyone else at the raging, comical figure who cannot move without sticking to everything he touches. It is certain that he will not be following anyone for some time. Our spy will be too occupied with trying to remove the honey from his clothes and hair.

———◆———

As if on cue after Aziz's prank, the clouds now begin to clear. At last, Najib rejoices.

"We will go, now," he cries, "and leave our belongings here with the servants!"

Kaysan, Uncle Chad, and I leave the scene of the sticky man and scramble to catch up with Najib.

On a near run, Najib leads us through narrow streets and clogged alleyways. At times the buildings hide our heavenly guide from view, but not for long. And after only about four minutes, Najib holds out his hand.

"Stop!" he says. "This is the house. The star is no longer moving. I'm sure of it."

Kaysan concurs, and we stop.

The house before us is a simple one, set in a row of desert-brick dwellings that share common walls. Nothing like Herod's palace, this is the abode of a common carpenter. The proof is in the array of tools and half-finished furniture that sits just outside the entrance. The workman must be inside taking a midday break.

Kaysan and Najib approach the doorway and call out, "Does a carpenter live here?"

After a moment, a man appears. "Yes," he says, "I am a carpenter. May I help you?"

Joseph (I'm certain it must be Joseph) steps outside. "May I know what you need me to make?"

Kaysan asks, "Do you have a son?"

Joseph hesitates at the odd question, but he replies, "Yes. My wife and I have a son. He is just an infant. Why do you ask?"

Najib explains. "We have come a long way to see him. We believe he is a special child."

Mary appears at the door, holding the infant. "Joseph," she whispers, "they know."

"But how?" Joseph whispers back. "How can they know?"

Uncle Chad replies, "We are visitors from far away, who have followed God's call to come here. Your child is not an ordinary baby. Angels, scripture, and the stars have made it plain to us. We have come to honor him."

"Yes," says Kaysan. "We have come to worship him, for he is the God-child!"

Joseph looks at Mary, and she smiles. "Invite them in, Joseph," she says.

Najib holds up his hand. "Wait," he says. "We will return. There is something we must do first."

He and Kaysan bow and retreat, and we follow them. I wonder what needs to be done.

As they hurry along, Kaysan and Najib chatter quietly between them, and I can see the emotion in their gestures. When we arrive near the well, Kaysan calls out orders to his servants. They scatter to comply, and Uncle Chad pulls Dad and me to our spot by the tree.

Aziz is nearby, keeping watch over the donkeys and camels in his charge.

"What is it?" Aziz calls to me. "Have you found the child?"

"Yes, the child is here," I tell him. "My Uncle Chad and your lords have returned here to get something."

Aziz scurries back into his camp and disappears.

In contrast to the flurry of activity in the camp next to us, Uncle Chad seems calm. He asks Lawrence and me if we have fed the donkey this morning, and I answer no.

"There's only enough feed left for today," I tell him. "You will need to buy more at the market."

"Of course," says Uncle Chad. "But for now, could you two make sure he is fed?"

Lawrence tells me, "Come on, Alexander. I'll help."

And while we are feeding the donkey, I notice that Mom and Laura have been recruited to help Uncle Chad and Dad consolidate the food that remains in our shoulder bags. When the job is finished, Mom and Laura stash three food-filled bags into our tent. Then Dad and Uncle Chad shoulder the remaining two bags that now hold only our treasure and the coins that Uncle Chad traded for our gold ring at the money-changer's booth.

"It's not a good idea to leave these bags at camp while we're gone," murmurs Uncle Chad.

Within minutes we are all following the flowing robes of Kaysan, Najib, and their muscular guard Wazir. Behind us are the humble, tunic'd Aziz and four heavily loaded donkeys. It strikes me as odd to see us, in our sweaty, crumpled, rummage-sale clothes, sandwiched between these obviously well-off members of the wisemen's party.

Others find our company odd, too. Our strange parade draws attention from the villagers, who watch with curiosity as we make our way back to the house we have left.

When we arrive, Najib calls out, "Carpenter, we have returned."

Joseph appears and invites everyone in, away from his neighbors' curious, prying eyes. Aziz and the guard remain outside with the animals as my family, Laura and Lawrence, and Uncle Chad come and take our seats on carpets that line the floor of the small room. Although it gives off heat, an oil lamp has been lit for our convenience.

Joseph offers wine, but the wisemen decline.

Kaysan speaks. "We have traveled a great distance to come and honor your child. His star tells us that he will be a king of kings! His life is held and guided by the Almighty One."

Najib adds, "We represent not only ourselves, but many others in our country and beyond. We are their emissaries, as well as our own. And we come with gifts."

With a gesture of his hand, Najib signals for Wazir and Aziz to carry in the items borne by the donkeys. One by one, Kaysan and Najib describe their gifts as they are presented.

"Frankincense," Kaysan says, and two small, fragrant boxes are set on the floor. "Sacred crystals of noble resin that burn with the smoke of God's presence."

"Myrrh," says Najib. The guard opens two small chests filled with more crystals and ointments and liquids. "For the healing of wounds and relief from pain. For dispelling bad air. For sacred anointing. And for preserving and embalming at life's end."

"Gold," says Kaysan. The last chest is larger and is opened to reveal coins that fill it from top to bottom. "The glittering ore that never loses its luster, whether for decoration or for trade. The wealth of kings."

Uncle Chad whispers in my ear, "Those gifts are very rare and precious! They are worth a fortune."

When the servants withdraw and Kaysan and Najib bow to the child, Uncle Chad whispers to Dad, "Give your bag to Lawrence," and Dad transfers his sack.

Uncle Chad stands and motions for Lawrence to follow him. "Bring your bag," Uncle Chad tells him.

Lawrence rises but then halts for a second. I can see that he suddenly realizes what Uncle Chad has in mind.

Now Lawrence trembles as he and Uncle Chad move forward.

Together, they place the shoulder bags among the chests given by the wisemen. Uncle Chad opens and empties one of the bags onto the floor and announces, "We, too, bring gifts. We bring treasures from times long past and from the future. May this wealth support and sustain you wherever you go."

The eyes of Kaysan, Najib, and their servants grow large when they see the gold and jewelry we have brought. It is obvious that they have had a humble opinion of our financial means. Our wise companions regard us, now, with greater respect than they have already afforded us.

In the beauty of the moment, Uncle Chad kneels and prays silently— and the trembling Lawrence falls to the floor and weeps.

Laura moves forward and kneels beside him, and Lawrence whispers a prayer: "Oh, most gracious Son of God! I don't deserve to be in Your presence. And yet, for some reason, You have brought me here. You have known my wicked heart and yet You have offered me forgiveness and redemption—among my friends and before You. And now You even lift from me the fruit of my evil greed and turn it into good. Lord, it may seem that I am the one giving the gift, but in truth it is You who are The Gift—to me and to the world. Thank you for taking my burden, and thank you for coming to Earth to save us all!"

# Chapter 37

## Goodbyes

When we get ready to leave the home of Mary and Joseph, I see that Kaysan and Najib are leaving not only their precious gifts, but also the donkeys that have borne them. And I gasp to see that they are also leaving the sword-bearing Wazir and the donkey-keeping Aziz!

I hear Najib tell Joseph, "You will need protection for your new wealth. Wazir has volunteered his sword to guard you. And with him is Aziz, our stable boy, one who is small but who is strong and powerful in heart. Aziz will take care of your animals and dispense the grain we have left for them. And you need not worry; both servants have received payment for their service."

Aziz grins happily. He looks excited to serve the family of the new king. I smile my congratulations to him. On an impulse, I run to him and empty my pockets of all of Laura's taffy that I have stuffed there. "For you," I say, "to enjoy and remember me by."

"Thank you, friend!" Aziz exclaims. "I only wish I had something to give to you."

"Your gift to me will be to remember me and tell your children about this day," I say.

Aziz assures me that he will tell of our friendship. Then Aziz seems to think of something, and he laughs. "I do have one comical thing for you to remember me by." He reaches into his pocket and giggles as he holds out his fist to me.

"Hold out your hand," he says.

I put out my hand, and Aziz drops something very light and hairy into my palm.

"It is from Jasmina," he says with a giggle. "Now you can pet her whenever you wish!"

When I realize that the little braided camel Aziz has given me is crafted from fur that he has curried from Jasmina, I laugh.

"You are right, Aziz! Whenever I pet her, I will think of you!"

We grip shoulders and say our goodbyes.

And now the wisemen, Uncle Chad, my parents, Laura, Lawrence, and I approach the Christ child once again. Mary allows us to kiss his feet in our worship, and Kaysan and Najib ask for his name. Mary replies, "His name is Jesus."

———◆———

There is no star to follow now. We simply follow Kaysan and Najib back to our camp sites beside the Bethlehem well.

"We must leave to go home," says Kaysan. "And we are *not* going to return to Jerusalem as we had promised King Herod."

"No, we are not going to revisit Herod," says Najib. "An angel told me so, in a dream," he says.

Kaysan sniffs. "It was *my* dream," he says.

"And it was my dream too," Najib insists.

"But we cannot both have the same dream," reasons Kaysan.

As they continue to argue before us, Uncle Chad intervenes. "It is possible to share a dream," he says. "My family has experienced such a thing."

Kaysan and Najib listen with interest as Uncle Chad explains. "Our friend Lawrence, here, fell from a steep ledge when no one was near. He was badly injured and cried for help, but no one could hear him. We did not know what had happened. At the time, my family and I lived many miles away. But that night, all four of us heard Lawrence's cry in a dream—we had exactly the same dream. And we all felt compelled to go and help him. It took us thirteen hours to get to Lawrence and rescue him, but we did. We were amazed that such a thing could happen. But Lawrence is alive today because of our dream."

"Is this so?" Kaysan asks Lawrence.

"Yes. I would not be alive if they had not dreamed the dream and come to find me."

Mom and Dad and I repeat, "Yes, we all dreamed the same dream."

Kaysan nods as he absorbs our claim. "Very well," he says. "I guess that such a thing is possible."

Now Kaysan asks Najib, "What did *your* angel say?"

"He said, *Do not return to Herod.* It was very plain and very simple. And I believed him," said Najib.

Kaysan nods his head. "It must be true, for those are the very words the angel spoke to me. And so, Najib, it is confirmed that we must go home and not honor our pledge to Herod."

"Yes," says Najib. "I believe that Herod is an evil man and has evil intentions."

"In fact..." (Kaysan lowers his voice.)

"In fact," he says, "we have captured one of Herod's spies!"

At sight of my eyes grown wide, Kaysan chuckles.

"As your young man knows, a hireling of Herod's has been trailing us since we left Jerusalem. Our stable boy conspired with your Alexander to keep the man from following us to the carpenter's home."

I smile nervously and, before Mom can scold me for doing something dangerous, Kaysan shares, "The sticky man is safely slung over our last donkey and will not be able to return to Herod for a long time."

Uncle Chad instantly guffaws and calls out, "The honey incident! Of course! Bravo, Alexander!"

I quickly relate that the honey stunt had been conceived and carried out by Aziz, with my blessing as my only involvement. My mom still frowns.

"It is true," says Kaysan, "Aziz slowed the man down, and Wazir helped to execute the kidnapping."

"What will you do with the man?" Mom asks.

"Oh, he will be fine," says Najib. "We will take him with us for a good, long while before we turn him loose. He won't reach Herod anytime soon. If anyone asks, we will say that we caught him following us, like a potential thief."

Dad shakes his head. "The man's certainly getting more than he bargained for. And Herod is getting nothing!"

Kaysan and Najib smile broadly. They are content to have been able to thwart Herod's plans. I wonder, however, if they will ever hear of Herod's unthinkable, murderous response once he learns they have tricked him.

Kaysan and Najib now instruct their servants to complete the final arrangements for departure. And as the servants run to do their bidding, Najib points our eyes to the sky.

"Do you see that the star is gone?" he says. "I noticed it the moment we left the carpenter's house. By the time we departed, the sun had moved by nearly an hour. The star should have remained in its place because it had stopped over the carpenter's house. It should still have been visible to us. But instead, it is gone. It is nowhere. It has completed its task and has disappeared.

"No other star has traversed the sky like this one. It has led us here, and now its mission and ours are complete. We do not need its light for our journey home."

Najib asks Uncle Chad, "Will you also be returning home?"

"Yes," says Uncle Chad. And when Najib asks, "where is your home?" I am surprised to hear Uncle Chad tell him that we will return to Ohio, our land.

"I do not know this land," says Najib. "Is it far?"

"Very far," says Uncle Chad. "But like every return trip to home, it will go quickly. We have accomplished what we set out to do, and the joy in our hearts will make the journey light."

Now Kaysan says, "You are a wise man, my friend. How I wish you could join us at our library back home. We could study the stars and the earth and learn together."

Uncle Chad bows his head and replies, "You flatter me, friend. I think that all of us have moments of insight that outstrip our everyday knowledge. But I have work I must return to."

Kaysan nods but is not entirely satisfied. I feel his gaze settle on me, and he says, "If you cannot come, perhaps your young nephew would enjoy the adventure of traveling back with us and joining us in our library."

Thankfully, Uncle Chad replies for me (and I can only imagine the expression on my mother's face), "Alexander's gifts are already being employed in the learning centers of Ohio. He has always been interested in the skies, and he studies how various stellar bodies travel in them. We tease him that one day he may simply lift off the ground and fly through the stars!"

Najib and Kaysan laugh, and Uncle Chad sneaks a mischievous grin at me. And although they do not really understand, Kaysan says, "We understand. We are all dreamers. But if you should ever pass our way, we would be honored to have you as our guest and fellow-searcher of the skies."

Now Najib produces a large roll of parchment. "This map shows where we live. As you see, we are here—and this is where we are going soon."

Uncle Chad and I recognize the shapes on the map, but the names are different from those on the maps I have seen of Asia.

"Who knows?" says Uncle Chad. "One day, we might come to see you." Then he adds, "Such chances are very slim, of course. After all, we are so very far apart."

"But," says Najib, "we are close in the heart."

———◆———

Finally, Jasmina and Shazad kneel so that their riders can take their places in their special saddles and summon the camels to rise. We say our last goodbyes, and Uncle Chad calls out, "May the Almighty give you a safe journey. Many blessings as you travel home."

Then we watch as our wise friends make their deliberate way south, not north toward Jerusalem. When they are a good distance away, I ask, "Does this mean that we are going home now?"

Uncle Chad replies, "We should wait a little bit. It will be dark soon so that we can slip away unseen. We don't want to cause a stir."

Mom pulls out the bag that contains our cookies and dates. We snack as we sit, and we watch people come from the village to fill their water jugs before the sun gives way to the moon.

The minutes pass slowly, and Mom asks, "Does the Bible say anything about how the wealth from the wisemen and the gold we brought changed the lives of Jesus and his parents? I've always heard that Jesus was poor. But with everything we and the wisemen have left for him, he and his family could live like royalty."

Uncle Chad answers, "Tonight, an angel is going to visit Joseph and warn him to leave Bethlehem to avoid Herod's murderous rage. In the middle of the night, Joseph and his family will begin a long trip to Egypt. Our gifts will help them in exile for the two or three years before Herod dies. Then they will return and live in Nazareth."

"It's a good thing the wisemen left them some donkeys and helpers," I say. "They will need them to travel so far away."

"Yes," says Uncle Chad. "That will help them travel quickly."

I picture Aziz loading the donkeys in the dark. I pull the little braided camel from my pocket and picture Jasmina and Shazad carrying Kaysan and Najib thousands of miles back to where they started on their remarkable journey. And I picture four donkeys carrying Mary, Joseph, Jesus, and their treasures to Egypt. Aziz may never see his home again, but I like to think that he will see Jesus grow up and tell His stories. Perhaps Aziz will join the disciples and see the crucified Jesus once He has risen again. I hope that it is so.

---

The stars finally pull the night covers over the sleepy town of Bethlehem. Every door is shut, every lamp is snuffed out, and every eye is closed. The air is chilly, but we light no fire.

Instead, we gather noiselessly in a shivering little circle. And like fading shadows or wisps of smoke, we click our stones and rise from the earth and disappear.

---

When we arrive home and Laura turns on the living room lights, we look at each other and burst out laughing.

"Do I look as silly as you do?" Mom asks Dad.

"Have you ever seen such a wrinkled mess!" Laura giggles.

"Look at that rag on your head! You look like you pulled it out of the trash," Dad tells Uncle Chad.

"Can you believe we went anywhere dressed like this?" Lawrence laughs, and Laura realizes that he is back in his wheelchair. She kneels beside him with concern in her eyes, and our laughter fades away.

"I'm so sorry," Laura whispers. But Lawrence says calmly, "It's all right. I knew this was going to happen. I knew that the chair would be waiting for me. But I also know that I'll be leaving it soon, as I continue to heal."

Laura gives him a kiss and declares, "That will be nice, won't it?"

Because he doesn't want to remain the object of everyone's sympathy, Lawrence points to a pile of clothes on the sofa. "Are those mine?"

It is enough to break the spell, and Mom and Laura begin to return everyone's proper clothing to them.

Once we've dressed, we gather again in the living room to face the present. Dad ceremoniously presents Lawrence with the onyx stone he wore on our trip. "You should have this," he says, even though Lawrence objects.

Mom is relieved and says, "Yes, you should keep the necklace. And we should be getting back to the cabin so we can pack up and go home. We need to let you two newlyweds have some time alone."

"Oh my!" exclaims Uncle Chad. "In all of the excitement, I totally forgot that we started all of this on your honeymoon!"

Lawrence mugs an angry face and growls, "Yes, it's about time we had some time alone!" And then he grins. "But we do hope you'll come again."

"Of course, friend," says Uncle Chad. "Congratulations on your new beginning."

# Chapter 38

## Home

At home, I continue to think about all that we have seen and done together. Mom and Dad and I often remark on various experiences from our trip, and we comment on how remarkable it was that we could all share it, together.

As far as I know, Uncle Chad has not taken any more onyx-stones adventures, but I wonder if the day will come when he and Lawrence will write a book about some event from the past. And the world will read one thing, and Mom and Dad, the Foxes, Cricket, and I will read between the lines! And I hope that Lawrence and Uncle Chad will share with us any new discoveries that no one else will ever know.

After all, who else would believe the tales we can repeat whenever we get together!

# Epilogue

Just before school starts in September, forty people, including my parents, Uncle Chad, Cricket (with Hero on her lap), Marlene Grace, William, and friends and teachers from school, gather in the sun on the junior high football field at three o'clock in the afternoon. Even Laura and Lawrence are here; they have brought news that Laura is expecting and that Lawrence will be visiting a gifted hand surgeon soon.

Dad is busy videoing everything and Mom clicks photos on her cell phone as Uncle Chad and I recheck all of my rocket connections.

I have already presented a portion of my research paper to the crowd, and now I direct all attention to the 29-inch model that sits on its launch pad. Uncle Chad and I have removed the safety cap, and I have slid the launch lug over the launch rod. I've made sure the rocket slides freely on the rod. Now we attach the micro-clips to the igniter wires and move back the full fifteen feet of launch wire.

Uncle Chad nods and I announce to my friends and family, "Once I insert this safety key to the arm of the launch controller, we will have five seconds to lift off."

The crowd grows quiet, and I dramatically wave the key and insert it. Then I count in a loud voice, "Five! Four! Three! Two! One!" When I press and hold the launch button, the engine ignites.

The rocket lifts up from the pad and heads skyward. The crowd cheers and applauds as it accelerates rapidly and gains altitude. At approximately 500 feet the engine burns out, and tracking smoke follows it the rest of the way to its approximately 700-foot apogee, or peak altitude. At that moment, the ejection charge activates the delivery system and we watch as the parachute opens to return the rocket safely to the ground.

All has gone well. My inspection of the fired craft shows that the rocket is in good shape for reset and relaunch at a future time. When I carry it back to the launch pad, I pose with it for photos. Then Uncle Chad quiets everyone to share closing thoughts.

He says, "I have watched this young man diligently work his way through the Youth Rocketry Program, and this is the last of the Youth series of launches. Alexander is now eligible to enroll in the Advanced

Model Rocketry Program. In this phase of his pursuit, he will be challenged to further study the properties and changes of matter, chemical reactions, motions and forces, and transfer of energy. He will learn about technological design and employ mathematical measurement, analysis, and problem solving. I have no doubt that my nephew will continue to advance in this field and will one day be listed among the NASA greats. Watch for him, my friends! On this wonderful occasion, I wish him well in everything he sets out to do."

Amid a chorus of cheers and applause, Mom and Dad stand with me so that Uncle Chad can take a picture on Mom's cell phone. I know that soon the framed photo and my achievement certificate will stand on display in Uncle Chad's workshop, next to my successfully-fired solid-fuel rocket and a copy of my research paper.

And although this 29-inch rocket will someday look small and insignificant, it will always remind me of the year that we traveled to the stars, rescued Uncle Chad, delivered Lawrence's gold to a humble house in Bethlehem, and worshipped the Savior who came to rescue us all!

# Note from the Author

## ANGELS AND MAGIC?

It would be easy to think that angels and magic are the subject of this book, but they are not. Instead, the focus of this story is God's desire to draw us to His salvation. Magic is not in charge: God is! The transport stones are simply a fictional device to draw us into God's story—to show God's power, judgment, and redemptive love. And Josh, the fictional angel in the story, does nothing more than what angels have always done: carry out God's bidding on our behalf in accordance with His purposes. Sometimes angels are invisible to us, even when they help God get our attention. But on rare occasions we might see them. And always they are sent to guide and protect us. Psalm 91:11 says, *For he will command his angels concerning you to guard you in all your ways.*

## LOCATIONS OF THE RED SEA CROSSING AND MT. SINAI

As of the writing of this story, no one has proven definitively where the Red Sea crossing took place. There are many suggestions, including the north end of the Gulf of Suez, the Straits of Tiran in the Gulf of Aqaba/ Eilat, and a land bridge across Aqabar at Nuweiba. In a similar way, many claims are made regarding which mountain was Mt. Sinai. Included are Jebel Musa in southern Sinai—the traditional location of Mt. Sinai and current location of St. Catherine's Monastery; Jebel Al-Lawz in Saudi Arabia; and Jebel Sin Bishar in western Sinai. For the purposes of this story I have chosen to place the Red Sea crossing at the north end of the Gulf of Suez and Mt. Sinai vaguely in Sinai and not in Arabia. You can research the many possible locations and the many arguments for and against each. I believe that one day evidence may be found for the crossing and the mountain, but even if it is not (after all, the exodus took place three thousand years ago and evidence is minimal for a tent-dwelling people), we still believe that the biblical account is true. The Hebrew-inscribed clay tablet piece in this onyx-stones story is fictional.

# About the Author

With this second *Onyx Stones* adventure for teens and adults, Debby L. Johnston transports her readers into the ancient Egyptian desert to search for someone who may be lost in time. Under the backdrop of the Exodus and the Exodus miracles, and against overwhelming odds, Debby's two young characters attempt the impossible—only to find that when they succeed, there is more to be set right. "Life is like that," says Debby. "Issues are always more complex than we expect. And God wants a full and perfect resolution that may stretch us but is vital for teaching us the full scope of Christ's grace." A graduate of Judson University in Elgin, Illinois, and wife of a retired pastor, Debby now resides with her husband in Southeastern Ohio.

# Reader's Discussion Guide

1 – In our story, Cricket Dalton is a remarkable quadriplegic young teen who surprises Alexander with how much she knows and is able to do. Are you physically challenged in any way, or do you know someone who is? What special gifts do you or your challenged friend possess that others might not expect?

2 – Uncle Chad's journal is key to discovering where to find him. Have you ever kept a journal of special events or journeys in your own life?

3 – When Lawrence Traeger steals Uncle Chad's treasure, he thinks it will make him wealthy and prosperous. And he tries to hide his crime by claiming it is a pirate treasure found on his property. But his claim runs into trouble. Have you ever tried to hide something that you have done wrong and had your attempt backfire?

4 – Why do you suppose that the mysterious Josh takes Uncle Chad into the Hebrew past? What does Uncle Chad see there that he had not believed in before?

5 – Alexander has a hard time believing the story in Uncle Chad's journal because it isn't *scientific*. Although we, as readers of the story, know that it is indeed fiction (although a good story), it does make us wonder if there might be some things in life that can't be explained scientifically—for

example, God and his work in the human heart. Can you think of other things?

6 – Uncle Chad, and later Alexander and his friends, see miracles take place among the Israelites. Do miracles still happen today?

7 – Do you think that some of the events described among the ancient Israelites could have happened the way they are described in this book? Keep in mind that although the story's events are based on what the Bible tells us, some things in this fictional story are conjecture. We can all imagine what it might have been like to be part of the Bible's stories, but we can only speculate on certain details that aren't specifically spelled out in Scripture. It might be good to reread the real story in the Bible so you can tell what the author of this story has imagined and which things are exactly as the Bible shares them. See Scripture references at the back of this book for help in locating the passages.

8 – Do you think the Christmas pageant costumes that Alexander and his friends wore to go back in time would have been realistic enough to pass without suspicion? What might the ancient Israelites have done if they had seen William using matches or his flashlight? What might they have thought if they had spied one of Marlene Grace's plastic food bags?

9 – Alexander and his friends see many skills and types of work being done among the Israelites at the foot of Mt. Sinai. Some of these activities included pottery making, metal melting, fabric weaving, thread dyeing, carpentry, and more. You might want to research these and other ancient skills to see how they differ from similar skills today. Did it surprise you to learn that one of the Tabernacle roof coverings was sealskins?

10 – What do you suppose the guiding pillar of cloud and fire was like? Might it have been like it is described in this story? Or do you think it might have been different?

11 – Can you imagine eating only manna every day for months, even years? What do you think manna might have tasted like?

12 – We learn in this story that Uncle Chad's onyx stone burned Lawrence severely when he tore the necklace from Uncle Chad's neck. And the worst part was that Lawrence couldn't let go of it! That's a pretty good picture of sin. Once we do something wrong, sin sticks to us and continues to hurt us! Only Jesus can forgive and heal us from its effects. Have you ever asked Jesus for His forgiveness and healing from sin?

13 – In this story, we read that Cricket was not healed of her quadriplegia, and Lawrence still needs surgery on his burned hand. And there are other examples of God's working in ways we might not expect. Has God ever answered one of your prayers differently than you expected?

14 – Have you ever read about anyone using the Heimlich Maneuver to save a life in the way that Marlene Grace does in the story? Have you been trained in what to do if someone you know starts to choke on food and can't breathe?

15 – When Alexander realizes that an airplane flight to Cairo is going to take eleven hours, he wishes he could just click the onyx stones and be there. But then he realizes that because of the length of the trip, he gets to spend time talking with his dad and uncle, and he learns things about their lives that he had never known. Sometimes we get impatient to hurry and do things when there are advantages to taking our time and getting to know each other better. Have you ever slowed down and found that you learned something you might not have learned if you hadn't taken time to listen and watch?

16 – In the story, Alexander's family shares a mutual dream about Lawrence crying for help. Although it is rare, mutual dreams have truly been known to happen. Later in the story, the wisemen are guided by a dream and told not to go back to report to Herod after they find the baby Jesus. Can you think of other dreams (mutually shared or not) that are mentioned in the Bible?

17 – Alexander finds that his assumptions about Lawrence's crime have not been totally accurate. And Alexander is surprised that Uncle Chad is willing to forgive Lawrence. Have you ever had a hard time forgiving someone who has hurt you? Have you asked God to help you forgive them?

18 – The star that led the wisemen to Jesus was unique and is still a mystery among astronomers. You may want to reread Scripture's description of its appearing and movement. The actions of Kaysan and Najib in observing the star are fictional—as is the idea of following it by day. What we do know is that God directed the wisemen—just as he guides people today in many aspects of life. Often his guiding is through his Holy Spirit in our hearts. Have you or someone you've known been guided by God to learn some special truth or to be in the right place at the right time to help someone?

19 – In the story, the author has pretended that Alexander and his family and friends join the wisemen in traveling to Bethlehem and, in the story, that they give Lawrence's stolen gold to the baby Jesus. Of course, this is purely fictional, but some parts of the story of the wisemen are true. Did you know that the wisemen did not visit Jesus on the night He was born? You might want to read the story of the wisemen again so you can pick out the facts from the fiction.

20 – We learn by the end of the story that Uncle Chad, Lawrence, Alexander and his parents have accepted Jesus as their Savior. Like them, have you asked Jesus into your heart? If you would like to do so, you can pray to him something like this: *Lord Jesus, I ask you into my heart and to forgive my sins. I know that you died to pay for my sins. And I know you rose from the grave to prove that you are able to save me. I know you are the Son of God and the Lord of all the Universe, and I trust you to count me as one of your children forever. I give you my life from this day forward. Amen.* Once you have prayed this prayer, be sure to tell someone—perhaps your pastor—about the decision you have made. Remember, you can always ask your pastor to explain whatever you don't understand about becoming a Jesus-follower or about what asking *Jesus into your life* means.

21 – Where do you suppose the onyx stones will take Cricket and others next? Whether or not there is another onyx stones story, you can always take your own journeys into biblical history by reading the stories in the Bible. Perhaps you will want to visit King David or the Apostle Paul. There is a wealth of places you can go and people you can meet, and in every Bible account, you will learn more about God and His eternal purposes.

## WHERE IS IT IN SCRIPTURE?

God promises Abram (Abraham) that his descendants will be freed and wealthy after 400 years of slavery: Genesis 15:13-14

Moses asking Pharaoh to release the Israelites from Egypt: Exodus 7

The plagues on Egypt: Exodus 7-12

The Passover and the beginning of the Exodus: Exodus 12

God guides as an angel of cloud and fire: Exodus 14:19-20 and Exodus 23:20-23

The crossing of the Red Sea: Exodus 14

Gathering manna in the wilderness: Numbers 11

Camping at Mt. Sinai, and God giving Moses the Ten Commandments: Exodus 19-20

The Tabernacle is set up: Exodus 10:17

God's presence comes to rest over the Tabernacle: Exodus 40:34-38

The wiseman following the star and visiting the baby Jesus: Matthew 2 and Luke 2

Some of the prophecies about the birth of Jesus (as referenced in chapter 35): Numbers 24:17; Isaiah 49:6; Isaiah 9:6; Daniel 7:13-14; and Micah 5:2

God's desire that no one should die (perish) in sin: 2 Peter 3:9

The basic message of salvation from sin through Jesus: John 3:16-17

AND, here are several other Bible verses that outline God's plan of salvation: Romans 3:23 (everyone has sinned), Romans 6:23 (everyone faces judgement for their sin), Romans 5:8 (Jesus Christ, God's Son, died in our place and for our sins), Romans 10:9-10 (we are saved by believing in Jesus and confessing it with our mouth), Romans 8:1 (as believers in Jesus, our judgment and condemnation for sin is removed for eternity).

The Onyx Stones:
Mystery of the Underground People

Debby L. Johnston

**Yes! There is the prequel to the story you have just read. In book one of the Onyx Stones series**—*The Onyx Stones: Mystery of the Underground People"*—you can read Cricket Dalton's story. How did Cricket come to possess an onyx-stone necklace? Where did she and Hero travel on their initial onyx-stones journeys? What did Cricket learn about the End Times and about God's love for her?

To purchase this book, visit Amazon.com; BarnesandNoble.com; Christianbook.com; or other online sources.

*www.DebbyLJohnston.com*

Printed in the United States
by Baker & Taylor Publisher Services

Printed in the United States
by Baker & Taylor Publisher Services